THE LEGACY OF THE HEAVENS
BOOK ONE

THE SONG OF ALL

TINA LeCOUNT MYERS

Night Shade Books
New York

Night Shade books may be purchased in bulk at special discounts for sales promotion, corporate gifts, fund-raising, or educational purposes. Special editions can also be created to specifications. For details, contact the Special Sales Department, Night Shade Books, 307 West 36th Street, 11th Floor, New York, NY 10018 or info@skyhorsepublishing.com.

Night Shade Books® is a registered trademark of Skyhorse Publishing, Inc. ®, a Delaware corporation.

Visit our website at www.nightshadebooks.com.

10 9 8 7 6 5 4 3 2 1

Library of Congress Cataloging-in-Publication Data

Names: LeCount Myers, Tina, author.
Title: The song of all / by Tina LeCount Myers.
Description: New York : Night Shade Books, 2018. | Series: The legacy of the heavens ; 1
Identifiers: LCCN 2017006722 | ISBN 9781597809238 (softcover : acid-free paper)
Subjects: | GSAFD: Fantasy fiction.
Classification: LCC PS3612.E3365 S66 2018 | DDC 813/.6--dc23
LC record available at https://lccn.loc.gov/2017006722

Cover illustration by Jeff Chapman
Cover design by STK•Kreations

Hardcover ISBN: 978-1-59780-942-9
Trade paperback ISBN: 978-1-59780-923-8

Printed in the United States of America

AUTHOR'S NOTE

The Song of All is a work of fiction which draws upon various Saami languages spoken in the northern regions of Norway, Sweden, Finland, and extreme northwestern Russia. The author incorporates Saami words and concepts in this work with the utmost respect for the Saami languages and cultures and with the hope of their preservation for future generations. The relevance of a language should not only be measured by the number of speakers, but, in the spirit of communication, should also seek to embrace the multiplicity of experience, honor the insight offered, and safeguard what is irreplaceable.

Kiitos, äiti.
You were right.

Part One

THE EIGHTH SEASON
OF SNOW

CHAPTER ONE

I RJAN WALKED WITH SOHJA in silence. Their footfalls made no sound in the powdery snow. The cold air squeezed the breath from him, and the sun, veiled now by the gods, offered him no warmth. By the end of the moon cycle they would be plunged into such darkness that even the weightless snowflakes would become a burden.

But rather than consider the coming shadows, Irjan tried to focus on the sleeping babe snuggled in his wife's arms. Their boy, Marnej, would be their light in the coming darkness. But it scared him to think that so much of their hope rested in such a tiny body. Irjan drew his arm around his small family, pulling them close, as if, by doing so, he could ward off his regrets.

Sohja looked up at him and smiled, her contentment radiating like the brightest of stars. It was too much for Irjan to bear and he looked away, searching the path ahead for an answer to the question that continued to gnaw upon him. *How could he tell his wife that he lived each day with the knowledge that others had died by his hand?*

~

Sohja's smile faded as Irjan stared ahead. She leaned in closer to him as they walked and he tightened his arm around her. She was grateful for it, because she suspected his thoughts strayed to the past. They'd spent two full seasons of snow together before the baby had arrived, and she'd often seen him staring into the distance. She worried the call of the tundra and thundering herds would overtake him once again, and he would disappear as suddenly as he had appeared.

~

In the moon cycle of *Skábmamánnu*, the dark period, Irjan had arrived at the farm seeking shelter and work. Sohja's father could offer him no work, but the old man welcomed the sound of another voice. In the dying firelight the two men had talked nightly, and as days grew into weeks, she'd listened.

He said he'd traveled for six seasons of snow with the *binna*, caring for them as they moved along their ancient routes. The reindeer had given his life its every shape; they'd been his food, his shelter, and his marker of time. He had lived in accordance to moon cycles of molt, rut, and calve, and his life had been measured in their age-old rhythms, in their births and deaths. He had cared for them and they had sustained him.

As the weeks passed through the moon cycles, Irjan told her father stories of the endless nights, much deeper and darker than their own, where the changing lights painted across the black heavens came from the breath of the gods.

"*Badjeolmmoš*, did you not fear this breath of the gods?" her father wondered.

"*Boanda*, I feared not the night sky, but rather the endless sun of the time of *Geassemánnu*. In these days there are no signs in the heavens to know where you are. You must know the trees and the rocks and marshes, but these things change over time." He paused. "The stars in the heavens do not. To be lost on the *Pohjola* is to die on it."

"Well, herder," the old farmer chuckled, "on the farm it is only old age you must fear. For it will surely kill you."

The farmer struggled to his feet from his chair. "Child," he called, "lead me to my bed."

Dutifully, Sohja rose and helped her stooped father cross the room. She glanced backward at Irjan's face, lit by the dying flames. But in her mind, it seemed the breath of the gods lit him also.

～

On the snowy path they now walked, Sohja looked up at her husband's lined features. The scruff of his beard hid his gauntness. She thought of those long-ago nights and his stories, and wondered if perhaps the gods were darker than their night sky.

He kissed her upturned forehead absentmindedly and seemed to come back to himself, saying, "Wife, I am sorry you have to walk this morning."

"I am content to walk with you. The snow is too light to use the sleigh."

He nodded.

"In a short time we will have all the snow we need. Are you sure you are both warm enough?" He pulled her closer to him.

"It is the first snow, husband. It is hardly cold, and you have us layered so tightly in reindeer *duollji* the wind cannot touch us."

Irjan smiled broadly, which made her laugh. He squeezed her again, and the baby yawned. They could see the village in the distance, and heard the peal of a bell.

"I hope the gods know I do not like sharing you both with them," he said, still smiling.

Her eyes narrowed. "It is not the gods you should worry about. It is the rest of the village. You have been one of us for only two seasons of snow; the others still look upon you as a stranger, a reindeer herder, and not a member of the *girkogilli*."

"And if I worship at their altar with them long enough, this will change?"

"Yes. There are many who are still frightened by you. You came from the Pohjola. Few have been to the Northland. Most have never left their farms."

"You do not mention that many would have gladly left their farms for yours," he replied.

"All the more reason to attend worship and make your place in the girkogilli strong," she said.

"I belong to you, and to no group of men," Irjan said with more force than he intended.

CHAPTER TWO

"WE HAVE, EACH OF us, a duty to the gods beyond prayer, beyond offerings. From the moment our souls arrive, carried upon the wing of the bird, until the moment they claim them for their own, the gods demand we find the light in the darkness and fight against evil in all its forms. We, the *Olmmoš*, are their chosen. We are their soldiers in this mortal realm of Davvieana."

The *Apotti's* exhortations echoed in the narrow wooden temple. The burning braziers belched thick smoke, smelling of rich smoldering pine. The Apotti stood in front of the chosen and tried not to see the tired faces of farmers and tradesmen, but rather an army of the gods.

As the last of his words reverberated, he felt his heart beating wildly. The blood of a believer coursed through him. He was a child of the church, a son of a priest, and a man, as his father had impressed upon him, destined for greatness within the Order of Believers.

"And, as soldiers, we must remain ever vigilant." His voice rose to the rafters. "As we enter the dark time we often become vulnerable. Doubts and fears prey upon us and we can lose our faith, fearing the light will never return. In these moments, I ask all of you, the gods' chosen ones, to remember the battles of our forefathers. Remember the blood they shed to fight evil, to fight those who tempted them to look away from the gods, to fight the *Jápmea*. These so-called Immortals, these abominations, strove to bind us to their wickedness and have us believe them to be our true gods. But we saw through their lies, for only the gods are immortal, and we slew these false deities. And in shedding our own blood, we cleansed ourselves of their tainted promises." The priest sagged after his crescendo to catch his breath.

"Remember, *mánáid*, children of the gods, the battles may have ended, but the war for your souls continues." The priest closed his eyes and let silence take over the room.

~

After the sermon, the faithful stood and shuffled toward the door. The priest, however, did not move forward to greet his worshipers. Instead, the priest's acolyte stood with his outstretched arms, ready to receive the varied offerings.

"The Apotti thanks you as you thank the gods," the acolyte said softly to each person.

Waiting to leave, Irjan and Sohja spoke to those they knew in the village. The women cooed over the baby, and a few of the men clapped Irjan on the back. He was accepting their congratulations when a voice whispered, "Brother, the Apotti thanks you as you thank the gods."

Irjan faced the priest's assistant and replied, "I am thankful to the gods and their messenger the Apotti." He handed the acolyte the cured and folded reindeer skin.

The acolyte accepted it. The corners of his mouth pulled up into a pained smile, as if someone stood behind him tugging at strings. "Brother," he said through strained lips, "the Apotti would like you to call upon him in his sanctum. It is a matter of importance to the village." The acolyte then nodded solemnly.

Irjan continued forward through the open door and into the cold.

Sohja smiled. "You see? I was right!"

"Yes." Irjan smiled back. "You were right."

"Go to him," she urged. "Hurry!"

"The only reason to hurry is to see you and the baby get home and out of the cold. The Apotti can wait," Irjan said, raising his voice.

"Shh. Do not! You have gained the Apotti's notice. Do not court the attention of the rest of the girkogilli for being rude. I will be fine. I will walk with the neighbors, and then it is a short distance home."

Irjan raised his hand to guide Sohja down the steps. "No. I will take care of my family first."

Sohja brushed his hand away. "You are doing so by going to see the Apotti."

Irjan knew by the look in her eyes he could no more change her mind than he could stop the falling snow.

Reluctantly he watched his wife hurry off to catch up with the others. He watched her retreating back until he could no longer distinguish it from the snow. He felt a hand on his shoulder.

"This way, Brother," the youthful acolyte said with some command.

Irjan followed, but his thoughts remained with his wife and son.

At a large, rounded door, the acolyte stopped and knocked softly. It seemed impossible anyone could hear such a light touch on such a stout door, but from inside a voice granted entrance.

The young cleric pushed open the door. The iron hinges groaned with strain. A fire blazed on the far side of the room and the priest sat beside the hearth, gazing with interest at his guests.

"Good," he said. "Send the Brother forward, Siggur. Your duty is done. The gods thank you."

The acolyte stopped abruptly, then lowered his head, murmuring, "As I thank the gods." Silently he retreated.

The priest gestured. "Brother, come sit beside the fire. We have important matters to discuss."

Irjan took the proffered chair. Even with the light of the flames, he could only see the Apotti's face. Whatever cloaked the priest's body, its details remained hidden in blackness. In contrast, the priest's face was ageless and luminescent, framed with golden white hair. His eyes were icy pools. Irjan felt as if the Apotti looked through him as if he were mist, with no solid substance to stand in the way. Suddenly, Irjan feared those same eyes were trying to bore into his thoughts, into his soul, where desire and fear intertwined.

"Brother, you have skills we are in need of," the priest said.

"Apotti, I do not understand. I am a boanda, one of many farmers, and certainly not the richest in crops or livestock," Irjan answered cautiously.

The priest blinked.

"Brother, don't think I cannot see your soul, your history," he replied. "You are not a farmer; you are a *Piijkij*, one of the Brethren of Hunters."

The statement hung in the air. One man refused to accept it and the other refused to retract it. The silence grew to fill the room, pushing out what little air the fire had not already consumed.

"Apotti, you are mistaken," the man finally said. "I am not a Piijkij. I was a reindeer herder before becoming a part of this village."

The priest's face darkened. "Am I mistaken? Are then the gods mistaken? They are the ones who speak of you. You may deceive others with your tales of traveling with reindeer in the North. The gods are not fooled, nor am I."

Irjan's throat ached to deny, to lie. And yet, he sensed it was useless. The priest's penetrating gaze told him he somehow knew the truth. Had the gods betrayed him? If so, why?

Irjan's mind raced to avoid being engulfed in the past. "Apotti, I was a Piijkij," he finally admitted, "but I am *no longer* among the

Brethren of Hunters. I made a vow to the gods I would never again hunt, never again kill."

The priest stared at Irjan, his face taking on the color of the flames. "You remain a Hunter, Brother. It is what the gods want. It is what the gods ask of you now and forever."

"I cannot," Irjan protested. "I am no longer a young man. I have a family, a wife and a child who need my care, and a farm to keep."

The priest rose abruptly from his chair. The rush of his robes fanned the flames and his voice parted the darkness. "Hunter you were born. Hunter you remain. You may not choose your destiny. It has been chosen for you."

"And if I fight my destiny?" Irjan asked.

"Hunter, you will lose," the answer came back, as if from the flames themselves.

CHAPTER THREE

SIGGUR WAITED IN A gloom-filled alcove. The shadows hid his burning humiliation. *Exclusion.* His mind churned on the slight. *Exclusion is my reward for being a faithful acolyte.* The Apotti's door creaked, startling him. He peered out from the shadows and watched the bearded farmer emerge. He glared at the man in disgust.

What can a farmer offer the Apotti or the village? Turnips?

The man walked down the corridor and Siggur stepped out of the gloom. He considered knocking on the priest's door to see if he could be of service, but then he froze.

Service? I have been of service to that man since I was a boy.

Another voice in his mind, smooth and sibilant, answered, *And that is how he still sees you—as a child.*

Siggur spun on his heels and followed the man out of the temple. He watched as the farmer headed. . .not toward his farm, but toward the village.

"Where do you go?" Siggur whispered to the distant figure, curiosity nudging him along.

∾

Out in the cold air, away from the priest's eyes and his fire, Irjan could breathe again. He staggered forward, pushed by his own questions.

How had the Apotti discovered his secret? He'd told no one, not even Sohja's father, who, on his deathbed, had begged to know the secret of Irjan's life before the binna.

"What of life before the reindeer?" the old farmer had asked.

On that night, as on all the others before it, Irjan had answered, "There was no life before the binna."

Irjan had told the old man the truth. No life existed before the reindeer, because there had only been death. The hunt. The capture. Death.

The Apotti had called him by his title, a Piijkij. The Bird of Prey. The Hunter. The Man Who Takes the Souls of the Immortals.

Irjan stumbled over his visions of the past—one body after another, over what seemed a lifetime. With each one, Irjan had stood and watched until the life force dissipated and the ravens came to pluck out the eyes and carry away the soul. And with each one, a little more of his own soul flew off with those same birds, until one day he looked down at the bloodied and distorted face of a Jápmea and saw himself, a twisted shell of a man turned killer. There was no trace of the boy he'd been before the Brethren had turned his fear and heartache into something black and burning. He was dead before he'd ever lived, and now not even the hatred that had fueled him remained. He was empty. On that day, he turned his back on the Jápmea Immortals and ceased to be a Piijkij. He walked into the Pohjola praying to find his soul again.

But here he stood, in the midst of the village, trailed by a past that not even the thunderous tracks of the binna could erase. . . How? Why?

Irjan found himself standing outside the travelers' hut. He opened the door and walked into the smoky room. The men greeted him and the women looked up from their circle, but no one beckoned him to join them for a *juhka*. He got his own ale and found a stool in the corner, away from the chanters, but the room resonated with the chanter's *joik*. The song was strong and vivid, and Irjan struggled to keep the images from his mind. He had more important things to consider. But the joik could not be ignored.

Irjan heard the hooves of the binna and the wind rushing past them. He heard the ice cracking and thundering as the voice continued to sing of endless expanses. Irjan hung his head and released the breath he had been holding since leaving the priest's chambers.

If I'd stayed with the binna, I would not be in this room. Regret washed over him. The chanter's voice rose, then stopped suddenly. The room pulsed with silence. Irjan buried his face in his hands, trying to wipe away the vision before his eyes, but the truth remained.

Were he not in this room, Irjan would be standing in front of his wife, lying. He could see Sohja's expectant face and the baby asleep in the corner near their bed. A new wave of remorse washed over him. He would have to lie to her. It could not be otherwise. To tell Sohja the truth would be to lose her forever. A woman could not knowingly remain handfast to a killer like himself.

As if to hone the point, the soft chanting of one of the women swelled to fill the murky room. Her clear, sweet voice pierced Irjan's heart as she sang of the wind that spoke the courting promises of her husband, lost to her after a lifetime together.

"I had no idea, Brother, you were interested in the joik of your neighbors," a sly voice cut through the ballad of love and longing. "Perhaps you will sing your own."

Irjan looked up, surprised to see the priest's acolyte hovering before him. The young man quickly sat down beside him.

He smiled, but, to Irjan, the grin seemed to hold more cunning than warmth.

"I am afraid, Brother, that I do not have a voice for chanting," he replied with care.

"Brother, it is not the voice that matters, it is the story it tells."

"Well then, Brother, in that case, no one would be interested in the tales of a farmer."

"But Brother, it is well known you have traveled in the Pohjola. Few of us, here in the South, have gone any distance from our familiar world. Surely, you must have seen a great many things that we can only dream of."

"Dreams and nightmares are close cousins, *Amanuensa*," Irjan answered, using the young man's title in deference, while looking for a way to leave.

The acolyte, his face bright with mischief, drew in close, blocking Irjan's exit. He called for another drink for them both.

"Brother, tell me some of the things you have seen," he said with a truthful eagerness.

"What is it you expect to hear, Amanuensa?" Irjan pretended to scoff. "Stories of demons and ghosts and—"

"And the Jápmea," the acolyte finished.

"The Jápmea? Why them?"

"Because they are said to live in the Pohjola. You have traveled in the Pohjola. Surely you must have encountered them."

The acolyte lowered his voice, though there was no need to hide it in the din of the room. "How are we humans to fight this evil if we do not know its form? Its ways? Please, Brother, I must know something of what I will face in the future."

The acolyte had guessed well, or he had been sent by the Apotti. Either way, Irjan suspected he could not escape without giving him something, and yet he was determined to try.

"You are speaking of the past, Amanuensa—a distant one. Besides, you are more acquainted with the ways of Jápmea Immortals than I. You have been educated. You have learned the history of the ancients. I am a farmer who traveled with the binna."

The acolyte shook his head forcefully. "Stop," the young man ordered. "Your attempts at humility only confirm what I suspect. The Apotti has sought your counsel because you have encountered them."

Would that it were that simple, Irjan silently wished. To the acolyte he said reluctantly, "I have seen them."

The young man lowered the cup from his mouth. "What do they look like?"

Irjan glanced around the room and lowered his voice. "They look like us."

Appearing slightly crestfallen, the young cleric went on, "The Apotti says that when the Jápmea sought immortality, they offended the gods, and the gods punished them. Surely, those who are blighted cannot look as we do, Brother."

"Would you have them distinguished by some mark of evil?" Irjan demanded, taking another hasty drink. The warmth of the juhka flowed through him and his mind momentarily swam with thoughts and faces and long-forgotten memories. A part of him wanted to tell this young cleric everything, to air out every dark corner of himself. He wanted to confess and wash his hands free of the blood that, though not visible, coated his callused skin, thick and red and sticky as sap. But the part of him trained to survive rose to the surface and took control.

"Do you believe they should have horns like the reindeer or fangs like the wolves?"

The acolyte's face reddened. "How then do you know you have seen the Jápmea?"

"Because they do not move like us," Irjan continued, holding the acolyte's attention. "They move in all measures of space."

"How can that be?" The acolyte pushed back, disbelief flashing across his face.

Irjan leaned forward. "Some say they exist in the shadows, but that is not true. The shadows have substance. Darkness occupies its space. The Jápmea cannot hide where there is no room for them. Instead, they exist in the gaps."

"How can you know this?" the young man pressed.

"Have you ever seen something out of the corner of your eye so fleeting it made you doubt yourself? Or seen something and thought you had seen it before, but could not place when or where? This is where the *Jápmemeahttun* exist. We can share the same world, the same sun, the same air and water, and yet we need not touch."

"But if what you say is true"—suspicion crept into the young cleric's voice—"how is it that you have seen them?"

"Amanuensa, I tell you truly, I do not know. If you say it is a gift, I will tell you it is a curse. They live apart from us for a reason."

"Because they are evil. We fought them back into the darkness!"

"Not into darkness, Brother. Darkness has no room for them; they still live among us because we give them room."

"No, Brother! We, all of us, must not give them any room to live. We must follow the faith of the Believers. We must remove this evil creeping around us, threatening our souls."

"Noble sentiments, Brother." Irjan snorted, coughing up a bit of rising bile. "How do you propose we do that?"

"We kill them!" the acolyte spat.

"How?"

"If they are as you say they are, like you and me, can they not be killed?"

"To be truthful, Brother, they can be killed, but I wonder if you would be capable of doing the killing." Irjan leaned back and drained his cup, replacing it on the table with an awkward thump.

Before the acolyte could answer, Irjan stood up and swayed, then walked out of the travelers' hut.

Outside, he bent over, sickened. When he stood up, he wiped his mouth with the back of his hand. His conversation with the acolyte had left him shaking. The maze of his past was closing in on him.

If he had been wise, he would have gone straight home and told Sohja everything. But he feared losing all he had worked so hard to gain, his freedom, his farm, his family. He thought again of his wife and child waiting at home, safe and warm. He could not allow anything to harm them.

Irjan quickened his pace, reminding himself that only one man knew his true calling: the Apotti. And the priest could not make him do something against his will. As for the acolyte, he only knew a small part of the story. But suddenly the thought occurred to Irjan, *What if the Brethren knew about him?*

And then Irjan ran.

CHAPTER FOUR

DARKNESS SLID DOWN THROUGH the trees, engulfing the small farmhouse. Sohja paced the floor, stopping every few steps to wring her hands. Her husband's audience with the Apotti could not have lasted this long if there were not a serious problem. Marnej stirred in the cradle, his cries becoming increasingly more insistent. Sohja picked him up and held him against her breast. He was rested and fed. She had done everything for his comfort, and yet he still cried.

Sohja rocked in place, chanting her joik, hoping the sound of her voice would soothe her son. Her song brought to life the tale of the everyday, caring for those she loved and knowing that one day she, too, would be loved and cared for by her children. As her last words hung upon the still air, Sohja rested her cheek against Marnej's downy head. He was hot.

She removed the duollji pelts she'd swaddled him in. Out of the furs, he suddenly felt so small in her arms, so unprotected. Her thoughts cracked like spring ice. What could the priest want with her *käällis*? He was a farmer now. They were too far south to have need of a reindeer herder.

Whatever he wanted, she told herself, she should be gratified. The Apotti had said the village needed her husband and that should suffice. But her fears lingered. Irjan never wished to discuss his life before the binna. And when he did speak of it, his confessions were unsettling. For him, he had said, there had been no life before the binna.

Sohja put her son back in his cradle and paced the room until she felt a cold sweat trickle down her back. She moved closer to the fire. The flames roared, and yet still she felt chilled. All the questions she had feared to ask now rose to the surface. She pushed each one down frantically. But one refused to be suppressed. It screamed in her mind until she could no longer avoid it.

What if my fears are only the start?

Sohja stared at the fire until she could no longer abide her own stillness. She grabbed the broom beside the hearth and began to sweep. When she finished, she began again, seeing dust and grime where there was none. When she started to sweep the room for the third time, she stopped herself and sagged against the rough handled broom.

Sohja looked at Marnej sleeping fitfully. She walked over and sat hesitantly upon the bed, unsure if she could find any rest. She looked at the supper on the table—the stew had a grey skin of congealed fat upon its surface.

The crunch of quick footsteps outside propelled Sohja off the bed. Before she reached the door, it swung open. Irjan rushed in and she fell into his arms, holding on to him as if she would never let him go.

～

Irjan dropped the knife he gripped in his hand and held on to Sohja even tighter than she held on to him. When she released him, he pulled back and saw her face shadowed and lined with fear.

"What has happened? Have they come?" he demanded, quickly picking up his knife again before rushing to his son's cradle. Seeing the boy sleeping, he spun to face his wife.

"I am sorry, my love!" she suddenly burst out.

Irjan twitched with surprise. "What have you to be sorry for?"

"I should not have pushed you to make yourself fit where you did not want to."

Sohja hid her face behind her hands.

Irjan stepped forward, placing his knife upon the trestle table before gently pulling aside Sohja's hands. He brushed back the hair that had escaped her pale braid.

"It is all I want, my heart. To be with you here, in this life, and see our son grow. I swear to you I will do anything to make that happen." This time Irjan fell into his wife's arms and held her tightly, wanting to feel her reassuring embrace, wanting to believe that they were all still safe.

~

The Apotti sat and peered into the fire. He clenched his teeth, thinking of the man's pathetic attempts to deny his past. *How dare he?*

He may have been a Piijkij, but he was obviously a fool when it came to the power of the Order of Believers. There had been no divine intervention; rather, Rikkar had made inquiries accompanied by the correct compensation. True, he wore the robes of a priest, but Rikkar was a man of his world, and in his world, one either wielded power or cringed beneath it, and he'd experienced both.

But while he much preferred being Apotti over acolyte, Rikkar had to admit that he now found little satisfaction knowing the villagers of Hemmela placed their souls in his hands. They were sheep, easily corralled and led, and what power did the shepherd really have? He desired something more befitting his skills, his talent. With a Piijkij in his service, he would not only have access to the Brethren's closely guarded knowledge, but he would also have access to the Immortals themselves.

Rikkar momentarily savored the vision of depositing one of those vile creatures at the foot of the Vijns.

The High Priest would be compelled to offer him a position within the Court of Counselors. Rikkar smiled at the thought, then eased back in his chair, warmed by both the fire beside him and his own smoldering ambitions.

CHAPTER FIVE

RIKKAR AWOKE WELL BEFORE dawn to pray. His prayers, however, had swiftly resolved into a plan. Destiny beckoned him to reach higher and farther, and he would not entrust his future to chance. His own hand needed to guide him forward.

Rikkar crossed the temple's threshold and shivered in the wan morning light. He tightened his cloak about him. From the corner of his eye, he saw something move. He whirled in the direction of the flash, but saw only wispy fog. He moved cautiously into the courtyard and slowly circled. Finally satisfied he was alone, Rikkar walked toward the outskirts of the village.

As he passed the last of the central structures, he looked over his shoulder one more time, and then headed toward the woods lining the path. It would take him longer to travel the uneven and snowy ground, but he could not risk being seen by any who traveled to the last trading market.

∿

"I do not like to leave you," Irjan said. "Especially when I can see your heart is still heavy from yesterday's trouble."

Sohja shook her head, saying, "Yesterday is gone. I am much better. You cannot miss the last market."

"We are stocked for the dark time ahead. We need little else to be well prepared."

"Do not look so dour," she chided him. "There are things we still need. Go and get them." Sohja gently pushed him toward the door.

"I do not like to leave you," Irjan repeated with an insistence that almost sounded like pleading to Sohja's ears.

She shook her head at her own strange thoughts. "Go now, or you will miss the others."

Irjan tried to protest, but she cut him short with a finger to his lips. "I have much to do today, and by the time you are back, I will have finished and we can sit down together before the fire as we did when we first met." She gave him a shy smile and a nudge.

Irjan kissed her and then their son before finally heading toward the door. Just before he stepped through he looked back over his shoulder and smiled. "I will hold you to that," he said, before closing the door with a firm pull.

With Irjan gone, Sohja focused on the day ahead. She put behind all her silly speculation and concentrated on the tasks at hand. Her husband's assurances the night before had calmed her fears. In fact, in the morning's light her worries seemed silly. He loved her.

Marnej began to cry. Sohja went to pick him up, but saw he moved within his dreams. She walked to the hearth and stoked the fire to boil wash water. As she waited, Sohja cut up potatoes and turnips along with the rabbit she would serve her husband when he returned. She sang softly to herself as she peeled and cut the vegetables, then salted the meat and set it aside to rest. The rabbit skin hung on a line, to cure. It would make a fine little cap for the baby.

While waiting for the water to boil, Sohja sat down beside the fire and picked up her mending. As a little girl, working next to her mother, she had imagined a moment such as this.

"One day you will be a mother yourself, with a home and a handmate to honor you and children to love," her mother had said.

As a child, Sohja had nodded, believing her mother.

But as she grew older, and a desirable handmate was not forthcoming, Sohja despaired. Then her mother became ill. Sohja could do nothing but try to offer her peace at her death.

"Do not carry worry in your heart to the other side, Mother," Sohja soothed. "I will choose a good handmate. Our children will grow strong and care for Father in his old age."

But Sohja did not become handfasted after her mother's death. Instead, she cared for her father in his dotage.

And then Irjan arrived, out of the darkness and into their home, and eventually into her heart. At first, Sohja was cautious. The stranger could have been like most of the men in the village, more interested in her father's land than in truly sharing a life with her. Sohja watched and listened, and in the end she knew before he did that his heart belonged to her.

Warmed by the fire, Sohja smiled to herself and drifted along with her thoughts, her needle moving ahead without her attention.

The knock on the door startled her out of her reverie. She stood and went to the door, but paused, her hand hovering above the pull. She opened it warily. The Apotti stood before her. Sohja shrank back.

"Good morning, Sister." The priest bowed slightly.

Sohja gave him a bobbing curtsey. "Good morning, Apotti."

"I hope I have not come too early, or found you in an inconvenient moment," he continued evenly.

She cast her eyes down, smoothing the front of her apron. "No, no," she stammered.

"I have come to see your husband."

Sohja tried to steady her gaze upon the man in front of her. "My käällis has left for the market."

The priest looked disappointed, but then his expression lightened. "Then perhaps I might take a moment to speak with you, Sister."

He stepped forward toward her.

Sohja stood frozen in the doorway. An awkward silence filled the small gap between them.

"Sister," the Apotti leaned in to confide, "it is a matter of great importance." His voice whispered, but it felt far from comforting.

Sohja stirred and haltingly took a step back into the house. "Of course. Please come in and warm yourself by the fire."

The cleric brushed past her and she jumped back.

He strode toward the fire, but spied the cradle and changed his direction. Sohja shot out her hand as if to stop him, but pulled it back again just as quickly. He leaned over the sleeping infant and touched a gloved hand to his face.

"I marvel at the beauty of innocence," he said, facing Sohja once again.

Sohja moved to stand near the fire. "You must forgive me, Apotti, we are not used to entertaining those of your standing."

"Please, Sister, do not concern yourself with matters of conduct. I am a man of humble origins and now find myself with the most humble task of all—serving the gods."

Sohja could not meet his eyes and gestured to the priest to sit. The cleric took her mending chair and she her husband's. The chair felt cool and unfamiliar. She never sat in it. It was her kääl-lis's. Her hands brushed along its smooth edge and then fluttered from her knees to her throat and back again. Finally, she clasped her hands in her lap.

"Would you care for tea, Apotti, to warm you after your walk?" She gave her guest a fleeting glance before fixing her attention upon the fire, feeling the priest looking at her.

"Something warming would be most appreciated." The priest smiled.

Rikkar could see the woman was nervous. In her brief glances he discerned uncertainty and apprehension lurking behind her eyes. She feared him, he realized, and he swelled with satisfaction. His task would be simpler than anticipated. It was always much easier to reap the rewards of fear than to sow them. But he was not averse to using a heavy hand this day to obtain what he wanted.

When it seemed she could delay the moment no longer, the woman handed him a steaming cup.

"I thank you, as the gods thank you."

"It is I who am thankful," she answered. "To have a messenger of the gods in our home is an honor."

Rikkar smiled at the rote compliment, and carefully sipped his scalding tea. "Yesterday, I sought conversation with your husband. Did he speak of it to you?"

"Yes, Apotti. I mean no," she mumbled. "I mean, yes, I know my käällis joined you in your chambers for an audience, but no, he did not speak to me of it when he returned home."

Rikkar digested her words. The man had not told his wife of the conversation. It suggested she did not know the truth of her husband's past.

The priest tested his theory.

"Your husband has unique talents which could well serve, not only the girkogilli, but also the gods."

"What need does the village have for a farmer or a reindeer herder? Or the gods, for that matter?"

The priest sat quietly with his suspicions confirmed. "Sister, your husband is much more than a boanda or badjeolmmoš. He is a Hunter."

"But so is every man in this village, Apotti."

"True. But your husband is not merely one of many. He is a Piijkij."

The woman's face clouded in confusion and doubt. "What do you mean?"

"Sister, your husband was born with a destiny to fulfill. He is the agent of the gods in the struggle against evil."

The woman shook her head. "No," she whispered. "He is my käällis. He is father to his son. He has chosen to become a boanda."

"It is one role, among many, he has played in his life so far. He may pretend otherwise, but your husband is first and foremost a Piijkij, a Bird of Prey. He is a Hunter, a slayer of Immortals."

The woman's eyes widened and seemed to look into the face of every fear she held in her heart. "No. That cannot be true," she whispered.

Rikkar let her denial crumble into silence. He could see she did not believe it herself.

"I know this must be difficult for you," he soothed. "But you must realize it is not I who asks your husband to fulfill his destiny. It is the gods. We each have our calling."

She raised her chin in an attempt at defiance. "And what would the gods have him do?"

"To take up his mantle once again," Rikkar said with passion. "To punish those who enslaved us when were weak and in need of compassion. To avenge those who died in the wars to free us from the Jápmea."

Her eyes narrowed. "And why are you here today speaking to me?"

"I am here to enlist your voice on behalf of the gods. Speak to your husband. Help him understand that the gods are in need of his service."

"If you need my help, then my käällis must have refused to answer your call. I will not urge him to do what he does not desire to do." Her voice gained strength and clarity, but her hands shook and she spilled her tea.

"Sister, I have clearly upset you, which was not my intention." Rikkar rose to his feet, standing before her. She trembled. Rikkar reached down and took her empty cup from her hands.

"Let me fill this for you," he said.

The Apotti stood in front of the fire. With his back to the woman he pulled a flask from his pocket. He continued to speak as he emptied a murky liquid into the woman's cup. "I understand the hardship I am asking you to face. It would be natural for you to think of your child, who needs a father in the dark time, and yourself, in need of a husband and a protector." He stirred her newly brimming cup and faced her. "I can only ask you to think of those who came before, who had the courage to stand up against cruelty and injustice and offer up their lives. I ask you to remember that those who are willing to make sacrifices are richly rewarded by the gods."

He handed the woman her tea, but remained standing.

The woman looked down at the cup before looking up.

"I do not think of myself or my child. I think of my husband. If he has turned his back on the rewards of the gods, who am I to seek it for myself? As you said, Apotti, we each have our calling. Mine is to stand by my käällis and honor his decisions."

Rikkar allowed himself a brief smile. "Sister, it is a noble destiny you have before you. I will not stand in its way. I only hope you can see that in coming here today, I answered the call of my fate to serve the gods in whatever they ask of me."

Rikkar bowed to the seated woman. "We are both wiser today for knowing the truth that lies in our hearts."

The woman remained watchful, but kept her own counsel.

"Sister, I thank you, as the gods thank you," Rikkar said, and strode to the door.

~

Left alone again by the fire, Sohja drank deeply of her tea and let its warmth push away the cold fear filling her. Her heart pounded, and yet, for the first time since her käällis had appeared as a stranger on their doorstep, she felt sure of who she was.

CHAPTER SIX

A FOG ROLLED OVER THE still-sleeping rooftops and ran headlong into the first rays of daylight. Aillun looked up at the waning moon and then at the village surrounding her. She wondered about the Olmmoš who still slept and the lives they led.

She had been Outside before, but never alone. Once, she had stood encircled by the ancient ones, safely hidden within the Song of All, listening to the Olmmoš speak. Aillun had been surprised she could understand them. They had a thick, round accent, as if they had a mouthful of berries and feared losing one. She had stared at them in wonder and it had struck her that the Olmmoš were not so very different from herself, except that, given the opportunity, they would have killed her. But the Song of All had kept her and the circle safe, and for a brief moment she and the Olmmoš stood together as her kind had done before, long ago.

Although she knew she should not be in the village alone, Aillun could not resist her curiosity. Besides, she had not journeyed out of her way to find it. Rather, the village had grown up along the route she traveled to her Origin. It had not been there at her birth, for her return song mentioned no villages. But the Olmmoš grew like the lichen upon which the binna fed, spreading from rock to rock.

Some Jápmemeahttun sang of the Olmmoš as a blight upon their world, but the voice was weak and in the background. A stronger, cautionary voice reminded them of the consequences of their own conceit—when their ancestors had grown so many in number that they had brought themselves to the brink of extinction.

But as their ancestors had scattered to find food and water to sustain themselves, the gods had pitied them and had given them the first *oktoeadni*, the first of their kind to transform from female to male after she gave birth.

Aillun would sing the song of the oktoeadni when her time came. The life growing inside of her would come into the world to its sound—the birth song of all the Jápmemeahttun.

As the snake eats his tail, the circle of our life closes.
We exist in balance.
We live on in harmony.
The death of one.
The birth of one.
The life of one as All.

The life of one as All. Aillun took in a deep breath. If she stepped off her sled and walked out into the snowy drifts, she would quake with the energy of all below her—the rocks, the plants, the earth, the hidden springs. It would all be there, humming with life—reverberating through her, as much a part of her as the new life growing inside.

It was the Song of All. And she had her part as well. But Aillun couldn't help wondering about the impact she made upon the world around her. She was one voice among a chorus, one chord vibrating among all these others. Did she matter?

The path she followed belonged to all those who preceded her, to her Origin. She would give birth where she had been born and if she lived long enough, she would return to be a life bringer for another. The cycle would complete itself. But would she matter? Would she fulfill the promise of her birth?

Aillun could not remember her own birth, although some Jáp-memeahttun said they could. But she knew her birth story. Her *biebmoeadni* had shared it with her throughout her childhood.

"*Bieba*, please!" she would beg.

Her guide mother would relent after some protest and begin the story in the same manner each time.

"My child, the whole Song is important, because it sustains us. But, since it gives you happiness, come and listen to your part of it."

"You were delivered to my arms in the dark time by your oktoeadni, your birth mother. She had returned from her Origin ready to take her place as an *almai*; her time as a female was over. You were a small bundle wrapped in duollji. When she pulled back the reindeer furs, I could see you were as pale as the snow in which you were born, but your eyes were clear and dark like the heavens, and your cheek held the smallest black dot. And like a star it has stayed with you, unchanged." Her guide mother would caress the mark upon her cheek.

"Bieba, more!"

And with a sigh, more a laugh, her guide mother would continue.

"Your oktoeadni placed you in my arms and sung the story of your birth, how the ravens descended to give you your soul and how the wolves circled, watchful of a new Immortal entering, and that day a wish went out into the heavens for you to have a future like the bright North Star. That day your oktoeadni became an almai and you became my *mánná*."

Her childish request fulfilled, Aillun always hugged her biebmoeadni and ran off to play with the other mánáid, content in her uniqueness and belonging.

But this story no longer quelled her fears, nor answered her questions. At the moment, she wondered how she would give birth outside of the Song and then return, to leave behind not only her child but everything she had known and experienced.

Unwilling to look at her future any longer, Aillun nudged her reindeer, and the sled moved beyond the sleeping village. In the shadows of the trees, Aillun retreated into her memories, where she still lived happily, training to be a healer.

Aillun had been one of several apprentices taken on by Okta, the oldest and most experienced healer. The tasks of the apprentices had been mundane, but were no less crucial for their everydayness. They had gathered herbs, ground roots to powder, and distilled tinctures. Aillun understood the kitchen chores, but each task also contained a profound lesson when explained by her teacher.

On her first trip to gather forest herbs Aillun had felt impatient. The inexperience of youth had led her to believe she knew how to pick plants. She had reached to pluck one from the ground, but Okta's shout had stopped her short.

"You cannot take a plant thus!" he reprimanded her. "You would rip it from the earth and all its properties of healing would be lost in the act of violence. To gather plants is to ask them to join you in the process of healing. You must acknowledge their existence and the sacrifice you are asking them to make. Take the time to listen to the plants. They will tell you their strength, their weakness, and their willingness. They will guide you."

Aillun was embarrassed by the censure, but possessed enough wisdom not to let her pride stand in the way of her future.

She lowered her eyes. "Yes, Okta."

When she looked up, she saw the healer's benevolent smile. But more importantly, Aillun saw the grinning face of Kalek, another apprentice. She was so surprised by the almai's expression she barely took in the healer's next words.

In the following moon cycles, Aillun and Kalek worked side by side and when not with Okta, they spent their time in happy companionship, their shy tenderness nurtured by quiet ardor.

Kalek had been by her side when she received her first mánná. Holding the sleeping infant and looking up into Kalek's smiling face, Aillun finally understood the meaning of love: being loved and loving in return.

In the hushed snowfall, Aillun clung to this memory, and shivered against the cold and her own growing apprehension. She looked up through the treetops, hoping for the comfort of a blue sky, and cringed when she saw the frosty gloom staring back.

Although it was only shortly past midday, she was tired. The life growing inside of her seemed to be requiring more and more of her strength. Aillun stopped the sled and climbed out by a circle of birch trees, listening to the hum of all life. She placed her hand upon the bark of the closest tree and willed the energy to flow into her. Somewhere off in the distance, she heard a wolf pack readying itself to hunt. She shivered again.

Aillun foraged the wood close to her, too tired to travel farther. She squatted before her small pile of branches and carefully pulled out her tinder pouch. Her hands fumbled it, but with effort she was able to get a spark started. The wind blew out the nascent flames. Aillun choked back her instant panic. *What if I can't get a fire started? What if I freeze here?* Her hands trembled as she struck the flint with her curved firesteel. The spark shimmered and she quickly huddled forward, protecting the flame as if it were her child.

The flames grew and quickly gobbled the twigs she fed them, and soon Aillun sat before a small hungry fire. She eased back, looking down at her swelling body. Only days before, the roundness had been less noticeable. She had tried to conceal the change for as long as possible, dreading the future it heralded.

Of course Okta had known, but he had said nothing and instead had waited for her to say something. He understood. But Kalek—Kalek had not.

～

"I wanted to protect you," she explained in the quiet gloom of the apothecary.

"I do not need protection," Kalek retorted.

"Fine then," Aillun snapped back, "I wanted to protect myself from heartache. If I did not admit what was happening, then it could not be so."

"So you denied truth, and you denied us the chance to face our future together."

"What future is there?"

"There was the future of every minute we lost in a lie you told yourself."

When she did not respond Kalek continued, "I could have shared it with you. I could have prepared you."

"Prepared me for what?" Aillun argued. "To go Outside? To leave everything I have ever known and come back to become someone not even I will recognize?"

"Yes! Yes, I could have done that. I have done it myself. Why did you never ask me?"

"I thought we would have more time. I hoped we would have more time."

Kalek's anger receded, and seemed to hollow him out. "But we do not." He sighed. "They are gathering the Council now. No doubt you will be summoned soon to the Chamber of Passings."

~

When the Council had called her forth, Aillun had been prepared, not to answer the call of her destiny, but rather to present a long list of excuses to postpone it.

"Sister, your time has come," the Voice of the Council intoned.

"But I have just become a biebmoeadni," Aillun protested. "My mánná is still a baby."

"Do not worry, Sister," spoke another voice from the Council. "The babe will have a guide mother. One of us will take her."

"But she has not yet heard the song of her birth."

"She will hear it from her new guide mother," said another from the Council.

"But I did not choose this! I am not ready!" Of all her protestations, this was the truest.

The Voice of the Council embraced her and let her cry. When no more tears fell, the Voice said, "Sister, to be Jápmemeahttun is to transform. Remember the first Oktoeadni. To give birth Outside is a test we must all endure to protect those within the Song. Think of all of us when you say you are not ready. We are so few, and we are scattered like leaves upon the wind. You may believe us to be cruel, but none of us gets to choose our time. Some of us stay guide mothers long enough to see the rebirth of our Life Star, *Guovassonásti*, many times, and others, like you, no sooner walk between *nieddaš* and biebmoeadni than you must cross over to oktoeadni and almai. But this is our way; this and our Song have allowed us to continue to live on when other creatures of the gods have perished."

They sat quietly. Aillun's acceptance numbed her. She would leave to give birth.

On the dawn of her departure day, the Council gathered once again. She had placed her mánná in the arms of her new guide mother and sung the child's birth song for all to hear. Aillun gathered her supplies for the journey and was embraced by all of the Council. In these final moments she asked with despair, "How can I do this alone?"

"You will not be alone," the Council comforted her. "The chosen *Taistelijan* will guide you."

"You mean the warrior will journey with me." Aillun grasped on to this slim hope.

"No, sister. You journey alone. The Taistelijan will find you at your Origin."

"How can that be? How can the warrior know where my Origin is?"

The faces of the Council smiled for the first time since they had come to her.

"He will find you at your Origin, because it is his as well."

CHAPTER SEVEN

IRJAN RETURNED TO THE farm at nightfall. The market had taken longer than expected, and the snow falling throughout the day had made the journey home harder. Irjan declined the invitation of his traveling companions to stop in the village to warm himself. The previous day's events made him anxious to return to his farm and family.

From a distance, Irjan could see no smoke rising from his dwelling. An inexplicable feeling of dread washed over him. Irjan dropped what he carried and ran headlong to his house. He staggered heedlessly through drifts until he burst through the door. His heart sought to believe his wife had merely fallen asleep upon the floor, but his eyes told him otherwise. Even in the darkness, Irjan could see Sohja's limbs were cast about her in an unnatural way.

Irjan ran to her, dropping upon his knees to pull her into his arms. Her skin burned with heat and she moaned.

"My love," Irjan shouted in panic, shaking her.

Sohja groaned again faintly.

He pulled her to him and rocked back and forth, making silent bargains with the gods. "Please," his voice escaped his lips. Repeatedly he begged. "Please."

Sohja drew in a ragged breath, sounding as if she were trying to draw air from water. He caressed her feverish face, and rejected what he knew to be the outcome. "No. No. No. No."

In the midst of his canting, Irjan stopped in terror. He scrambled across the floor to the cradle, dragging his wife's limp body. He reached his hand into the cradle and felt the cold body of his son. In his panic, he overturned the child's bed and the small lifeless body spilled onto the floor.

Irjan cried out and the house, and everything around it, filled with the sound of heartbreak.

He pulled Marnej to rest between his body and his fevered wife. Again he rocked silently as tears fell down his face.

Throughout the night Irjan clung to everything he had ever loved in his life and felt it slip through his fingers. When Sohja drew her last breath it felt as if his own had been taken from him. He waited and willed her to breathe again, shaking her as if he could somehow dislodge the hand of death that held her.

Finally, Irjan let go of her lifeless body, and sat still in the darkness of the night.

One thought pushed out all other thoughts in his mind.

Why?

Over and over again, he repeated the word until it lost meaning and became only sound. But in his heart, Irjan knew why. This was no work of the Brethren. This was the work of the gods. This was his punishment.

∾

In the morning, Irjan awoke holding on to his family, but the question of why had faded. In the hollowness of his heart, he knew he was to blame for what had happened. He had failed in his duty to protect his family. He had failed them the moment he believed he could escape his past.

Irjan curled up in a ball and let his grief creep through his limbs like a slow, squeezing serpent.

When he woke, his breath escaped him in raspy clouds. He caressed his wife's face and his son's. Both were tinged blue with cold, as if their blood had frozen in their veins. How long had he been lying there? A day, or more? He didn't know.

Irjan stumbled to his feet and went outside. The goods from the market lay half buried in the snow where he had dropped them. He passed them by as he crossed the yard toward the barn. Animals, anxious for their forgotten food and water, greeted him. He released them from their pens and went in search of his tools.

He grasped the metal pick and spade, and their cold surfaces burned him. He flinched but held on tighter. He walked out toward the tree at the far end of the yard and thrust the spade into the earth's newly frozen crust. Again and again he stabbed the ground in rage. He pulled the earth away from its resting spot as if tearing at his own flesh, trying to find the source of his pain.

Irjan burned with the sweat of his labor. He tore open the furs protecting him against the cold, and cast them aside. Again he dug deep into the ground. At the end of his labor, he stood surrounded by the short walls of the grave. He shivered and pulled himself up out of his self-hewn abyss. He looked back across to the house and saw his wife as a memory, passing before his eyes.

It had been early spring and she was still pregnant. She had come out to fetch him for a meal. Her one hand waved in the air, beckoning his attention, the other cradled around her belly, embracing their unborn child. Irjan fell to his knees and felt the wetness of the snow soak in. If he believed his wife and child were waiting for him in the afterworld, he would have lain down and let the cold drain away his life. But he now knew himself to be cursed by the gods. They had seen to it—a lifetime of punishment. Death held no reward for him.

Irjan stood and gathered his clothing. He slowly walked toward the house. He paused at the threshold, then stepped in and shuffled toward the bed. He rested his hand on the blanket and closed his eyes, trying not to see Sohja carding and spinning its wool. He gently guided the blanket to the floor. He lifted his wife's stiff body and laid it upon the waiting shroud, then folded its corners, leaving her face uncovered.

He pressed his hand to where her heart had once beat. He stared at Sohja's face, not so he would remember it, but so he would never forget it. He took his knife from its sheath and cut a swatch of the fabric to place in his pocket; then he kissed her one last time before finally covering her face.

Irjan took Sohja's needle and thread and painstakingly bound together the edges of the fabric. He carried her to the grave and returned for his son, Marnej. He made his son a shroud like his mother's, using the blanket from the cradle. The blanket was like the one upon their bed, the palest of blues.

He folded the soft wool around the tiny body, feeling the contours of the form beneath. Marnej looked as if he still slept.

Irjan gathered the child in his arms and trudged to the waiting grave. There he knelt and tried to place the child beside his mother. But he could not. Every part of him fought against it. His outstretched arms shook under the tiny weight. Irjan groaned and pulled Marnej back to his chest. He hunched over and rested his forehead upon the ground, feeling his tears begin their icy journey to the waiting snow. Then he heard something, like a whisper in his ear or an echo of a long-ago thought.

Irjan stirred and raised his head to listen. As he concentrated, he looked down and saw the death before him. He squeezed his eyes tight, trying to find consoling darkness.

But there was no darkness, only the disappearing vision of his dead wife and child, encased in their meager shrouds. And yet, his thoughts still flashed, fragments of light and life.

Irjan tried to grasp on to them to see where they would take him: To his childhood? Before he'd lost it? Was he meant to find some hope in his past, to carry him into the future? His thoughts took him to the village of his boyhood, where smoke choked him, and flames pierced his flesh. He remembered a hand stopping him—thick fingers with a single carved gold ring.

"There is nothing you can do," the priest had said, looking down at him.

Behind him, another man spoke. "Brother, do not leave this boy with no hope. There is always something that can be done in the face of such evil." The second man touched his hand to his sword. "You can fight."

Irjan shrank from the memory. Death surrounded him. The family of his boyhood had died, and he'd been spared. The family of his manhood had died, and yet again he'd been spared. He dared not look upon the reasons. And yet, he could not look away.

The day his parents died, Irjan had turned his back on the flames and left, hand in hand with the man who'd urged him to fight. He learned and trained and became a Piijkij; he fought and killed until he could no longer remember the purpose behind the killing. When Irjan discovered his parents had become a distant memory in his heart, his rage became emptiness and he dropped his sword and walked away into the forest. Irjan could not have saved his parents; he could only avenge them. But he could have saved his family. If he had fulfilled his destiny as the Apotti had asked, then his wife and child would still live. To be sure, they would not have been his, but they would have been alive.

They would be alive, echoed in his mind.

Suddenly, Irjan saw flashes of another time, another person, a woman.

He heard the refrain. *I am the maiden.*

A vision of a baby loomed before his eyes.

I am the bringer of life.

Irjan thought he saw the woman die.

My transformation serves the future.

A man rose in her place.

My transformation reflects the past.

The man turned away.

I walk alone, but count myself among the many who walked before me.

When the vision released him, Irjan was panting. "A Jápmea."

Clarity took hold, and he knew what he must do. Irjan stood and returned to the house. He gathered the few possessions he deemed important. He then worked flint and tinder into a small fire, which he spread throughout the house by use of a torch. With the house ablaze, he returned to the graveside.

This time he did not have to turn his back on the flames, for they were already behind him. His life as a farmer was over; he was a Piijkij. He would find her, this Jápmea of his visions. He would fulfill his duty to his son. With each shovelful of dirt he cast upon the grave, he swore a new oath.

"This shall be righted."

~

The smoke from the burning farmhouse drifted into the noon sky, which was already fading into gloom. It took time for the girkogilli to see the signs and raise the alarm. Those closest were hidden by the tall forest, and last to realize something was amiss.

When the first villagers reached the farm, they saw the house consumed by flames, and at the very end of the yard, freshly turned soil and the marker of a grave. When shouts raised no response, the villagers drew back in dread. An evil walked among them, whether the work of man, or of something else, they cared not. They cared only to keep the evil from their own homes. The bravest among them bowed their heads to pray for the souls of those who once lived upon the farm. The rest ran away.

Irjan heard the shouts and the voices in the hush of the forest. He looked back in the direction from which he'd come, but could see nothing, which was just as it should have been. Nothing remained for him at the farm. Everything he valued he now carried with him.

In the distance, Irjan thought he heard something else. He stopped to listen. Was it at a distance or much closer? He could not tell. Suddenly, as before, the sounds reached him in images in his own mind. *I am the maiden,* a baby; *I am the bringer of life,* he saw the woman die; *my transformation serves the future,* and then appear as a man; *my transformation reflects the past,* and the journey; *I walk alone, but count myself among the many who walked before me.*

~

The insistent banging on the temple door brought Siggur out of his chambers. The acolyte trudged down the corridor, muttering curses against whoever disturbed what little time he had to himself. Siggur pulled open the door, and was assailed by a breathless plea.

"Brother, there is a fire at the farmhouse of the traveler of the Pohjola. No one there answers our cries. There is a grave. They have died. Brother, a great evil is walking among us. Apotti, you must come and cleanse the site or the evil will spread."

Before Siggur could answer, he felt a presence behind him, and a stern voice resonated. "Brother, calm yourself. No evil can spread if our hearts are closed to it. Return to your home, care for your family, and attend to your prayers. I will do what is required by the gods."

"Yes, Apotti," the chastened messenger responded. "I thank you."

"As the gods thank you," the priest answered, then withdrew.

The villager remained on the steps, dumbfounded.

"Do as the Apotti instructs," Siggur commanded, anxious to follow his superior.

"Yes, Brother," the messenger mumbled, and staggered off the steps toward his home.

Siggur quickly closed the door and hurried toward the Apotti's chambers. His mind raced. Before he got halfway to his destination, he heard banging along the narrow corridor. This time the sound came from an entrance door he had already passed on his way to the Apotti's chambers.

Siggur wished to ignore it, but he knew that if the knock went unanswered, the Apotti would hear and it would draw his ire. He could ill afford to anger the priest if he hoped to gain his confidence. Siggur backtracked and heaved open the door. His ready admonishment fell silent when he saw the traveler from the Pohjola.

The man pushed past him into the corridor. Siggur protested, but he could tell from the man's movement he would not be stopped.

Siggur entered the priest's chambers on the heels of the visitor. He bowed. "Apotti, I could not stop him."

"There is no need to stop him, Siggur," the priest replied from behind the shadows of his desk. "I am pleased to see him."

Siggur shifted his attention from the priest to the man beside him, taking note of his mud-covered leggings and the frayed satchel draped across his back.

"Leave us," the cleric ordered.

Siggur bowed deeply, casting another appraising look at the man beside him. The stench of sweat rose from him, carrying with it the scent of barely contained danger.

"Yes, Apotti," Siggur answered and withdrew.

He closed the door softly, careful to leave a sliver of an opening so he could listen to their conversation.

"Your presence, though pleasing, is unexpected," the priest said evenly. "I understood our conversation to be at an end."

"Today I offer you a different answer," the man replied.

"Please, sit."

～

The man remained standing, staring both at the priest and through him. For the first time since he had embarked upon his plan, Rikkar understood the power of the man in front of him. He was unshaven and dirty, lacking refinement, and yet he radiated a force unlike any the priest had previously encountered.

"Stay as it suits you," Rikkar conceded, rather than remain silent in the face of the pillar before him. He delayed before asking, "What is your answer, Brother?"

"I am a Piijkij and will do what the gods ask of me."

The priest let out the breath he had been holding. "And why today do you answer the gods, when just a pair of days ago you would not?"

"Because they are the last to have use of me."

Rikkar leaned forward, but strained to keep the eagerness from his eyes and words. "Do not doubt your value to others, Piijkij. The future will speak your name and know your part in bringing an end to the Jápmea."

"Do not flatter me, priest. There remain no voices in this world I care to hear speak my name."

"We have much then to discuss." Rikkar leaned back in his chair.

"There is nothing to discuss."

"But I must know of your plan and your intended course of action."

"You have no need for my plan or course of action. You need only know that I will fulfill my duty to the gods." The man's voice grew colder in his defiance.

"But what proof will I have that you have done what you have been asked?"

The man's eyes narrowed. "The gods need no proof. They will know what has been done in their name. As for you, I will bring back the carcasses so you can scavenge from them what you need."

Rikkar did not protest the man's frank response. They understood each other. It was enough.

"You look to have few supplies about you. What needs might a humble servant of the gods give to one of the Brethren of Hunters to aid him in his cause?" Rikkar spread his hands in a gesture of benevolence.

"A sleigh, a horse, and a sword."

"And coin?"

"I do not intend to buy the Jápmea, Apotti. Besides, I find the point of the sword more effective than the rounded edge of the coin."

Rikkar snorted. "Quite right, Piijkij, quite right. You may draw foodstuffs from the rectory kitchen. The sword you may choose from our armaments."

"Your armaments, Apotti?" the man questioned, showing an expression for the first time since walking into the priest's chambers. "What need has a spiritual servant of the gods for armaments?"

"You of all people should know, Piijkij, the battle against evil is dangerous and often fought with body and soul. As for the sleigh, that will require coin. I could give you mine, but I doubt its finery would suit your purpose."

"Actually, it would suit my purpose entirely." The man looked at Rikkar to gauge his reaction, as if he wanted to know what Rikkar was willing to sacrifice for whatever he thought he would gain.

Rikkar hesitated, then smiled. "Whatever the Piijkij requires."

Rikkar drew out a small piece of vellum from a scattered pile upon his desk. He hastily scribbled out instructions, the scratching of his nib the only sound in the room. He added his seal with a flourish before handing the scroll to the man. "Give this to Siggur, my acolyte. He will see to it that you have what you need."

The man unrolled the document, scrutinizing its contents. He raised a brow. "You make reference to a sledge and not a sleigh," he said evenly, his gaze sliding up to meet Rikkar's.

It was the priest's turn to be skeptical. "How is it that a Hunter can read?"

"The Brethren seek to sharpen minds along with their swords," the man said, handing the scroll back to Rikkar. "I'm sure you meant to write sleigh."

~

Irjan walked out of the priest's chambers, shifting the satchel upon his back. He had gotten what he needed. He looked up in time to see a figure receding. He shook his head. He would not play a game of shadows with the acolyte. If the priest chose to keep secrets and his servant chose to seek them out, the game was theirs alone. Irjan cared only to get started before he lost the trail of the voice. He followed the corridor until it jogged; there he ran into the acolyte walking in his direction.

"Brother, you have finished your discussion with the Apotti?" the acolyte asked, with an almost convincing tone of boredom. From the casual sound of the young man's voice Irjan knew the acolyte had indeed been spying. An uninformed man would have naturally been more curious.

"Yes, Brother, my audience is finished," Irjan answered, "but I am in need of your assistance."

The young man's eyes suddenly sparked to life. "I will serve you as best I can, Brother."

"The Apotti has allowed me use of his sleigh and horse as well as my choice of his armaments and whatever foodstuffs I require," Irjan said.

The young man wavered. Irjan could tell he struggled to find the best way forward.

To ease the acolyte's burden Irjan added, "You are welcome to read his instructions while I wait." He proffered the scroll but it remained unclaimed.

The young man blushed. "That will not be necessary. A Brother such as yourself, in the service of the gods, would not lie or seek to make gains from falsehoods. Follow me to the armory. We can then visit the kitchen and prepare the sleigh."

The young man took down a candle from the sconce and cradled its flame.

Irjan bowed his head in mock appreciation, but kept the bite out of his words when he said, "I thank you, Brother."

Irjan trailed behind the young man as they made their way through the dim corridor, passing many doors. They stopped in front of the last, and the acolyte drew a key from within his robe. He pulled the chain over his head, catching his hood and tugging awkwardly to release it. He straightened himself before sliding the key into the lock, then swung open the door and lit the torch inside with his candle.

The torch cast a weak light across the small room, but all around the walls, metal dully reflected the colors of the flame. Axes, pikes, and swords lined the walls evenly, just like the soldiers destined to hold them. Bows hung staggered by height, and arrows stood in regiments.

Irjan drew his hand up the fletched end of the arrows and imagined them flying along with the birds whose feathers adorned the shafts. *Birth and death, together, as always.*

"You are a Piijkij," the young man blurted at Irjan, apparently unable to curb his curiosity.

Irjan took down a sword and tested its weight and feel. "Yes," he answered, without taking his eyes off the blade.

"That is why you have seen the Jápmea. Because you hunt them and kill them."

"Yes."

He replaced one sword, then gently removed the satchel from around his shoulders. The acolyte moved forward to take it, but Irjan abruptly turned his shoulder, placing the satchel carefully upon the ground himself.

The young cleric drew back as if he had been struck.

Irjan noted his recoil, but focused his attention on the swords upon the wall. He drew another down and cut the air with quick, broad strokes.

"That is what the Apotti has asked of you," the young man concluded.

"Yes."

"Have you killed many?"

"Yes." Irjan chose a casing for the sword and fastened it around his waist. He wiped the blade on the folded ends of his cloak before seating it at his side.

"What happens when they are killed?" the acolyte probed.

Irjan crouched down and laid his hands upon his satchel. Seated on his haunches, he looked up at the young man.

"Nothing. They die like us. They cry out in agony. They void themselves, and their lifeless bodies serve no one but the worms."

Irjan lifted the satchel with care, repositioned his possessions on his back, and stood.

The young man's face glowed with wonder. "One hears tales of a golden light that can transform men into immortals."

Irjan cut him short. "There is no light, only a gasp."

It was a lie, but he did not have the time or the desire to encourage this boy. Confirming tales would not serve his purpose.

"What then of the sleigh and food?" Irjan said to forestall further speculation.

Chastened, the young man extinguished the torch in the bucket of water by the door and took hold of a candle once again. "Follow me," he said, trying to regain the dignity of his position.

Irjan did as he was bidden and felt grateful for the silence. He had no wish to go into the tales of ghosts and spirits. Mothers told their children these stories about the Jápmea to exact good behavior, but in every tall tale, truth flickers like a distant flame. The stories reminded the Olmmoš they were not alone, nor their own masters.

In truth, the Jápmea no longer sent out killers to rid the world of the Olmmoš, but they did travel out in the world and were dangerous. As any hunter knew, certain prey could become deadly when cornered. The Jápmea were no different. They would kill to protect themselves. The scars crisscrossing Irjan's side attested to that fact. But regardless of the risk, he bristled with resolve. He would once again seek the Jápmea, to balance the scales of life and death.

CHAPTER EIGHT

DJORN PREPARED TO ANSWER the summoning. The Taistelijan warrior had journeyed as long and as far as any,
but one task remained. He sat quietly in his modest
quarters, listening to the Song of All. It flowed through him,
though no sounds passed his lips. He could no more stop it than
he could his heart. The Jápmemeahttun had survived because of
the Song of All and it reminded him of how much suffering they
had endured.

Djorn stood and moved to the slit of a window. He drew back
the leather flap covering it against the gusts of snow and wind.
Looking out upon the tall trees, he watched the snow fall upon
the branches and felt the branches' burden as his own. Guovassonásti, their Life Star, whose comings and goings measured the
length of their existence, was on its descent. Soon it would be
gone. As would he.

Suddenly, pain twisted him as if his flesh sought to pull away
from his bone. He leaned against the wall, gasping. The intervals
between these episodes drew closer. He could postpone his journey no longer, and yet he hated to leave. Outside he would only
have his voice to sustain him.

Djorn withdrew from the window, letting the leather cover
fall back into place. He gathered the supplies he needed for his

last days: a small amount of food, his furs to protect him, and his *miehkki*. Guovassonásti had risen and set more than twelve times since his blade had been used in battle. *More than one hundred seasons of snow*, he thought to himself as he hefted the blade. So much time had passed.

At the gate, Djorn made his farewells. His loved ones shed tears and held him close, while his compatriots clasped his hand but said nothing. Nothing remained to be said. The cycle must be completed.

Djorn walked through the gates and looked back at his home. All that remained for him lay Outside. He patted the reindeer beside him.

"Come, old friend. One last journey."

The animal took up its burden, and together the warrior and his steed rode into the forest.

As he traveled west, he wished he could feel the sun's warming rays on his back, but he would not live to see another summer. His time had come in the season of snow. In some ways, he thought it fitting his end should coincide with the darkness. It put him in the right frame of mind. He thought of the next part of the Song. Instinctively the refrain came to him.

I return to my Origin to share my life force.
My life ends so that a new life begins and another transforms.
I leave as I entered and the whole is unchanged.

He wondered what it would feel like when he finally gave voice to those words. Would he feel himself part of the child to be born, or the nieddaš becoming almai? Would any vestige of his essence continue in the world? He thought back to when he had become almai. He remembered feeling frightened. The *boaris*, the old one, who had joined him at their Origin, had tenderly reassured him.

"I do not know what awaits me," the old one had said, "but what awaits you is both sacred and profound. Today you end your time as nieddaš. Tomorrow you will give birth to not only a child, but to your new self. You are asked to remember all you have experienced thus far, so that as almai, and later boaris, you understand the needs, hopes, and destinies of all."

But Djorn had forgotten much of what life had been like before he'd become a Taisteljian. He'd spent so much time at war and in battles, he worried his own words would not be adequate for the nieddaš who awaited him.

At the edge of a clearing, he stopped and tethered his binna to a tree. The reindeer nibbled at lichen growing upon the bark and ignored him as he walked out into the vast expanse of white.

Were anyone to happen upon this place, they would not know of the tragedy that had occurred here. No rock cairn marked the great battle waged upon this spot. There had been so many battles that the memory of both the Olmmoš and the Jápmemeahttun had collapsed them into a single endless war. But now, as Djorn stood on the field surrounded by hushed snowfall, it almost felt as if the war had never happened.

Long ago, when the Olmmoš had first walked out of the eastern sunrise, the Jápmemeahttun had looked into their large, wide-set eyes and had seen innocence. Their kind taught the new-comers how to survive in the world—how to live upon the ice and snow and find light in the endless darkness.

But over generations, the Olmmoš, like mánáid, grew quarrelsome and resentful of guidance. They rebelled and denounced all Jápmemeahttun as abominations, and claimed the gods as theirs alone, even as they slaughtered neiddaš and biebmoeadni, along with their charges.

Djorn's hand moved to his miehkki. Feeling the hilt's contours, he remembered that time, and the blood that later dripped down its long blade.

In those distant days, when the almai had answered the Elders' call to take up arms, he had stood at the edge of many clearings such as this one and readied himself to meet his end. He had run onto the fields determined to take the lives of as many Olmmoš as he could, and had screamed with vengeance as his comrades fell beside him. But time and again, Djorn had lived to fight another day. Until the Elders came forward and spoke of a different way.

"It is a gift of the gods," they had said.

The Song of All could hide them.

While the Jápmemeahttun has always sung, to pass on their knowledge, to commune with their gods, to honor those they loved, it was only when Elders had listened deep within themselves as they sang that they understood what was truly possible.

"We are one," the Elders had said, their faces expectant as they explained.

Djorn had scoffed but he had slowed his breath and quieted his heart as the Elders had instructed. Then with a rush like cascading water, songs too numerous to count had flooded into him, threatening to drown out his own. Mercifully they had coalesced and Djorn had understood what the Elders had meant when they said they were all one. He had glimpsed the veil that could shield them. The Olmmoš would never be able to single out the Jápmemeahttun song.

Then the Elders said that their kind had a choice. They could continue to wage war, or they could withdraw and make a new life for themselves. And as war-weary as they were, the Jápmemeahttun were willing to listen.

Their kind chose a new life. They vanished before the eyes of their enemies, who celebrated, believing a scourge had been wiped cleanly from their world. But the Jápmemeahttun remained. Deep in the Song of All, they stood in front of the Olmmoš unseen. To the Jápmemeahttun, the Olmmoš became like the distant shores—visible but unreachable. Olmmoš and Jápmemeahttun could then live in the same world and yet never have to touch.

This gift of the gods had saved the Jápmemeahttun, but at the time Djorn could not accept it. With blood-lust running through his veins, he said it as a weak-willed trick, a sign of cowardice. And many Taistelijan agreed. They wanted to fight, to teach the upstart Olmmoš their place in the world. For almost one hundred seasons of snow, discord threatened the peace of their kind, as rogue warriors continued to hunt and kill the Olmmoš without sanction.

Djorn had been one of those rogues who refused to fade into the mists of obscurity when the dead needed to be avenged. And while Djorn and his comrades had foresworn peace, it did not mean they had not used the Song of All to their advantage. Early on they had discovered it was possible to shift back and forth between the two realms.

At first, only a few had the skill to make the shift. For most, the challenge of bringing their focus back to the All proved disastrous. Those who fought in battle were often too intent on the fight and were unable to hear the Song. For other Taistelijan, when they tried to escape by finding the Song, they often forgot to wield their swords, finding death in place of the other realm's safety.

The archers loosing arrows from the shadows found it easier. They were already focused on hiding. But in the end, the archers did not prevail among the ranks of the rogue warriors. A Taistelijan who elected to remain outside the Song of All could not choose to hide in the shadows and cast arrows. For these Taistelijan, the sword or the knife became the weapon of a true warrior and the arrow the sign of a coward.

Djorn was never a coward.

CHAPTER NINE

THE SNOWFALL GREW HEAVIER, blocking out the day's remaining light. Large flakes drifted into Irjan's beard and became imprisoned in the tangled dark hair. Today reminded him of so many days from his past. How many times before had he set out as he had today, determined to find his quarry? He could not remember. Some Piijkij were considered successful if they tracked and killed a handful of Jápmea in their lifetimes. Granted, those lifetimes tended to be short. They became victims to the elements, wolves, and the Jápmea themselves.

If a Piijkij was a Hunter, then so too was he hunted. Although encounters with the Jápmea were less and less common, the danger they presented was no less daunting. Many Hunters who went abroad never returned. Sometimes they would be found frozen in the moment of death, and other times only remnants of their human forms remained, along with their weapons.

The Piijkij carried a mark of distinction upon each sword for just this reason, so the swords of the fallen would make their way back to villages and from there to the Brethren of Hunters. A ceremony of passing would be conducted and prayers would be offered to the gods. The next day the training would continue as if nothing had intervened.

Following the end of the battles, when the Jápmea still actively ambushed the Olmmoš, the early Hunters encountered hundreds of them. But with each successive season of snow, the number of Jápmea killed declined. It appeared the Immortals had grown wary, rarely traveling openly. As a Piijkij, Irjan had been luckier than most. At least that is how he described it when his exploits drew attention.

As a young Piijkij, he had been required to provide proof of his deeds upon his return. More often than not, the presentation of a gruesome talisman heralded his homecoming. As a youth, he thought the head a fitting declaration to his efforts. But his first summer foray, with its long warm days and its swarms of flies, quickly convinced him rotting relics were best kept small.

As Irjan's proficiency grew, relics became superfluous. His testimony and his reputation sufficed. The Brethren bestowed honors upon him many times. On those occasions, they spoke of his destiny, his duty, and his rewards. But they did not mention the methods they'd employed to make him into a Piijkij.

Irjan did not dispute that the Brethren made him into a skilled tracker. He could see without seeing, hear without hearing, and feel without touching. But they'd driven him without mercy to exhaustion then punished him for any weakness. When he was a young boy they'd left him blindfolded in unfamiliar woods leagues away, and tasked him with finding his way home. Finally, they'd forced Irjan to kill or be killed, to relieve him of all compassion. Irjan passed all their tests. He surmounted all the obstacles.

When the Brethren were satisfied and ready to send him out to hunt for the first time, they brought Irjan to the battlegrounds of the old wars. They intended to inspire him with his hallowed history. As they stood in the open meadow of green springtime, the gathered Brethren intoned a prayer to the gods.

We have taught as you have bidden.
He has learned as you have required.
May his blade strike glory upon the heavens.

May his blade draw the blood of those who call themselves
　　Immortals.

Irjan heard voices. But they weren't those of the Brothers at
his side. Rather, he heard the far-off voices of the dead below him.

I stand before the gods ready to fight.
I stand before the gods ready to die.

These thoughts of long ago came back to Irjan as he glided
easily over the fresh blanket of snow. Though his mind traveled
the ether, Irjan remained seated squarely within the comfort of
the Apotti's sleigh. If any had seen him passing, they would have
wondered at the incongruity of the man and his means of travel.
The beauty of the sleigh, with its wooden curves and golden fil-
igree, stood at odds with Irjan's harsh angles and rough appearance, but not a soul passed to make comment.

Irjan listened to the sounds of the world he moved through:
the snap of the leather reins, the quiet shushing of the rails along
the snow; the punctuated rhythm of the hooves, and the gentle
wheeze of breath. In syncope, these sounds filled the air, until
something broke its cadence.

A voice.

Abruptly, Irjan brought the sleigh to a halt. He jumped off
and concentrated on the drifting refrain. His eyes flew open in
frustration. Where was the voice coming from? With a singular
focus, Irjan scanned his surroundings, looking for anything to lead
him in the right direction. He searched for any tracks or traces.

From past experience, Irjan knew that when the Jápmea traveled on their own they struggled to remain hidden from Olmmoš
eyes, and sometimes they left traces: footprints, tracks, embers
of fires, bits of meals forgotten. They would be nothing out of
the ordinary. Often, Irjan had followed these signs and found his
own people, traveling, hunting, or lost. But other times, he had
followed the tracks and seen the flashes.

The first time he had glimpsed a Jápmea, he'd been young. He stood watching without moving as an almai disappeared into the summer forest. When the young Irjan regained his composure, he chased after the Jápmea. He ran through the thickets; branches snapped him in the face, causing his eyes to water and yet he ran on.

A flash appeared on his right and then disappeared. The leaves on the birch trees rustled and mixed with other sounds to drown out the footfalls of the hunted, and still, Irjan ran on. Blind and deaf, he ran deeper into the forest, until he was lost. Winded, he bent over, trying to catch his breath. When he straightened, the almai flashed ahead of him, bow and arrow aimed. In a shimmer of light the Jápmea disappeared. The arrow loosed by the Immortal grazed Irjan's shoulder, ripping his sleeve and binding the fabric to a tree behind him.

This time, there was no arrow. Nevertheless, Irjan felt pinned to where he stood. Though his heart beat like the running hooves of the binna, Irjan stopped looking about him and tried to winnow his thoughts until only one remained. One wordless thought vibrated within him, until he and it could not be separated—like a ringing bell. *At first it resonates in the ears and then in the body, until the sound and body are one and the same.*

CHAPTER TEN

AILLUN HEARD SOMETHING. SHE stopped. She stepped off her sled and away from the snorting breath of her binna to listen. Could it be the call of her Origin? Perhaps she was closer than she thought. Or, perhaps she heard the song of the Taistelijan awaiting her. She closed her eyes, trying to hear the voice, but the images in her mind made no sense. *A baby at a crossroads. A boy blindfolded wandering the woods. An Olmmoš racing through the forest, chasing another. An arrow flying through the air. A sword piercing the heart of a fallen one.*

Aillun's eyes flew open. In her vision, the fallen was Jápme-meahttun. She raced back to her sled, her heart pounding. She fumbled with the reins, dropping them into the snow, before jerking them to a start and heading down the path.

Aillun shivered, but not from the cold. She knew she'd heard a voice, but clearly not the Taistelijan. The images she'd seen were like a story told to caution the mánáid and the nied-daš about the world Outside. The voice, however, did not feel Jápmemeahttun. Although she could not explain why, it felt like an Olmmoš.

But the Olmmoš could not sing among the Jápmemeahttun, she told herself, urging her little reindeer forward.

That voice should not have reached her ears, and she should not have been able to see their images. And yet she had. Her mind raced to find reason. Was it a warning from one of her kind, or some trick to lure her into a trap? She knew the Piijkij still traveled in search of the Jápmemeahttun. Aillun, however, could not let herself believe she had heard a Piijkij. To do so would mean facing one of two grim possibilities: either she was hunted by the Piijkij, or—a more devastating prospect—the Olmmoš had finally crossed into their realm.

Although darkness made the path slow to travel upon, Aillun did not stop. She thanked the gods she need not use her eyes to find her way, for indeed she had never seen the path to her Origin. The last time she had passed, she'd been a baby in the arms of her oktoeadni. She now traveled as her instinct guided her, but could not help glancing back over her shoulder to see what followed.

The unknown song faded to a faint whisper sometime in the waxing night and then disappeared; however, Aillun still felt its impact upon her. As she pressed on, she tried to take comfort in sound of only her song. But the words and images of the other continued to cloud her mind.

~

Irjan came to a fork in the path. He drew back on the reins. The shaggy horse came to a stop with a shake of its head. One path led in the direction of the long-forgotten battlegrounds. He remembered the voices of the fallen. They had guided him in the past and he still felt the pull of the place upon him, but today he was driven by the dead. He looked toward the forgotten battlefield once again and then chose the other path.

The moonless night, however, made the track he traveled impassable, and Irjan reluctantly stopped. He gathered his furs and satchel from the sleigh, then withdrew the stout kitchen axe. Using the axe's broad side, he dug down through the soft layers of snow to make an embankment under a pine's wide-reaching arms.

He gathered the outlying twigs and small fallen branches, then withdrew the tinder pouch he always carried.

Irjan struck a spark and lit a small fierce fire, which, if well tended, would keep him warm and serve to keep curious wolves at bay until dawn. Only then would he actually sleep, and only then for a brief respite. He removed his satchel and placed it against the tree trunk for protection. He burrowed up against it. It had been eight seasons of snow since he'd turned his back on this life, and he hoped he retained enough of his stamina and training to see him through.

~

Somewhere beyond those who moved across the snowy landscape, a voice grew in strength.

We are the Elders.
We are chosen to guide.
We listen to the voices of the gods.
We seek to avoid the mistakes of the past.

All Jápmemeahttun recognized the well-known chorus. But its familiar refrains now contained an unusual element, a warning.

The birth of our undoing is at hand.

CHAPTER ELEVEN

DJORN LOOKED UPON DEATH as an old friend. It had been his constant companion upon the battlefields. He had witnessed scores of his kind die in the wars, and cradled countless bodies next to his as they took their last breaths. And yet, his old friend death had never taken him into its embrace. The Jápmemeahttun who passed in Djorn's arms on the battlefields had done so in the realm of the Olmmoš, their spirits lost forever. The greatest fear of his kind was a death without rebirth, but Djorn had not feared this type of death. He had grown to understand it. It would be the end. A final end. No more fighting ever again. But now, he realized he was not so very different from the rest of his kind. Like them, he too feared the unknown, but for him, rebirth, not death, presented the greatest mystery.

When the first signs of the coming change bore down on Djorn, he sought the counsel of the healers.

"Dizziness, sudden weakness, and the gripping pain," he said.

The healers nodded and spoke among themselves before giving him their recommendation. They advised him to seek out the Elders.

"This is no sickness or passing malady. It is the sign your end time draws near," the healers explained.

Djorn ignored them. He knew himself better than they, so he returned to his activities and waited for the illness to pass. It did not pass. The bursts of pain grew in frequency and in strength—leaving him breathless and unable to deny the healers' conclusion. His ending time had come. As he should have done from the start, he took counsel with the Elders. In the quiet of their chambers they gathered together and placed Djorn before them.

Standing among the Elders, Djorn felt the same sickening anticipation he had felt a lifetime ago, waiting to enter a battle.

A lifetime ago, he thought. *My lifetime ago*.

"For countless seasons of snow you have sung the song of a warrior," one voice intoned. "We have listened to it and heard its breadth of timbre: Valor. Sadness. Vengeance. Acceptance. Your heart speaks them all now."

"The time has come for a new song, warrior," another spoke. "We ask you to listen to the wisdom of the gods and learn."

Together the voices of the Elders joined as one, and Djorn did not so much hear them as feel them.

To be Jápmemeahttun is to transform.

Once we believed ourselves to be like the orbs in the heavens, permanent.

Our self-deception brought tragedy. But the tragedy helped us hear the true voices of the gods, and we changed.

We learned the power of transformation.

The head of the Council of Elders stepped forward, his weathered face lined by experience, a testament to wisdom. The *Noaidi* held up the ancient, deerskin drum in his hand. The other voices died away. The Noaidi began a low, steady drumming that matched the beat of Djorn's heart.

"Our renewal began with the first boaris and the first oktoeadni," the Noaidi's deep voice shook with quiet power.

"They were two of only a few souls clustered together for survival."

Like a gathering storm on the Pohjola, the drumming picked up momentum.

"One soul prepared to leave the world," the Noaidi said, looking directly at Djorn.

"The other to bring a new soul into it," he trailed off, even as the drum beat grew in strength.

"Birth and death met as the old one died." The drumming came faster and faster. "His life force passed to the waiting unborn. But the small body could not hold the power."

For an instant, Djorn feared his own heart would burst as pain flared in his body.

But the Noaidi's voice was relentless. "His spirit passed through all of the assembled Jápmemeahttun. Those too weak exploded in a burst of light filling the night skies for all time."

The drumming stopped abruptly, but the air surrounding Djorn still vibrated with its thunderous force.

Barely above a whisper, the Noaidi said, "When we look to the heavens of the dark time, we are reminded of the power of transformation. We see the true meaning of the Jápmemeahttun."

One of the Elders stepped forward. He placed his gnarled hands on Djorn's shoulders. The old warrior who had been so fearless in battle, quaked with pain and sudden uncertainty.

"You will journey away from here, to your Origin," he said. "In the final transformation, you will reenter the Song of All and, like the first of our kind, your life force will bring about the rebirth of the Jápmemeahttun. You will awaken the soul of the baby to be born and the seed of the almai inside the nieddaš. You will complete the cycle, and the whole will remain vibrant and unchanged."

Another of the Elders came forward and spoke. "Although you will travel alone, you will carry with you the future of all of us."

Irjan awoke suddenly when the cold began to seep into his bones. His fire had gone out, and the wind had picked up. He quickly looked around his carved circle of snow, then sat up under the branches of the fir, and saw nothing disturbed. He leaned back, hurriedly searching for his satchel. It was still there. He took a deep breath and released it slowly. His sense of relief, however, faded immediately, overshadowed by anger.

I should have stayed awake. How can I be this weak?

Irjan gathered his possessions and burst up through the branches protecting him. The snow they had kept at bay showered down.

"Gods be cursed!"

He stood, unsteady, and groped to gather the sleigh's harness.

His heart pounded beyond his control. He leaned against the sleigh. The carved wood dug into his back.

I have traveled less than a day, and I am already failing! Are eight seasons of snow enough to wipe away the preceding twenty?

"Or am I being punished by the gods for disavowing my oath?" he spoke out loud.

But which oath? The pledge of a small boy distraught by the death of his family, or the promise of a man grown weary of killing?

Aillun had traveled through the night, and yet the day looked to be little different. Her energy ebbed, divided as it was between herself and the baby growing within. She stopped the sled and stepped off, listening carefully but hearing only the sound of a lone bird. She looked for it, but could not find it among the branches. She felt a kinship with the solitary creature. They both journeyed alone. The bird's call stopped and it leapt into the air in a rustle of snow and leaves. She looked at the sky behind her, and followed the bird with her eyes until she lost sight of it.

Aillun grasped the tethered binna and led it off the path toward the copse of trees. A few moments of rest, she told herself, and then she would be off again like the bird. She needed to eat to keep up her strength and nourish the life inside of her. She stomped her feet and waved her arms about to feel the tingle of blood warmth, then wrapped herself even more tightly in her furs. But even so, she felt the cold winding its way through the maze of layers, intent on finding her skin, prickling it with its chill, determined to reach the new life within her.

Aillun drove back the cold with the force of her will before crawling back inside her sled and burying herself deep in her firs.

"A few moments," she repeated to herself, and quickly drifted off into a dreamless sleep.

When she woke with a start, Aillun reeled with confusion. Then she heard the song. It came from somewhere behind her, far enough back to seem faint, but close enough to make it clear she was followed. Her heart raced as two separate rhythms and Aillun realized her baby shared her fear. She tried to calm herself and keep to the Song of All, but panic broke like waves upon her, carrying away her defenses as if they had been made of riverbed sand.

Aillun pushed herself off the sled and, in her haste, fell upon the snow. She pressed through its whiteness, and found herself deeper within it. Finally, her hands felt something unyielding, and she used its solid surface to right herself. This time, as Aillun stepped, she moved with care. She reached for the reindeer's harness and used the animal to steady herself. The quiet of the woods, which had nestled her in slumber, suddenly became ominous, as if only she and her pursuer existed. Her step faltered, and she floundered again. This time, the sturdy reindeer kept her on her feet.

The voice grew stronger.

Aillun jumped inside her sled and snapped the reins with urgency. The animal snorted, and they fled the trailing song and its images of death.

～

Irjan had traveled for hours, looking for tracks and concentrating on the details he saw around him. Had he lost her? Had he imagined her? This last thought filled him with dread. If his search stood upon a foundation of wild ravings, then truly all was lost. He would wander aimlessly until death claimed him and the snow covered him.

Irjan was taking some comfort in seeing his end, when he heard a sound, fleeting and choked as if something had interrupted it. He stopped to listen, but heard nothing save his own heartbeat and the welling of anxiety. And then the voice broke through his darkness.

I am the maiden. I am the bringer of life. My transformation serves the future. My transformation reflects the past. I walk alone but am pursued by another.

Irjan froze. The song had changed. She knew he followed, but how? How could she know of actions behind her?

She could have been warned, he offered himself as explanation.

Irjan drew the two likely men before his mind. The Apotti had set into motion the path Irjan traveled, and stood to gain from his success. He would have no reason to warn the enemy. *Moreover*, Irjan thought, *if the priest had contact with the Jápme-meahttun, he would have seized the opportunity to rid the world of one of its kind.*

This left the acolyte. The young man had eyes for advancement, like his mentor. He could not have betrayed Irjan and hoped to take glory for himself.

Irjan's mind circled endlessly around the possible machinations of the two men, and yet he knew, somehow, they played no part here. Then another explanation rose in his mind. It broke down his internal resistance, until nothing else remained but to give it voice. She had heard him, as he had heard her.

"It's not possible," he said aloud.

He had successfully hunted and killed countless Jápmea and they had all died with surprise in their eyes. Yet, she knew he was coming.

Why now? Why in his moment of need had his gift deserted him? He snapped the reins with more force than he intended and the horse jerked forward.

Then, just as suddenly, another thought occurred to him. Irjan pulled the horse to a lurching stop.

What if there was more to his gift than he imagined?

~

Djorn felt the pull of his Origin strengthening. He must be close. He stopped and closed his eyes as he listened. An unfamiliar note caught his attention and he focused on it. It wasn't the Origin calling out, it was the nieddaš.

Djorn opened his eyes and immediately picked up his pace, thinking she must be close to her journey's end. But her voice remained faint and distant. He stopped again and listened.

I am the maiden.
I am the bringer of life.
My transformation serves the future.
My transformation reflects the past.
I walk alone, but am pursued by another.

Djorn stood still, puzzled by what he heard and saw. He shook his head. *Meandering through the past has given new life to old fears.* He listened again. The sound of the song hung in the air for a moment, but did not repeat. Djorn waited to chide himself for being foolish and old. The very air around him seemed to come to rest with him, as if it too were waiting.

The song came again, faint and clear.

I am the maiden.
I am the bringer of life.
My transformation serves the future.
My transformation reflects the past.
I walk alone, but am pursued by another.

This time Djorn's heart skipped a beat. This was not some ghost from the past, but a living danger that threatened the nieddaš. Suddenly, all his memories of the slain innocents flooded back and he felt his long-ago rage resurfacing. Djorn had believed it gone from his soul, but he'd been wrong. It had remained dormant, deep within him, awaiting one more battle.

Djorn regarded the path ahead. *Perhaps this is as close as I will ever get.* His life had been full. However, the nieddaš's had just begun, and if he failed anyone, then he would fail her—a possibility he found unbearable.

His voice rang out into the universe.

I am the warrior.
I am the survivor of the battles of the Olmmoš.
My sword serves our kind in death,
My knowledge our continued life.
I come to protect you.

Djorn traveled with the swiftness his aging body allowed him, and he prayed he would be in time.

~

Aillun drove her binna hard and hoped it would be enough to elude her hunter. She shuddered. She'd seen the images of his song: the boy blindfolded and forced to fight, the man racing through the woods like the wolves themselves. How could her bows, meant to

hunt small animals for food, battle against the steel and determination of one who lived to kill?

Her head whipped from side to side as she looked for anything
resembling sanctuary. Aillun knew of no special cave or stone
outcropping to serve as even a temporary reprieve. She traveled
like the blindfolded boy of her vision. Her eyes could not pick out
familiar landmarks or alternate routes. Panic tightened its hold.

He was within the Song.

This thought echoed in her mind and dogged her every
attempt to push it aside. She had nowhere to hide. She could only
go forward, and she knew only one route, the one instinct presented.

"Oh, gods!" The cry escaped her lips, and she clamped a hand
over her mouth. Every possibility she considered ended in death:
her own, the baby's, the Taistelijan's. And yet she traveled on
as fast as she could, holding on to the small spark of hope the
unimaginable would happen, and she would be saved.

CHAPTER TWELVE

IRJAN STOPPED IN THE blinding white storm. He could choose to wait it out or continue to travel on foot, but he could not go ahead with his sleigh in the present conditions. Either way, he risked losing his quarry.

Irjan chose to wait, at least for the time being, and keep the advantage of his transport while he still could. There would probably come a time when it would no longer serve his purpose, and he would need to be ready for that eventuality.

Irjan drew himself, the sleigh, and the horse under the cover of a tree, and used its shelter to ride out the storm. He continued to listen for the song of the female Immortal, but the wind crowded out all other sounds, even those that seemed to come from inside of him.

Once he thought he heard her—a fragment, and something he had not heard before. Only one word sounded clearly—*survivor*. Irjan did not know its meaning other than it suggested she remained close at hand. Irjan felt the cold seeping into his body, bringing along the tendrils of doubt. He burrowed deeper into his furs.

"I will find you," he said to himself, and repeated the promise to fend off the storm that raged both in his mind and in the world around him.

~

Across the snow-covered distance Aillun heard the words in her mind.

I will find you.

And then another voice layered upon the first.

I will protect you.

The second voice continued.

I am the warrior.
I am the survivor of the battles of the Olmmoš.
My sword serves our kind in death,
My knowledge our continued life.
I come to protect you.

Aillun let out the breath she had been holding. The Taistelijan had heard her. The wind created eddies of fresh powder on the ground as Aillun looked about her. The storm deepened. She needed to take shelter before it got much worse, but she felt anxious stopping, knowing she was being hunted. On the other hand, she had to admit that to go on blindly, even with her intuition to guide her, would be a greater folly.

Aillun took cover in a copse of tall trees, moving her sled and binna through the soaring trunks. She looked up and saw that the lowest branches hardly moved, even though the highest swayed in the strong winds. She crawled deep into her furs, taking some comfort in the fact the Taistelijan had heard her. She wished she knew where he was, but she could not change her course even if she did. Only one path existed, the one toward their Origin.

Aillun wanted to call out to the Taistelijan, to let him know her location, but she suspected he would not be the only one to hear. Her song could be a beacon for the other to follow. At least the warrior knew her destination, and perhaps, if her luck held, he would find her before the Hunter did.

Hidden behind the flurry of falling snow, Aillun finally closed her eyes and tried to calm her trembling body. She focused on the Song of All. If she could stay veiled for a while longer, perhaps it would be enough.

~

Djorn pushed on through the merciless storm, listening for the nieddaš. He knew he risked himself if he continued, but he feared more what would happen if he did not persist. He looked for signs of her within the Song of All, and felt her presence. Her voice was there, but so too another, a voice that threatened.

I will find you.

This voice spurred him on until, blinded and nearly frozen, he sought shelter. Djorn drew himself deep within his furs, hunkering in his carved snowy cave, praying to the gods this delay would not prove fateful.

He heard again the voice in his mind:

I will find you.

To which he answered aloud, "I will be ready."

~

As soon as the storm passed, Irjan came to life. His body, tense with waiting, sprung into action. He readied the sleigh and checked the horse's harness. He drew himself up into the sleigh, but stopped short. Without a direction to follow, he could not go forward with any hope of success.

Irjan let loose a yell that came from his core. He jumped out of the sleigh and paced through the drifts of powdery snow. He needed to find the connection. He stopped pacing and took a deep breath, trying to still his mind and listen deep within.

The sounds around him pierced through his concentration. Irjan took another deep breath, and this time released it in a long slow stream. His heart seemed to slow with each passing moment. Something nudged him from within. He dug deeper into himself, clawing inward to the sounds he heard. Something lay so close at hand, but he could not grasp it. From high above, a bird cried out, and Irjan's eyes flew open, his heart beating wildly.

He felt compelled to move quickly and let his instinct lead the way. He settled himself within the sleigh and gave the horse a quick snap of the reins, taking the path open to him.

As the hours grew, one upon the other, Irjan's vigilance wavered. He continued to scan trails and paths, looking for signs he had chosen wisely. On occasion, Irjan's excitement peaked, but was then quickly dashed as he discovered the tracks were made by foraging animals. Although he would have loved to put some fresh meat upon the fire, he had no time to hunt for it, so he moved on. He scanned for broken branches, disturbed snowbanks, anything hinting at a presence, current or past.

Suddenly, when weariness gave way to despair, Irjan saw something—just a flash, but enough. He leapt from the sleigh, seeing exactly what he had hoped for.

The female was not a trained warrior and could not easily hide. She was unprepared and scared. He had seen it before. He had fought many Jápmea whose fear had left them stunned.

Irjan took a running step and then stopped, frozen. He had never before hunted a female. Although he had known from the beginning who his target was, when faced with the immediacy of her capture, Irjan hesitated. As he did so, something else flashed past him.

This was no female Immortal, but the slashing of a sword.

In the corner of his eye, the blade flashed like a ray of light, then slowed until Irjan swore he witnessed it bisect a single snow-flake. Before he could give it another moment's observation, Irjan felt pain radiating through his arm where the blade sliced into his body. He staggered, pulling out his own sword. He clumsily cir-cled the spot he occupied. His heart pounded, refusing to listen to the commands of his mind, but his attacker was gone.

Irjan waited for whatever would come next, but nothing hap-pened. He tried to slow his thoughts and break through to what-ever power had guided him previously.

He felt the unmistakable hum take over, and yet, when he looked with fresh eyes, he found himself alone. His attacker was gone.

Irjan squatted down and looked for tracks in the snow. He saw two sets: a pair led off in the direction whence he had come and another carried on ahead. The ones moving forward were larger and deeper—the attacker's.

Irjan retraced his own steps. The female would be easier to find, and she did not wield a sword. Irjan, however, felt sure he would encounter his assailant again.

∾

Aillun stood paralyzed. The Olmmoš man loomed between her and her sleigh. She would have to continue on foot. A small voice in the back of her mind screamed at her to run. Aillun took one halting step and did as the voice commanded. She ran through the snow, whispering a prayer to the gods for her strength to continue.

Aillun glanced back and was startled to see a Taistelijan warrior behind her. She watched him pass from their realm into the world of the Olmmoš with a shimmer that could have easily been mistaken for a trick of the light. But there was no light, only the gloom.

The warrior raised his arms high over his head, holding a sword. Aillun felt a rush of relief suffuse her body, but she did not stop running, nor did she see if the warrior reemerged in the Song.

~

Djorn saw the nieddaš running in the distance. Her hood had fallen back; her hair flew free. Concern for her gripped him, but he could not let it stop him. Djorn left the sounds of the Song and plunged into the leaden world of the Olmmoš with his sword swinging. The warrior felt immediately disoriented by the shift, but more importantly, he felt his sword finding its intended mark, the Olmmoš man.

Djorn pulled himself back to the Song before rage clouded his mind and prevented his return. He watched the man stagger and whirl in a circle, one hand choking his outstretched sword, the other holding the wounded arm where blood seeped through the cut in the furs.

Djorn had wanted to deliver a death blow, but the passage of too many seasons of snow had dulled his skill. He cursed himself and prepared to finish what he'd begun. He readied his sword and took a step forward. As he did, he stumbled, feeling his head spin in a wide circle. He kept his thoughts upon the Song and waited for the feeling to subside. Had it really been so long since he'd last entered the world of the Olmmoš?

Djorn felt as he had in the first days of retreat—his insides jumbled and his mind clouded by the power of the shift. He stepped back and again felt uncertain upon his feet. In this state, he was no use to the nieddaš. The best he could do was offer her a chance to escape by drawing the man away.

Djorn staggered off. Looking back, he saw his visible tracks and this spurred him to move faster.

~

The power surging through Irjan's heart faded. His pace slowed. He was tired and cold, but he staggered ahead, intent on the pursuit. Then, without warning, the world tilted and he found himself falling forward. In the last moment of his consciousness, he felt the weight of his satchel on his back, and then nothing else.

～

Aillun finally lost the momentum of hope. Exhaustion and the heaviness of her heart acted like anchors, dragging her down. As she stood in the snow, the path forward looked the same as the path behind her. Both would carry her to her death. Tears welled in her eyes, but she willed herself to keep going. *You cannot stop.*

She took another step and sank deeper into the powdery white expanse. She struggled to free herself, then stopped. *Just a moment to catch my breath,* she promised silently, cradling her swollen belly, feeling the pull of the drifting wind.

Aillun saw herself at home, holding her child and singing to her the song of her birth. She was handing the baby over to her guide mother and taking the hand of her love—Kalek.

He smiled and looked into her eyes. "You have come home," he said. "You have come back to me."

She smiled back and rested in his embrace murmuring, "I never wanted to leave."

～

Djorn came upon the nieddaš lying in the snow. He fell to his knees and pulled her limp body toward him. Shallow breaths escaped her blue-tinged lips. She moaned weakly, and her eyes fluttered open.

Djorn pulled open his furs and hers as well. He encircled her in his warmth. He could feel her weak pulse. He had made it in time. He rested his chin on the top of her frost-covered head, losing himself to his memories of love forgotten and love left behind.

When Djorn finally felt warmth spreading through the nieddaš's limbs, his warrior's instinct returned. He refocused his mind on their needs: shelter, a fire, rest, and food and—above all—to remain behind the veil. He parted from her, rewrapped her furs and held her gaze until it steadied.

"We must move ahead," he said, trying to infuse her with his own strength.

She nodded, then took his hand to rise and gave him a weak smile—her last reserve of hope.

Djorn led the way, but he kept a cautious eye and ear to what, if anything, followed them. So far, both directions had been clear of danger. The nieddaš's weakness, however, would not allow them to go much farther. The last time he had asked whether she could continue, her nod seemed to take all her concentration. He needed to find shelter soon.

Djorn scanned the distance. He wanted more than a copse of trees for protection, but if the surroundings had nothing else to offer, it would have to serve.

Djorn led the nieddaš in the direction of the densest circle of trees. He used his sword to trim the low-lying branches, then layered them on the snow and set her upon them.

"Rest while I prepare for the night," he said.

She said nothing in response, but sat down.

Djorn used his hands to dig the snow and form a small cave. He cut small pine boughs, and lined the cave with them. He took the lightest of his layered fur and laid it upon the branches. He gestured for the tired nieddaš to come and lie within the cave. When she was settled, he covered her with more boughs, then left her to gather the makings for a fire.

From beyond the copse, he looked back. They were well hidden. Even if the veil fell, it would take a practiced eye to find them. Of course, having no fire would further ensure their safety, but he needed to keep himself and the nieddaš warm. Djorn could only hope his attack had proved mortal to the Olmmoš. Perhaps then the cold would be of equal danger.

Djorn returned to their camp and set about making a fire. When healthy flames licked the air, he sat back against the blanketed body of the nieddaš. She moved against him. They would make it to the morning, he vowed to the trees above, and the stars and gods beyond.

CHAPTER THIRTEEN

THE SOUND OF THE wind brought Irjan back to himself. He rose up and saw an owl in the branches ahead of him, its luminous eyes staring downward. Somewhere behind him, he heard the protests of a raven, but could not pick out its shadowed frame in the dark sky.

Had the owl prevented the raven from taking his soul? Irjan wondered. His body prickled with cold and resisted the idea of movement. His arm throbbed—the dark patch upon the snow could only have been his blood. He was lucky the wolves had not yet picked up its scent, or perhaps they had and were on their way to investigate. Either way, he could no longer stay hunched upon the ground.

Irjan rose slowly and repositioned his small satchel. He steadied himself against a wave of dizziness. He looked down at the patch of blood. The pool must have gone deeper than he first suspected.

He started forward and scanned for his sleigh. It was gone, carried off by the unattended horse as he rested between the worlds. He staggered ahead, looking for any shelter in the distance. He needed to find a place to rest and bind his wound before he could begin to hunt again. At the same time, he couldn't lose the trail. He was close. He could feel it.

Irjan moved slowly in the pale semblance of morning. The embers of his fire sputtered in the rising wind. He took the few remaining twigs and added them to the glowing cluster, then leaned forward with his face inches from the heat and breathed life back into the flames. He took a scoop of fresh snow in his metal cup and placed it in the fire to boil, needing the water to warm his insides and wash off the cut in his arm.

He reached for his satchel and carefully opened it to take out a small swatch of fabric. Irjan stared at it as if he had last seen it a lifetime ago.

The fabric had been part of the blanket his wife had woven for them when they were first made handfast. Sohja had asked him to trade for wool at the market and had taken the soft strands and carded them and spun them. Finally, using the summer berries, Sohja had dyed the yarn a soft blue like the sky in spring. Irjan had held her in his arms under its warmth, and four days ago he had wrapped her lifeless body in it. One memory lingered like a dream, the other rose up like a nightmare.

As he waited for the water to boil, Irjan slid his arm out from his furs. With difficulty, he pulled himself free from his woolen vest and under shirt. The cold stung his exposed skin. Dried and crusted blood covered the length of his arm, but Irjan could not waste the water to wash it off. He needed the precious liquid to cleanse his wound or it would fester and rot him from the inside out.

He poured the hot water on the hardened ooze along the cut and it softened. Using a handful of snow, he wiped away the loosened scab. A fresh supply of blood ran from the gash. He was thankful the sword had been sharp and had not left a jagged wound.

Irjan poured the scalding water on the piece of fabric and applied it to the wound. The heat burned his chilled flesh, and again he followed up with a handful of snow. The shift from one extreme to the other caused him to inhale sharply through his gritted teeth.

He scrutinized the tree bark around him, finally spotting what he needed. Irjan placed his knife in the embers and waited for the blade to glow. Then he removed it and plunged it into a congealed amber liquid that had long ago oozed free of the bark. He pulled away some of the sap and returned to the fire where he melted it on the blade.

When the first drop hit the fire, he pulled it out and applied it to the wound. Irjan cried out as he seared his own flesh, using the tree's blood to stop his own. Over time, the sharp stunning pain subsided to a background throb that matched his drumming heart.

Irjan bound the cut with a strip torn from his shirt, then replaced his arm in the layers of clothing. He sank into the momentary comfort, then removed his cup from the fire to sip the scalding water. He took a piece of dried reindeer meat and chewed thoughtfully—meager fare, but he had few options. He couldn't turn back.

When Irjan finished, he stood and threaded his injured arm through the strap of his satchel. He moved gingerly. Luckily, it was not his fighting arm. He refastened his weapon and kicked snow across the spent embers of his fire. Habits from his past slowly infiltrated his actions. Although Irjan had no need to hide, he couldn't ignore his training. Caution had served to keep him alive. But the need to find the female, and possibly her partner, now outweighed his desire to complete his routine.

Irjan walked out from under the sheltering trees and stood in the clearing. The wind hurried around him, but the snow remained in the embrace of the clouds.

He closed his eyes and tried to ignore all distractions. He thought only of slowing his heart. When he could no longer hear its beat, he listened for the sounds that came from beyond his silenced world. His effort was rewarded when the wind carried a fragment to him, but it was more a hum than a true sound. It came from the east and traveled away from him.

When Irjan came back to himself, he was dusted in whiteness. He had been gone long enough for a flurry to pass him by, and yet, he had not been aware of it. A deep sense of disquiet welled up. In the past, he had experienced short gaps in time when he had stilled himself—a moment or two perhaps had been lost—but he had never experienced anything like what had just happened.

Irjan backed away from the event's meaning the way a mare shies from a snake. He shook off the coating of snow, but he couldn't shake the feeling he had taken a step into the unknown.

CHAPTER FOURTEEN

AILLUN AWOKE STRUGGLING TO fill her lungs. She emerged from sleep to find the warrior draped across her. She pushed against his weight. Her sudden movement startled him. He rolled awkwardly onto his knees, grasping the hilt of his sword in readiness. Aillun shrank back into the little snow cave.

The Taistelijan released his sword, and his shoulders slumped. "You are safe."

Aillun gaped at him, unable to find her voice.

"Are you all right? How do you feel? Are you hungry?" he fired off questions.

"Yes," she stuttered and moved slowly toward him.

"We cannot waste the time to make a fire, but we have time to take some sustenance," he said, not rushing his words this time. "I am afraid it's not much, but it should give you some strength," he continued, and then, looking at her midsection, added, "and the baby as well."

The Taistelijan reached inside his fur jacket and pulled out a small parcel. He unfolded the soft leather wrapping and removed a piece of dark bread, to which he added a slice of hard cheese and a long sliver of dried reindeer meat. As he prepared their meal, Aillun observed the warrior.

Despite the protection of his hood, wisps of greying hair caught the wind, and Aillun saw his face was creased with lines; some she could imagine came from grimaces, others from laughter, and still others she could not guess. His hands, though deft with his knife, were gnarled and bent, as if a lifetime of holding his sword had molded them to its shape.

He handed her the food, which Aillun gratefully accepted. She took a tentative bite and received little for her effort. She then grasped the bread with her teeth and pulled sharply, ripping off a morsel. As she chewed, she reflected on how much her life had changed. A few days earlier, she had enjoyed warmed honey on soft cheese and tender reindeer meat, roasted with potatoes. But she found that what she ate now was no less delicious to her hungry palate.

The warrior fumbled with the folds of his furs and took from them a flask. Held close to his body, it had not frozen.

He handed it to her.

"This will help you chew the food," he said encouragingly.

Aillun took the leather flask from him and drank from it sparingly. The water was neither warm nor cold, but refreshing, and it did relieve the dryness of the food.

"What do they call you?" she mumbled between bites.

"My name is Djorn."

"Djorn," she repeated and chewed in silence. When he did not speak, she continued, "I am named Aillun."

"We should break camp. You finish eating. We have still a distance to travel, and now that we are on foot, it will take us longer. We do not have much time."

"Because we are followed?"

"Yes, and because our time draws near."

Djorn finished the last of his food and took a swallow of the water. He offered it to her once again, and gathered their belongings. While eating, Aillun watched Djorn tear apart their camp.

"What are you doing?" she asked.

Djorn continued to work. "If the one who seeks us comes upon this by chance he will know we have been here." He sat back on his haunches and considered the skies above them. "Unless the snowfall begins again." He pressed himself to his feet.

Djorn drew his sword and cut off a long branch from a fir tree heavy with needles. He dug a small hole in the snow with his heel and shaved off the small twigs into the hole. When he was done, he covered over the hole again. Aillun watched him in silence.

"Are you ready to leave?" he asked.

She nodded.

Djorn unfastened the belt holding his sword. He took the belt and tightened it around her waist above the bulge of the child, leaving a fist's width of room.

Aillun struggled against his actions. "What are you doing?" she demanded.

Djorn did not answer, but pulled back on the belt. He raised the base of his whittled branch upwards between her belt and her back until the bough would just drag across the ground.

Aillun stopped protesting.

"I will walk ahead," Djorn explained, "you will walk in my footprints. The branch will cover our tracks with snow. I will try to walk at a pace to suit you, but you must understand the urgency with which we travel."

"But the Song. . ." Aillun started to say.

"The Song may not hold us." Djorn looked at her to make sure she took his meaning.

Aillun's breath caught but she managed to nod. Djorn stepped forward and she followed in his footprints. She looked back over her shoulder and across the snow.

"I think he might be a Piijkij," she said suddenly.

Djorn stopped abruptly. "Are you sure?"

Aillun felt the warrior's eyes boring into her. "No."

For a long moment silence filled the space between them.

"We should hurry," he said finally.

~

True to his word, Djorn kept the pace just slow enough for Aillun to follow, but just quick enough she could never catch her breath. When the sky showed the first signs of a storm, Aillun thought they would stop and seek refuge, but the warrior kept walking. She contemplated protesting, but remembered who followed them.

As if he had read her thoughts, Djorn stopped. She could not see his face, hidden within the hood of his furs. His voice hit her like a blast after the hours of silence in which they had traveled.

"We should continue," Djorn announced. "The fresh snow will help to mask our tracks."

Aillun looked down and watched the footprints appearing in front of her and her own small feet attempting to fill them. She counted the steps and could not imagine how many more still lay ahead of them. But she drew reassurance knowing each step forward was one step away from what followed them.

Aillun hadn't heard the voice since taking company with Djorn. She hoped the warrior's attack had proved fatal to the Olmmoš, but feared it hadn't, and her concern spurred her to remain focused on the Song of All. She did not want to give the Hunter any room to enter her mind again.

As the storm intensified around them, Djorn's figure became obscured. His footprints were her only tangible link with the Taistelijan beyond her reach and she struggled to move through the deepening drifts. Finally, when she thought she could go no further, she ran into the back of the warrior, who had suddenly stopped.

"We shall take refuge in that small ledge over there," he said.

Aillun looked to where he pointed, and discerned nothing resembling shelter. Djorn removed the branch she trailed, and the belt holding it in place.

"Head in that direction." He gestured ahead.

With difficulty, Aillun made it to a tumble of rocks, which supported a small stone roof. Djorn used the branch he carried to sweep away snow from under the ledge, then trimmed the closest trees of their lowest boughs to make a nest on which they could sit.

When he finished, he helped her down. Aillun burrowed as far under as she could to make room for him, but he did not join her right away. Instead, he gathered more branches and laid them against the small ridge, forming a sort of tent. With the wall of branches almost completed, Djorn drew himself under the stone roof and pulled the undergrowth behind him as if closing a door. His long frame bent upon itself to fit in the tight space. He loosened his sword belt and let it lie upon the floor of their safe haven.

"Come closer," he urged Aillun, opening a layer of his coverings. "I will keep you warm."

Aillun hesitated.

"Come."

Aillun eased into the space he had created for her and he encircled her with his arms. She felt the hint of heat growing where they met, but she was embarrassed by their closeness. Few had held her as the old warrior did now. She could not see his face and was glad her own was shielded. Djorn said nothing. His heart beat at a regular rhythm and his breath rose and fell with hers. Aillun wondered if he slept.

Aillun closed her eyes and thought of home. She saw herself walking in the woods of springtime, collecting flowers to distill into elixirs. Kalek walked beside her, carrying the basket. When she stooped to gather the pale blue Petals of Forgetting, he leaned against the tree and looked up at the clouds. They were happy and in love. They spoke of their future together with knowing looks.

In her mind's eye, Aillun looked up at Kalek from her vantage on the forest floor. Kalek's eyes were closed, his face smiling toward the shining sun. A breeze wound its way through the high branches and a few leaves floated down between them.

~

"Aillun," a soft voice called out to her. "Aillun, we must go."

Aillun awoke to find herself, not in the spring forest in the company of her love, but rather in a snowy refuge with a stranger, who would in a short time forever alter the course of her life.

Still held by the wisps of her dream, she asked, "Did you leave someone behind when you left?"

"No," the warrior answered, beginning to remove the branches in front of him.

~

Djorn looked down at Aillun, and saw her as if for the first time. Her dark hair was knotted and tangled with pine needles. One small black dot stood out upon her otherwise snowy cheek, and her eyes were dark, but they could not conceal their fear and uncertainty.

She is so young, he thought to himself. Had he ever been that young? For a moment, Djorn wanted to tell Aillun the truth that he had left behind love and family and friends but the difficulty of it all overwhelmed him, and he lied.

"No," he said, "there was no one."

In truth, the whole of his existence was marked by those he left behind. In his wake trailed the echoes of all those he had cared for: his sisters, his child, his lover, his wife, his comrades. He had left so many. They all did—those who lived as long as he, those who lived to become Taistelijan. Perhaps, Aillun would one day understand, and do as he had done and lie. But that would only be possible if they managed to elude their pursuer on this day and each succeeding day.

"Come." He held out his hand. "We still have far to go to reach the Origin."

CHAPTER FIFTEEN

IRJAN TRIED TO TRAVEL on, and not think about the time he had lost. He walked forward, but he kept coming back to the impossible nature of the event. He thought back to his youth with the Brethren of Hunters and what they had taught him. As he walked through snow drifts, the droning lectures of his teachers came back to him in pieces.

"They are the unseen and the immortal pretenders," the oldest of the Brethren had ranted. The ancient Brother had exuded a barely-contained madness. Irjan remembered his eyes. Rage seeped through their milky masks.

As a boy, Irjan had made the painful blunder of mistaking blindness with unseeing. He and others had grimaced and mimicked the Brother behind his back only to find out too late the Brother did not need his orbs for sight. The old one unleashed a powerful blow against those who mocked him, and no one dared to repeat the folly.

But even with his ears ringing from the boxing he had received, Irjan still managed to hear the man say, "The Jápmea cut through our very air, stretching it, to walk through to another world."

Irjan had not understood how it was possible to stretch air, but at the time he had been too afraid to ask, lest his ignorance be construed as impertinence.

The old man had rattled on, "The gods gave us time, the length of sunlight and the length of darkness. As moon cycles pass from one to another, all sunlight gives way to all darkness, only to release us again to all sunlight. Light and dark are equal forces, whose gains and losses are measured and balanced."

"The Jápmea have disavowed time and have angered the gods. As faithful servants we must avenge this wrong, to purge this evil, and restore the balance."

Throughout his training, Irjan had come back time and again to the fundamental question of how it was the Jápmea Immortals traveled into another realm. His cohorts did not find it important to understand how or why, only what—what they were expected to do. But Irjan hadn't been satisfied. He sought those older and wiser than himself for answers.

"Brothers," he begged, "how is it the Jápmea leave our space and return to it?"

Their explanations had varied depending on their studies. The alchemical Brothers said they transmuted their flesh into flesh of a different kind—tree, rock, earth. Those who charted the heavens said they controlled time.

"They live the full length of time. While we see only the beginning and the end points and must connect the two together," the astronomers said, "they have learned to split time."

But Irjan could still not fathom this possibility, and his further questions branded him a troublemaker, for which he paid a high price. He received more beatings, less food, harsher conditions, and merciless ordeals, yet he persevered. On the one hand, he had nowhere else to go. On the other hand, he would not allow himself to be broken.

Irjan read everything written on the subject of the Immortals, from crumbling treatises on their war tactics, where he could barely make out one word in five, to the firsthand accounts of returning Hunters. His doggedness was rewarded in the end, not only by the satisfaction of his curiosity, but more importantly, by his success as a Piijkij.

Irjan came to understand what it meant to split time—the slowing of his heart, and the reaching out into the world as he went deeper into himself. But what had happened earlier in the day was not the splitting of time. He believed in his heart he had actually stretched it. The old Brother's explanation ran through his mind again.

"The Jápmea can cut through our very air, stretching it, to walk through to another world."

With a sense of wonder, Irjan allowed himself to consider the possibility he had, in fact, stepped into the timespace of the Jápmea. The idea, at first uncomfortable, suddenly emboldened him. If he had done it once, then he might be able to do it again.

Irjan quickened his pace through the deepening snowdrifts, conscious that if any hope of redemption existed, it lay ahead.

❧

Irjan took a moment to rest on his haunches. He shifted his satchel. It weighed nothing, and yet he felt a burden—a cruel measure of oaths. As a boy, he had been compelled to honor the pledge of the Brethren of Hunters—to purge the evil and restore the balance. As a Piijkij he had satisfied his promise. As a man he had offered a vow to the gods that his hands would no longer be the instruments of death, and he had made true his words. But of all the declarations he had made, only his last, whispered over his son's body, came from his heart.

Irjan stood quietly, thinking on that promise, and then stilled his thoughts and his heart, until they became one, until he became one with the wind, the snow, the trees—everything around him. In that moment Irjan heard a song. The voices in it spoke directly to his soul, filling him with so many thoughts, emotions, desires and fears; he felt as if his heart would explode and crack his chest wide open. What his heart heard, his mind translated:

We are the Jápmemeahttun.
We are the guardians of the world.
Our memory stretches back to the start of days.
Our vision reaches beyond all tomorrows.
We sing together as one, so that our one may always survive.

Irjan's very essence surged with the consciousness of every-thing—past and present and future. And then, the song was gone.

Irjan found himself upon his hands and knees in the snow, unsure of where he was. Had he crossed over, or had he returned? He scrambled to his feet and looked about. Nothing had changed, at least nothing he could discern.

Irjan examined himself. He looked the same. But in truth, he still felt uncertain. Without another soul to confirm it, he could be in either realm.

⌒

Aillun followed in the footsteps of the old warrior once again, knowing instinctively they moved along the right path.

"You have been there before, have you not?" she asked, breathless from the forced march.

Djorn's head snapped to one side as he walked. "What was that?" he asked.

"I said, you have been there before."

"To the Origin?"

"Yes."

"In another lifetime."

"Then you know this path?"

"Yes. As you do. From a memory laid across our souls at birth."

"Do you not recognize any landmarks?"

"The world changes."

When the old warrior added nothing else, Aillun persisted. "But can you tell if we draw close?" Her question was clipped by her staccato breathing.

"Each step draws us closer. If you need to rest, then tell me so."

"I need to rest," Aillun panted.

Djorn scanned their surroundings. "We can find some coverage ahead and to the left. Can you make it there?"

"Yes."

Aillun set off ahead of Djorn, but he easily caught up with her, and they walked abreast for the first time since they'd met. A fallen tree lay snow-covered near their path. Aillun pushed the shelf of snow off the log.

"Stop!" Djorn hissed.

Aillun shrank back from his advance.

"Any break in our surroundings gives him a clue to our location and direction. We cannot know if the Song holds us."

Aillun nodded, standing still.

Djorn sighed, gestured for her to sit, and reluctantly joined her. He reached inside his layers and pulled out the flask, then offered it to her.

Before she held it to her lips, Aillun asked, "Why must we be here alone?"

"We are alone so that we can protect those who remain." Djorn reached into another pocket to retrieve the food pouch.

Aillun handed back the leather flask. "Why would they be in danger?"

Djorn opened the pouch. "The giving of a life force is a powerful event, shared by all present."

"But I have witnessed death," Aillun insisted.

"The deaths of which of us? Mánáid? Nieddaš? Beibmoeadni?" Djorn seemed irritated.

"And almai!" she retorted, feeling slighted.

"But not boaris, Taistelijan, the old ones," Djorn snapped back and then quickly added, "I am sorry." He handed her a piece of bread awkwardly. "The others can release their life force within the Song of All, and it can be absorbed by those who already exist. But the boaris and the Taistelijan have lived too long. Our life force cannot be taken in by those who exist and remain unchanged. Our energy is meant to bring in new life even as it leaves us, so the balance is preserved."

Aillun took the proffered food, and looked at it for some time before speaking. "But who will protect us?"

"It is my job to protect you."

"And when you are gone?"

"It is my job to prepare you for that."

"And what if I am not ready?"

"You will be ready."

Djorn shook his head, as if to banish some thought. Aillun was about to press him when he spoke.

"There is much I must convey to you. I had hoped this time would be a Sharing. But the circumstances are dire, and I feel as if I must act as the master and not merely the guide."

Aillun gave Djorn time to continue. When he did not, she tried to decipher his thoughts.

"Are you afraid to die?"

"No."

"I am," she admitted.

"You will not die," Djorn assured her. "A whole new life stretches out before you. You will become almai and then perhaps a Taistelijan."

"But I don't know what that means. I don't know what that feels like."

"None of us knows what our future feels like."

"And it does not frighten you?"

"Yes. I know I will die. I know my passing will allow a new life to begin and yours to continue. But I do not know what it will feel like. I do not know what lies beyond. But I do know that to be Jápmemeahttun is to transform."

"Then I suppose we are together in our aloneness," Aillun concluded.

"At least for a little while longer," Djorn replied, and then let the silence grow between them before adding haltingly, "If you have rested, we should continue on a bit more before making camp for the night."

"I am rested," Aillun replied, and stood to follow her guide.

CHAPTER SIXTEEN

"TELL ME WHAT IT is like to be a Taistelijan," said Aillun.

Djorn smiled sadly and regarded the campfire he had built. "I have thought of nothing else since beginning this journey. There is no simple answer. My past may not be your future. So much has changed in my lifetime that I can only expect your future will change as well."

"Did you want to be a Taistelijan?" Aillun asked, rubbing her hands in front of the little blaze to warm them.

"Yes."

"Why? Why did you want to?"

"Because I wanted to protect our kind." Djorn looked off into the distance as if seeing a scene from his past. Neither of them spoke for a while.

"Did you fight in many battles?" Aillun finally asked.

"I fought in all of them."

"Did you kill many?" her voice wavered.

"I killed more than I can remember." Djorn shook his head as if in disbelief.

"How did that feel?"

The old warrior paused and looked at Aillun, his face half lit by the fire.

"It felt sickening and satisfying and then thrilling, and finally I was numb."

"Did you regret your decision?"

"What? You mean to become a warrior? No!"

"Do you regret killing the Olmmoš?" Aillun's voice barely rose above a whisper.

"Some, yes. Some." Djorn poked the fire, and the wood crumbled into embers. "You should sleep," he said, arranging the furs near the fire. "I will keep watch, and at moonrise we will continue on."

᠉

As he watched her sleep, Djorn found himself revisiting the questions she'd asked. The questions were not new—he had posed them all to himself many times. But Djorn had never heard his voice answer them out loud. To his own ears, he had sounded so sure of himself. He wondered if the conviction came from his desire to remain strong for those who depended on him, or if it really still burned within him? Truthfully, he was no longer certain. At Aillun's prodding, he had voiced his doubts, giving them new vitality.

From the moment he had become a Taistelijan, fear had accompanied him. And now, with the battles fading into dim memory, regrets also kept him company. Djorn told the truth when he said he had never regretted becoming a Taistelijan. Nor did he lament his actions on the battlefields. He had been no fiercer than his enemy—no less just. Regret came after the war, when Djorn joined the brigades of dissatisfied Taistelijan who continued to hunt the Olmmoš.

At the time, he had felt the righteous indignation of a forfeited rank. While the Olmmoš walked proudly, the Jápme-meahttun had gone into hiding. To those who wished to continue fighting, hiding was a needless sacrifice. Like his comrades, Djorn acted the role of a warrior, but with no war he was little more than a brigand. He wished he could claim he had been young and rash, but he'd been neither, merely a warrior in his prime with too much bloodlust to stop.

For too long, Djorn had thrived on the danger and uncertainty he faced. Even now, he could not deny the thrill of the chase, the sense of aliveness which hunter and hunted brought one another. Djorn's sword had rusted, hidden in his chambers for more seasons of snow than most Olmmoš lived, and yet the stirrings of a warrior eagerly rose within him. In some ways, he took comfort in knowing his end time approached, because there had been no place for him in a world not at war. Whatever his dreams may have been, they ended the moment he picked up the sword; but perhaps for Aillun it would be otherwise.

The moonrise took Djorn by surprise. He had been lost in his thoughts—lost in the past—unaware he was observed by Aillun until he saw her unblinking stare. He gave her a weary smile, which she also seemed to consider before she spoke.

"What made you stop?" she asked softly.

The question appeared open-ended, but Djorn suspected her intent.

He hoped he was wrong. "What do you mean?"

"What made you stop killing?"

Djorn looked around their camp, then busied himself with gathering together their things.

"The war was over."

"And you turned your back on it all and went home."

Djorn snapped around, his jaw tightening.

"There was no home to return to," he growled. "We had to leave it to the Olmmoš and forge a new existence for ourselves."

"And did you? Did you find a new way of living for yourself?"

Djorn was taken aback by Aillun's sincere interest. There was no judgment, only the determination to know the truth.

"Yes," he finally said. "But it was a life of halves—half-lived hunting and half-lived hiding."

"So you never stopped, then."

"No. I stopped."

~

"What made you stop?" Aillun circled back to her original question.

Djorn stood still.

Although Aillun could not see the emotions playing across his face, she knew he was conflicted.

She dropped her voice. "Djorn. Please."

"Of what value could my shame be to you?"

"So I might understand what it means to be a Taistelijan." The resolve in her answer surprised Aillun.

The hushed nighttime forest encircled them, two strangers united by soul paths decided somewhere in the stars. They shared nothing from the past. Destiny fated them to share a singular moment in the future, after which their connection would cease to exist.

"If you really want to understand, then I will sing its song to you."

Djorn closed his eyes and his chant filled the still air. As Aillun watched, his craggy face and stooped shoulders transformed before her eyes into a younger, stronger, and more fearsome man. His hair flew back from his shoulders in ribbons of black. He ran quickly, deftly dodging obstacles. He hunted. Her inner vision shifted from him toward his prey, an Olmmoš. The Olmmoš ran as if weighed down.

Suddenly, the Olmmoš stopped and spun upon his heel. His chest rose and fell with a labored breath; his eyes, all the while, ablaze with rage. He pulled forth his sword.

Djorn slowed to a deliberate walk, his own weapon drawn.

"I will send you back to whatever hell you sprang from," the young Olmmoš spat out. His face was flush with anger and his voice shrill with recent boyhood.

Djorn sneered. "A world occupied by the likes of you is hell enough. And it is I who will dispatch you to join your brethren in the underworld of the Pohjola."

Djorn sprang into the air and brought the full force of his sword down on his adversary. The Olmmoš deflected the blow, but it took all his strength to do so. The man staggered back, then scrambled to his feet, lunging at the Taistelijan.

The sound of metal against metal filled Aillun's mind, as the swords clashed again and again. But the Olmmoš was tiring. After each attack, his recovery grew slower, his own assaults fewer. He breathed as if the wind held no air. Defeat registered in his eyes, but he summoned whatever courage remained and charged headlong at Djorn.

The Taistelijan parried easily and spun to rake the backs of the man's legs. The Olmmoš fell to the ground. Red lines of blood trailed toward the brown earth. Djorn stood over the young man as he grabbed fistfuls of dirt in his attempt to crawl away.

The warrior used the toe of his boot to kick the Olmmoš over onto his back. The man grunted. His face shone with sweat; his features twisted.

Djorn placed the tip of his sword upon the exposed neck below him. A prick of blood grew.

Aillun could feel the warrior's heart beat in her own. It pounded. She looked from one to the other. Both pairs of eyes glowed with righteousness.

"What do you wait for?" the fallen Piijkij screamed. "Add my death to the others and claim your rewards in hell!"

Djorn dropped to his knees next to the Olmmoš, tossing aside his sword and grabbing his dagger in its place. He slid the blade across the man's throat.

"Watching you die is my reward!" the warrior hissed through his teeth, as blood streamed from the mocking smile of a wound, until life drain from the man's eyes.

Djorn, blade in hand, slumped forward, exhausted. His back rose and fell with each breath. The muffled cries of a baby broke through the vision. Djorn shot to his knees, rolling the dead Olmmoš onto its stomach. The cries became piercing. Djorn could see something writhing beneath the fabric lashed to the man's back. He cut the sashes and pulled apart the fabric, exposing the red face of a wailing baby.

Aillun's breath caught. Djorn stared at the infant. Its tiny hands waved in helpless fury; its fingers curled into fists. Aillun wished she could take the child into her arms and comfort it, but she could do nothing but watch the past unfold.

Djorn replaced the fabric across the infant's face and raised himself up off the ground. He bent and picked up his sword, wiping its blade and that of the dagger before replacing them in his belt. He began to walk away.

Aillun found herself crying out, "No!" But she was within Djorn's song and without a voice of her own. Hot tears ran down her cheeks.

The infant continued to cry, uncomforted. Aillun's heart broke within the memory. She looked at the warrior's back. He seemed hardened to not only death, but also to innocent life. Djorn continued to draw away. Aillun knew she could not close her eyes and will away the vision before her. It was the Taistelijan's song and she had asked to listen.

When she could take no more, Aillun begged him to stop. As she did the warrior of her vision stopped and spun to face the fallen Piijkij. She saw tears streaming down his face. Slowly, Djorn retraced his steps, his movements stilted and shaking. When he reached the body, he knelt down and carefully removed the cover from the baby. He took the small body into his hands and haltingly brought it to his chest.

The song stopped. The old warrior stood silently with his head bowed. Aillun wished she could comfort him, but found herself at a loss.

Djorn looked up and met her gaze. His eyes reflected his pain.

"What happened?" Aillun finally asked.

"I took the baby to the nearest Olmmoš farm and placed him upon a doorstep to be discovered and hopefully cared for and loved," Djorn answered. "Then I returned to the Song of All."

Aillun felt ashamed she had pressed the warrior to recount this tale. She looked away and wiped away her brittle tears.

"I am sorry," she whispered.

"You were not wrong to ask. It is important to remember, even that which is most painful. To be a Taistelijan is to acknowledge all."

Djorn sang to himself softly.

I am the warrior.
I am the survivor of the battles of the Olmmoš.
My sword serves our kind in death,
My knowledge our continued life.
I walk alone, but count myself among the many who will travel after
  me.

He smiled at her. "You will travel after me. Come."

~

Irjan recognized the feeling immediately. The voice conveyed pride and remorse mixed in an uneasy union. He clung to the feeling because it seemed akin to his own.

He swayed in the moonlight and contemplated the possibility that hunter and hunted were not so different. And yet the Jápmea *were* different—they were immortal; he was not. His bones would crumble to dust and himself be forgotten along with all that he had loved, while they lived on.

But the chorus seemed so familiar, so much like him.

Irjan was on the verge of accepting their oneness when the quiet communion he felt exploded into visions too quick for him to comprehend. The voices in his mind screamed, and the visions swam, and then he saw it clearly: a Piijkij sword clashing with that of a Jápmea.

Irjan's heart raced, as if he were himself in the fight. Now the Immortal stood over the wounded man, who struggled to crawl away. Irjan willed himself to enter the nightmare, but it was unlike a dream; he could not partake. He stood frozen as the Jápmea slid dagger across the wounded man's throat.

Irjan shook with uncontrolled emotion. He reached out and clawed at the wretched Immortal. But nothing changed. He tried to close his eyes to wipe away the images, but his mind's sight forced him to watch as the Jápmea rolled the Piijkij upon his face and then cut open the fabric on the fallen Hunter's back.

Suddenly the face of a baby loomed before Irjan's eyes, and his chest caved as if the wind had been knocked from him. The babe's angry squalling visage bored into his mind, and he saw his own son in its likeness. The pain drove Irjan to his knees; his hands reached up to cover his eyes. But eyes covered or not, the illusion continued.

The Jápmea looked at the crying infant and then replaced the fabric. To Irjan's horror, the Immortal stood and walked away. Irjan longed to bury his own sword among those murderous bones and slice open whatever heartless core existed. He struggled to move, and then he heard the piercing scream.

"No!"

Suddenly the scene before his eyes disappeared, and he was alone in the moonlit night. There was no baby, no fallen comrade, and no heartless killer. Irjan stood alone with the echo of a woman's voice.

CHAPTER SEVENTEEN

DJORN CRESTED THE SMALL rise in the pale imitation of dawn. Below him lay their Origin. In the snowy landscape, it was hard to remember the time of sun he'd once encountered here. He wished for Aillun's sake she could have made the passage in warmth, as opposed to this frigid world.

Djorn looked behind, toward her approaching figure. Her pace was slowing. He was thankful they neared the end of their journey. Aillun needed to rest and prepare for what awaited her and the baby. Djorn's relief, however, was tempered by the knowledge they were followed. He'd hoped to give himself and Aillun enough time and distance to complete the transformation, but his experience with the Olmmoš taught him the Piijkij were relentless, like wolves, hungry and intent on their kill.

∼

When Aillun reached Djorn, he stretched out his hand for her to take, and she drew upon his strength. Hers was waning, but a sense of urgency pushed her to continue. With one hand firmly grasped, Aillun felt Djorn's arm encircle her back and gently guide her up the snowy slope. Aillun knew they were close to the end of their journey. The sense of belonging grew stronger with each step she took, though she could not have explained why. She recognized none of the landscape. As she crested the small hill with Djorn at her side, Aillun immediately felt as though she knew every rock, tree and shrub before her, as if she had lived with them her entire life. Even the snowy coverage could not obscure her connection to what lay beneath.

Her breath caught, and the old warrior mistook it for pain.

"Are you in discomfort?" he asked, concerned.

"No," Aillun whispered, shaking her head. "I am home."

The two of them took in the vista, soaking in the meaning of her words. When she was ready, Aillun walked down the embankment toward a circle of tall trees. Djorn followed behind her.

As she walked into their ring, she placed her hands upon the stalwart trunks on either side. She felt life pulsing inside of them. She savored their song.

We wait.
We watch.
We mourn.
We rejoice.

Aillun smiled in wonder, and went to stand in the midst of their towering presence. She looked up to see where they touched the sky. The wind whipped around their tops, but she felt calm in the center of the circle. Djorn joined her in the grove.

"They are beautiful," she said with reverence.

"They are a part of us," he replied, looking up at the towering majesty around them.

Aillun eyes widened. "What do you mean?"

"These trees contain a part of every soul who has gone on. They are the ones calling us back." They stood silently. "I will prepare our camp," he added.

Aillun watched as Djorn went far beyond their circle of trees to harvest branches to make a carpet against the cold. She sank down into the soft powder, heedless of the cold. She felt impervious. For the first time since she had set out, she was at ease. She knew great challenges awaited her, but for the moment she felt calm and confident.

Djorn returned and resumed his tasks with his usual attention and care. Soon Aillun sat comfortably in front of a small fire. As she ate, she observed her guardian. Earlier in the morning, Djorn had been withdrawn. Aillun now felt a twinge of guilt; she had pushed him too far. Their future was precarious enough, and she had added the weight of the past. When Djorn sighed, Aillun redoubled her silent lament. She should have kept quiet.

"I have neglected to ask you about yourself," Djorn said, clearing his throat. "If I am to help you, then I should know more of you."

Surprise caught hold of Aillun and she suddenly felt shy.

Djorn pressed on, "Tell me your birth story."

She looked at him, hesitating before beginning the song of her life.

Djorn closed his eyes.

When she had finished, she waited to see his reaction.

"Tell me about your life as a mánná," he said.

Aillun did not know what to say, and yet she felt compelled because she had demanded the same of him.

"As a child, I was happy," she answered, thinking of that time. "My biebmoeadni loved me very much. She and I lived alone. But I had many friends and was never lonely."

"What did you fear?" Djorn asked abruptly.

Aillun roamed through her memories. "Nothing. I feared nothing." She smiled briefly. "I was not fearless. I did not jump from rooftops nor swim to the deepest part of the lake, but I did not have a worry to preoccupy me."

The warrior nodded as he listened. "As it should be."

Aillun did not ask him about his fears. She had learned enough of him to imagine what they might have been.

"What did you imagine your future would be?" he asked.

This time, Aillun could not rely on her memories to provide the answer. She had to look to her heart for her dreams. "I thought I would become a healer. I would live a long while as a biebmoeadni and see my mánná grow. I would heal the sick and. . ."

Aillun stopped, feeling her cheeks grow red with embarrassment.

"And?" Djorn prodded.

"And I would have the love of my beloved." Aillun hung her head trying to compose herself.

"I am sorry," Djorn said.

Aillun looked up. "There is no need to apologize. As you said, it is important to remember even what is painful."

Aillun took a sip of the tea Djorn had made for her. "I am sad not to fulfill those dreams. I was heartbroken to leave behind those I loved."

"But you can return to be a healer."

Aillun smiled but she could not keep the sadness from her voice.

"Yes, I can still be a healer. If we survive."

Aillun's misgivings drove Djorn deeper into his thoughts. He knew the upcoming transformation presented its own risks. The power he would produce, as he left the world, could be as destructive as it was transformative. It was why lifebringers traveled to their Origin for birthing. But they also faced the uncertainty presented by the Hunter. Even if both mother and child survived, they might be forced to contend with the Piijkij. Aillun would be a new almai. Her strength would be increased, but she would be untrained. Some of his memories would merge with hers, but he feared these would not be enough to protect her from a Piijkij attack. If they could run and remain hidden within the Song of All, they might succeed in eluding the Hunter. Djorn considered the odds. They were not good enough. And yet he could not think of an alternative.

He wheeled about abruptly and she jerked back startled.

"There is so much I need to tell you, and yet..." Djorn's eagerness gave way to doubt. "And yet...and yet I fear it will not be enough."

"You fear the Olmmoš who follows," she stated.

"Yes. I wish it were not so. I wish your transformation were to be like mine was. I wish it were in the warmth of sunshine with only a bright future to look forward to."

She regarded him evenly. "Even yours could not have been so unfettered."

"No. There was fear. I feared the pain of birth and unfamiliarity of a changing body, but the war had not begun. We still walked among the Olmmoš, and I did not have to fight a Piijkij."

"Perhaps he is not a Hunter."

Djorn studied Aillun. She was so very young, and what he needed to say would sound harsh to her.

"There are few others among the Olmmoš who would have the skill or the cause to seek us out. You must believe that somewhere behind us there is a Piijkij, and you will have to face him."

Aillun looked off in the distance. "How will I fight him?"

Djorn grimaced. "That is what I have been giving thought to. Your strength will be augmented, but you will be inexperienced. I cannot teach you all there is to know of fighting. That comes of training."

"But I will receive some of your skill with the sword, will I not?"

"Yes, there will be a residue, but it will not be enough to stand against a Piijkij." Djorn paused then continued. "Do you remember what you witnessed in my song?"

She nodded.

"I was already a Taistelijan. I had already fought in countless battles, and yet I almost died. Only a small mistake separated my triumph from a defeat."

"I have my bows. I know their use for hunting, and if my power is augmented, then I could unleash a lethal shot." Aillun's words tumbled out of her.

The old warrior reflected on her suggestion. *It was possible.*

"Yes, if you could hide within the Song and ambush the Hunter, you would improve your chances of escape. But what of your accuracy? You may only get one opportunity. You would have to remove yourself from the Song, take aim, make the shot, and return to the Song, all within a moment in time."

Aillun nodded quickly. "I can do that."

"If you do not—if you do not hit the target—he will continue to hunt you, and if you cannot return to the Song, because fear or rage clouds your mind, you will remain within the realm of the Olmmoš, making his mission easier."

The warning was cruel but necessary. Aillun needed to know the consequences. And yet, neither had broached the subject that she would not be on her own. She would be caring for her baby. Aillun truly faced the impossible.

Djorn noted her crestfallen expression. He knew he had disheartened her. He wished there were some other way.

Perhaps he could lay traps on the perimeter of the snowy glade and hope the Hunter fell into one of them. But what if the Piijkij did not become ensnared? Or what if he came upon Aillun on her travels away from the Origin? Djorn discarded the trap idea as an option.

He could leave Aillun at the Origin and venture out to hunt the Piijkij. For a moment, the idea spoke to his warrior's heart. But what if he did not find the Hunter, and the Hunter found Aillun instead? She would be at her most vulnerable. Even if he found and killed the Piijkij, what would become of Aillun and the unborn if he began his ascension and he was far from them? He could not leave her side now that they had found each other.

Djorn despaired. It seemed the only option that remained was to wait and see if the Piijkij found them. He kicked at the snow in frustration and drew back his foot again, but stopped. If he could not go out to seek the Hunter, couldn't they hasten to bring the Hunter to them, and ensure he fell into their trap?

Djorn glanced up to see Aillun's expectant look.

"Tell me again what you experienced before we joined together," he demanded with a hint of excitement.

"I do not understand." Aillun shook her head.

"You said you somehow knew you were being followed and that it was a Piijkij. How did you know this?"

"I saw him."

"He was close enough to you that you saw him and recognized him to be a Hunter?"

"No. I saw him in my mind."

Aillun seemed to reflect on the recent events, and Djorn waited for her to continue. "I heard something and I stopped the sled. I got out and listened. I saw images in my mind. I saw his life."

"How did you know it was a Piijkij?"

"I saw his sword—its markings. His sword was driven into the heart of a fallen opponent. . ."

"Olmmoš or. . ."

"Jápmemeahttun."

"And you are sure he was a Piijkij?"

"Yes." Aillun faltered, then added excitedly, "his sword was the same sword as the one in your song."

"And you say you heard him?"

"Yes."

As Aillun's silence grew, Djorn drew his own conclusions. "He has traveled in our time." The implication of what he had said hit him. "The Song alone will not protect you," he spoke his thoughts as they occurred to him. "But perhaps it can be used as a weapon. If you heard him, then could he not hear us? If we should call to him. . ."

Aillun shrank back in alarm. Djorn realized her fear and tried to assuage it by explaining his intent.

"If we could lure the Piijkij into a trap, I could dispatch him with no danger to you. We could be finished with this threat. We could enter our transformation with clear minds and hearts."

"But what if you fail? Could we not hope that he will not find us?"

Djorn looked at Aillun, trying to gauge her true fortitude. It was perhaps unreasonable to ask a nieddaš, about to give birth, to enter into a risky scheme like the one he proposed, but he had never been one to rely on hope.

"It is possible I could fail. I am old. My reflexes are not the same as when I was young. But I am still a warrior. I have not failed in my service yet."

"But if you do," she persisted, "what then?"

Djorn reflected upon the possible outcomes. "If I fail to kill him and he kills me, he will come for you. If I succeed in killing him and die in the process, my life force will not be transferred. The baby will be born, but will never take a breath of life. And you. . ." He hesitated. "And you will not become an almai. But you will no longer be a nieddaš either."

He could see by her expression she did not understand the importance of what he was telling her. For the first time since he had found peace, Djorn damned the gods and the ways of their kind. Why must he explain the ritual of birth and death?

"I would return home then," Aillun concluded, "unchanged."

"No," Djorn said decisively. He saw her confusion, and it broke his heart. He took her hand in his. "You would be unchanged, yes, but you could not truly return home. Even if you survived and you managed to make it back, you would fail the *dákti* and the gods would give you no new song. You would be a *rivgu*, neither almai nor nieddaš. You would be cast out."

"But why?" Aillun's voice became high and thin.

"Because you would break the balance. Your death would never give birth to life. For all of our kind, you would be one who takes life force, but can never return it."

Aillun was shaking. She drew her hand back from his. "You said, 'if I survived.'"

"When you give birth, you may lose much blood, and my life force is meant to sustain you and replenish you. Rarely does one survive the birthing without some sacrifice."

Djorn did not know how to comfort Aillun, to lessen the harshness of her fate, their shared fate; no kind reassurance or embrace could soften the blow he had delivered with his pronouncement.

Aillun sat in silence and peered into the fire, her food forgotten at her side. "There is no other option," she said finally.

The old warrior could not tell what conclusion Aillun had reached. He waited for her to tell him of her decision. In the end, the choice was hers; his own fate was sealed. He would surrender himself to her future.

"We should call to him," she said.

Djorn nodded. He stood and looked down at her, but she would not return his look. Instead, she watched the flames in front of her.

"I will begin the preparations." Djorn walked away from their circle of firelight. He needed time and space to think where best to lay their trap.

~

The morning passed in silence. Irjan traveled along an easterly path, hoping to find an indication the Jápmea had traveled in this direction. He scanned the trees, looking for broken branches. He watched for disturbances in the snow that might indicate tracks had been made or covered, but he had seen little to give him confidence. An honest assessment of his situation would force him to admit the chances of success were diminishing.

Irjan, however, refused to accept defeat. He focused his mind on the Immortals and what would come after. If his future could be shaped by intent alone, then he would succeed. Then he suddenly remembered his earlier vision—that of the Jápmea warrior. The cruelty and heartlessness of the Immortal, leaving the child behind to die, firmed Irjan's resolve. The wrong could be righted—one life for another. He would see to it.

The sound of hooves distracted Irjan from his thoughts.

Far to his left, a small herd of binna gathered speed as they cut through the forest into the open space before him. Only a dozen or so animals ran, but their sound filled his ears. Although the snow softened their impact on the ground, Irjan could feel the vibration of their movement. He thought of his time with the binna, and it filled him with regret. They had given him a focus and a structure, but not a sense of completeness, nor a feeling of connection. Irjan had found that connection when he left the herds and wandered to the doorway of the old farmer and his daughter—his beautiful Sohja.

From the moment he saw her, Irjan had known she was the answer he sought. He spent so many nights in front of the fire with her father, praying his feelings were shared. He would steal glances beyond the old man to where Sohja sat, her face obscured by the shadows, hoping his words communicated more than the essence of his tale, because he imbued each one with his love for her.

Night after night, Sohja sat sewing, her paleness at times lit by candlelight—so close to him, and yet, it seemed, unreachable. And then the impossible happened. When had he realized she loved him? Irjan tried to remember the past, even as his feet carried him forward into his future.

He had been returning from the market in the peak of summer. He'd gone in place of Sohja's father, who had grown too weak to travel. As Irjan drew close to the farm he saw Sohja open the door and rush out. He smiled and waved. She hesitated and then shyly lifted her hand to wave back, only to retract it quickly and smooth the front of her apron. Her reticence lifted his spirits. Irjan had felt like he soared upon the sweetest wind. Even now the memory was powerful, but the reality of her death overshadowed his memory of momentary joy. Her death was his fault.

Before he could delve deeper into his thoughts, Irjan heard something that made him stop. *Was it them?* Indecision took hold. If he concentrated on the sounds and stilled himself, he might find himself frozen in time again and unable to pursue. But if he did not concentrate, he would lose the thread connecting them. In the end he chose to listen, hoping he would be able to follow should he find he had lost time again.

His heart slowed, his breath slowed, and the strands filtered into him.

I am the maiden.
I am the bringer of life.
My transformation serves the future.
My transformation reflects the past.
I walk alone, but count myself among the many who traveled before
me.

Another voice joined it.

I am the warrior.
I am the survivor of the battles of the Olmmoš.
My sword serves our kind in death,
My knowledge our continued life.
I walk alone, but count myself among the many who will travel after
me.

Together the two voices became one.

We are the Jápmemeahttun.
We are the guardians of the world.
Our memory stretches back to the start of days.
Our vision reaches beyond all tomorrows.
We sing together as one, so that our one may always survive.

Irjan opened his eyes and took a tentative step. Their song continued.

We return to our Origin.
We return to begin anew.

One life to begin.
One life to change.
One life to end.

Irjan heard all this and yet it seemed no time elapsed. The sky appeared unchanged, the world the same as he'd left it. Stillness brought no surprises this time. Irjan took a step forward and another, and then he ran, mindful of the direction of the voices, gathering speed as he gathered determination. *It will soon be over*, he told himself.

CHAPTER EIGHTEEN

THEY STOOD TOGETHER IN a momentary embrace. They both knew the roles they were to play. When they parted she held on to his hand.

"Thank you, Djorn," Aillun said. "I know you are a true warrior and are willing to make this sacrifice to fulfill your duty, but it should not be made without hearing my heartfelt gratitude."

"That you and the baby live on is all the gratitude I need." He touched her cheek gently. "You can do this, Aillun."

She nodded and tried to keep her doubt from showing.

"You know what you must do," he encouraged her once again, then took both her hands in his.

"It is time."

They closed their eyes and began to sing their songs. To each, the refrain of the other seemed to hang in the air before being carried off by the wind. When their songs merged, Aillun felt a jolt of courage rush through her. She realized then what it meant to be part of a history that began with time and the gods. Theirs was a heritage of heroes and brigands, and a legacy of great acts of compassion and the small deeds of everyday sacrifices. Aillun now understood she was one part of an unfolding universe, one part that made the whole.

When they finished their verses, Aillun opened her eyes to find Djorn watching her.

"You should go now," he advised. "We do not know how far the Piijkij needs to travel to find us. It may be a long wait, and you must be prepared."

When Aillun did not immediately release his hands, Djorn squeezed hers again.

"If I should fail. . ."

She looked directly into his eyes. "You will not."

Aillun let Djorn's hands drop and walked away. She knew the details had been planned as far as possibility would allow. Djorn had made false tracks leading toward a small clearing in the woods, which looked as if he were running and confused. If the Piijkij followed Djorn's tracks, he would be led to the empty circle, where Djorn would be hiding, waiting to attack. It was not the choice of a proud warrior, but the reality of those who wanted to live. All that remained now was for her to enter the Song of All and stay hidden.

Aillun carefully wound her way through the trees, erasing her tracks as she went. She knelt among their sturdy trunks in the hidden shelter Djorn had made for her. From her little den she could see the clearing where the warrior still stood. Although Aillun worried she might be discovered, Djorn reassured her that even if she became lost to the Song, it would take a discerning eye to see her. Aillun joined the Song of All and watched and waited. Djorn removed himself from sight behind the trees on the far side.

~

Irjan ran on, following the strands of the voices he heard. They seemed close, but he could not be certain. Then, the voices ceased. Irjan stopped running. He slowed his heavy breath. Nothing. He could not risk losing time now. He raced up a short incline, his satchel jostling against his back. When he reached the crest, he scanned the terrain ahead. He knelt and touched the snow—powdery and fresh. He descended the rise, keeping his eyes trained on the snow for tracks. His mind remained with the wind, listening for their voices.

Irjan's heart raced in spite of his efforts to remain calm. He had been away from the hunt long enough that the excitement of a close quarry surprised him. He imagined he could smell them—smell their fear and feel the blood coursing in their veins. They may have been immortal, but their core was no different from his.

His eyes caught a change in the snow's reflection off to the left, and he moved quickly to examine the discoloration, finding a footprint, large and deep. Irjan looked ahead and saw more, widely spaced and uneven. They belonged to the one who had attacked him, the male. It appeared as though the Jápmea were running.

Irjan stood and followed the steps at a run himself. When he reached a small clearing in the woods, he became wary. He stepped carefully, mindful of movement in the woods around him, trying to read the patterns in the snow.

❧

When Aillun saw the Olmmoš, she clapped her hands over her mouth, fearing a noise would escape and betray her presence. She tried to keep herself focused on the Song of All, but she felt her heart pounding wildly and she desperately wanted to run away. She watched the Hunter's cautious movements.

He scanned the trees, and she feared his gaze would penetrate her thicket. When he focused in her direction, it seemed his eyes bored right through to her. *He can see me. He can see me.* A panicked voice arose within her and competed with the Song for her attention. Aillun struggled to remain still and hidden. When the Hunter's scrutiny shifted from her position, she sagged in relief.

The Hunter's head snapped around. Aillun prayed it was due to an animal stirring.

She heard the Piijkij call out.

"Show yourself!"

She froze.

"I know you are here," the Olmmoš shouted. His voice echoed through the silence of the woods. He continued to pace about the clearing looking for signs.

Djorn had not revealed himself.

Suddenly, the Piijkij stopped his circling and drew his sword from his scabbard. He stood motionless in the center of the circle. Aillun sat transfixed. Had the Hunter divined the nature of their trap? Was he attempting to create his own by taunting them? For an instant Aillun's fear shifted her focus away from the Song. Her guard dropped. The voices ceased to resonate. Numbness grabbed hold of her body. Aillun reached her hand forward to steady herself, and a branch snapped.

The sound exploded in her ears. She shot a look toward the Hunter, knowing he must have heard her, and yet praying that he had not. His eyes seemed to peer into her shelter and hold her spellbound.

Slowly the Hunter walked in her direction. Only then did Aillun realize the significance of his movement.

She burst from her hiding spot like a rabbit flushed from cover, stumbling forward and falling on the ground. The world around her was dead. There were no voices, no hum of life. She felt as if her legs were made of stone, but she willed herself to get up, thinking only of putting distance between herself and the Hunter.

From behind, Aillun heard the muffled sounds of running. She glanced over her shoulder, and saw Djorn emerging from the circle of trees, with his sword raised above him. The Hunter spun with sword drawn.

Djorn let out a thunderous roar and appeared ready to bring down his sword with vengeance when he collapsed, as though struck by some great force.

Aillun froze, watching the great Taistelijan fall to the ground.

He struggled with his limbs, trying desperately to stand. The Hunter, seeing his attacker rendered helpless, marched forward, deliberately.

"No!" she screamed, and loosed an arrow as she ran toward the two startled combatants.

The arrow missed the Olmmoš, but it succeeded in transferring his attention away from Djorn. Aillun drew another arrow from her quiver as she stumbled forward. She set herself and loosed it.

The Olmmoš threw himself to the ground, and the arrow sailed over his head. Aillun didn't know what she would do when she stood face to face with the Hunter. She only had a knife meant for skinning. Her advance, however, halted when Djorn's song washed over her. Her eyes filled with tears and she ran headlong, heedless of the Hunter who stood between her and her warrior.

The Taistelijan's voice reached into the sky.

I return to my Origin to share my life force.
My life ends so that a new life begins and another transforms.
I leave as I entered, and the whole is unchanged.

The chorus repeated again in a chant. The Hunter appeared momentarily transfixed, but regained himself and scrambled toward Djorn.

"Leave him be!" Aillun yelled, loosing another arrow.

～

Irjan felt the stab of an arrow break through his flesh, trying to find bone. He fell to the ground and screamed in agony, but he would not let the pain stop him. He stood and staggered to within reach of the chanting Jápmea.

Irjan cast aside his sword and tore his satchel from his back. He ripped it open with the force of frenzy and brought forth a small bundle of fabric. As he lurched forward, the fabric pulled apart, revealing the face and small body of his son. He held his baby ahead of him as he moved.

In that instant, the Taistelijan burst into a blinding light, knocking Irjan to the ground. As Irjan fell, he encircled his son in his arms and protected him from impact, accepting the warmth of unconsciousness.

～

Aillun had released her last arrow and was gratified to see it hit the Piijkij. But then she saw the Olmmoš rise to advance again. The force of rage and frustration propelled her forward. She would stop him with her bare hands if necessary.

Aillun unsheathed her knife and charged ahead. She saw the Piijkij throw down his sword and tear open his satchel. When he exposed the small folded blanket she stopped in her tracks.

Before she could react, Aillun crumpled in the explosion of light. She felt as though every inch of her body had been lit with a flame. Aillun collapsed to the ground, only to be seized by a spasm that shook her to her core, leaving her gasping. No sooner did her breath return to her than another spasm wrenched it away again; her mánná was making its way into the world.

Aillun panted as she raised herself to her knees. She glanced at the world around her, but it appeared hazy and far off. She knew she needed to prepare herself to deliver the baby, but she could not summon a clear thought. Everything slid and shifted. She held out her hand to grasp something solid, but found nothing.

A spasm took hold of her. This time its significance helped her to focus. Aillun tore at her furs to open them. The dense layers resisted before falling wide, and she clutched at the folds of her skirt. She raised them and tried to untie her leather and woolen leg covers, but her fingers fumbled with the lacing.

Aillun's curse of frustration became a howl of pain. She fell upon all fours. The pain ebbed, but before she could take a breath it swelled, threatening to rip her apart. Her breath was pulled from her body, and she struggled against what was happening. She sobbed—her heart crying out to make it all stop.

And then, it did.

In a final push, her pain gave way to relief. She lay upon the cold snow. She wanted to rest, but a thought broke through her exhaustion.

Aillun struggled to sit up. A small body lay silent upon the snow in a pool of blood, its hands tightly clenched and its eyes closed. The weight of dread settled over her heart. The baby had not drawn the breath of life. She grasped the infant's body to hers, wrapping its tiny frame in the warmth of her furs. Her voice became a keening whisper of denial.

"You must live," she said repeatedly. Aillun rocked back and forth with this thought until she collapsed. The silence in the circle of trees was complete.

CHAPTER NINETEEN

IRJAN AWOKE TO FIND himself holding the body of his little
boy. He did not know how long he had been unconscious.
He quickly pulled apart the layers of the shroud to reveal his
son's serene face. He stared, trying to discern signs of life. The
baby did not move. Irjan moaned in despair, and then he saw the
shallow rise of the fragile chest—a breath. His heart almost burst
with excitement as he continued to stare at the tiny frame, willing
the rise and fall to grow more robust. It did not, but it continued
nonetheless, enough to raise his hopes.

He removed the shroud entirely, then cut a piece of the inner-
most layer of his own furs and fashioned a bunting for the baby.
When it was finished, he held his boy close, and with his head
bowed, he silently thanked the gods for their mercy.

Assured the baby's breath would continue, Irjan looked
around. The Jápmea warrior had vanished. His sword lay in the
snow. Irjan revisited those last moments in his mind. As he did,
he felt the throbbing of his shoulder. He reached his hand over
and felt the jagged edge of the arrow shaft. The arrow brought
him abruptly back to the present. Behind him, to the left, the Jápmea female lay upon her side in the snow, unmoving.

Irjan stood and, holding his baby close, walked over to her.
When he reached her, he knelt. She did not move, but she lived. A

knife rested by her side. He tossed it away. Her body lay wrapped in furs. Irjan nudged her shoulder. She remained still, but tears trickled from the corners of her eyes.

For the first time since he had become a Piijkij, his hand moved to comfort a Jápmea. He heard a baby's muffled cry, and he looked to his son in his arms. The boy slept. Shocked, Irjan bent over the young female and gently pulled apart her arms and the various layers of fur.

Under their protective warmth, a newborn pressed its face against its mother's chest and struggled to breathe. He looked upon the mother and child, stunned. The Jápmea baby cried out again, and the cry shook Irjan from his stupor. Although he loathed letting go of his son, he did so, placing him gently on top of the snow. He quickly took off his outermost layer of clothing and made a blanket upon the snow, on which he placed his son. As he lifted the protesting body of the other baby, he could see she was a little girl, and still connected to her mother by the gods' cord.

Irjan took his knife from his belt and cut the bloodied cord, tying a knot as he had done for his son when he'd entered the world. He laid her near his own baby and then cut another piece of fur to fashion a bunting for the girl. Irjan covered them both deep within his furs.

The female Immortal stirred. Her eyes fluttered open, but she did not appear to recognize him.

"I have come home, Kalek," she said, her voice a hoarse whisper.

"I am not Kalek," Irjan answered softly.

"Then I am not home." She closed her eyes again, and new tears welled in the corners.

"No, you are not at home. You are in the woods, where you fought bravely and gave birth to a beautiful girl."

The Immortal heard his words and they seemed to give her strength.

"She lives?" the barely conscious female marveled.

"Yes, she lives."

Irjan leaned over and placed the now mewling infant in her mother's arms. The Immortal's hands struggled with her front dress lacings. Realizing what she meant to do, Irjan stood abruptly, feeling suddenly uncomfortable, and walked to the shelter that had once hidden the young Jápmea. He looked at its construction and decided it would serve the immediate purpose of providing a refuge for the two babies and the new mother. Irjan trudged back across the clearing, then carried his sleeping son to the shelter and gently made a comfortable spot for him, before returning to the female's side. She lay still and whimpered while her child cried, red-faced with need.

He placed his hand upon the female's shoulder, and she stirred.

"I am going to move you," he told her.

She nodded, but said nothing. Her child, however, howled like the wolves.

Irjan bent down and cradled her and the babe in his arms. Her lightness surprised him. When he stood, blood pooled across the length of the indentation her form had made. To him, it looked like more blood than an Olmmoš could lose and hope to survive. *On the other hand,* he thought, as he laid her in the shelter, *she is a Jápmea. Perhaps she is truly immortal.* He rested the two infants, one squalling and the other sleeping, against her for warmth. He hesitated a moment before taking out his knife and cutting the laces of her dress. He placed the Jápmea infant in her arms, then left to gather wood for a fire.

❧

Aillun awoke to darkness. A fire flickered in front of her and she was comfortable and warm. Her thoughts, however, swirled around her like thick mist. She recalled the Taistelijan, their flight, and the trap. She remembered Djorn's hands holding hers. Her heart skipped a beat.

"Djorn," she said out loud.

Something stirred beyond her vision.

"If you speak of the other," the disembodied voice said, "he is gone."

"Gone," she repeated.

"He burst into light," the voice explained.

"He ascended."

"I thought it was death."

A figure drew into her line of sight.

Aillun looked at him for a long time. Slowly, a sense of recognition spread across her mind. Her eyes widened and her lips parted to speak, but no sound escaped.

"Do you know who I am?" he asked.

Aillun tried to draw away, but could not make her limbs respond. "You are the Piijkij!"

"I was a Piijkij. I am no longer a Hunter."

"But you hunted us. You were going to kill us."

"No! I was searching for you. I did not want to kill you. I wanted you to bring my boy back into the world of the living."

"Your boy?" she asked, then dread fell upon her like a great crashing tree. "My daughter!" she screamed.

"She lives," the Hunter assured her, lifting a bundle for her to hold in her arms as she lay upon the ground.

Aillun clutched the infant to her chest where her own heartbeat rose to meet the welcomed weight. She raised her head with effort and saw a wide yawn in the babe's otherwise pinched face.

She let her head fall back to the ground as relief claimed her body. She turned her attention to the Olmmoš who cradled a child in his own arms. Aillun vaguely recalled him with outstretched hands as Djorn ascended.

"He lives," she said finally.

The Olmmoš took it as a question. "Yes. Yes he lives," he nodded.

"How?" she asked, her disbelief sounding more like an accusation.

"Among the Hunters there is a legend that the Jápmea mating releases the miracle of life. It is said the miracle can restore an ailing man to vigor and bring back life to the dead."

Aillun shook her head.

"It is true," he insisted. "You see."

Aillun looked at the Olmmoš infant, then turned her head away.

She closed her eyes and rested briefly, then opened her eyes suddenly, startling the Olmmoš when she spoke. "Sleep feels too close to death to be comforting."

She turned her head to regard him. "Why do you call us by that name?"

The Olmmoš frowned. "What name? Jápmea?"

"Yes, that. Why? We are the Jápmemeahttun."

"It is how you are known to us." The man shrugged weakly.

"It sounds ugly to the ear! Can you not speak our name properly?" A flush of anger brought heat to her face. When he did not answer, she said, "If you pride yourself on taking the lives of my kind, then you should speak of us as the gods intended."

The man dropped his head. "I do not pride myself on what I have done."

Seeing his troubled face, Aillun's resentment drained. "How did your child die?"

"I do not know how my child died. I returned home and my boy, Marnej, was dead. His mother was dying upon the floor; she had moments to live in my arms. I discovered nothing of what happened to them in my absence. I had not wanted to leave them, but my wife insisted I go." His voice trailed off.

"You had expected to live your lives together," Aillun said.

"Yes."

"We have no such expectations. I left my beloved behind to journey here. I knew when I left him I would not be with him again. Perhaps it is less cruel."

The Olmmoš said nothing in response, but seemed to be considering the possibility that she was right.

"What was the name of your beloved?" she asked.

"Sohja. Yours?"

"Kalek."

"Who was your mate?" the man asked.

"My mate? Oh, Djorn was not my mate. We shared the same destiny and the same Origin, but we were not mated."

"Why was he with you, then? Was he your guardian?"

"No, he was not intended to be my guardian. His purpose was to share his life force with me and the baby." She held the child a little closer to her and felt its reassuring warmth. "He gave her life and made me almai."

"I don't know what that means," the Olmmoš said.

But Aillun found she did not have the strength to explain. As her eyes fluttered closed, she thought it must be a dream—a Jápmemeahttun talking with a Piijkij. Otherwise, the ways of the gods were indeed strange.

~

Irjan watched the female's eyes flicker closed. Thinking she had died, he reached his hand to touch her face. A soft exhalation of air came from her gently parted lips.

She lived.

He removed his hand and savored his sense of relief and marked its revelation.

The infant resting in her arms squirmed. Its mouth puckered with hunger. He did not wish to wake the mother, but if the hungry girl did not eat she would call down the heavens with her screams. Irjan nudged the Jápmea female, but she did not awaken.

He knew what needed to be done, and yet he hesitated. He was like some shy stripling embarrassed to see the breast of someone other than his mother. Irjan chided himself for his foolishness. He pushed aside the Jápmea's furs and brought the little girl to the nipple. She needed no encouragement. She suckled with the same fierceness as she screamed.

Irjan sat back and looked down at his son. Marnej was waking, but there was no breast for him to suckle upon with his mother resting in her grave. For an instant he wondered if he had done what was best for his child or if he had acted only from his desire not to lose all love from his life.

Irjan placed his metal cup in the nest of glowing embers. He added a handful of snow and a piece of dried reindeer meat, and made a broth.

Irjan looked at the Jápmea baby in her mother's arms and momentarily thought of putting Marnej to the other breast. He told himself she would never know. He told himself it was the only way to save his son. He told himself Marnej deserved the milk as much as her daughter did. But in the end, Irjan knew he could not force his will upon her, not when she was helpless and so close to what might be her own end.

He took the small blue swatch of cloth he still carried with him and dipped the fabric into the heated broth. He held it above the cup and let it cool. Irjan let a drop fall upon his own skin, and, when he was certain the temperature would not scald, he held the soaked cloth above his son's lips until the babe took it into his mouth and sucked the wetness from the rag.

Irjan repeated this process until the cup emptied and then searched through his meager possessions for something more for his son.

"Give him here," a hoarse voice cracked.

Startled, Irjan looked up to see the Jápmea female staring at him. "She is finished and I have more milk."

Irjan was about to speak, but his gratitude overwhelmed him and seized his heart. He brought Marnej to her other breast. The boy latched on and Irjan sank back, his relief as profound as his shame.

"Why did you hunt us?" she asked. "I do not mean now, but in the past."

"It is what I was trained to do," Irjan answered uncomfortably.

"But you take care of me now. Surely you were not trained to pity your enemies."

"You are not my enemy."

"But I am Jápmemeahttun."

"The Jápmea," he started to say, and then corrected himself, "The Jápmemeahttun ceased to be my enemy eight seasons of snow past."

"What happened to change your heart?"

"Death changed my heart. I was tired of death. I wanted to live. I wanted to give life, not hunt it and take it. I made a vow to the gods I would not take another life, but death seems to follow me."

"You mean your mate and child?"

"Yes, and the family of my childhood before. They were killed by the roving Jápmemeahttun, but somehow I was spared. I was taken in by the Brethren of Hunters. They took the suffering of a small boy and sculpted it into hatred."

"I know," she whispered. "I saw it."

Before he could ask how, she spoke.

"I saw the blindfold. I saw the woods. I saw you chasing another. I saw you put the sword through the heart of a man." Her voice trailed off.

A chill ran through Irjan. It was as if every act of violence had been witnessed and tallied and he faced a reckoning.

"How can you know that?" His voice roused her.

"I heard your song," she whispered, her eyelids closing again.

Irjan shook his head. "But I have never sung."

"You sing with your heart and your soul, and you do not even realize it," she said before falling asleep.

Irjan wanted to press the female to explain herself, but he knew she needed to rest. He tried to intuit what she meant by singing, and with the heart, no less. *Impossible.* And yet, she had been uncannily accurate. Some of it she could have easily guessed, like the sword through the heart. Likely a Piijkij such as himself could have killed in that manner. But what was singular and unpredictable was her mention of the blindfold. None but the Brethren knew of its use in training.

Irjan tried to reflect back to see where he might have revealed the information, perhaps in an unguarded moment. But he kept coming back to the fact he had maintained the unbroken secrecy of what had truly happened to him.

Irjan removed the dozing infants from the Jápmea and covered her bare breasts with her furs. He placed the two infants at her side for warmth. Looking at the two sleeping babes, the divide between Jápmea and Olmmoš was hard to discern.

The female stirred. Irjan felt her forehead and cheeks and they felt cold to the touch. He added more wood to their fire. He made some more broth and when it cooled, he shook her gently.

"Can you take some broth?"

It took her longer to come to her senses this time, but her eyes finally fixed on his face.

"Yes." She accepted the cup he handed her. Aillun lifted her head to sip. The broth trickled down her neck.

"Here." Irjan took the cup from her. He knelt beside her and scooped his arm behind her head. He slowly tilted the cup so the liquid inside made it past her lips without spilling. After each sip, he lowered her head and allowed her to rest and absorb what strength the broth could provide.

When she slept again, the dull throb of his arm reminded Irjan he had yet to deal with the jagged arrow shaft that still jutted from his body. If he did not tend to it now it would likely fester, and his own end would not be far behind.

As he boiled more water, he finally eased himself out of his furs, wincing when they caught upon the shaft. With his arm exposed, he saw the arrow had not fully buried itself in the meat of his arm. The barbed ends of its base rested above the skin. But he saw his shirtsleeve threads were caught in the pucker of the wound.

Irjan placed his fingers gingerly on either side of the arrowhead and slowly edged it back and forth, sucking in air through clenched teeth as he did. When he finally slid the metal tip out, some threads still clung to the wound.

"Gods be cursed," he swore softly, as he poured some of the boiled water over the arrow tip. Irjan pried open the wound with his fingers, and using the arrow point, he scraped at the open gash until nothing but blood and flesh remained. Adding some snow to the boiled water, he rinsed out the wound, turning the snow under him a pale pink hue. To numb the pain, Irjan scooped a handful of clean snow, and clamped it against his arm. The cold seared where the hot had scalded. Finally, he used a strip of the swaddling he had cut to bind the wound tightly. As he cinched the cloth, a gasp of pain escaped his lips.

One of the infants stirred, and their care diverted his attention. When they settled, Irjan clothed himself again. He checked on the female. She seemed comfortable. The faint flush in her cheeks could have been a trick of the firelight, but Irjan suspected it signaled something much worse. As he considered her face, her beauty struck him. His wife had been the light of his heart and yet she shared none of what he saw before him. The Immortal appeared to be the perfect embodiment of a man and a woman, a blending of the best qualities of each. Plus, she had a recognizable set to her face he could not place.

Irjan tried to dredge up a thought or memory that carried her likeness, but nothing sprang to mind. After a while, he gave up trying to remember. He added more fuel to the fire and shifted the infants closer to the young female to rest their small bodies between his and hers.

That night, as the fire sputtered, untended, Irjan dreamed of his childhood before the Brethren. He was running through the forest, not in fear or in pursuit, but out of joy. By his side he could see his brothers and sisters, smiling and laughing at the game they played.

He looked again, and his brothers and sisters were gone, and in their place were the infants. He looked around for their parents, but saw none. He knew he needed to find someone to care for the infants, yet he could not leave them to find their parents. Irjan was afraid that if he did, he would not find them again in the woods, and they would die. He tried to pick up both to carry them in his arms, but, a child himself, he was too small and could not. He placed them upon the ground again.

Irjan had to make a choice between them. He could carry one, but not both. He had to choose. One would live and one would not. He looked between their sleeping faces for some sign of the right answer. He picked up the girl and carried her off, not daring to look back at the one who remained behind.

Irjan woke with a start, the tendrils of a dream still curling around his thoughts. He remembered having to make a choice, and the memory filled him with dread. He looked quickly at the infants and the Jápmemeahttun. She still slept, but the infants stirred, no doubt with hunger.

Irjan nurtured the fire back to life, and repeated his food preparations from earlier in the evening. With the broth ready, he moved himself into position to cradle both infants.

With a sudden jolt he realized he was looking into his son's wide-open eyes for the first time since he had left on that fateful day for the market. The staring orbs blinked and moved his heart. Marnej was alive. His sweet, beautiful son lived.

Irjan broke down and sobbed with relief. His tears cascaded down his face until his mouth tasted their salty wetness, but his gaze never wavered from the tiny face before him.

Finally, Irjan gathered the child into his still-shaking arms and carefully helped him take the meager nourishment. When Marnej was sated, his eyelids drooped and closed. Irjan replaced his son at the Jápmemeahttun's side and went to pick up the sleeping girl.

He froze as the horror of his dream came back to him in full. He recalled again having to make a choice. He remembered picking up the girl baby and turning his back on the other as he walked away.

Irjan recoiled from the sleeping girl, and laid a hand on his son to reassure himself of his solid reality. The slow rise and fall of the boy's chest gradually calmed him.

The female Immortal stirred and shifted with some distress. Irjan moved to her side, but remained watchful of his son. He smoothed the hair from her face, wiping an icy sheen from her brow. A soft moan escaped her lips, and her eyelids flickered, then stilled. She was growing weaker.

Irjan had assumed the blood in the snow had come from the birth. He had not checked for other wounds. He now regretted his haste. He was loath to expose her to the cold air to see where she was injured; on the other hand, if he did not, he could in no way determine the source of her discomfort.

Irjan spoke to her softly. "Were you injured before I found you?"

She did not rouse herself to respond.

"Can you wake up for me?"

She still appeared to sleep fitfully.

Feeling he had no alternative, Irjan opened her furs. He felt for wet areas indicative of bleeding and looked for traces of darkened fabric where a wound might have bled. He saw nothing on her front.

He pulled back on her furs and then gently rolled her onto her side away from the fire, and removed her arm from her sleeve. With her back exposed, it was obvious she still bled. The fabric of her skirt shone with the wetness of fresh blood. Either she had been wounded in her belly, or she continued to bleed from the birth.

Her baby's relative health suggested she had not been harmed while in her mother. Therefore, a puncture to the belly was unlikely, which meant the female continued to bleed from the birthing.

Irjan's seasons of snow among the binna had given him the opportunity to see all manner of difficult births. Some he had been able to assist in and correct, and in others he had stood aside as the animal died, and so condemned its newborn to a short existence. From the blood he saw and what had been left in the snow, Irjan suspected the casing holding the unborn within the Immortal must have ripped.

He carefully replaced the Jápmea's arm in her sleeve and rolled her onto her back. He refastened her furs, making sure her skin was covered entirely with the exception of a small sliver of her face.

If, indeed, she continued to bleed from within, he could do nothing but try to keep her comfortable until death claimed her. Irjan held out the hope he was wrong, but the first light of the day revealed her shadow was not shadow at all, but rather made of blood.

The female stirred and called out to him.

"I am here beside you," Irjan answered, taking her hand in his.

"The baby?"

"They are both sleeping."

"I have such a thirst."

Irjan took a scoop of snow and set his cup in the fire. As soon as its whiteness faded he removed it and tested its heat with his finger.

He gathered her head in his arms again, and lifted the cup to her lips.

She drank deeply and then sank into his arms. "Thank you. It is strange that I was training to be a healer and yet it is you who works to heal me."

"We are far from help." Irjan didn't know what else to say.

"And even if we were not, you could not bring forth a Jápme-meahttun for treatment. Nor could you carry us all. You would have to choose."

Irjan recalled his dream with clarity.

"I will not leave you."

"When I first heard your voice upon the wind saying you would find me, my heart shrank in fear. Now when you tell me you will not leave me, I find my heart is grateful to you."

"Earlier you said you heard my song, and just now you said you heard my voice speaking to you across the wind. I do not understand. How is that possible? I was at a distance from you. No shout could carry that far, and I certainly did not yell my intentions to the winds."

"How did you find me?" she asked. "How did you enter the Song of All?"

At first Irjan missed her meaning. He assumed she was slipping from reality. But then it occurred to him where he had seen her before. The maiden. The baby. Her journey. The young man so much like her. He had seen her image and it had been in his mind.

"I saw you," he exclaimed in surprise.

She nodded. She closed her eyes and let her heart sing her song.

I am the maiden.
I am the bringer of life.
My transformation serves the future.
My transformation reflects the past.
I walk alone, but count myself among the many who traveled before
    me.

"I hear you," Irjan replied in disbelief. "You are silent and yet I hear you. But it is more like images to the eyes than sounds to the ear."

"Yes." She opened her eyes again.

"This is how I found you. I listened and saw the pictures, and followed their fragments. But you knew I was coming."

"Yes. You told me you were."

"Is it only you that hears me?"

She shook her head. "No. I believe Djorn heard you. That was why we tried to set a trap for you."

"The Piijkij he killed and the baby he condemned to die," Irjan said, leaving off the rest.

Aillun coughed and pain squeezed her features. "No! He sang that story of his life to me to explain why he never took up his sword again. He killed the Olmmoš, but the baby lived."

Irjan shook his head. "I saw him walk away."

"But he came back. He came back and took the baby to a village where he believed it would be discovered and taken in by a family who would care for it." Aillun coughed again. "You two were not so dissimilar. You both made the decision to value life."

Although he did not want to say it aloud, Irjan saw the truth of her assertion.

"When you hear us, is it as we are now? Together here? Talking?" she asked abruptly.

"Do you mean, do I see you in my mind as I see you now?"

"No. Can you enter the Song of All? Is that how you can hear us?"

"The Song of All? I don't know what that is."

"It is what keeps us separate."

"You mean you use a song to hide? Like some magic incantation?"

"The Song of All is not sorcery!" A spark of life blazed in the female's wan face. "It is the gift of the gods that's protected us from the likes of you!"

"The likes of me?" Irjan bristled, his sudden flare of anger feeling both familiar and unwarranted. When his irritation finally subsided, he was able to think upon what she had said.

"The Song of All?" Then it struck him what she was asking. "Yes!" he answered excitedly. "I think I can enter it."

Irjan wanted to understand more, but her eyes were closed again, and he knew her strength ebbed with each passing moment. Her child shifted—her eyes open, watchful even, as if they searched his heart, looking for the truth of his being. Was he a Hunter? A herdsman? A farmer? What was he? He couldn't say, because he no longer knew.

Irjan observed the child's mother, who slept fitfully. He knew there would come a time soon when she would not wake again. He had seen many of her kind killed, but this time it was different. He wondered what awaited her at the crossroads of life and death.

She stirred again, and Irjan placed the child at her side. He took dregs of the broth from the child's earlier meager meal and fed it to her mother.

～

Aillun struggled back to consciousness to take the nourishment the Hunter offered her. She realized she still thought of him by the name of his trade, and it seemed wrong, when he worked to keep her alive.

Though it took effort for her to speak, she managed to ask him his name.

The man looked surprised and embarrassed. "My name is Irjan."

"Irjan," she said, reaching out her hand toward him.

The Olmmoš put down the cup he held. He took her hand in both of his, warming it with his touch.

"I am called Aillun." She looked directly at him, and then her eyes wandered to her side. "I must ask you one last kindness. . ."

The man seemed ready to interrupt her, but Aillun would not let him.

"I know you will say I will live. I do not need to hear your words to know your thoughts now. I know I will not live, and perhaps it is better. It is closer to the ways of our kind." Aillun stopped to gather her strength.

"I need you to learn the birth song of my mánná," she said finally, "and sing it to her when I am gone. You must promise me that. You must promise to sing it to Dárja."

"Dárja. Is that what you call your daughter?"

Aillun shook her head slowly. "No. It is what the gods have called her. But I approve." She felt a smile grow across her face. "Will you do as I have asked?" she said, drawing his focus back to her request.

"Yes. But I am afraid I will not be able to sing it properly."

"If it comes from the heart, it is enough."

In a soft voice Aillun started to sing.

Daughter of the gods.
Sister among the Jápmemeahttun.
You started your life at your Origin, with sadness and joy as your companions.
You braved dangers and met enemies and can see the truth of friendship.
Go into the world to meet your destiny, knowing that the stars watch over you.

When Aillun finished, she looked at the man expectantly. He shook his head.

"Say it after me." And the two alternated, until the refrains became natural to him.

"Now you alone," Aillun said.

The man held on to her hand and began to sing. Aillun closed her eyes and prepared herself to listen. She heard the first notes of her daughter's song, then she heard the unexpected—the song of Irjan's true soul.

Daughter of the gods.
I am the son of the gods.
Sister among the Jápmemeahttun.
I am brother among my kind.
You started your life at your Origin, with sadness and joy as your companions.
I started my life at a crossroads.

You braved dangers and met enemies and can see the truth of
  friendship.
I traveled the winding path of those who are lost.
Go into the world to meet your destiny, knowing that the stars
  watch over you
I will return to fulfill the forgotten destiny of one who should not exist.

Aillun opened her eyes to look at the Olmmoš beside her,
or rather what she had thought was a man. His birth song swept
through her. He was someone who should not exist and yet did.

As Aillun stood on death's edge, she did not see her own life
play before her eyes. Instead, she saw the life of her mánná and
the Hunter who would be her guide mother. Djorn had said, to be
Jápmemeahttun is to transform. Aillun saw this truth now in her
vision, and she stepped into the stars surrounding her.

～

Irjan held on to Aillun's hand and watched her as he finished the
last refrain of her child's song. He thought her eyes had momentarily blinked open to bore deep into his soul, but as he looked
closely at her, he could see they were shut.

Holding on to her, he felt life slip from her hand as the beat
of her heart slowed and its pulse ceased to throb. He was not sure
what he had expected—perhaps the spectacle of light that had
brought his son back to him—but she did not ascend. She quietly
eased into whatever lay beyond for her kind.

Irjan put Aillun's hand upon her breast and took her daughter
into his arms to sing the child's song to her once again. His voice
filled the morning air, and he felt proud to honor his promise to
the young mother—a small consolation to those of her kind that
at least one Jápmemeahttun had experienced the mercy of a Piijkij.

When Irjan finished, he placed the girl alongside his son and
allowed the two to slumber together. Once again he faced the

task of burying someone who had become dear to him. Irjan was stilled by the knowledge that Aillun had a place in his heart. Just the day before, she had loosed arrows, intending to maim, if not to kill, but she had been driven to act out of love, he believed, just as he himself had been.

Aillun's arrow was not the first to pierce his flesh. Its scar would join the ranks of the others he had acquired in his pursuit of the Jápmemeahttun. Her true mark upon him was the resurrection of his compassion. Irjan had thought it dead and buried with his wife's body. To his surprise, compassion filled his heart now as never before. Perhaps he was lost in the Song of All, as Aillun had called it. Or, perhaps he had known her a lifetime in his own timespace and he now mourned not the passing of a day, but the end of an era of friendship.

CHAPTER TWENTY

I N THE DAYS SINCE Irjan had buried his wife, the ground had
frozen many times, and he had no tools to dig into the hardened earth. And yet he would not leave Aillun's body to the
wolves.

Irjan searched his surroundings for an answer. The wood was
too wet to make a proper pyre; it would smolder and not burn hot
enough to consume her flesh. He looked about the ground. The
snow concealed the rocks and stones he might have used to build
a mound over her. He was at a loss. The best he could offer her
body to protect it from the elements was to cover it in packed
snow.

Irjan lifted Aillun as gently as he had done his wife. He
removed the outer layers of her clothing—she had no more need
of warmth—and the leather belt at her waist. It once sheathed
the knife she would have gladly sunk into him, given half a chance.
In the single layer of her woolen dress, Aillun looked small and
frail, unlike the Immortal she had been.

Irjan bent and picked her up. He brought her to the mound of
large stones and laid her beside him as he set about to work. He
took his knife and, using it and his hands, he carved a space next
to the rocks. When he managed to clear an area large enough for
her body, he gently laid her next to the great marker.

Irjan raked snow upon her body and finally her face, and pressed it firmly against what remained of her. Again he heaped snow and packed it until the boulders' contour extended far from its original boundaries. The wolves might be tempted to dig, but in the end he hoped they would be discouraged, and eventually give up and seek an easier meal.

Irjan had brought both babies close to where he labored, so he could hear their cries. When he finished, he dripped with the sweat of his effort. He took off his furs and removed the inner-most layer, replacing it with a drier outer one. The wet layer he used as a final covering, and he expected it would dry over time with the heat of his body.

Irjan looked at the sleeping babies and his meager supplies. He needed to act swiftly to ensure the babies would have proper nourishment soon. He knew he was several days' walk from his village, and he had no desire to return there. Nothing remained of his former life to welcome him back, except perhaps the Apotti, and, Irjan knew he could not reappear with the daughter of a Jáp-memeahttun and expect the Apotti to take mercy on the helpless infant. Moreover, he could not begin to explain how his own son once again could be counted among the living. *No*, he thought to himself, *I cannot go back*. He could only go forward.

Irjan left aside future concerns for those more immediate. With the sleigh gone, he would have to travel on foot. To do that, he needed to devise a way to carry both infants. Irjan looked down at Aillun's garments. The sound of her name in his mind felt strange, but he could not stop to consider why.

Instead, he bent down and laid out the pieces of clothing. He wrapped one baby in one layer and the second one in another layer, using the belt to make a sling. With Dárja draped across his back and Marnej at his chest, Irjan secured his sword and the meager food stores he retained. He thought of his dream. In the nightmare, one child came away with him and the other remained behind. The recollection caused a fresh welling of dread, but he willed it aside — he was a man and not a boy. He could carry both babes.

Irjan stood by Aillun's grave and offered a prayer to the gods who had taken so much from him and from her. For just a moment, he wondered if they shared the same gods. Had these gods made them enemies and forced them both to make such sacrifices? He walked to where Aillun's companion had disappeared. The warrior's sword lay in the snow.

He bent down and picked up the weapon. The cold of its hilt seeped through the fur protecting his hand. He examined the blade. He had no need for another sword, carrying death at its heart, but for Dárja, it would be a connection to the world from which she came. So he carried the two swords, along with the two young lives, next to his body in a delicate balance of life and death.

Irjan walked northwards—heading for the crossroads. He'd been anxious to start, but now, emptiness haunted each step. Unbidden, Dárja's song rose in his mind. As he sang it aloud, he realized there was something profound in the notion of a child's song.

Irjan thought of his wife's joik. Sohja often sang it in the quiet evenings by firelight. When Irjan told her he had never felt the need to sing a life song, Sohja had looked at him in amazement.

"It is the sound of your soul," she had encouraged. "The story of who you are."

But he had lost his soul long before they'd met, at the precise moment when his sword pierced the heart of the first of many Jápmemeahttun.

Irjan still didn't feel the need to sing his own song, but suddenly, he knew it was important for his son, Marncj, to have one. Though not gifted with words, Irjan let his love for his child speak.

The refrain rose.

Son of my heart.
Vessel of a father's soul.
You journeyed into the realm of the dreams of the dark sky,
And traveled back in a blaze of light.
Go into the world to meet your destiny,
And know that you have been touched by the gods.

The song flowed with ease, as if it had always existed within him. It was as his wife had described it to him. For the first time in eight seasons of snow, Irjan felt free of darkness. The moon cycles ahead would be shrouded in gloom, awaiting the return of the sun, but they would be filled with the tasks of the living. The lives of two babies had given new meaning to his life. They had given him back a part of his soul—a reason to sing.

Irjan walked on, singing to both children.

❧

A world apart from those who walked through the dark night, the Elders of the Jápmemeahttun shared another song.

We are the Elders.
We are chosen to guide.
We listen to the voices of the gods.
We seek to avoid the mistakes of the past.
Our undoing walks among us.

Part Two

DREAMS OF
THE DARK SKY

CHAPTER TWENTY-ONE

IN HIS QUIET CHAMBERS, the Apotti dipped his quill in the ink before him. His hand hovered in midair a moment as he considered what to say, and his thoughts wandered back to youth and promise, when he had entered the Order of Believers and his future had been boundless. Back then he had been the honored son of a priest and gifted with his father's faith and passion. His sermons had roused the spirits of the Believers, and delivered the faithful to the fold. But with the passage of each season of snow, his efforts failed to gain him a rise in position. His lament had gone unheeded, until one day an acolyte much his junior told him, "Rikkar, you will get nowhere by faith alone."

To which he had stammered back, "But what else is there but faith?"

The youth with the pointed nose and sparse whiskers had snorted and walked away. It had taken Rikkar, the Apotti Hemmela, far too long to learn the truth of the young acolyte's advice, but he had learned.

The quill nib touched the vellum and softly scratched against its surface.

"It has been five days since my agent left to do the gods' will. Although it is too early to tell the nature of his progress, nothing distracts him from his cause. My faith assures me his abilities will bring honor not only to you, the Brethren of Hunters, but to all of us who seek to rid this world of evil, and, in doing so, serve the gods. I thank you as the gods will thank you."

Rikkar signed the document with his title, and sealed it with his mark. He leaned into his chair's hard wooden back and considered the weight of the missive in his hand. It seemed inconsequential in its physical essence, and yet it represented so much more. The letter was another step toward escaping the small isolated village, with its simple farmers, their sniveling children, and their pathetic desires.

Rikkar reflected with pride on his actions; he had not shied from opportunity when it had presented itself. As a result, *he* had forged an alliance with the Brethren. The church, either out of blindness or pettiness, could not see the value of what the Brethren could offer. But *he* had. Rikkar had realized the Brethren could give him what the Believers could not—first-hand knowledge. The church could only provide the crumbling texts of pious scribes, which he had already scoured for anything of use.

But more importantly, *he* now wielded the power of a Piijkij. Rikkar had to admit he'd been slow to see the arrival of the stranger from the Northland as the sign from the gods. He had initially disregarded the whispers about the stranger, believing the gossip to be the idle mutterings of jealous farmers. But when he saw the man for himself, he could not deny there was something unusual about the stranger, something special.

Rikkar knew it was his duty to report his doubts and concerns to his superiors among the Order of Believers, but he had not. Instead, he had sought answers in the darker corners of his world. Experience had taught him that money bought silence, and when it could not, a knife would do. It had been a long road, but Rikkar now measured the price of truth in men's lives. And by his calculation, the knowledge he had gained came at a bargain.

Although anxious to have the missive on its way, he dared not entrust it to his assistant. Siggur had grown too curious and too brazen for his own good. The priest would need to give this letter to someone whose loyalty could be ensured—someone ruled by coin or fear, and preferably the latter; however, Rikkar did need to send forth his meddlesome assistant to ensure he was none the wiser regarding the priest's intentions. To this end, Rikkar composed a second letter, one more suited to the prying eyes of his subordinate.

The priest placed this second letter alongside its twin and marked their differences. One letter contained the spirit of a man who had seen his destiny and eagerly waited to grasp greatness. The other letter was the product of a loyal servant, fated to be lost in the squalor of a remote village.

Rikkar's hands rested lightly on each of these missives, and he considered them like a man at a crossroads. The priest, however, was not at a loss for which direction to travel. His path was clear. He placed one letter in the drawer of his desk and locked it with his key. The remaining letter sat alone upon the great expanse of smoke-darkened wood, awaiting its messenger.

With his next course of action determined, Rikkar felt his patience strained and stretched, as he waited for the arrival of his acolyte. He wished he could seek out Siggur, but he understood it was better to allow the young man to come to him and preserve the dynamic of their relationship.

The priest rubbed his hands in front of the weak fire. This would be one of the first things to change when he was given his due. A man of his understanding and vision should not spend his days attempting to keep the cold at bay. The crackle and smoking hiss of the flames punctuated his thoughts.

"Demon's eyes," Rikkar cursed, "where is that motherless cur?" The priest pushed himself up to pace about his chambers just as sharp rap resonated upon the door.

"Enter," he called out into the dimness of his room.

A shadowed figure entered. From a bowed head a voice spoke.

"I have brought the books of account for you to review, Apotti." A face beneath a hooded cloak looked up.

"Good. Good," the priest answered, trying to keep his anticipation at bay. "I will review them." Rikkar took the proffered book and opened it. Without looking up, he spoke to his assistant.

"Siggur, see that this letter is taken to the High Office of the Order." The priest kept his voice even and low. He held out the letter and waited for Siggur to take it. When he no longer felt its weight, he turned a page of the book in front of him.

"And Siggur, deliver it yourself. Do not entrust it to anyone else." Rikkar looked up when he heard no movement from the young man.

"That is all." Rikkar dismissed his assistant with a wave of his hand.

~

Siggur bowed and retreated into the shadows, closing the door behind him with a soft click. In the hall, the acolyte threw back his robe and held the letter to the torch, lighting the dark recesses. He could make out no words, but he knew he had time to discover its contents. He reasoned to himself that at this late hour it was too dangerous to travel abroad, especially by horse. After all, the Piijkij had taken their best sleigh not five days before.

If the task of delivering the letter could not be entrusted to another, then it should not be risked in a nighttime foray. Better to wait until the morning, when proper consideration had been given to the rest of the messenger and to the document in his hand. As he retreated to his own quarters, the young man could not help but enjoy a small smile of satisfaction.

Siggur stood in his room with his back to the solid wooden door. A candle in the corner lit the spare dim space. On one side of the room sat a low bench-like bed and on the other a diminutive desk and stool.

He crossed the small chamber and sat down at the desk that housed all his worldly possessions: three religious texts and a small rabbit-pelt pouch, inside of which was a tiny bronze ring, a lock of golden hair tied with a now-faded thread, and a few coins. *The sum total of his worth*, he snorted to himself.

Siggur measured the meanness of his current state and his insides burned with a bitterness he could almost taste. He was the fourth-born son of a vast landholder, and so given to the church as much out of practicality as out of piety.

No sooner had he been he issued from his mother's loins than he was given to a wet nurse, charged with bringing him to the Order of Believers. Siggur had no memory of it, but the endless hours spent kneeling in prayer on cold earthen floors had fueled his imagination as much as it had inculcated his faith.

In his mind's eye, Siggur saw his family in their warm homestead, content after a filling meal. They listened to the joik of one or more of their members. He often wondered if anyone sang his joik, the song of Siggur, the son sacrificed to the gods for their continued benevolence.

His rancor flared, and he cursed his luck. Since he had arrived at Hemmela, he had been searching for a way to advance and escape. The Apotti had made it clear he was content to keep Siggur in his current station. And while the priest had never said it explicitly, implicitly Siggur had been made to know he should be thankful for his lot in life.

Denied his master's confidence, Siggur was forced to skulk in the shadows, looking for any morsel of information he could use. And he'd had some minor successes, the most promising being his recent encounter with the farmer in the travelers' hut. The man, his tongue loosened by drink, had let slip that not only was he a Piijkij, but he was in the employ of the Apotti. Granted, the farmer could have lied, but Siggur believed the man told the truth. Unfortunately, he had no way to prove it. Were he to take this information to the High Priest of the Order, he would surely be denounced, if not by the High Priest himself, then at least by the Apotti. He was not willing to make that gamble.

He needed evidence—something tangible that could not be dismissed as hearsay or his own idle conjecture. He took the letter entrusted to him by the Apotti and scrutinized its exterior, particularly its wax closure. If he wanted to know its contents, he would have to break the seal. He withdrew his knife from its sheath, placed the tip of the blade in the flame and waited for it to glow a pale red. When he was satisfied, he slid the blade through the middle of the seal, careful to leave the vellum unscathed. Siggur held his breath as he unfolded the pages, praying the gods were with him this time.

CHAPTER TWENTY-TWO

F AR AWAY IN THE night, as if it traveled from another time, a song could be heard for those who had heart and soul to listen.

We are the Jápmemeahttun.
We are the guardians of the world.
Our memory stretches back to the start of days.
Our vision reaches beyond all tomorrows.
We sing together as one, so that our one may always survive.

Irjan stood in the light of the moon, his face raised to the sky, but his eyes closed to the wonders above. The wind blew enough to release the snowflakes that had fallen upon his hair—the only movement about him. To any who might have happened upon him, he would appear to be the dead standing again; but he was very much alive, and, at that moment, he was lost in another time.

In the world of his body, his heart beat a slow and even pace. In another world, he felt the thrum of everything surrounding him. Using every sense available to him, he searched for any knowledge that would help him survive the challenges ahead. In a distant part of his mind, he heard voices. He focused on them, and following the voices like a thread he wound his way to the songs of the Immortals.

Many conflicting choruses encircled him, and in his stillness he was frantic to find what he needed to hear.

And like a flash, one chorus suffused his mind.

One voice is lost to us.
One voice sings with the gods.
We seek the ones without words before their stories can be written.
We journey to find them.
Our future is not our own without their end.

A cold fear grabbed Irjan's heart, and his breath seemed to stop. In that instant, he regained the awareness of his world, only to find himself upon his knees in the snow, gasping for air.

Irjan pushed himself up to stand, and staggered headlong into a copse of trees. In their midst, he found two small forms sleeping in tightly bundled furs, unaware of the events of Olmmoš and Jápmemeahttun.

Irjan knelt down next to them and felt the tightness in his chest release. For the moment they were safe and his—one the child of his flesh, the other the child of an Immortal.

Had it been foretold this moment would come to pass, Irjan would have scoffed at its impossibility. Yet, here it was, before him. His son lived as a result of the very Immortals he had once hunted and killed; and he was now nursemaid and father to an infant of their kind.

As Irjan looked at Aillun's daughter, Dárja, he saw the many who had died on the way to this moment. And for an instant, it occurred to him to wonder in which world he found himself. His or theirs? The howl of a far-off wolfpack brought him back from the edge of unknowing.

Irjan added more wood to the fire and curled himself around the two slumbering infants. He hoped their dreams were warm and comforting. For him, tonight would be neither. Irjan feared the Jápmemeahttun sought them, and he was not sure where to seek safety for himself and those he protected.

As the fire died down, a song emerged wordless and instinctive. It flowed from the soul of the man, a Piijkij, an anointed Hunter, and entered the heavens for others to hear.

I am the son of the gods.
I am brother among my kind.
I started my life at a crossroads.
I traveled the winding path of those who are lost.
I will return to fulfill the forgotten destiny of one who should not exist.

This verse was added to Song of All, and its chorus chilled the hearts of the Elders who listened and understood.

Irjan emerged from a fitful sleep to find a pair of dark eyes staring at him. They belonged to Aillun's daughter, Dárja. He held her unblinking gaze and wondered what she saw. Did she see the man responsible for her mother's death, a man so foolish as to betray the gods and then hope to escape their wrath? Had he not, though? Had he not brought his Marnej back from the land of the dead?

Irjan shifted and saw his son still slept. For a moment, panic gripped him. Perhaps the boy was not sleeping after all, and death had reclaimed him. Irjan put his hand upon the small body and waited breathlessly for the slight rise and fall signaling life. When he saw Marnej still lived, he turned his attention back to the squirming body of Dárja. Her face had reddened and looked ready to release a storm of discontent.

Irjan quickly rose, scooped her up in his arms, and began rocking her to and fro, hoping to forestall her wrath. As he gently bounced her, he spoke in soft comforting sounds. Then he thought of Aillun and the baby's birth story.

Daughter of the gods.
Sister among the Jápmemeahttun.

You started your life at your Origin, with sadness and joy as your companions.

You braved dangers and met enemies and can see the truth of friendship.

Go into the world to meet your destiny, knowing that the stars watch over you.

The sadness of the song struck him, as did his part in it. Irjan told himself it was not a role he had chosen, but rather one that had been forced upon him, but he heard his own lie and had to admit it. He had chosen vengeance, and he had chosen betrayal. All his actions had their consequences, not the least of which included caring for an Immortal's child.

Suddenly, a piercing scream shattered the peaceful environs. Irjan put Dárja at arm's length. No amount or rocking would soothe this fury. To add to his woes, his son, rudely awakened, chimed in and gave a howl worthy of a wounded beast. Irjan accepted his defeat and pronounced loudly, "You will both need to scream a bit longer since your food is not ready."

Silently he thought, *At least this commotion will serve to keep the wolves at bay.* He unswaddled the girl and removed her soiled cloth. As he did so, he recoiled at the odor and added to his earlier thought.

If the howling doesn't repel the wolves, then surely the stench will.

He cast aside the dirty fabric, replaced it with a clean piece, and rewrapped the girl. He turned his attention to Marnej and repeated the process, but this time, he steeled himself for the assault on his sense of smell.

By the time Irjan finished the ordeal of changing soiled garments, the water had boiled, and he divided it into three: one part for the babies' broth, one part to warm himself, and the remainder to launder the sullied strips of fabric.

It seemed like hours of preparing and packing before he was finally ready to put more distance between his little trio and the events of the preceding week. *One week*, he thought, *short time to wreak so much havoc in so many lives.*

With the babies finally secured to his body, Irjan began walking. He held a steady pace, which he hoped to continue until the needs of his little ones forced him to stop. With any luck, they would be leagues away from where they now stood.

CHAPTER TWENTY-THREE

THE HUNTER, SLEEPING ALONGSIDE his small charges, could not have dreamed the course of his life and the world around him would shift as the result of the actions and ambitions of one young man.

In fact, the young man who sat alone in his quarters reading the Apotti's unsealed letter began to doubt the scope of his own future. The missive to the High Office of the Order contained the dry ramblings of a dutiful servant of the church. The priest's obsequious greetings and fawning inquiries galled Siggur. In the same position, he would not have stooped to ingratiate himself to obtain advancement. In his mind, a man who did not show his strength and power would not be considered worthy of receiving more power. *No wonder the Apotti remained in a barren backwater of a village like Hemmela.*

As Siggur read on, it became clear the letter would be of no value to him and, in fact, he had taken a great risk for no reward. He looked at the open letter and cursed his luck once again. He refolded the pages with care and examined the seal, looking for a way to return it to its unbroken state. Admittedly, he hadn't planned on resealing it. Rather, he had hoped the letter would contain such vital information he could take it openly to those who could use the information and advance his cause in return. But his hopes now stood dashed.

The letter would need to be convincingly resealed and delivered as expected. Siggur leaned in closely to look at the work of his heated blade, a clean line through the black wax and the impressed insignia of the Apotti. It was possible a simple heating of the seal would meld its edges seamlessly.

Siggur looked about him to find a suitable instrument, but found nothing save for the candle and his knife. He briefly considered letting the candle wax drip into the gap of the seal, but he dismissed this out of hand, recognizing the color of candle wax would be noticeably different. Again he was at a loss.

Siggur regarded his knife, examining the tip once more. Hope flashed in his mind. The blade could be heated again and perhaps its flat edge used to knit together the sides of the wax seal. Siggur placed the very tip of the knife in the flame and waited for it to heat up. He pulled it out before it began to glow, then placed the knife along the slice and slowly, painstakingly, drew the blade broadside back toward him. He kept his face inches away from where he worked to evaluate his process. When he finished, Siggur examined his handiwork. The seal was whole again, but even to a less discerning eye, it was clear a repair had been made.

Once more, Siggur cursed his ill fortune. His only recourse was to gain access to the wax and the seal and remake the closure on the letter. He hoped the late hour worked to his advantage. The Apotti should be cloistered in his personal room and away from his official chambers, where he kept the wax and seal in the desk. On many occasions, Siggur had witnessed the priest bringing them forth or replacing them once a business matter had been concluded. He also knew the drawer housing them was kept locked, but he fervently prayed for some way to overcome this obstacle.

Siggur rose from his desk and felt the tension of his body. He listened at his door before opening it and entering the hall. The noises he heard were those of any night—the crackle of a torch and the distant whistle of wind making its way through the chinks of the ancient building.

Siggur moved forward, and his footfalls sounded like thunder in his own ears, even though he knew he took the lightest of steps. When he reached the door to the Apotti's chamber, he placed an ear to its rough surface and listened for sounds emanating from inside. He heard nothing. He tapped lightly, on the off chance the priest remained inside. He wanted to make at least a credible attempt of forthrightness if any explanation of his nocturnal wanderings was required.

His soft rap went unanswered and he gently opened the door to the priest's chambers. The dying embers in the fireplace glowed and left the rest of the room to its shadows. Siggur quickly entered and closed the door behind him, checking the darkened corners for another presence in the room.

When his eyes grew accustomed to the gloom and he had assured himself he was alone, Siggur approached the desk and walked around to its far side. He gave a gentle tug on the handle of the drawer and was not surprised when it did not give way. He felt for the lock's surface, and in blind hope inserted the one key given to him. It spun without result. He removed the key and slid it into his pocket, then crouched down on his knees to draw himself into the space below the desk.

Lying on his back, Siggur reached up to feel the under surface of the drawer. His fingers sought out any imperfections and his reason examined each for its potential use. An initial review left him panicked. His mind leapt ahead with questions and outcomes that looked extremely unfavorable. Fear pushed him to check again and again until desperation led him to bang his fists against his wooden enemy. The sound echoed in the room, and Siggur held his breath, waiting to hear if his rashness would be his undoing. He listened for what seemed like a lifetime, but his banging had not been heard.

Relieved, he looked up again at the drawer. A small shadow darkened the back of the drawer. His hands found the spot, and much to his surprise one of the planks had been loosened. He pushed on the piece and it gave way with a sharp crack. A piece had broken upwards.

In frustration, Siggur rapped his head on the hard earthen floor. When the blinding pain receded, a moment of insight took its place. If he could dislodge the piece and then replace it, he could gain access to the contents of the drawer, and could hope his purpose would not be discovered. A reasonable hope, considering the break rested toward the back, and it would be inconceivable for the Apotti to find himself in the same position as himself, on the floor, on his back and looking up at the underside of the desk. Siggur steeled his nerves and pressed forward, tempting fate, believing he had experienced the worst it could offer.

He wiggled the piece of planking until he heard the snap of the final woody tendons holding the piece in place. He carefully pulled it down and set it aside. Siggur reached his bared arm into the hole and gently rooted around. His fingers glided over the few contents of the drawer, and in short course he found both the wax and the seal. He carefully extracted them, and then took a moment to lower his head to the floor and let relief wash over him.

Siggur crawled out from under the desk, and by the glow of the embers he set about restoring the letter to its original form. His grand scheme had started out as the key to a brighter future and had quickly spiraled downward through risk and possible ruination.

Siggur melted the wax and let it drip upon the old broken seal, then pressed the Apotti's emblem into the newly warmed wax. He pulled it free, gratified to see an unmarred seal of office. Using caution, the young man let the wax cool fully before attempting to replace the tools and repair the wooden piece.

The young man pulled back the sleeve of his cloak, and with a bare arm, to prevent any threads from catching on the splintered wood, he took the wax and seal and returned them as best he could. As he pulled his hand back, his fingers slid across another sealed letter. Siggur froze momentarily and considered his next course of action.

Despite his earlier mishap, curiosity gained the better of him. He felt around the drawer for other letters, but it appeared there was only the one. He withdrew it and pulled himself close to the fire. He examined the new letter, in outward appearance the twin to the one he had been entrusted with. Disregarding his earlier laments and curses, Siggur heated his blade in the embers and then drew its glowing tip through the heart of the newly sealed letter. The page opened readily, and this time, as he scanned the contents he knew he had found his opportunity.

Without giving it another thought, Siggur took the first letter and slid it into the drawer. He painstakingly aligned the splintered edges of the plank, using the knife blade to gently pull the board into place. Siggur could not get the piece flush with its neighbors, but again he was certain the Apotti would not have cause to examine the drawer that closely.

The young man withdrew from his position, and placed the new letter safely in the folds of his cloak. Again he listened for the telltale sounds of his superior, but silence told him the Apotti still slept. Siggur retraced his steps to his chambers, and this time when he entered the room he did not alight on the meanness of his lot. Rather, he saw the room with the eyes of one whose fortunes were about to improve.

CHAPTER TWENTY-FOUR

A T THE FIRST LIGHT of dawn, Siggur left to deliver his missive. Not long after, the Apotti departed to seek out another messenger to do his bidding. Through the gloom of the darkened forest, the Apotti made his way to the blackened property that had once been the home of the Piijkij. A man was already hard at work, shoring up the remnants. The priest's footfalls were silent. Caught off guard by the priest's greeting, the man whirled around.

"I see you have wasted no time in making yourself at home," Rikkar commented dryly.

The man glowered. "I'm doing what must be done before the next storm comes." He stared at the priest and wiped his mouth with the back of his hand, as if the meekness of his reply was distasteful to him.

"Yes. I can see that." Rikkar took in the surroundings. "I am afraid it must wait. I need you to take a letter to the Brethren of Hunters for me."

"But I can't leave," the man protested. "I haven't finished."

"Biera, do you forget yourself? Do you recall how you came by this land?"

Cowed, the man looked down. "Yes, Apotti."

"Good. You will leave at once and wait for a response, which you will bring to me. Discreetly. Is that clear?"

"Yes, Apotti."

The priest handed him the letter, which the man placed within the folds of his furs. Rikkar made to leave, but hesitated.

"And Biera, I hope I do not have to remind you of the importance of secrecy. I truly wish you a long life where you can enjoy the fruits of your labors here. The gods thank you."

"As I thank the gods," Biera murmured.

~

Watching the Apotti walk away, Biera drove his axe into the wood before him. He spat and went to find his nag. The sooner he started, the sooner he would get back. He squinted at the sky and prayed the storms would not come before he finished the work he'd started.

Acting as the priest's messenger, Biera had long hours ahead of him to curse the man, lessening his own part in the matter. While it was true he'd always coveted Álbe's land, he'd had little opportunity to gain access to it. The old man was friendly enough and accepted Biera's gestures of kindness, but his snooty daughter, Sohja, did not.

How many times had he caught her weighing his value, only for it to come up short, time and again? And then the stranger had come, and suddenly Álbe didn't need Biera's kindness, and the daughter followed the reindeer herder like some lovesick moose.

Well, she got hers in the end. Didn't she?

And he did as well. Biera was now the landholder, and the stranger had disappeared. Biera had taken some chiding when it became known the land belonged to him. He had bristled and replied, "You give me grief for caring for land that will support this village, when that stranger probably killed Sohja and the baby! He probably killed the old man, too!" There were murmurs of disapproval, but in truth Biera had spoken aloud their fears and their doubts.

"Cowards!" Biera said to himself upon reflection.

He would not be made to feel bad for taking advantage of the opportunity presented to him. If the Apotti had approached any of the other landless men, they too would have jumped at the chance to gain land, and with it some standing. Being the priest's lackey rubbed him wrong, but he hoped the Apotti would soon find what he sought and would then leave him to his land and his future as a farmer.

Biera pushed his work horse as much as he dared, wanting to discharge his duty and return home before the next storm came.

"Arrogant prayer mumbler," he swore under his breath, and urged the beast on once more.

~

Biera arrived at the Fortress of the Brethren of Hunters tired and embittered. Each mile had added to the righteous indignation he felt at being obliged to another's whim. He pounded his fist upon the gate, demanding entrance. When his call went unheeded, he redoubled his efforts. Suddenly the gate swung open, and the point of a sword greeted him.

Biera's bluster deserted him, and he flinched back in fear.

"I do the gods' bidding," he cried out. "I do the gods' bidding."

"Drop to your knees then," the gatekeeper commanded. "Perform your duties in a manner befitting what you claim."

Biera immediately dropped to his knees, his hand fumbling in the folds of his furs.

"Choose carefully your next action," the gatekeeper said, flicking the tip of his sword toward Biera's eye.

Biera's mouth opened and closed like a landed fish, before any utterance materialized. "I bring a letter from the Apotti of Hemmela," he sputtered, proffering the evidence.

"Show me the seal."

Biera dropped the letter onto the snowy ground. He lunged for it, and then handed it upwards, turning the missive so the man could examine the seal.

"Rise and enter," the gatekeeper ordered. "And bring your mount with you."

Biera stood, grasped the reins of his nag, and did as ordered. The gate noiselessly closed behind him by the hand of unseen forces. With a nod, the gatekeeper called another guard forward.

"Follow him and keep your mouth shut," the gatekeeper said in parting.

Biera did as he was told, following the second guard into a great hall, more impressive for its trimmings than its size. Swords covered the walls; even more swords dangled from the rafters. The blades turned slowly as the wind from outside rose up to meet them. Forgetting himself, Biera blurted out, "What *is* this place?"

The guard spoke over his shoulder. "*It* is the Hall of Trophies. These are the swords of the Immortals—at least the ones who have died by our hand."

"And how many of them're yours?" Biera pried, wishing to gain some of his courage back.

"Enough that you should not forget to whom you are speaking." They stopped and knocked on the door in front of them.

A distant voice from within bade them enter. The guard pushed open the hulking wooden door and proceeded into the room. Cold air immediately struck Biera as he stepped inside. No fire blazed in the hearth, and the occupant of the chamber stood before an uncovered window, dressed in what Bierra assumed to be battle garments, although he couldn't be sure, never having been in battle himself.

The guard bowed before speaking, "My *Avr*. The messenger bears a letter from the Apotti of Hemmela."

The man pushed himself away from window opening. "Step forward, messenger," he commanded, "and discharge your duty."

Biera balked but lurched toward the armored man when nudged by the guard. He held out the letter, which shook in his unsteady hand. The man in battle garments took the letter and dismissed him with a nod.

Biera wavered, "I. . .I was told to return with an answer."

Biera felt his head snap forward with pain. The guard had cuffed him in the back of the head and moved to take him from the room when the other man spoke.

"The Apotti will wait for my answer, as will you, until I have finished with more pressing matters," he replied.

Any thought of protest died in Biera's mouth when he looked into the face before him. He shivered as he realized his future was more precarious than he had first believed.

"Viellja, take this messenger where he can warm himself," the Avr instructed. "He is obviously not accustomed to hardship, nor cold."

The guard bowed to his superior and roughly pushed Biera from the chamber. Biera looked back at the leader of the Brethren of Hunters, who held the letter in his hand, unopened.

~

Alone once again, the Avr dropped the letter upon his desk and took up his place at the window. He closed his eyes and inhaled cold air. He could discern the scents of the different trees, the age of the snow, and the fear of an animal close at hand. What eluded him was where next he should lead his men. Dávgon needed to find the Jápmea. He needed to find them before his order became irrelevant. The church, though it preached against the evil, did not see it much, and, as such, gave less credit to the value of the Brethren. The Order of Believers cared more for the richness of their cloth and the weight of their coffers, than protecting the borders of Davvicana.

Their memory is short, he thought.

Had not their fathers' fathers waged great bloody battles against the Jápmea scourge? No more than twenty seasons of snow had passed since the Brethren had finally driven back the lingering marauders. The Piijkij had been too effective, and the spirit of the Jápmea appeared to have receded into the mist. In his last encounter with the High Priest of the Believers, Dávgon had suffered indignities built upon the success of the Brethren.

At that meeting, the small, rat-faced priest, who petted his robes as if they were loved ones, had had the audacity to ask with rhetorical wit, "Is there a need for the eagle when there no is longer a plague of mice?"

Who was that insolent whelp of a clergyman to question the leader of the Brethren of Hunters? The Piijkij had made the world safe for upstarts like him.

Dávgon drew the leather flap across the window, dimming the room around him. Neither sight nor sound nor scent gave him what he needed: more men, more coin, a worthy adversary to remind priest and peasant alike the Piijkij were their only protectors. He would be twice cursed if he let the demise of the Brethren happen while he still drew breath. Dávgon strode across the room to his desk where the letter from the priest of Hemmela waited, creamy yellow in the light of the flickering candle.

He picked it up, snorting in disgust. He cast it down again and cursed himself for needing to associate with village priests to secure the rightful position of the Brethren. Teasing out church secrets from the Apotti of Hemmela made Dávgon feel as if he were no better than a pig rooting around in the mud and filth for a morsel of food. And cajoling the man into preaching against the Jápmea threat had left a foul taste in his mouth. But the priest had presented him with an unexpected opportunity. He claimed he had in his midst one of the Brethren, one of those thought fallen. His description had intrigued Dávgon, because the man he described had once been the most talented and heralded of the Piijkij.

Dávgon himself had brought the man to the Brethren as a wild-eyed child who had lost his family to the Jápmea, or so he had been led to believe. Fear and vengeance had proven to be a powerful combination for the boy's upbringing and training.

Before this past moon cycle, Dávgon had not thought of Irjan since his supposed passing. Seven seasons of snow had come and gone since Irjan's sword had been found in the woods by a fisherman about his trade in the early spring thaw. The fisherman had returned the blade to the Brethren and had received compensation. That night a prayer had risen among the Brothers and the name Irjan had been entered into the records of brave and fallen Hunters.

Dávgon had been part the ranks of the Brethren on that day, not yet having risen to the position of their leader. He had mourned the loss of a Brother. When he rose to become the Avr, shortly after, Dávgon had cause to mourn not just a Brother, but probably the most talented Jápmea hunter the Brethren had ever known.

The Brethren needed a man of Irjan's skill to carry on their cause and keep their brotherhood intact, but as the seasons of snow passed, none materialized. No one equaled Irjan. And then the first letter had arrived from the Apotti of Hemmela. The priest's words had leapt off the page. A Piijkij had taken refuge among his villagers.

Dávgon's initial curiosity quickly transformed to rage when he recognized whom the Apotti described—their fallen hero, Irjan. But apparently, Irjan was neither hero nor fallen. He lived and did so as a traitor to his brothers. Dávgon had been furious, but his anger had not clouded his understanding of the chance presented to him.

Irjan had chosen betrayal, but he could still be made to serve a purpose. With the Apotti of Hemmela as a go-between, Dávgon planned to once again make Irjan the instrument of the Brethren, without him, or that nettlesome High Priest, being any the wiser. The subterfuge appealed to his desire for a reckoning, while it served to fill his need for a truly talented Hunter.

Of course, initially, the unctuous Apotti of Hemmela had been eager to meet with the Avr to discuss what he should say to the villagers about the Jápmea, but Dávgon convinced him otherwise.

"Secrecy assures success. And success is the key to all hopes," he'd written back to the priest. Fortunately, a hint of position and power had been enough for the Apotti to see reason and remain content with their correspondence.

Most recently, the Apotti had indicated to Dávgon that he had devised a means of leverage, assuring Irjan's participation in their grander plan. It had amused Dávgon to let the priest believe he understood the grander plan. Nevertheless, the Avr had encouraged the Apotti to move forward with haste. That had been nearly seven days past, nearing the full moon, and Dávgon assumed the priest's letter today contained an update on his conspirator's progress.

Dávgon picked up the letter and slit the seal. He opened the page. The salutation made it clear he held something not intended for him. The salutation was to the High Priest of the Order of Believers and the contents of the missive were a summation of accounts and events pertaining to the village of Hemmela.

"Useless," Dávgon swore. If there had been a fire in the hearth he would have burned the page in frustration. Instead, Dávgon balled up the piece of parchment and threw it across the room. The letter lay in a corner and Dávgon stared at it. As he looked at it, he thought about its significance.

On one hand, it could mean the messenger had misunderstood the priest's instructions and arrived at the door of the Hunters rather than that of the Order.

Which only a fool would do, he dismissed.

On the other hand, it could mean the Apotti had confused this letter with another, which meant, not only was the priest a man of small discipline, but, more importantly, the letter intended for the Avr now potentially rested in the hands of another, quite possibly the High Priest of the Order of Believers. The damage this confusion could bring about would depend upon the discretion of the letter and the meaning understood by its reader.

Dávgon's mind immediately jumped to a third and more ominous possibility.

"A saboteur," escaped his clenched jaw.

Who?

He paced his chamber, each step building tension within his already taut frame.

A knock upon the door exploded his thoughts.

"Enter!" he yelled.

The door opened slowly. The sentry entered and spoke to the Avr, but his word went unheeded.

Dávgon was once again trying to find his way through the maze of possibilities before his mind's eye. In the end, he concluded that regardless of the cause, either carelessness or connivance, the result was the same. If the letter intended for him fell into the hands of the Order of Believers, an undeniable shadow of suspicion would be cast upon the Brethren. Dávgon could not idly wait for the Order to take action against his Brothers.

The Brethren of Hunters will not be disbanded by men who have never wielded a sword, nor drawn the life blood of another to preserve their own.

Dávgon would do whatever it took to preserve the Brethren—to preserve what he had dedicated his life to.

CHAPTER TWENTY-FIVE

I RJAN WAS TIRED. HE wished he had been able to retrieve the sleigh. The babies were not a physical burden, but they restricted the amount of ground he could easily cover. Moreover, his reluctance to take well-traveled paths, exposing himself and his charges to discovery, forced him to walk in deep snow, where his footfalls, with their added weight, caused him to sink to his knees.

Early in this day's trek he realized the need for a staff, so he cut and trimmed a straight, lean, low-lying branch. As the day progressed, he found himself relying more and more upon the staff to move forward. Darkness surrounded him for the better part of the day, weakening his resolve to continue.

Just two seasons of snow away from the rigors of traveling with the binna and I have lost my taste for hardship.

Irjan looked up to the sky. The stars were barely visible. But by what he could see, he knew he still had some time to go before he could truly claim it to be too late to travel farther.

Step upon step, forward he went, with a rhythm that broke the silence around him. Pole. Step. Sink. Push. Step. Pole. Step. Sink. Push. Step. Irjan continued in this manner throughout the encroaching dark of the day. The monotony of his advance was broken only by the needs of the babies, which more often than not refused to coincide.

Irjan found that he repeated the needed tasks within a matter of steps of each other. With the approach of true night, his energy waned. His patience for the contrariness of children's requirements reached its limit, but he bit back his frustration and carried on walking through the squalls of both babies, until he found a suitable place to stop.

Irjan cut branches and laid them upon the snow. He removed the writhing bundles and placed them carefully upon their evergreen bedding. He stretched his weary body toward the sky above him and breathed in the chilled air. He dug a snow cave to shelter them all, and started a small fire to prepare their food.

When the babies had been fed and cleaned and wrapped together for warmth, Irjan covered them with the extra furs he had taken from Aillun. When he was sure the infants slept comfortably, he raised the fir bough walls around them, then withdrew to seek answers from the nighttime world.

In a small clearing, close enough to hear the babies' cries, Irjan stilled himself and opened his senses to the world around him. Footfalls echoed in the distance—a quick four-step trot, probably a scouting wolf. The smell of rotting flesh assaulted his nose. The flesh had had time to age and feed other creatures. Irjan listened closely again. Tonight he heard no voices. He wondered if, perhaps, he had dreamed the voices of the previous night. It could have been the wild imaginings born of great stress. Irjan wanted to believe this, but his heart told him he had truly heard at least one of the voices or songs of the Jápmemeahttun.

Irjan released a long breath and felt his tension drain away. His heart slowed and his thoughts quieted. He drifted downward within himself as if trying to reach the depths of a calm lake. Before he touched bottom, however, the silence of his mind erupted in a chorus of sounds and emotions that overtook his body.

Irjan felt himself vibrating with life itself. He opened his eyes and tried to push aside his sudden panic. He worried the sensation would not pass and at the same time worried it would. He looked around. Everything glowed in a way that could not be explained by the pale light of the moon. He blinked, trying to clear his eyes. The glow dimmed into blurriness, as if one world were placed upon another. Irjan lifted his hands to his eyes and was startled to see that even he himself had become blurred. He felt lightheaded.

Irjan took a step forward and stumbled to the ground. When he righted himself the glow was all gone. He whirled around, looking at trees and rocks. He threw up his hands in front of his face. Their glow was gone. The haziness with which he had seen the world no longer clouded his vision.

Panic assailed his thoughts, as he paced about the snowy clearing, trying to explain to himself what had happened. His mind looked for a rational explanation. He was exhausted, and he had not really slept since he began traveling with the babies. Moreover, he had not eaten enough. These were all solid answers, and yet they did not satisfy him. But where Irjan's rational mind failed to give him the answers he needed, his soul whispered the truth with inner knowing. *It was the realm of the Jápmemeahttun.* The whisper grew in strength until it became Irjan's own understanding, one that both repulsed and attracted him.

Irjan took a deep breath to clear himself of his recent experience, surprised to discover a faint odor of smoke. He quickly looked to his own fire, which was not the source of the smell. The air carried the scent of old, dried wood mixed with herbs and the deep sootiness of the bogs.

Irjan looked up and saw wisps of smoke trailing upwards and disappearing into the night sky. He looked at the moon for a long while, feeling his earlier discomfort replaced with the habits of training. The halo around the moon grew. It would snow—if not tonight, then tomorrow. In either case, it would be best to find proper shelter before it happened.

Irjan was torn. He wanted to scout for the fire and learn something of its source, but he could not leave the babies vulnerable to animals and environment. He considered his choices and, in the end, decided it best to take the infants with him, but leave the weight of the camp behind.

He needed to know if the smoke represented a threat or a haven, but, he knew he was taking a grave risk. If the babies awakened and cried out, they would alert the maker of the fire to their presence, and, be he friend or not, Irjan saw the danger in the possibility. In the best case, the fire maker would find it curious to hear a babe's cry in the midst of the forest and perhaps might repeat the tale at a travelers' hut or gatherings. The strangeness of the tale had the power to give life to rumors, which might reach the ears of those who searched for Irjan. In the worst case, the fire-maker and hunter were one and the same, and Irjan and babies were walking into a trap. For so many seasons of snow Irjan had been that man, the Hunter. It was easy for him to believe the worst. But he needed to know.

With sleeping infants strapped to his body, Irjan set out from his camp and moved as quietly as possible. By the wisps of smoke he saw, he judged the fire to be less than half a league away, and he hoped to cover the distance as quickly as possible. He headed in the direction of the smoke, ever watchful of the halo around the moon and careful not to jostle the babies awake.

As he neared his goal, Irjan slowed his pace further and looked for a strategic approach. He wanted as much cover as possible, given his bulky profile. Drawing closer, he found himself holding his breath and praying for the silence of the babes he carried. He moved forward, to where the dense forest gave way to sparse coverage. Irjan feared he would not be able to move closer without exposing himself to whomever had made the fire.

He strained his eyes to see ahead. Clouds swirled across the previously clear sky. Snow was coming. When the clouds passed, the moon reappeared to give light. Smoke rose above the treetops, but he could not see the glow of a fire. He tried to look beyond and through the trees to what lay ahead. Without the infants, it would have been a simple task to slip ahead unnoticed, but from this vantage point, he could only hazard a guess. He squinted and looked for any movement.

The babies stirred, but did not wake.

Irjan moved forward more boldly, eschewing the need for hiding spots. The trees finally gave way to a wide clearing which surrounded a small, sloped farmhouse. The structure could be no more than a single room. This discovery buoyed Irjan's spirits, because it meant all potential dangers could be assessed at once. There could be no one lurking in another room to ambush him. But once again, needs pulled Irjan in different directions. He wanted to know who and how many people occupied the dwelling, without being detected, but he feared he could not learn that with the infants strapped to him. On the other hand, he needed to keep the babes with him, because he could not safely leave them behind.

Irjan silently cursed. He'd never had cause to worry about the care of others on his earlier forays. He had traveled alone or with other Piijkij, and, while he'd always been willing to give aid when required, he'd never had to place the needs of another before the task at hand—particularly the needs of defenseless babies. He was not a defender. He was a Piijkij, a Hunter.

Finally, Irjan made his decision. He would continue with the children. If attacked, they were together, and if they perished, they would do so together.

Irjan moved out from cover and quietly crossed the open snow. When he reached the corner of the structure he checked to make sure the babies remained asleep before proceeding to circle the building. Their chests rose with soft and restful breaths. Irjan kept his shoulder to the wall. He loathed his large profile, but he could do nothing about it. As he crept forward, he noted there was a break in the long length of logs that formed the hut wall. *A window.* But as he neared the window he saw, to his disappointment, it was covered with stout wood planks, and not a leather flap as he'd hoped. There was not even a chink in the wood for him to put his eye to.

He passed by the shuttered opening, careful not to jostle the infants, and continued to circle the cabin looking for other opportunities and potential sources of danger. As he came around the far corner, he saw another small window. But it too was tightly shuttered. This time, however, there was a small gap in the wood where the planks had pulled apart.

Irjan stooped to place his eye to the crack. He could see the glow of what must be a fire, but there was no one in sight nor was there any movement within that he could detect.

He watched and listened.

The babies stirred, and he heard the unmistakable nattering of goats. Irjan looked away from the gap and realized the short wall beyond the window must be the hut's stable. The sounds from within the stable grew louder and more insistent, and he wondered if they sensed his presence. Irjan stepped cautiously away from the building, hoping the animals had not raised the alarm. He strode off in the direction he had marked for escape, keeping one eye upon the hut, while wishing he had the time and the means to cover his tracks over the open ground. Reaching the cover of the trees, he glanced up at the sky and took some comfort that, most likely, the coming snowstorm would cover whatever footfalls he'd made around the hut.

But to be safe, Irjan now took a fallen branch and attached it through the rear of his belt, allowing the rough pine needles to sweep away the signs of his presence as he doubled back to find his earlier path. If anyone was looking for him, he hoped this would be enough to prevent them from tracking him back to their small camp.

Keeping his steps even and measured, Irjan reached their shelter in time to feel the first snow beginning to fall. He moved quickly to situate the children. He gathered more fuel for the fire and readjusted the furs. It would be a long night, but he had much to occupy his mind. He needed to decide whether or not to seek shelter the following day.

In the tight space he'd made for the infants, Irjan hoped he could keep them warm enough. He was not worried for himself, for he'd endured worse. He filled a leather bladder with heated water, then placed the bladder under the folds of fur covering the babes.

He kissed Marnej lightly on the forehead. The child's smell reminded him of his wife and the warmth of their home, and as he closed his eyes and took in the scent, he believed for an instant he'd been transported back in time. He knew, however, he would have to open his eyes and let the vision go. When he did, he saw Dárja and felt a stab of guilt. Like his son, she would never know the love of her mother.

Irjan hesitated before leaning down and kissing her forehead as well. She smelled nothing like his son. He closed his eyes again and breathed in her scent: musky, like a smell from his own childhood.

Irjan sat up during the night, giving his full attention to the future and how best to proceed. Whatever doubts he had about traveling with the infants, they were redoubled as he listened to the increasing intensity of the storm outside. He would have to get them to better shelter tomorrow. He thought about the homestead and wished he could have discovered more.

CHAPTER TWENTY-SIX

S IGGUR SAT BY THE wide hearth in the rectory of the Order of Believers. He had pushed hard through the course of the day and had barely escaped the full onslaught of the storm that now raged outside. His late arrival made meeting with the Vijns of the Order inadvisable. He would have to wait until the following day to see the High Priest. But Siggur had good reason to feel content and confident that evening. He carried with him a letter authored by his superior, which he believed would serve his purpose more than it would his master's.

Siggur leaned forward and felt the heat of the flames before twisting in his seat to view the room. The difference in accommodations between Hemmela and his current surroundings was staggering.

When he'd arrived, Siggur had been surprised to be graciously greeted by the Chamberlain of the Order. The man had seen him to his quarters and then inquired as to any other needs the young acolyte might have. When Siggur spoke of his hunger, he had been escorted to the rectory, where the cook had given him spiced tea to shake off the cold before feeding him a filling and satisfying meal.

Siggur now sat comfortably, sated and covered in furs. It seemed to him the meanness of Hemmela had been replaced by soft comforts which beckoned him to remain and to flourish.

Lulled by the fire's warmth, he closed his eyes as he waited, thinking idly of how his life would change; how he would no longer be the lackey of a petty priest, and instead be given the station he deserved. As the dream world gently took him into its arms, Siggur felt the letter rustle in the folds of his robes. It broke free and grew a raven's black wings. The letter began to fly away, but Siggur quickly reached up and grabbed the letter-turned-bird. The creature grew in size and strength and began to climb into the sky with Siggur hanging on. In his dream, he drew himself up onto the the giant bird's back and they soared higher into the night sky. He felt as though he could reach out and touch the stars all around him.

Siggur felt a soft jolt and awoke to find the shrouded face of a Brother staring down at him.

"Brother, you must be tired after your long journey," he said. "Let me show you back to your quarters."

Siggur shook himself free from the world of dreams, and nodded. He stood up and followed the dark-robed figure. They left the rectory and climbed up the winding stairs. As he looked down to the room below, he wondered if he were still partly in his dream. But when his head finally hit the pillow he entered a realm of darkness and warmth, untouched by dreams, until dawn's call to prayers roused him.

For the first time since he'd entered the service of the Order of Believers, Siggur sang morning prayers with honest feelings of gratitude and faith. Among the murmured voices his stood out when the prayers concluded.

A heart and soul free from doubt is an open vessel for the power
    of the gods.
The gods shall reward those who believe and those who act
    upon faith.
We thank the gods.

After prayers, Siggur rose with the rest of the Brothers. He stood silently, at a loss for what to do next. The others all had tasks and schedules which did not include him. He remained motionless in their midst, until he felt a hand on his shoulder and heard a voice whispering in his ear.

Startled, Siggur jumped and found himself facing the broad chest of a Brother, possibly the tallest person he had ever seen.

"The Vijns requires your presence."

The softness of the man's voice was at odds with his stature — so much so, it took Siggur a moment to grasp his meaning. The tall Brother repeated himself slowly, as if Siggur were somehow enfeebled.

When the acolyte said nothing as he envisioned the upcoming meeting, the giant inquired if Siggur needed a little more time or assistance. Siggur assured him he was quite all right, almost confessing his nervousness, but quickly thought better of it. Better to leave off further communication, keeping his purposes and feelings to himself.

With as calm and serious a voice as he could manage, Siggur said, "I am at the service of the Vijns."

The giant of a Brother nodded and led the way to the chambers of the High Priest. Siggur noted with relief that no one observed their procession, because each step the statuesque Brother took required Siggur to take two and sometimes three steps to keep up. In fact, Siggur felt he would soon need to run just to stay within the giant's shadow. But Siggur was saved when the giant stopped and knocked upon a door. When the call to enter resounded, the Brother stepped aside and gestured for Siggur to proceed.

Under the watchful gaze of the man behind him, the young acolyte felt his nerves tingling. As he reached for the door, he worried it would not open for him and he would become the topic of ridicule among the Brothers. When the handle turned smoothly and the door opened with ease, Siggur let out a slow, silent breath of relief. He entered the chamber without a backward glance and strode forward to meet his destiny.

The Vijns stood with his back to Siggur, examining an open book upon the lectern at the far end of the chamber. The man was surprisingly small, his face on level with the open book. In any other context, the High Priest might have been taken for a weak or powerless man, but in this environment Siggur did not doubt he held sway. The opulence of the room and of the person spoke to his power.

Siggur stood quietly and waited. When the Vijns finally faced him, the pinched features of the man's face brought to mind a cunning Siggur had not expected.

The High Priest took his time before he spoke. "The Aman-uensa of Hemmela," the High Priest said, stating Siggur's title.

"Yes," Siggur confirmed, finding his tongue reluctant to add anything more.

"And what business of the gods brings you to us?" The High Priest took his seat with a flourish of his rich robes.

Throughout his journey to the Stronghold of the Believers, Siggur had practiced in his mind many openings to this conversation. Until this moment, however, he had not realized the true risk he embraced by daring to bring the letter to the High Priest. In the seconds between hearing the question and formulating the answer, Siggur saw the true challenge was not bringing the letter. Rather, the difficulty rested with presenting a betrayal as a service to the gods and not to himself.

"I bear a letter from the Apotti to the Office of the Vijns," he said and presented the letter with a formal bow.

The High Priest took the letter and dismissed Siggur, saying, "The gods thank you, as I thank you."

Siggur froze for an instant. This was not what he had envisioned, and he acted rashly.

"I beg the indulgence of the High Priest," he said softly, making another low bow, "but the Apotti charged me to wait for your response."

The Vijns snapped up his head to look directly into Siggur's eyes. "Am I to understand that the Apotti of Hemmela has conveyed to me something of such importance he requires an immediate answer?" The priest smirked.

Siggur balked, stumbling in his mind over what to say.

"With great regret I am forced to admit I do not know the contents of the letter, and must ask for indulgence. I hope my duty to the Apotti has not given offense to you, my Vijns, instrument of the gods."

Siggur felt the man's stare bore into him, and then he appeared to relent and accept the small compliment offered.

"Very well. I will review the letter presently and give my reply. You will wait."

Siggur nodded but said nothing, keeping his eyes down, hoping to hide his anticipation.

The young man heard the seal slit and the unfurling of the page. There was a pause and then a resounding bang of fists upon the desk, which caused him to look up.

The High Priest's face had closed even further into a scowl of rage.

"What is the meaning of this?" he bellowed, and charged around the desk to confront the messenger.

The page shook in front of Siggur's face, as he shrank back with very real fear.

"What is the meaning of this?" the High Priest demanded again. "Do not stand there with your jaw flapping like some fish."

"Truly, sir, I do not know," Siggur stuttered. "I was given the letter by the Apotti and told to deliver it to you and await your reply."

The priest glared at Siggur, and then he spun on his heel and drew across the room to his desk and focused his attention on the fire.

"What is your name, boy?"

"Siggur."

"Siggur, you are at a very dangerous crossroads. Your future rests upon your next words and the choice they reflect."

Siggur said nothing.

"You spoke of your duty. I would like to know to whom that duty is paid."

"To the gods," Siggur croaked.

"To the gods." A small smile perched on the Vijns's lips. "And naturally, you are willing to do whatever the gods ask of you?"

"Yes," Siggur whispered.

"Good. The letter you have presented me has given me much need of thought before I answer it. You will be required to remain with us until I am ready to devise a suitable reply."

Siggur nodded, but in truth, he was unsure if his plan had succeeded.

"Leave me now and return to your quarters." The High Priest focused on the paper in his hand.

Siggur bowed. Before he reached the door, however, the voice of the High Priest called out.

"One more thing, Siggur. You did not ask about the contents of the letter. It leads me to believe that either you are a most uncurious young man or you, in fact, have known the contents of the letter all along. Of these two possibilities I am not sure which I find more believable."

"It was not my place to be curious." Siggur bowed again, keeping his protest muted.

"Let us for the moment pretend it was the former and not the latter," the Vijns suggested. "After all, it is much easier to reward the dutiful servant than it is the faithless betrayer. The gods thank you."

"As I thank the gods," Siggur whispered, and disappeared from the room, leaving his fate behind in the hands of the High Priest.

CHAPTER TWENTY-SEVEN

DÁVGON, THE AVR OF the Brethren of Hunters, spent a restless night in contemplation. His mind surveyed possible futures and sought a way to protect his men from the Order of Believers. If the relationship between the Apotti of Hemmela and himself had been revealed, he had little time to ready himself and the Brethren for charges of conspiring against the Believers.

Dávgon scrutinized his own aims in this regard. He did not want to rule the priesthood. He had no desire to take on the role of Vijns. The clergy were cowards—content to let others bear the the sword's burden. He was a fighter and proud to have wielded a blade. But the role of the protector grew ever smaller. Dávgon wanted the Brethren to be exalted as they once had been. After lifetimes of service, he could not accept that the gods would repudiate all the Brethren stood for. He could not believe they had been sentenced to the whimpering death of old men.

Dávgon felt anger rising within him. He would not allow his life to lose its meaning and purpose. The Brethren of Hunters would not disappear into the mist like the Jápmea. Those who had died protecting their people would not be forgotten.

But Dávgon knew determination alone would not suffice. He needed a plan of action. However, he had none. He had never been at such a loss. He had always led with foresight, and yet now he hedged upon his next step. Dávgon pushed himself out of his chair and paced about his chamber; his thoughts moved with the same nervous energy as his body.

They could go against the Order of Believers and forestall any attempt to disband the Brethren, but that would be considered an act of war, and, while Dávgon readily accepted the loss of life it would require, he knew that if they did not succeed, then their end was assured. Moreover, he could not guarantee they would win a war against the Order of Believers. The Brethren had skill on their side, but the Order had the masses at their disposal.

Then there was the matter of Irjan. Up until the arrival of the Apotti's messenger today, Dávgon had been content to allow secrecy and patience to advance his cause, but now secrecy and patience had lost their advantage. He could no longer use the priest to foment fear of the Jápmea. He needed to find the Jápmea. In short, he needed to ensure Irjan's service to the Brethren. It maddened him to think he might be forced to openly align himself with a traitor, but, if the circumstances dictated it, he would do whatever was necessary. He also needed to find out what else the priest in Hemmela knew.

Dávgon opened the door to his chamber. The guard outside grew stiff.

"Send the Apotti's messenger to me, and instruct Vannes to accompany him," Dávgon said.

He did not wait for a response, but rather reentered his rooms and closed the door with a firm push. Dávgon strode to the window. He drew back the leather flap to inhale the frigid air. It carried something green in it that reminded him of summers past, where the cool wetness of rain mixed with the tang of sweat and steel and blood. The hardship and sacrifice of training had not been a folly. Their vigilance had kept threats at bay.

Dávgon retreated from the window, the thick leather cover falling back into place with a dull slap. He paused in front of the fire, unsure when it had been lit. *Probably during the night when*

I was too deep in thought to notice. As he walked past the fire to reclaim his chair, he looked at the ash that had swept out of the hearth. The cinders softly swirled about and touched down upon the floor, so much like snow. But unlike snow, the ash reminded him all things must come to an end. The mighty tree, reduced to soot.

Not yet, he thought. *Not yet*.

A knock upon the door broke the spell, and Dávgon called out to enter.

The man named Vannes entered first, and brought with him the reluctant messenger Biera.

"My Avr," Vannes said, bowing his head.

"Be welcome, Vannes," the Avr replied.

Biera remained silent and seemed to hope to go unnoticed.

"Biera," Dávgon pronounced his name, wanting the man to feel it in his bones. "It is time for you to fulfill your duty and return to the Apotti with my reply."

The messenger poked his head out from behind Vannes's broad shoulders.

"Draw forward, man," Dávgon commanded, "and leave Vannes's skirt folds."

Biera did as he was told, his hands fidgeting.

"You will leave today for Hemmela. You will take Vannes back with you and he will act as my personal emissary to your Apotti." The Avr regarded the man once more. "You will be rewarded for your efforts."

"There's no letter, then?" Biera asked.

Dávgon smiled, a sense of pleasure welling in him. "No. But you may think of Vannes as the letter and afford him the same level of care and attention."

Biera frowned, perplexed.

"That is all." Dávgon motioned for the messenger to leave.

When Biera did not do so immediately, Vannes stepped forward and laid a hand upon his shoulder. He wheeled Biera around, marched him to the door, opened it, and shoved him out. Vannes spoke in low tones to the guard and then came back to stand before Dávgon.

"What do you recall of Irjan?" the Avr asked when they were alone.

Vannes's heavy brows shot up in surprise at the mention of the name. "Irjan?"

"Yes."

Vannes let out a long breath. "He was here when I arrived as a boy. His training had begun before mine and so we did not associate much. By the time my training was completed, Irjan had been traveling as a Piijkij for many seasons of snow, and after that our paths rarely crossed. I was abroad when his sword was brought to us."

"His is alive," the Avr declared.

"Impossible!" Vannes exclaimed. "His sword. . ."

"Yes, his sword, but not his body."

Vannes shifted uneasily on his feet. "My Avr, the weather and the wolves are not kind to the remains of any man's body."

"That is very true. But I have received confirmation Irjan is, in fact, alive."

"But where has he been all this time?"

"Apparently, in Hemmela," the Avr replied, unable to keep distain from his voice. "At least until recently. Before that, he was with the binna, working as a badjeolmmoš.

"A reindeer herder?" Vannes's expression darkened. "Irjan left the Brethren to become a reindeer herder? He must have lost his mind."

"More likely his taste for blood."

Vannes snorted. "Not likely! Irjan was the most bloodthirsty of us."

"Vengeful, yes! Ruthless, yes! But bloodthirsty, no. I saw in his eyes that when he killed, he never enjoyed it. He did it to avenge his family and from a sense of duty to their memory."

"It is hard to believe one so skilled at killing the Jápmea had no taste for it."

"We do not always take pleasure in our gifts." The Avr took a deep breath. "Vannes, I need you to go to Hemmela and find out all there is to know from the Apotti. If Irjan is indeed alive, I need you to track him and find him."

"And when I find him?"

"When you find him, I want him brought back here to me."

"And the Apotti? What would you like me to do when I am finished with him?" Vannes asked.

"I believe it depends on his answers. It would be wise to exhaust his usefulness and to do it quickly. I am fairly certain we will soon be facing the scrutiny of the Order of Believers."

"I will leave immediately. How should I send word?"

"I will dispatch Bihto to follow you. He can bring me word. It would be good, Vannes, to have someone to be our ears in Hemmela. Perhaps you could persuade our friend Biera to do that for us?"

"I believe I can make him see the advantage of a close friendship." Vannes patted his sword. "Have you any further instructions, my Avr?"

"No. The Brethren thank you and I thank you for the service you are about to do."

"And the gods?" Vannes smirked.

"The gods," the Avr repeated. "It is unclear what the gods want."

Dávgon rose and clasped the proffered hand of Vannes. "But it is not the first time the Brethren of Hunters have been forced to act on their own."

CHAPTER TWENTY-EIGHT

THE SNOWSTORM HAD MOVED on in the night, leaving a heavy blanket of whiteness that muffled the sounds of the forest. Irjan had not slept, but rather had kept a watch over the babies. They had slumbered soundly through most of the storm, waking early from hunger. When he peered out from their shelter, Irjan found they were an indecipherable mound among many. In fact, only the tall trees still had a recognizable shape. The Hunter in him was comforted by the fact their tracks had been covered by the recent snowfall. If anyone had followed them, their cause was lost.

Irjan created a small chimney through the fur cover roof to allow the smoke to escape. He used the wood he had gathered the previous day to light a small fire, then cared for the two little ones.

In the short time they'd been traveling, there had been no chance to set up a routine. As a result, each new day dawned as unfamiliar to him as the first. As Irjan considered their future, it seemed likely unforeseen challenges would ensure no routine would ever be established. This was not a life conducive to rearing children, nor was it ideal for avoiding those who might want to find them. Whatever doubts lingered from the previous night's foray, the first light of day galvanized his decision. He would seek shelter, at least briefly, at the nearby homestead.

By the time Irjan finished all of his duties, it was well into the morning. More than ever, he was convinced he had to find a place to hide until he could safely ascertain who and how many might be interested in them.

Irjan set off in the direction of the homestead, hoping his assessment the night before proved correct. He took a winding route this morning, trying to obscure not only their tracks, but their intent as well. He wandered well wide of their destination, and then backtracked through his steps in reverse. He listened intently to the sounds around him, but dared not listen in the other realm lest he somehow alert the Jápmemeahttun to their whereabouts.

Finally, when he was satisfied, Irjan approached the farmhouse directly and with great noise. He wanted their arrival to be obvious and seem guileless. He reasoned that if he approached those who dwelled within furtively, they would look like fugitives and possibly prompt a violent reaction. With both children upon his body he would rather face a ready drawn sword than a hastily pulled knife.

It took a surprising amount of thought and energy to make sufficient noise within the snow-covered clearing. Irjan finally jostled the babies to elicit their disgruntled cries and give ample warning to those inside the hut.

Under the cover of his hood Irjan looked to see if anyone had taken notice. No one came forth. The Hunter and his charges continued their noisy approach. Still no one emerged. When he finally stood before the door, Irjan grew concerned. Had he walked into an ambush? Or, was the house merely unoccupied? He looked about the snow and saw no footprints to indicate an early morning entrance or exit. He hesitated, about to draw back and reconsider his decision, when the door opened and a wizened face with clouded eyes poked out.

"You are not from here," the old crone stated. "What is your business?"

Through the cries of the babies Irjan presented himself. "Forgive our arrival upon your homestead. It is true we are unknown to this area. I am from the North, and travel with my babies to rejoin our people."

"If you are from the North, why do you approach from the south?" the woman asked sharply.

"I have lost my wife in childbirth among her people and now I go north to find my sisters to help me care for the little ones." Irjan answered with half-truths. He looked down at the bundle in front and confessed, "I am without much skill in administering to the needs of babies."

The old woman snorted. "In my long life I have not known a man yet who could properly care for a baby. That includes my husband and sons. I should not doubt you are out of your depth, particularly with two."

The woman's milky eyes narrowed on Irjan. She stepped back into the room behind her and opened the door.

"Well, come in quickly. It is bad enough we have let the warmth escape, sizing each other up."

Irjan did as he was bidden while the woman continued to talk.

"I am an old woman and have chosen to believe no brigand would travel with babes, and so I believe you to offer no harm. Likewise, I am an old woman and cannot myself be a brigand, and thus we are both of us quite even." She shuffled to the fire. "Although in my youth you would have been wise to give me wide passage. My husband was not so wise." Her shoulders shook with her soft laughter.

"Bring yourself and the babes close to the fire. Let us see if we can calm them and bring an end to their caterwauling."

The babies, as if on cue, raised their voices in unison. Irjan hurried over to the fire and freed himself of his load. He knelt and unwrapped the infants and removed the soiled clothing. Their nearly naked bodies wriggled in defiance. He replaced the swaddling and allowed them to lie upon their furs.

"Not skilled. But not without attention and gentleness." She poured water into the pot that hung in the fire, eliciting a sizzle and hiss as cold and hot met. "It will not take much time for the water to be ready."

The woman sat in her chair and observed the scene in front of her fire. Irjan knelt upon his heels, and the babies quieted.

"What do they call you?" she asked.

"Irjan. My son is named Marnej and my daughter is Dárja." The Hunter faltered on this last part. In the time since Aillun's death he hadn't needed to define what Dárja was to him. She had been Aillun's daughter. But in that moment, under the watchful eyes of the old woman, Dárja became his daughter by his own words.

"I am called Gunná," she said, checking the kettle upon the fire. "The water is warm enough to drink. Use what you need."

Irjan thanked her and removed a cupful to make broth for the babies. He dipped their suckling rag in the liquid and allowed one and then the other to draw upon it. For a while, the only sounds in the room were those of the hungry babies and the fire warming them.

"Your children are very close in age, but they are not twins," Gunná commented.

"No, they are not twins. Nine moon cycles separate them, but my son was born at a time when we had little to nourish him. It is why we traveled south to my wife's people. We had hoped to give him and our new one a better life."

The lies became easier for Irjan, but they were no less distasteful. He consoled himself with the fact these falsehoods served to protect the infants.

"There is not much work in the north," the woman stated. "What did you do?"

"I was a badjeolmmoš."

"You traveled many seasons of snow with the binna?"

"Six."

His mind wandered back to a similar conversation he had shared with Sohja's father, when he had first left the binna in search of new meaning for his life. The memory of that time and of Sohja brought tears to his eyes.

Irjan dipped the now-empty cup into the warm water to make another drink for the hungry babies. He was grateful for the distraction, because it allowed him to not look into the old woman's eyes. He did not want to display a reluctance to talk, nor did he want to reveal his pain and bring more questions to her mind.

"Here now," she said, rising with a creak. "Let's get those babies something more than broth. I've fresh goat's milk from the morning's milking."

Before Irjan could think of a response, she'd turned her back to him and shuffled off to a corner of the room. When she returned to him, she was holding a wooden bucket of creamy white goat's milk. She placed it beside him and gestured he should take some.

"My husband was a badjeolmmoš as well," Gunná said with pride as she sat back down. "He traveled fourteen seasons of snow with the herds. Then he met me and became a farmer, but the binna were in his blood. I used to tease him and call him *binnalak-khi*, for he truly was half reindeer and half man. If you had seen him run, you would have thought the same." She gave Irjan a long look.

"You may be a binnalakkhi as well. But there is more eagle about you than reindeer. In any case, after five births and eight seasons of snow I saw he was yearning to run with the binna again, and I gave him my blessing. He traveled with the sun to them and with the dark to me. I can tell you it was a lot of work for me to farm and raise children, but I was young and strong and I did it, as one must do what life asks." Gunná sighed deeply and closed her eyes.

"But," she spoke in a whisper, "I would be waiting for the first scent of snow upon the wind. I knew it would bring my Ulvá back to me. The moon cycles of the dark time were the happiest for mc. We were all together." She opened her eyes again. "But that was a long time ago."

Irjan fed the hungry babies the goat's milk. They suckled and slurped greedily. "And your husband?"

"Ulvá died here not two seasons of snow past. My children have scattered, as they should. Some follow the binna like their father, others follow people, in search of work."

Irjan gave her a probing look.

"I know what you think," she said, lifting her chin to look down upon him. "I am an old woman, but I can care for myself. I did so before I became handmate to Ulvá, and I continue to do so."

Irjan said nothing and continued to feed the babies. Marnej wriggled and began to protest.

"Here," Gunná held out her arms, "let me soothe the little one."

Irjan hesitated. Gunná scoffed, "I have raised more babes than you. Give him over to me and allow me to comfort him."

Irjan blushed, and carefully picked up his son and put him in the arms of the old woman.

Gunná took the milk and the suckling rag and rocked Marnej, whispering to him until he quieted. Irjan watched the process, and realized it was the first time another hand had held his son since his wife's passing. A fresh wave of regret and bitterness washed over his heart.

"It is a small offering to know that in time the pain grows less sharp," she said, surprising Irjan with her insight. She regarded the sleeping boy in her arms. "No doubt you feel the weight of injustice. In your place, I would curse the gods. I had many seasons of snow with Ulvá. We built a life together." Gunná trailed off, and the hiss of the fire took over.

Irjan did not meet the old woman's inquiring gaze. He looked into Dárja's deep, dark eyes and tried to separate the strands of emotion running through him. He touched her soft cheek and soothed her brow. Its heat let him know she was warm enough.

After a long silence, Irjan spoke. "I do not curse the gods. But I wonder if the gods have not cursed me instead."

The old woman nodded in understanding. "Death makes us wonder what we have done to deserve it. And we drive ourselves mad the more we wander that pathway, because we do not find reason. What we find is the life of an ordinary person, with small crimes and prejudices balanced by moments of love and sacrifice. It is hardly the cause, and yet death is still there." She trailed off into her own recollections.

"I know it is hard now," she said, regaining the moment, "but the lives of your children will give joy, and their needs will fill your days."

Irjan nodded, but kept silent.

Filling the growing silence, Gunná said, "You must be tired from your travels, no less so for coming through the snowstorm. You should rest. I will care for the babes."

Irjan was about to protest that he was not tired, but the old woman cut him off.

"Go on now! Let an old woman feel that she is still needed in this life."

Although reluctant to trust the safety of these surroundings, Irjan was also aware of the burden he had carried since Aillun's death. He secretly yearned to be free of its weight, if only for a breath of time. Before he knew it, Irjan agreed with the old woman. He lay down upon the furs by the fire, telling himself it was only to rest his body. Soon, however, he was falling asleep. His last waking thoughts were of the sweet warmth of the fire, seeping into his bones.

In his dream, Irjan drifted down through a dark cavernous hole. When he reached the bottom, his feet touched softly upon the ground. All around, candles lit one by one to illuminate his surroundings. Four openings faced him, one in each direction, but he could not discern any difference among them. Irjan sensed he needed to choose one to go forward, but he did not know which way was best.

In his frustration, he called out, "I do not know which way to go."

"A Piijkij always knows which way to go," a disembodied voice replied.

"But I am no longer a Piijkij," he answered.

"You will always be a Piijkij."

Then Irjan whipped around, trying to find the source of the voice. He saw nothing in the shadows and nothing within any of the openings.

"Show yourself!" he demanded.

Silence.

"Show yourself!" he roared, spinning in a circle.

The stillness remained unbroken.

The soft voice of a woman came from behind him.

"Why did you not trust me?" she said. Irjan whirled around to see his wife, Sohja, holding Marnej in her arms.

"Sohja. I...I am so sorry, my love..." He dropped to his knees. "I am not a Piijkij. I was..." His apology was choked and tangled. "I stopped. I walked away."

Her voice floated down to his prostrate body. "You have deceived, but cannot deceive any more."

The voice had changed. Sohja was gone, replaced by Aillun.

"Where is Sohja?" he demanded. "What have you done with her?"

The figure looked at him with sadness in her eyes. "You cannot deny what you are. You must accept this."

"No! No! I am not a Piijkij. I only did what was needed to save my son."

Aillun knelt. "It is time." She laid Dárja in his arms and Irjan realized he also held Marnej.

"But I do not know what is best! I do not know which way to go!"

"Then do not go," she said, "Stay. Rest. Sleep."

And he did.

CHAPTER TWENTY-NINE

THE COUNCIL OF ELDERS was lost in the Song of All. They listened to the strands of individuals weaving in and out, making the Song whole. In earlier times, they would have rejoiced at the diversity they heard and enjoyed its beauty, but they had a greater purpose on this occasion. They searched for particular chords in the Song. They sought the voice of the one who should not exist. The voice had first appeared when Aillun's song ceased to resonate, and it had taken the Elders by surprise, giving them much cause for thought and discussion. The images they saw were confused with those of Aillun and her baby, and the Elders could not see any of it clearly.

But the second time they heard the unknown voice, it was unmistakable and disturbing. Since that time, the Elders had been in seclusion, seeking out the one who should not exist. But each day silence continued to greet them.

"We cannot keep this to ourselves," one of the Elders said finally.

"Are we sure?" asked another.

The head of the Council looked at the faces of those around him. The Noaidi saw the concern and doubt.

"I cannot speak for all here," he said, "but I believe we must consult with the Taistelijan. If the situation is as I fear, then we should not wait for our undoing, we should meet the threat head on." He paused, to see if he had swayed those with doubts. "I am willing to listen to all who have concerns about the one who should not exist, but let us at least ensure our safety while we continue this discussion."

"Noaidi," another member spoke, "do we not sow our demise by allowing our fears to push us to the warriors? We have honored Guovassonásti's rebirth a score of times since we required their services. The Song of All has safeguarded us in the interim. Can we not expect it to continue?"

The head of the Council of Elders gave the matter some thought. He did not want to appear as if he dismissed, out of hand, an important question; however, in his heart he knew he was right. He nodded.

"It is true the Life Star has shined peace among us for long enough to believe it has always been this way," the Noaidi conceded. "But we cannot depend on the Song of All."

Many in the room gasped.

"The one who should not exist walks in the world of the Olmmoš!" the head of the Council of Elders pressed. "And as we have seen, he has entered the Song. I do not believe my fear is unjustified."

The murmurs of the Council members hinted at a qualified victory for the Noaidi. In truth, he took no satisfaction in calling on the warriors. It had taken too many seasons of snow to finally quell those among them who preferred violence and bloodshed. Many had resented disappearing into the Song, and he wondered how many still clamored for the use of steel, even after all this time.

"Are we in agreement?" he asked the group.

"We are," the voices in the room resonated, but not without some hesitation. The Elders stood and filed out of the room. The

Noaidi lingered for a moment. Fewer and fewer of the old guard Taistelijan remained, which was a testament to the success of the Jápmemeahttun. War seemed to be a thing of the past. However, when the last of the battle-tested Taistelijan transcended, there would be few who remembered how vicious and cunning the Olmmoš truly were.

The Noaidi bowed his head and looked into his own memories. They stretched far enough back to remember the time of the arrival of the Olmmoš. He had been a nieddaš then, running with her sisters.

The head of the Council of Elders lifted his head and released his memories. So much had changed in his lifetime. He feared that if he were not careful, the coming events would make all that preceded pale in comparison. The Jápmemeahttun had more than once looked upon their end, and the Noaidi could not be sure they would survive another test of that kind.

He strode from the room, but he could not shake the feelings following him. The simple life of the Jápmemeahttun moved all around him as he walked. Mánáid, almai, nieddaš, they all went about their daily lives. There were petty quarrels and unsuppressed laughter, moments of joy and pain, and all of it contained within the Song. Their lives, present, past, and to some extent future, played out in a great unceasing melody. Its beauty sometimes overwhelmed him.

The head of the Council of Elders thought about all this as he headed directly to the chambers of the healer, Okta. The Noaidi did not bother to knock upon the door. He knew the old healer would be in the back, engrossed in whatever greenery kept him busy, and deaf to the calls of others.

As he suspected, the healer worked, hunched over his desk, creating some concoction. Okta was alone and humming to himself. Not wanting to risk alarming the healer by speaking, the Noaidi remained quiet, and waited for his presence to be acknowledged.

The healer hummed, reaching up to scan the bottles in his view, then whirled around and exclaimed, "Cursed fire of the gods! You scared the breath out of my soul, Einár."

"I see the world of herbs has not dulled your warrior's tongue, Okta," the head of the Council of Elders replied.

"Nor has your time as Noaidi given you enough wisdom not to sneak up on a soul unawares, particularly one as handy with the sword as I."

The healer moved forward and reached beyond his visitor's head, pulling down a jar filled with a muddy brown liquid.

"What can I do for you, Einár? That is, other than adding to your amusement for the day."

The brief moment of merriment faded as the Elder remembered his purpose.

Okta noticed the abrupt change, and left his work aside, forgotten.

"What is it, Einár?"

"Aillun was your apprentice, was she not?"

"Yes. Yes, of course. But she has gone, Einár. Surely you must know she is going through her change."

The Noaidi nodded. "Yes, I am aware. I am sorry to tell you this, but we believe she has left us. Her voice is no longer heard within the Song of All."

The old healer protested, but the other raised his hand to stop him. "There is more."

Okta looked frustrated, but nodded. "Unburden yourself, Einár, as you see fit."

"The story is long and confused, Okta, but I believe we are in great danger. At the time Aillun passed from this world, a new song entered."

"Her child's?"

"Yes, her child's song was heard. But there was another, which at the time we did not understand." The Noaidi lapsed into uncomfortable silence. The minutes dropped away like an eternity before he finally added. "Three days ago, we heard it again, and it confirmed our suspicions. We believe it is the song of Mare's child."

"Mare?" Okta repeated. "Djorn's offspring?"

"Yes."

"But Mare's child died at her Origin with Mare."

"We all believed it. But the Song is telling us Mare survived, at least to give birth. Okta, she gave birth to a male." The Elder emphasized the last part.

"Impossible," Okta scoffed.

"Not impossible. Mare always had trouble adjusting to life within the Song of All. Not unlike Djorn."

"You give attributes to Mare based on what Djorn became. That is neither just, nor right. If Mare strayed, her actions are upon all of us."

Einár became impatient with the old healer.

"Can you not see what is important here? Mare often journeyed Outside. Could she not have been with the Olmmoš?"

"What? And risk certain death? Einár, she would not have done that!"

"Well, how else do you explain the birth of a male child? There are many tales from the time before the war, of those who did not respect our boundary and tried to mix the blood of Jápmemeahttun and Olmmoš."

"But we are not meant to mix," the healer insisted.

"I know that. But could a half-child not exist? If not, then I am truly at a loss to understand what the Song tells me. . .what it shows me."

"If Mare had a child by an Olmmoš, why is it only now that you have heard him, or for that matter, how is he able to enter the Song?" Okta pressed back.

"Truly, Okta, I do not know. But I have seen the signs and they trouble me." Einár shivered. "The fact he does exist means it is possible he could find us within the Song of All." The Elder looked to see if his old friend grasped his meaning.

"If he can enter the Song, then he can lead others to us," Okta concluded.

Einár nodded. "There is more," he hesitated. "We believe he has Aillun's daughter."

Okta's face registered confusion.

"If she is allowed to grow up among the Olmmoš," the Elder began, "she will become as much of a threat as he is."

Okta shook his head in disagreement.

"You know what I say is true," Einár said, bringing force into his voice for the first time in the conversation.

"What is it you need from me?" Okta snapped.

Einár knew he needed to forestall a heated argument if he hoped to succeed in obtaining the healer's help.

The Elder softened his voice. "I need you to approach Mord and the old warriors, those who can be trusted. We must be prepared."

"A handful of Taistelijan would suffice to harass Olmmoš farmers and herders. But they are not even remotely enough if you are proposing war, Einár. Besides, why do you not approach Mord yourself?"

"I do not seek war, Okta. I seek to keep our kind alive." The Elder bristled. "The Song of All has worked until now, but I fear it no longer can be relied upon. I do not address Mord directly, because I do not wish to raise concern among us."

"And what would you have me tell Mord?" Okta demanded.

"Tell him to select those from the almai that have the Taistelijan soul."

Okta's face clouded. "That is a dangerous thing you ask."

"I know it is not without risk, but until we have located both Mare's offspring and Aillun's daughter, we must believe our future to be threatened. It is a greater peril I am endeavoring to forestall."

Okta nodded.

"If this is what you believe, then I will do as the Noaidi asks," he said, resuming his work.

The Elder came around the bench to confront him. "Okta, do not treat me like this. I no more want to reawaken the warriors among us than you do, but I see no alternative. We must find them, before they become our undoing."

The healer banged the jar down on the table. "And what then? What happens when we find them? Do we start the bloodshed then?"

Einár was silent as he stared at his friend. "What would you like me to say, Okta? That we bring them here? And then what?"

"And then we see what kind of a threat really exists!" the healer exploded.

"And what if it is too late?"

"It will be too late the moment you put them to the knife!"

~

After Einár left, Okta remained alone with his thoughts. He tried to focus on the task before him, but memories emerged from the dark corners of his mind. It wasn't contrariness that made him press the Noaidi to reconsider his plan. Rather, Okta understood the ease with which defense could become bloodlust. He had blocked out these thoughts for a lifetime, and now, when he least wanted to remember his part, it was all he could see.

If excuses were needed, Okta could have said he was young when he went to war. He was young. And he believed in the righteousness of their cause. The Olmmoš were a diseased limb that needed to be cut from the body so they, the Jápmemeahttun, could survive. In those days he did not examine what he was told. He did not question. He was told to act and he did.

Okta fought in countless campaigns, and killed many Olmmoš. And when the killing ended, he was no longer young, and he no longer felt righteous. When Okta walked off the battlefield into the Song of All, he did not want to look back. He wanted to leave death behind and embrace life. His wish was granted, and through a gift from the gods, he received an apprenticeship with a healer who took pity on the warrior.

The master healer, with one look, had known Okta would be a good student.

He explained it plainly, "One who is skilled in the way of imparting the death blow has good knowledge of the body and an even greater commitment to life."

At the time, Okta did not know if his master spoke the truth, but it was a chance to make amends for what he had done, and he applied himself with the same intensity he had given to each battle. Okta was the oldest of the master's apprentices, and a healer's skill did not come easily to him. He tolerated the laughter and the jibes. He felt lost and ridiculous. But he persevered. Now, in his old age, he understood his master's intent.

The mortar and pestle remained idle in Okta's hands, and after awhile he could not remember their need or purpose. He put them back on the shelf. It was clear to him he would not be able to concentrate until he had wound his way through his feelings. One conversation had undone the peace that his time as a healer had instilled in him.

Above all, Okta's heart was heavy with the knowledge of Aillun's death. She had been so beautiful, so full of joy, and she had shared that joy with him.

He recalled the last time he had seen her before she left to seek her Origin. Tears stained her pale face and she had trouble speaking. When her words finally emerged, they shook with sadness. "I am sorry, Okta. I must leave. I have been very happy here with you and wish I could stay. You have much work to do, and now I will not be able to help you with it."

He had wished for Aillun's sake he could have calmed her fears and told her what to expect and who would be waiting for her, but he could not, even though he knew who journeyed to meet her. It was to be Djorn, his friend and comrade. Djorn had recently paid him an unexpected visit. He had come to say his farewell and to ask to be remembered in his old friend's prayers.

They had reminisced about their youth and their folly. There had been some laughter, but also the sharing of great sadness.

"I wish I had chosen the path of life," Djorn had said in parting.

Okta had wanted to offer this once-great warrior the honor he deserved, and he hoped he had succeeded by telling him that, in the end, he would be the bringer of life.

To Aillun, Okta had offered similar comfort. "My child, you go forth to give shape to a new life." Then, he embraced Aillun and gave her a remedy to calm her nerves, before she set out.

As he bade farewell to both Aillun and Djorn, Okta kept to himself the understanding of who each was to the other. Their paths would cross in time. He told himself what he had always believed.

We are not meant to know the one who will sacrifice himself to bring in life and change our own.

There was movement in the vestibule of the workshop, and Kalek appeared before the old healer, who continued to struggle with ghosts and memories.

"Okta, you look unwell," the young almai apprentice said. "Here." He pulled up a chair. "You should sit."

The healer let himself be led. He sat in the chair provided by his assistant.

Okta looked at the golden-headed youth in front of him and thought of himself and Djorn as they had been so very long ago.

"We were not so different." escaped the healer's lips.

"What was that, Okta?"

"Nothing, Kalek. Just the ramblings of an old one."

"I trust, then, I do not need to note it for future reference." His youthful face broke into a broad smile.

"No, indeed. My mutterings are best left unmarked."

"That being the case, what shall I work on for you?"

The old healer's attention briefly returned to the work he had left.

"I am working on a dried *sarrit* reduction to use in these moon cycles to ward off sickness."

"Right." Kalek got to work gathering the necessary ingredients and measuring them carefully. Okta observed his assistant as he went about his tasks. His smooth, fluid movements signaled confidence. At the same time, however, Kalek was patient with the measurements, which indicated an awareness of the importance of precision. They were both good attributes and, when combined properly, they made for a successful healer and, some would say, a good warrior as well.

Okta enjoyed watching the young almai and wished he did not have to interject turmoil into his life. He wished there were some other way to do what needed to be done. He took a few more moments to convince himself that this was indeed the only recourse open to him. Okta knew he must honor his agreement with Einár, but he also knew he was bound to hold up the oath he had made to serve life. Kalek seemed to be the one option he had to honor both ends.

"It is quiet these days without Aillun," Okta began, as if it were a casual comment.

He saw the back of Kalek's head bob in agreement.

"You must have a very heavy heart," he added. Again there was the bob of the head. Okta suspected that too much emotion played upon the almai's face to allow him to confront his mentor. Okta knew Aillun had not included Kalek in her confidence. And for his part, Kalek, in his love-struck state, had not realized what was happening until too late, even though Kalek himself had gone through the change. Okta shook his head. It was the blindness of love—to not see that which was destined to separate and cause pain.

"Kalek, please forgive and indulge an old one. It is my place to pry and then to offer advice," Okta said.

The young apprentice stopped and hung his head. The healer waited. Finally, Kalek faced him.

"She has been gone a short while and yet I miss her," Kalek began. "But I am still angry that she did not share with me what was going on in her body." He reddened. "I could have helped her! I could have supported her! Now our time is over and I had no part in its ending. I was the hapless fool, tolerated but not trusted." Frustration pulsed in his voice.

"Kalek, you must know that you were more than tolerated. You were loved."

Kalek snorted in disbelief.

"I know the present cruelty is clouding your memories, but I remember. I remember the love Aillun showed you, and you her. It is not wrong to acknowledge both the love and the anger. It is strange how often they are mirrored twins in our lives."

"I know, Okta," Kalek answered. "I know my harsh words are unworthy. But it is hard to believe in a future, and then learn it will never come to be."

Okta nodded. "Yes. Yes, that is very true."

"Kalek," the old healer began and then fought against his overwhelming desire to leave matters as they were. "There is something I must tell you."

The young almai tensed visibly, and his face became rigid with concern.

"Aillun will not be returning." He let his meaning sink in. When disbelief flashed across his assistant's eyes, he met it head on.

"Kalek, Aillun died at her Origin."

The young apprentice sank to his knees. He struggled to find his breath. Okta leaned forward and rested his hand gently on the almai's shoulder. He said nothing, waiting, instead, for Kalek to speak. Both old and young were held suspended in time by their respective grief.

Kalek broke the spell when he looked up at the face of his master and asked, "Are you certain?" The question was barely above a whisper, but the power behind it was palpable.

"Yes, Kalek. The Council of Elders ceased to hear her song a few days ago."

"And the baby?"

Okta looked deeply into Kalek's eyes and tried to reach his spirit inside. He needed to know for sure he was making the right decision.

Kalek met his master's gaze with unwavering attention. The almai held back none of his anguish, but neither did he allow himself to be broken by it.

"The child lives."

Kalek let out a long breath. Relief seemed to take hold of him. "Thank the gods!" he exclaimed. But the reprieve was fleeting. Kalek scrambled to his feet and grasped the healer by the shoulders. "How is that possible? How is it possible that you know this?!"

Okta took his apprentice's hands from his shoulders and held them in his own weathered grasp.

"Kalek, I need you to listen to me. I need you to understand that what I am telling you is for you only." Okta scrutinized his assistant. He knew he needed to be circumspect about his plan if bloodshed were to be avoided.

"The Council has received word from another nieddaš, traveling to her Origin, that she had seen an Olmmoš traveling with a baby shortly before coming upon Aillun's body. The Origin seeker could not take the time to retrace the steps and follow the Olmmoš, because her own birth was imminent. She does not know what happened after." Okta mixed truth and half-truths in a way he hoped the young man would believe.

"He must have killed her! The cursed Olmmoš killed her!" Kalek broke from his master's grasp.

"Kalek!" Okta bellowed to get the attention of the almai. "Consider for a moment that perhaps the Olmmoš happened upon Aillun already dead or close to dying and saved the baby from certain death."

The apprentice stopped his pacing and stared at the master.

When the agitation seemed to drain from the young man, Okta continued. "The girl's song was heard, so the Council of Elders believes her to be alive."

"She must be found," Kalek declared.

"Yes, of course."

"What have the Elders decided?"

"Nothing, as of yet, other than they agree the child should be found." Okta winced inwardly as he threaded his lies and truths together.

"I must be allowed to go and find the child," Kalek demanded. "and the one who took her."

Okta narrowed his eyes. "I hardly think an apprentice healer would be prepared to take on this burden."

Kalek's face burned hotly. "I have been training with Mord for two seasons of snow now!"

"Ah," Okta drew the word out in consideration of what he had heard.

A new blush replaced the heat of temper. "I did not tell you I had begun to train with the Taistelijan because I did not want to hurt your feelings."

"I see Aillun was not the only one who lacked trust," Okta replied dryly.

The truth of the barb hit home and Kalek grimaced. "I struggled when I returned and didn't know what path was right for me. I thought the healing arts would serve the needs of all, but inside I felt I needed to push myself physically. Mord approached me and planted the seed to take up the calling of a Taistelijan. I was flattered, so I chose to do both." Kalek wrung his hands for lack of something better to do with them. "When Aillun started and we became. . .close. . .I knew I wanted to be a healer. I saw the art through her eyes and it changed how I thought of myself as an almai."

"But you continued with Mord."

"Yes," Kalek admitted with lowered eyes. "I made a promise to him to finish my training before I made up my mind."

"So, you shared your doubts with Mord, but not with me. That is very interesting."

To this, Kalek said nothing, but he stole a look at his master. Okta smiled at him.

"You are not upset with me?" the almai asked tentatively.

Okta shook his head. "No. In fact it would appear you have chosen the right path to face this moment."

"You mean, you think I am the right one to find Aillun's daughter?"

"Yes. Yes, I believe you are."

Kalek nodded, acknowledging he had been entrusted with the master's confidence.

"Should I approach the Elders and offer myself?"

Okta stroked his white beard and gave the matter some thought. "No, Kalek. I will approach the Council for you and lend my weight to your favor. I will get for you what is known of Aillun's location when she died. And from there you will need to find and follow whatever trail might exist."

"Then I should go to Mord and get myself prepared for the journey."

"Kalek," Okta called out. "A word about Mord. I think it would be best if you did not disclose the exact nature of your journey to him."

"But why not?"

"Because you are an almai and not a Taistelijan. Mord would not entrust you with this important task. He would give the duty to one of the veteran warriors, and you would be left behind to continue on as my apprentice. If you, yourself, desire to carry out this mission, then Mord must not know of it."

"But what do I offer him in place of the truth?"

"You tell Mord I have requested that you journey to the west, to seek our kind there and relay the herbs and tinctures required for the time of the dark sky. I will provide those items so your response is plausible, but not burdensome to your travel. When you have gone and there is no chance another may usurp your duty, then I will address Mord myself, confess my part, and take full responsibility." Okta paused and acknowledged to himself that his course was set.

"But why would you do this?" Kalek asked.

Okta smiled, in spite of his sadness. "Because I loved Aillun, too."

Silence descended upon them as they both thought of Aillun.

"Kalek," Okta spoke up finally, "what will you do when you find them?"

"I will bring Aillun's daughter back."

"And if the Olmmoš resists?"

"I will kill him," Kalek said without hesitation.

"But if you kill him, how will we know what happened to Aillun?"

"I will get the information from him and then kill him."

"I know you feel his death is righteous, but be careful not to mistake understanding for wisdom. I would strongly advise you to convince the Olmmoš to return with you and let the Elders decide the question of his life or death," Okta warned.

"What is the importance of one Olmmoš life, Okta?" Kalek demanded.

"This Olmmoš's life is as sacred as any of ours. When we choose who is to live and who is to die, we do not act as gods, we act as creatures who offend them." Okta softened his voice. "As a healer you are sworn to honor life—all life, including that of an Olmmoš."

"And should he not wish to return with me?"

"Within the herbs that I give you, you will have the means to change the most stubborn mind."

"So I am to drug him and bring him back?" Kalek objected.

Okta frowned, considering how long it had taken to instill peace in himself and others. "I do not speak idly."

~

Kalek walked out into the frozen garden outside of Okta's quarters, all the while thinking of Aillun. He cringed now at his earlier outburst. He had been angry with her, but Okta was right to call him out on his own dishonesty.

He knew Aillun loved him. To deny that truth had been the act of a coward. The real truth was, his last words to her had been harsh, and now she was dead and he would never have the chance to take them back.

Kalek's breath caught. He tried to release the grip of guilt clutching his heart.

"I am sorry I failed you," he whispered into the cold air, and hung his head to look at the ground.

Kalek knew Aillun's spirit now rested with the gods, but the part of him that ached with regret hoped his atonement would somehow reach her. Then, to reassure himself of his purpose, Kalek sent his voice up into the sky and out into the Song.

I am the seeker.
I come to find the truth.
I have lost my heart, but know I will find her legacy.
I have chosen the path of warrior and healer.
I will balance life and death.

CHAPTER THIRTY

Vannes, with Biera as his guide, arrived within a day's travel to Hemmela. He allowed the messenger to trot off to his farm, partly because he didn't want an observer when he confronted the Apotti, and partly because he could no longer stand to listen to the man's constant bellyaching. The Piijkij thanked the gods he did not have a life so meager that carpentry figured as the sum of his existence.

Vannes's approach into Hemmela drew the attention of the few who were about in the waning light and rising cold. He did not bother to acknowledge their stares, but rather continued to the temple. He dismounted near the stables and looked for someone to take his horse, calling out but receiving no answer. Vannes wandered into the dismal and dilapidated stables. A pair of nags took interest in him only as far as he might supply them with some forage, which he did, once he had seen to his own steed.

I might as well be in the Pohjola, he thought.

Vannes, with a pat to his horse's rough-coated flank, left the stables and strode to the temple. He considered how to approach the Apotti. He had the element of surprise in his favor, so it was a matter of how to best use it.

Vannes banged upon the side door and awaited entrance. When no response came, he let out a series of curses that concluded with a fiery end to whomever was this remiss in their duties. He moved to the back door and used his fist to announce himself and his frustration. Again he waited in vain. Vannes calmed his anger by clenching and releasing his fists. He examined the lock and the sturdiness of the door, and, though he wanted to vent himself upon the wooden obstacle, wisdom prevailed.

As he trudged through the newly fallen snow to reach the front of the temple, Vannes looked around, but saw no one about. He tried the door, expecting it to be open as an entreaty to the faithful of Hemmela. It too was locked. Although every part of him wished to seek a sturdy axe to fell the door in front of him, Vannes took a deep breath and banged upon the wood with the hilt of his sword. The sound echoed through the interior. He continued his barrage, if only to release some of the anger welling up within him.

The door suddenly swung wide, and a red-faced cleric stood in its opening.

"Siggur, your absence has been a grave mistake. Your position here. . ." the rest of the sentence trailed away into nothingness, as the priest saw whom he addressed.

"I take it you have noted that I am not the one deserving of this tirade," Vannes commented, keeping his rage barely contained. "Based on the great effort I have taken to gain entrance, it would appear the person I should also hold in contempt is this selfsame Siggur."

The priest struggled to regain his composure, but before he could, Vannes spoke again.

"Perhaps it would benefit both of us to consider the future of this wayward person within the warmth of your chambers."

At a loss, the priest stood back to allow Vannes into the temple. The Piijkij swept past him into the gloomy interior, and waited for the priest to catch up. In the interim, Vannes took the opportunity to drop to one knee and honor the gods.

"If you might give me an idea as to your business and needs. . ." the priest began, but was again cut off.

"Not that there will be much chance of us being disturbed," Vannes said, "but my business is best discussed in the privacy of your chambers. You are the Apotti of Hemmela, are you not?"

The priest looked at the man, trying to gauge the nature of his business, before inclining his head and agreeing to the request for privacy.

"If you will follow me, then," the Apotti said reluctantly, leading the way through one shadowed corridor into another. When they reached their destination the Apotti opened the door and stepped aside to let Vannes enter first.

Inside, Vannes saw nowhere to sit other than at the priest's desk. He headed in its direction, removing a layer of his furs, which he tossed on the seat before sitting down.

The priest protested. "I think you take advantage of the hospitality afforded to strangers by the Order of Believers."

"I think you will see we are not strangers at all, but in fact friends, of a sort," Vannes answered.

"Friend or no," the Apotti puffed, "I would ask you to leave my seat."

"And would you ask the same of your friend, the Avr of the Brethren of Hunters? He sends his regards, by the way." Vannes let a smile curl slowly across his face.

The priest stood as if frozen, speechless and gaping. Then a small smile crept up his lips and into his face before he spoke. "We are honored to receive an emissary from the Brethren of Hunters. I take it you are a Piijkij?"

Vannes laughed. "Yes, I am. Your knowledge of the Piijkij represents a lively topic of interest among our Brotherhood. No doubt this rare awareness aided you in discovering the one in your midst."

The Apotti relaxed enough to speak without hesitation. "Yes, until recently we have had a Piijkij in our midst, though it was not immediately apparent."

"And how, may I ask, did it become apparent?" Vannes leaned forward onto the desk to hear the priest's response.

The priest's composure wavered. "I feel remiss in not having asked this sooner. Our unlikely meeting at the door has occupied my attention until now, but I must insist you show me proof of your connection with the Avr," the Apotti demanded primly.

Vannes leapt out of the seat and over the table, his sword drawn and at the neck of the priest before the cleric could utter another word.

The priest drew back, but the blade followed him.

"I would suggest you make no further movements, because I cannot guarantee the safety of your throat otherwise," Vannes remarked with deadly calm. "I would also suggest you look carefully at this sword. It is the sword of the Piijkij, made by the very fire that gives name to our leader, and forged with the purpose of ending an Immortal's life. But I find it works equally well on traitorous, upstart priests."

The Apotti swallowed. Vannes dug the tip of the sword further into his neck.

"Are we now at an understanding that I am before you at the request of Dávgon, the Avr of the Brethren of Hunters?"

With an almost imperceptible nod the priest agreed.

"Good." Vannes removed the sword and secured it in his belt.

"I believe we left off our earlier discussion at the point at which you were telling me how you came to know of the presence of a Piijkij in your village." He withdrew to the chair, letting the priest stumble in body and in explanation.

"It is not often that. . .that a stranger comes to our town and stays. This man came in the dark time of Skábmamánnu, two seasons of snow ago. He made himself indispensible to an old farmer with a daughter who had not yet chosen a handmate. I thought it fitting to look into the matter, lest he prove to be a thief, or worse." The priest stopped talking and looked at Vannes. The Piijkij waved to him to continue.

"I learned he had traveled for many seasons of snow in the Pohjola, but had chosen to leave the Piijkij to once again join the world of men. An agent of mine tracked his passage through various villages. In one village, close to the edge of the Pohjola, he found someone who remembered the stranger coming into their travelers' hut and having a few drinks. The man told my agent he had overheard the stranger's mutterings. They made no sense to him, but he repeated them to my man, and I in turn heard it from him." When the priest finished rambling he glanced expectantly at Vannes.

"And these mutterings?"

"They spoke of a sword returned to the Hall of the Fallen."

"And what in this made you believe he was Piijkij?"

The Apotti regarded Vannes warily. "The mention of the Hall of the Fallen and the sword."

"And when did you contact the Avr?"

"As soon as my agent gave me this news."

Vannes stretched and allowed silence to fall upon the room. He stood up and walked toward the priest. "Thank you for letting me occupy your seat. I must admit the journey here taxed me more than I expected."

"You are more than welcome to rest a while longer," the Apotti stammered.

"No! I am quite refreshed after our little talk. Please, you should take your place."

The priest gestured his thanks with an uncertain nod. He moved to his chair and sat upon the traveler's furs, facing the man.

Vannes moved about the room, examining its features and shadows. "No doubt you must draw comfort from those to whom you minister."

The priest eyed him warily. "Yes."

"But I am also led to believe you have expressed a grander vision for yourself," Vannes added with a smile.

The Apotti of Hemmela kept his silence.

"I should have thought a man as ambitious as you would have made every effort to carry out his affairs with care and discretion." Vannes let his voice edge toward menace.

"I do not understand your meaning." The priest fidgeted in his chair, attempting piety.

Vannes walked to the door as if about to leave, but, instead of leaving, he slid the iron bolt across the stout door.

"Would you care to offer an opinion of how it came to be that a letter bearing your seal and signature, addressed to the High Priest of the Order of Believers, was delivered by your ill-mannered messenger to the Avr of the Brethren of Hunters?"

The startled priest sat slack-jawed. "That cannot be possible. I took the letter from my drawer and handed it personally to my messenger. The drawer is locked and I hold the only key."

Vannes moved slowly back toward the desk. "So, I am to assume you either take the Avr for a man who enjoys a joke, or you do not understand the danger of lying to me."

The priest drew himself back into to his chair, as if he could somehow escape Vannes's advance. "No! No! I can assure you, my respect for the Avr is of the highest order, and no less so for you and your Brothers." The Apotti's voice rose with his panic.

"I do not know how this came to pass. I wrote to the Avr to tell him of the developments with the Piijkij and to assure him I had convinced the man to take up my—I mean *our*—cause."

"Then how is it the letter he received contained sums and accounts relating to this speck of civilization?" Vannes leaned on the desk, towering over the priest.

"Sums and accounts?" The priest's face clouded in confusion. "I sent that letter with Siggur." A moment of clarity dawned upon the Apotti. He fairly shouted, "Siggur! My acolyte. I gave him the letter to take to the High Priest. It was of our accounts. He left here four days ago and was to have returned two days ago."

"This Siggur, then, is not the same Biera who appeared at our gates?" Vannes probed.

"No. I sent Siggur away, to the Order of Believers, so I might send Biera to you without raising the suspicion of my acolyte or having him wonder why I chose to contact the Brethren. Do you not see? Siggur must have somehow exchanged the letters."

The priest's deduction hung in the room as Vannes waited for the thrill of discovery to give way to realization. It did not take long.

The Apotti's eyes widened and he shot up from his chair. "The High Priest has the letter. The High Priest has the letter." The man repeated himself as if he needed to be convinced of the horror that had befallen him. When it sunk in, he drooped back down in the chair, stunned.

Vannes studied the slumped priest. "The price for your indiscretion cannot be measured in coin, but I can guarantee you will feel its dearness."

When his threat went unnoted by the priest, Vannes raised his voice. Only then did the Apotti lift his gaze to meet that of the Piijkij. Vannes could see the man was already defeated, but it would not stop him from taking what little was left of the Apotti of Hemmela.

CHAPTER THIRTY-ONE

BÁVVÁL, THE VIJNS OF the Order of Believers, had given a
few days' thought to the matter of the Apotti of Hemmela.
The letter he had received confirmed that the priest could
not be trusted. It was obvious he would need to be removed. What
was far less clear were the Brethren's motives. *What did Dávgon
really want? Because surely he had little use for a zealot like Rikkar.*

Bávvál sloughed off his heavy, fur-lined robes so he could pace
freely in front of the roaring fire.

Rikkar had always thought too much of himself, even as an
acoltye. Yet Bávvál had never figured him to be a man of action.
Words, yes. But action? No. And yet he had proof of the man's
conspiracy with the Brethren. But Bávvál could not immediately
see the man's appeal to the Brethren.

Perhaps it's not the man himself. Rather, the place, the High Priest
mused. He took a quick step back to avoid the hungry flames
that licked out of the hearth. *But a few farms and trade-huts hardly
seemed worthy of attention.* Bávvál repeated the village name in his
mind. There was something in the name. And then it came to him
like the crack of an errant spark. Hemmela's temple rested upon
the razed foundations of a Jápmea gathering site.

What had Rikkar found?

Bávvál began pacing again. Fresh tension added a spring to his step. Of course, when he got his hands on the man, he would soon enough know what the priest had been up to. But until then the possibilities would plague his thoughts.

Then there was the acolyte. The Amanuensa of Hemmela was clearly cunning, because he managed to betray his superior's intention while leaving himself above suspicion. The young man's wide-eyed surprise had surely been affected. Bávvál, however, could not help but be impressed by the ruse. The acolyte had managed treachery without its stain. This type of skill could prove to be both a benefit and a cause for concern, particularly in a role of increased power.

A knock at the door halted the High Priest's perambulation.

The door opened without entreaty or ceremony and the lithe figure of Bávvál's most trusted agent entered.

Áigin inclined his head. Wisps of long grey hair closed in around his face like threadbare curtains.

Bávvál had asked his spy to befriend the young man and ferret out the truth behind the facade.

"And?" Bávvál asked.

"Our young acolyte rankles at the unfairness of his fate, and believes himself capable of greatness. He is willing to deceive those he deems his inferiors, but has a respect for those who hold the key to his advancement."

The High Priest considered Áigin's assessment. "And do you feel he can be trusted?"

"I feel he can be trusted to do what is best for himself," the agent answered.

"He is no different than most."

"No, we are all ambitious," the spy agreed, "but he will work to curry your favor if you bestow it upon him. Dangle a bright future, but keep a firm grasp upon his reins. He will do what you need for as long as you need."

"Is this what keeps you loyal to me, Áigin?"

"Yes."

"And if another were to offer you a brighter future?"

Áigin's dark, almost black eyes caught the firelight and his thin bloodless lips curled back. "Who could offer me a brighter future than the instrument of the gods?"

Pleased with the answer, Bávvál slapped the table with his palm and let out a loud laugh. "Truth and wisdom, Áigin!" The High Priest's eyes narrowed. "Send the whelp to me. He is about to realize a dream." Bávvál shared a smile with his agent, and then Áigin left.

Bávvál sat down and began writing out the necessary orders for the new Apotti of Hemmela.

But what to do with the Brethren of Hunters, he wondered.

The Brethren had been like a small pebble stuck in his boot, irritating at every step and difficult to dislodge. Bávvál wished he could use his new underling to get more information about their plans, but he could not see how the young man could gain access to the Brethren while being so closely aligned with the Believers. Then again, perhaps it was not for him to figure out. He could charge the new Apotti with finding a way to gain the information, however he saw fit. The onus would be his.

As long as the new Apotti of Hemmela understands his future depends upon his success. . . Bávvál stipulated silently, continuing to write.

The fire behind him crackled. The High Priest sat back, satisfied, and waited for the Amanuensa from Hemmela to be brought to him. He did not wait long. A knock at the door brought forth the young man who had occupied much of Bávvál's thought this morning.

"Ah, Siggur," he acknowledged the acolyte.

The young man bowed deeply.

"The last time we spoke, I believe I mentioned you were at a crossroads," Bávvál said.

The young cleric swallowed, but remained silent, choosing to acknowledge the Vijns's comment with an incline of his head.

Bávvál enjoyed toying with the nervous youth before him. To the acolyte's credit, he maintained a calm exterior; only a shadow of fear played on his haughty features.

"It would appear you have chosen well," Bávvál continued. "Your gambit, and do not deny it, was a success. You have effectively discredited your Apotti without bringing disfavor upon yourself."

The young man seemed ready to protest, but Bávvál raised his hand to stop him.

"Siggur, do not evince false modesty. It is as detestable in the eyes of the gods as false pride."

Siggur kept his tongue.

"The letter you brought me is proof of your superior's deceit. As the Vijns and the protector of our faith, I cannot offer a blind eye to this kind of treachery. Believe me when I say, I take no pleasure in what I must do. I act as duty accords. Therefore, I command you to return to Hemmela and present this letter to your superior. The contents, to save you the trouble of discovery, demand Rikkar's immediate resignation and, as your fate would have it, your immediate ascension to the position of Apotti of Hemmela."

"I. . .I am speechless," the young man stuttered.

"Yes, that is apparent." The Vijns smiled.

Siggur stood straight and looked directly at the High Priest. "I am grateful for this opportunity, my Vijns. I will strive to be worthy of this honor you have bestowed upon me."

"I am glad to hear you say that, because the job does not come without demands."

"Of course," Siggur answered, keeping his head bowed as he listened.

Bávvál picked up a piece of creased vellum with only a shadow of its former seal, the wax having crumbled in its handling. "We have established you know the contents of this letter the Apotti entrusted to you. Your very presence here tells me you understood the importance of its subject; therefore, I think you are uniquely disposed to address the problem of the Brethren of Hunters."

The newly appointed Apotti of Hemmela hesitated. "Perhaps you could be more specific with your request, my Vijns?" he asked, looking up at Bávvál who let his eyes briefly wander across the words "bring honor" and "Brethren of Hunters."

"I would like you to find out what the Brethren think they know and how they plan to use it," the High Priest answered. "Is that specific enough?"

"Perfectly. And how would you like me to obtain this information?"

"However you see fit, Siggur. You have made it this far, and I have little doubt that you are resourceful enough to fulfill my one request."

Siggur's face clouded. "I see."

"And Siggur, you have your future success within your own grasp." As an afterthought, the High Priest added, "Not many men can say that."

"I can leave at once," Siggur answered.

"Yes, I believe you can." Bávvál handed over the sealed letter to the new Apotti of Hemmela. "Please keep me apprised of developments. I would hate to receive news from elsewhere that my faith in you has been misplaced."

"I will," the young man assured, taking the letter.

Bávvál remained seated after the young acolyte left. He could not be sure if his strategy would succeed, but it would cost him nothing to pursue it.

CHAPTER THIRTY-TWO

VANNES LEFT THE APOTTI of Hemmela when he was certain the man could tell him nothing more. Two days of precisely applied pressure had not revealed as much as he'd hoped. Threats had provided some answers, and pain had loosened the man's tongue further, but when the Apotti confessed to poisoning Irjan's wife and son, Vannes knew the man had nothing left to offer but his own sins; which, though interesting, were not useful for his purpose. When he could no longer endure the sobbing and pleading, the Piijkij cut the priest free and allowed him to wallow upon the ground in gratitude.

Vannes used the tip of his sword on the Apotti's exposed flesh to carve upon him a reminder of loyalty. The priest shrieked in pain, though the blade remained on the skin's surface. Vannes would have dispatched the man, but the priest's fate rested with the Avr.

Vannes left the Apotti to his whimpering and made his way to the kitchen, where he took supplies for himself before heading to the stables. As he drew close he saw Bihto, one of the Brethren, newly arrived. Bihto quickly dismounted and greeted Vannes, clasping arms.

"What news do I bring back?" he asked.

Vannes summarized events, adding, "I had hoped to use Irjan's wife and child as leverage, but it appears the Apotti, in his haste, has dispatched them."

Bihto said nothing, waiting for Vannes to continue.

"Tell the Avr I will seek Irjan's trail. Have him send a dozen men north along the main trade route to find me."

Bihto nodded. He grasped the reins of his horse and remounted. He looked down at his comrade. "Bring him back for all of us, Vannes." He jerked the reins to gallop off.

Vannes watched him disappear before retrieving his own mount from the stable. As he drew himself up upon his horse, he looked at the village ahead of him. He thought of Irjan and the choices the man had made. Toil in the field over honor. Vannes shook his head in disbelief; although, he considered farming better than following the shit-strewn paths of the binna. The shaggy horse beneath Vannes stomped its hooves impatiently, bringing him to the present. He needed to make one more stop before setting out.

∾

Biera looked up from his labor and groaned inwardly. He wished he could ignore the approaching Piijkij, but the man headed directly toward his farm. The cursed Hunter was worse than a blowfly on a carcass, and Biera took no pleasure in being reacquainted, but, he could do nothing but stop his work and stride out to meet Vannes.

∾

"I'm honored by your visit," Biera croaked.

"The honor is mine, friend of the Brethren," Vannes lied as he dismounted and tossed the reins of his horse toward the farmer. "I would expect you to show my mount the same generosity shown to you during your time with us."

Biera fumbled with the reins and led the snorting animal off to a small barn. Vannes followed the man, taking in the scenery around him. The house was charred, but repairable. The barn was intact, though there appeared to be no animals housed within it. He noticed the soft mounding in the snow on the otherwise flat surface surrounding the house. He walked over to it and kicked at the snow.

Biera eyed him. "That's where he buried them. She shouldn't have trusted him, but she was blind, just like the old man."

"And it does not bother you?"

Biera scowled. "The fault's not mine! I offered, but she didn't want me, and look what happened." The man stuck out his chin toward the mounded snow.

"And you believe he did it?"

"Yes! Who else could've? Or, would've?"

Vannes looked at him, but did not enlighten him. "When you are finished with my horse, bring a pickaxe and a digger," he commanded.

Biera began protesting, but seemed to think better of it. Vannes explored beyond the mound. He walked toward the surrounding trees, stepping with care. When he reached the edge, he viewed the farmstead from a distance. Again, the appeal of this life escaped him. But rather than try to fathom it, he assessed the plot of land as one seeking to escape.

The forest grew thickest on the northwestern quadrant, which would be good for a man on foot, but the Apotti said Irjan had taken his best sleigh. Therefore, Irjan had departed directly from the temple without a glance back at his former life. The fire had a sense of finality about it, as if someone had wanted to cleanse away a sin or purge a sickness.

If the Apotti were to be believed, Irjan had taken up the cause of finding the Jápmea. And if indeed the traitor sought the Immortals, he could have traveled in any direction. But if Irjan had taken the task in name only, he would more than likely head to where he knew he could hide: the Pohjola.

Vannes was not pleased about the prospect of traveling into the Northland, but if necessary, he would follow through. In the meantime, he would stop in the villages and travelers' huts between, in the hope Irjan had presented himself.

He walked back to the mound and waited for Biera. "The more you tarry, the longer I will keep you from your more pressing matters."

Vannes grabbed the digger from the dawdling farmer and waited for the man to bring the pick to bear upon the earth.

The farmer and Hunter worked up a sweat breaking through the icy ground and depositing a pile of frozen earth to the side. As they got deeper, Vannes stopped Biera's pick and tossed him the digger.

"Keep going," he commanded. "I will tell you when to stop."

Biera groaned, but said nothing.

Vannes kept a sharp eye for a sign of the body. The farmer lifted scoops of broken dirt up past his knees and onto the heap they'd made. For a time, there was only the sound of the wind and the slow work of Biera's tool.

"Stop!" Vannes called out. He stepped into the hole with Biera and brushed aside dirt until he revealed a shroud. He stepped back out and ordered Biera to dig along the outside so as not to damage the body.

"Damage the body," Biera snorted. "She's frozen through, there's no damage I can do that's not been done already."

Vannes clapped the man about his head with his boot. "If I say I do not wish the body to be damaged, then I want you to act upon that wish and not offer your opinion."

"I was only saying..." Biera protested but let it drop as Vannes drew back his leg for another sound thump to the head.

The farmer groused more, but dutifully avoided digging into the body. When he had uncovered it, both length and width, he stopped and looked to Vannes for further instruction.

"Bring her out," the Piijkij said.

"Maybe you lot of Hunters have some special powers, but unless you come in here with me and help, she'll stay where she is," Biera retorted, his temper getting the better of his judgment.

Vannes thought about teaching the man a lesson, but realized it would merely slow down his own efforts to gain more information. Besides, he had already seen that Biera lacked the wit to retain a lesson learned. The Piijkij climbed back into the hole, now widened and deepened, and prepared to lift the shrouded woman out of her resting place. After a graceless heave, the body landed upon the ground opposite the hillock of exposed dirt.

Vannes climbed out, as did Biera. The Hunter sat on his haunches, slit open the stitching, and pulled back the shroud to reveal the woman. Biera recoiled, as if expecting her to come to life. But when he saw she was not resurrected, he leaned forward and looked closely at the face. "That's her."

"And you thought there would be someone other than she in this grave?"

The Piijkij ignored the farmer's disgruntled expression and focused on the woman—Sohja. She was young, though she looked too old to have been considered a maid. Her blond hair was woven into a neat plait that curved around her neck and onto her breast. Vannes had the impression the braid was done after her death, as a tribute to her from her husband. Vannes found it hard to reconcile his memories of Irjan with the man who would have taken the time to comb and braid his woman's hair. The display of sentimentality suggested Irjan no longer wore the mantle of a dispassionate Hunter. For Vannes, this meant Irjan might make mistakes that would make the job of hunting him easier.

Vannes stared at the woman's features. The cold had kept them intact. He reached down and cracked open the frozen eyelids, and saw redness of blood coloring the white. Her blue irises were clouded like watery milk. Vannes pushed the eyes closed, then squeezed her cheeks so her mouth opened. He saw even teeth, which he pulled apart to look at the tongue—swollen and blackened. He closed the mouth and pulled back the shroud.

An edge had been cut from the cloth. He was unsure of its meaning. Vannes studied the woman's clothing: lightly worn, perhaps the first or second winter's use. No outer garments or furs. Her feet were covered in light reindeer skin boots, laced up. He concluded that she had been indoors when she died. It was not an inspired deduction, but all pieces were useful when one assembled a larger picture. He stood up and looked at the whole of the dead woman, Irjan's wife. A thought struck him. He looked quickly at the grave and back at the woman's body.

"Did she not have a son?" Vannes demanded of Biera, who had moved off to sit on a fallen tree to rest.

"Yes," Biera answered, looking up.

Vannes jumped into the pit with the digger and set to work unearthing another hardened layer of soil. There was nothing. Again he set to work. He found himself sweating and uncomfortable, but he continued.

Biera came over and observed, leaning over and resting his hands upon his knees. He watched Vannes pushing aside loose dirt.

Finally the Piijkij stopped and rested upon the digger. "He is not here," Vannes said, more to himself than Biera.

Mistaking the comment as meant for him, Biera replied, "Well, I don't know anything about that."

Vannes pulled himself out of the grave.

"We all thought he'd killed both of them," Biera went on.

The Piijkij considered the man's response for a long time. "Perhaps you are right, Biera, and I would mark it as the first time."

The farmer's expression made it clear he was unsure of the nature of the comment—compliment or insult. "I'm not sure I understand."

"And again, a truer statement could not be uttered," Vannes agreed, slapping the man on his shoulder. He walked away from Biera toward the barn. Inside, he patted the flank of his mount, who foraged contently. He led the horse out of the barn and raised himself upon it.

Biera trotted over. "And is that it?" he complained. "You're leaving and I'm left with a body and a hole to deal with."

The horse circled impatiently. Vannes looked down at him. "Take comfort in the fact it only takes one man to roll a body into the hole and cover it again," he said and took off in the direction of Hemmela, leaving a muttering Biera in the distance.

They'd spent the better part of a morning unearthing the contents of the grave, and Vannes burned with impatience. He wished to be on his way, but felt stymied by the mystery of Irjan's son. What had become of him? The Apotti had said he had taken two lives in his attempt to persuade the former Piijkij to resume his duty. Biera and the other villagers believed the grave contained two bodies, and yet, he had discovered only one. No child lay with his mother. It was possible the child had been buried elsewhere, but Vannes doubted it. It would have been too much work to dig two graves. Besides, it would appeal to a sentimental Irjan to keep mother and child together in death, as they had been in life.

Then again, perhaps the son lived, which would present an interesting development. If Irjan traveled with an infant child, he would be forced to move more slowly and more carefully, aware of the baby's needs. The child would need food, rest, and shelter. Irjan would more than likely need to travel through villages to resupply, and a stranger with an infant would stand out in the minds of villagers weary of seeing the same neighbors every day.

But the question remained—which direction? Vannes had already told Bihto to have the Brethren find him along the northern route. As he edged toward the crossroads outside of Hemmela, he tried to think as Irjan might have done. He imagined himself bereft of wife and son—a man who'd lost the life he had struggled to find. *Where would he turn?*

The Pohjola. He had done it once, and he would do it again, if only for the comfort of a life he recognized. But Vannes wondered, if Irjan had his son, would he still choose such a rough world? Or, would he attempt to strike out in a new direction, to build a fresh life for the two of them someplace easier?

This question nagged Vannes as he headed northwards. Between him and the Pohjola were immeasurable leagues. With luck, he would have plenty of time to decide what he would do with them, should he find them both.

CHAPTER THIRTY-THREE

IRJAN'S PLANS DID NOT come to fruition. He thought a day's rest would allow him to continue onwards to the north, perhaps to the Pohjola. But a day's rest became two, and the two a week, and the week grew to into another. The widow Gunná had argued at first that it was silly to travel while a storm raged, and when the storm abated she pointed out that Dárja felt too warm to the touch and could be sick. By the second week it became clear the old woman needed Irjan and his family as much as he had needed Gunná and her homestead.

Despite the old woman's protests that she could take care of herself the way she always had, it could not be ignored that she did, indeed, need some help. Firewood needed to be chopped, and repairs to the structure, which had long been passed over, had to be made.

Irjan did these tasks and more. He hunted, bringing back fresh meat to supplement the stores the old woman had laid up during the cycles of sun and light. And he added the care of her small herd of goats to his daily routine. The goats were not so different from reindeer; though smaller, they shared the same stubborn-mindedness. The animals lived by their own rhythm and purpose, and Irjan drew comfort from this. They ate, they bickered among themselves, they slept and waited for the light to return so they could once again be outside to forage. Irjan had forgotten what it meant to be part of a herd, even one that was not migrating.

Recently, Gunná had insisted she needed to travel to Ullmea. Her youngest daughter lived in the nearby village, and the girl was expecting her first child. The widow wanted to check upon her daughter and also to satisfy her curiosity about the goings on of the wider world, even if it were just village small talk and petty gossip.

She had swept his caution casually aside. "Irjan, I will be fine. I would be doing this regardless of you being here, so pretend you are not here and do not worry."

"Perhaps we should not be here," Irjan suggested.

"Oh stop your silliness," she reprimanded. "You are just disgruntled because you cannot make an old woman see your wisdom."

"Well, at least you admit what you are about to undertake is not wise."

"My own wisdom is not in doubt here, and I will not be bullied." Gunná stood her ground with her arms crossed.

Irjan snorted and stomped off.

"Where are you going?" she asked, concern rising in her voice.

Irjan kept walking but called out over his shoulder. "I am going to hitch your sled to the nag so you will a least make it there with some speed. Because if you had to go by your hobble, it would take you a week's worth of moons!"

"Impudent son of a moose," she yelled after him, smiling.

～

Sitting by the warmth of the fire, Irjan felt Gunná's absence. She had been unclear how long she would be gone, but she'd said it would be more than a few days. He wondered if he had done the right thing by staying. It had been good for the babies to have the comfort and security the homestead offered. They seemed to have settled into a relaxed schedule of napping, feeding, and soaking up the warm embraces and tender endearments Gunná lavished upon them.

He watched the two pink bodies sleeping next to each other. They were so different, and yet linked in a way he feared he would never be able to explain. Marnej's pale yellow hair looked like the first frost upon the summer wheat fields. Dárja instead had dark hair, like her mother, blacker than the darkest sky of *Juovlamánnu*. The two were as different as the night and the day.

A sound from outside broke into his musings. Irjan sprang up, immediately on guard, his instinct fighting against the complacency the refuge had created.

Irjan crept to the door on the eastern side of the hut. He listened and then slowly opened the door enough to peer out. He looked toward the path the old woman had taken when she left. Nothing caught his eye, nor did the horizon reveal any sign of movement. Irjan weighed his options. He could go out and examine the perimeter, but he did not want to leave the infants alone. Once again he was struck by the familiarity of this dilemma. And once again Irjan concluded it was better to stay together, but he wondered if this would always be the case.

Irjan had had neither interest nor opportunity to seek the other realm since they had come to stay with the widow. Even now he resisted considering it, but, with Gunná's being absent, he had to admit this might be a rare chance. It occurred to him she might come upon him while he searched the other timespace, but he was fairly certain her arrival would rouse him. Balancing the profit and the harm, Irjan decided to try and reach out.

In the quiet of the hut, he stood still and closed his eyes. He deepened and slowed his breath, listening to the beat of his heart. The rhythm beat steadily. Irjan counted each beat until they fell away in his mind. He became aware of all the sounds and sensations around him. The fire crackled in the hearth. A fox padded softly in the surrounding woods, searching for a meal. Thankfully, he detected no sounds of men.

Irjan let silence take over his mind and he reached farther out.
He put himself into the dark sky and the dreams and fates it held.
Suddenly, his ears and body filled with the rush of song. At first,
he heard so many voices he could not understand any. It was a
cacophonous jumble he could make no sense of. He tried to focus
and find one, but it was like trying to watch one drop of water in
a downpour. Then he heard clearly:

We are the Jápmemeahttun.
We are the guardians of the world.
Our memory stretches back to the start of days.
Our vision reaches beyond all tomorrows.
We sing together as one, so that our one may always survive.

The chorus continued, flowing about him as more and more
voices joined in. Irjan's whole body vibrated with the words
he heard. The song swelled, and he thought it would burst and
explode into countless pieces. He fought to stay with all the
voices, even as he felt his body begin to weaken and quiver.

Then, as quickly as the voices had come to life, they faded,
save for one, which remained strong like his own pounding heart.

I am the seeker.
I come to find the truth.
I have lost my heart, but know I will find her legacy.
I have chosen the path of warrior and healer.
I will balance life and death.

Irjan's eyes flew open. He looked at the objects in the room,
but his eyes refused to focus. He swayed as the voice continued to
wash over him. He moved to sit down and the world shifted under
him. The last thing he saw before darkness and silence claimed
him were the babies, lying in the glow of the fire.

Part Three

THE BURDEN
OF CHOICE

CHAPTER THIRTY-FOUR

IN THE WILDERNESS, FAR from the dying fire that warmed Irjan and his new family, another voice reached out into the void of ever-dark sky. Kalek traveled Outside to accomplish the impossible. He journeyed to find Aillun's daughter. Okta had prepared for him the misdirection he needed to be free of unwanted questions, but Kalek had not been prepared for how it would feel to lie. When he approached Mord for the requisitions needed for his journey, the old warrior had not raised a brow. When he'd asked for the fastest of the binna, Mord objected, but relented when Kalek explained, "Okta wants me to travel and return as quickly as possible." It was one of the rehearsed rationales offered by Okta for Kalek's use. The lie tasted bitter, but Kalek swallowed it, knowing the end it served.

Kalek, now three days out, had yet to hear for himself the child's song, but he quieted his fears, recalling the journey had just begun. Using the directions and the stars Okta had shown him, Kalek focused on the Song of All. Although he traveled as quickly as the conditions allowed, he worried it would not be fast enough. He knew each step forward took him closer to his goal, but he could not outpace his doubts. Begrudgingly, he admitted to himself he could not predict how long it would take him to reach Aillun's Origin; moreover, he could not be sure there would be a trail to follow once he found her Origin, or if he would be able to recognize its signs.

Kalek shook his head and tried to focus his thoughts elsewhere, but the passing storm gave him fresh cause for concern. Any delay meant Aillun's daughter drew farther away.

Kalek kept moving as the storm passed over him. He used his one hope to push back all his doubts into the smallest corner of his mind.

Her song has been sung. She is alive.

~

Time weighed heavily on Okta's mind. He had put off talking to Mord for as long as he could without jeopardizing his agreement with Einár and the Council of Elders. He hoped he'd given Kalek enough time to put distance between himself and their community

Okta stood outside the Taistelijan's quarters. It seemed like a lifetime of moon cycles since he'd lived among them. The warriors who remained carried on the traditions and practices, often staying apart from the other Jápmemeahttun. Some said it was aloofness born of pride, but Okta knew better. He'd once been one of them, and knew it was not pride keeping them at a distance, but rather apprehension. Those old enough to remember battle feared no one would understand their experiences, and though their story still echoed in the Song of All, fewer each season of snow could appreciate its true meaning. For those others who had chosen to train with the old warriors, there was indeed something akin to pride—a need for honor. But for those, like Okta, who had lived the life of a Taistelijan, the pressure of loneliness among one's own kind pushed them to the fringes of daily life.

Okta felt the long-forgotten feelings of his homecoming after the wars, when everything he had believed in, everything he had sacrificed, had been betrayed by the Elders and their decision to hide rather than to continue the fight. At the time, he could not fathom why they had expended so much effort, and lost so many lives, only to withdraw when they might have won. But now, as whiteness overtook his beard like the first snows of the dark time, he understood.

Where he had once seen a failure to press for victory, Okta now saw the preservation of the true Jápmemeahttun spirit, and he feared this ideal was now in jeopardy as their leader, the Noaidi, sought out the Taistelijan. The paradox was not lost on him. In the prime of his life, the Noaidi's decision would have been a reason for rejoicing; whereas now, as an old one, it filled him with foreboding. In the end, Okta could not relinquish the hard-won belief that all life was precious, no matter what the Council of Elders believed.

Okta drew in a deep and unsatisfying breath and entered the domain of the warriors. He wandered through the main hall, looking at the artifacts of his past: swords and millstones, bows and arrows. The younger Taistelijan looked up and nodded to him, but continued with their work. They knew Okta as a healer, and he preferred it this way.

Okta moved through their work space and into the armory. It remained well stocked and neatly ordered, as if waiting for an army to be raised. The image caused him to cringe. This was, in fact, what he was charged to do—help raise a small army. Okta shook his head in amazement at the mire he found himself in.

"Cursed Einár," he said under his breath.

"You must be a dodderer if you have taken to talking to yourself," a voice boomed from behind Okta.

The healer faced his heckler.

"Mord!" Okta spat. "I am not surprised that time has not improved your manners or your propriety."

"If my observation stung, Okta, I would hate to see what my sword would do!" The warrior enjoyed himself.

"Again, such wit! It could use some sharpening. Perhaps a turn on the millstone?"

Mord laughed and slapped Okta on the back. "Same as ever! Pinched and pickled in your own brine!"

Okta let the comment pass in the hope of ending the repartee at a stalemate.

Mord gave him an appraising look. "What brings you to the home of warriors?"

If he'd intended his question as another barb, it missed its mark and served to bolster Okta's belief in the virtue of his plan.

"This is a fine collection of weapons," the healer said. "What of their handmates? Are they as honed and hardened?"

This time the Taistelijan bristled. "Have you left your hut of herbs to come here and impugn men who are your betters? I can, with wholehearted pleasure, say there is no place for you here!" Mord fairly growled as he spoke.

Okta clenched his fists, barely managing to restrain his anger. "While I know your memory has suffered from the many blows you have received, some of which I recall coming from my insignificant hand, you would do well to remember who you are talking to."

"A healer." Mord snorted.

"A healer, with a message from the Noaidi and the Council of Elders."

Okta knew Mord dearly wished to scoff at the implication; however, the warrior was still beholden to the Council of Elders, and so, bit his tongue.

"What does the Noaidi need to tell me that requires an intermediary?" Mord asked, allowing himself to withdraw into a sullen stance.

Okta picked his way through a maze of truth and deceit. "The Noaidi seeks to know your numbers and readiness."

"And for this he cannot appear himself?"

"That is right, because he wishes to ascertain the current threat the Olmmoš present to us."

"The Olmmoš?" The warrior looked surprised. "They are as ever—dim-witted as sheep, but as dangerous as starved wolves."

"Have you had much contact with them?" Okta took down a blade and examined its weight.

"We have not formally scouted in several seasons of snow, Okta. You know that. What is this about?" Mord's eyes narrowed.

"The Noaidi would like to know more about the world Outside." The healer winced inwardly at the half-truth. "He would like for you to ready yourselves for this, and to begin as soon as you can. Naturally, he would expect there to be enough Taistelijan to remain here to protect us in the absence of those who would be sent to gather information."

"That would mean training more almai, and it would take time." Mord paused, his mind seeming to wander into logistics. "We could begin as soon as the dark time ends."

Okta shook his head. "That will be too late for the Council of Elders."

"Gods' curses, healer, you know as well as I do a warrior cannot be trained overnight."

"I know, Mord, and said so myself to the Noaidi, but he is determined and would not be dissuaded from his plan. He wants to see action soon."

"If this is his wish, why did he not come to me himself?"

Okta silently thanked the gods for the chance to be truthful before adding aloud, "The Noaidi was concerned a conference between himself and the leader of the Taistelijan would be misconstrued and start rumors and panic among the others."

"And he chose you to deliver this message because. . ."

"Because he knew I once belonged to your ranks, and because it would cause no comment for a healer to enter these halls."

"Am I to understand you will continue to intercede for him?"

"For the moment, yes."

"A lackey and a coward." Mord spoke under his breath.

"Believe what you will, Mord. I do what the gods require."

The Taistelijan snorted. "Tell the Noaidi we will begin training immediately, and when I feel we are prepared, we will begin patrols."

Okta prepared himself to tell Mord the truth—that an immediate search party was required—when the old warrior raised his hand to interrupt. "And the next time you need Kalek to travel at speed, come speak to me first. I cannot always allow luxuries, particularly in light of the Noaidi's new request."

Okta bristled, but resolved himself to honor his commitment.

"And," Mord continued with a malicious gleam in his eye, "you should get used to not having Kalek around, because when he returns he will be needed here."

"I am aware of the sacrifice I must make," Okta snapped, brushing past the Taistelijan on his way out of the room.

He retraced his steps through the workshop, nodding curtly to the warriors. Okta had meant to present the truth, but Mord's insufferable arrogance had undermined his resolve. *Damn the hide upon his bones!* It was only a matter of time before this treachery would be revealed. Okta accepted the consequences for himself, knowing he honored the gods and his vow to them. But what of Kalek?

～

Kalek moved forward, driving himself toward Aillun's Origin, bullying his uncertainty into submission. For Aillun, the journey would have been within her, as a map upon her spirit. For Kalek, however, whose own Origin lay far to the north, the territory he traveled was uncharted.

As Okta's apprentice, Kalek had traveled Outside to visit other groups of Jápmemeahttun. He had also traveled with Mord as part of a training party, but this current journey held dangers he had never before faced. This far south, the chances of encountering Olmmoš increased with each step he took.

Kalek kept himself within the Song of All and, as a further measure, moved within the trees wherever possible. At times, however, he could not avoid crossing through wide-open spaces. In these moments, he offered a prayer to the gods and hoped the Song held him.

After days of silent travel, Kalek stopped and surveyed the area around him. His spirits rose momentarily when it seemed he had reached the place Okta had described, but then an upwelling of grief overtook him. He couldn't help thinking *this is where Aillun died*. He dismounted and peered into the shadows. He knew he was supposed to be looking for signs of the Olmmoš and Aillun's daughter, but more than anything Kalek wanted—no, he needed—to see Aillun, if only her body, one more time, to make amends.

Kalek scanned the surroundings for unnatural formations, admitting to himself that the snows could have easily covered a body, but refusing to let go of his hope. He walked over to the nearest tree and cut a straight lithe branch, trimming its twigs and greenery until he had a staff. Kalek began pacing parallel paths through the wide clearing, using the staff to feel for a solid presence. Although frustration threatened to take control of him every minute, fear of failure kept his feet moving. As the murky day progressed into the night, he continued to search, telling himself he was seeking clues to where the Olmmoš might have taken the baby.

Finally, when exhaustion bore down on him and he could no longer pull the staff free from the snow, tears of disappointment rimmed his closed eyes. If he couldn't find Aillun, how could he ever hope to find her daughter? He'd been foolish to believe he had the necessary skills. He should have left it to Mord and the old guard to do what they had been trained to do.

Kalek looked up at the stars and anguish pulsed through him. He wanted to shout curses at the gods, but knew they would come out as sobs—the pathetic wailing of heartbreak and failure. His feet moved on their own toward his binna. He couldn't make camp where Aillun had died. He pulled himself up on the snuffling beast and snapped the reins. The animal slowly picked its way across the open field. Kalek glanced back over his shoulder one more time. He saw the staff he had used, stuck in the snow where he'd left it. It stood as a monument to his shortcomings. He turned back around and hunched over against the cold. There was nothing for him but to return home.

CHAPTER THIRTY-FIVE

WHEN VANNES FINALLY LEFT, Rikkar gathered enough strength to crawl over to his desk to search for clues as to how his acolyte had succeeded in betraying him. The lock remained intact and its surface revealed no scratches. Rikkar pulled at the locked drawer, and it stood as solid as ever. He pulled forth the key he kept around his neck and opened the drawer, which slid out easily. He felt along the sides and found nothing. He let his hand slide over the bottom and everything seemed in order until he reached the very back of the drawer. A splinter lodged itself in his palm and he shouted in pain.

Rikkar pulled the drawer out. He grabbed one of the tapers and held its flame close to the surface of the wood. A slat in the back rested at an angle. From the underside he pushed upon it and it gave way, revealing how Siggur had obtained access.

In his anger, Rikkar rose quickly to his feet, ready to rush headlong at whatever stood in his way; but the punishment wrought by the Piijkij had weakened him to such a point his legs would not support him. He fell back into his chair crying out in pain.

"May the gods pluck out your eyes and feed them to the ravens," the priest called out to no one.

～

Less than a week later, Rikkar lashed out with the same abuse, this time face-to-face with the object of his rage. Siggur's smirk taunted the priest throughout his tirade. When Rikkar finished, the acolyte pulled from his new vestments a letter from the Vijns of the Order of Believers.

Siggur read the letter, his voice tinged with pious distance. "Rikkar, you are forthwith removed from your position as the Apotti of Hemmela and hereby charged with the crime of treason against the Order of Believers."

"That. . .that cannot be," Rikkar stammered.

"The letter was written by the Vijns himself, made secure with his sacred seal and entrusted into my care to be presented to you." Siggur refolded the piece of parchment into thirds and replaced it in his vestments.

Rikkar struggled against the hands restraining him. "Entrusted! I hope he knows what kind of vulture he has cast favor upon!"

"Apparently, the same could be said for you. In which case, if I were so inclined, I might thank you for teaching me a valuable lesson. But I am not so inclined, and will instead ask you to remove your robes and rings of office." Siggur smiled menacingly. "You will be confined to your quarters. On second thought, you will be confined to my old quarters until someone from the Order of Believers arrives to take you to the Vijns and to whatever future awaits you. I would imagine it will not be a future you will enjoy."

～

Rikkar lay upon a hard bunk, confined to quarters. The injuries of the Piijkij's assault still hobbled his body, but the insult brought back by his acolyte caused him even greater pain. Rikkar's thoughts ran wild with the injustices he had suffered at the hands of these two men. He cursed them to their darkest day. Then, not satisfied, he hurled invectives at the uncaring, unhearing gods, to whom he had pledged himself.

Rikkar could not understand how they could reward all his efforts with pain and disgrace. If his faith had wavered or he had not acted in their example, he could understand how this fate might have befallen him, but he modeled faith, he lived for faith! He had acted only to safeguard true belief. He did not deserve to be cast down.

Unable to believe the gods had deserted him, the priest unleashed the full force of his anger on his recent young acolyte. Siggur was to blame. The fallen Apotti cursed him and his family and anyone who had ever called the blackguard a friend, including himself. How could have been so blind? Had he really been lax in his efforts to safeguard his plans? In truth, he had not. He had taken all possible precautions to keep Siggur's curiosity at bay. He could not have foreseen that the disingenuous cur would break into his desk and steal what he intended to hide.

As he rested upon the bunk, Rikkar wondered how much time he had before someone from the Order of Believers would arrive, but he knew with certainty it would be a matter of hours and not days. Patience did not count among the Vijns's many attributes.

Rikkar knew he would need to find a way to escape Hemmela soon. He shivered. Stripped of his robes, he had little to keep himself warm in the drafty chamber. The priest drew himself up to a sitting position. His muscles screamed from the pain of the bruises inflicted by the Piijkij. He took his time and let the waves of dizziness subside. As he did, he looked about the room for anything that might help him to escape. The spare quarters contained a desk, which housed a few books, a candle, and a small pouch.

Rikkar slowly raised himself up and took a few tentative steps toward the desk. He felt light-headed as hunger tightened its grip. He grasped the back of the chair to steady himself and glanced at the books, but did not pick them—he had no use for worn spiritual texts. Instead, he reached for the pouch. He pulled apart its leather ties and shook the contents upon the desk: a few gold coins, a ring, and a lock of hair. The priest snorted at these meager treasures. In frustration, he swept his arm across the desk and knocked its contents to the floor.

Cast into darkness when the flame sputtered and died, Rikkar groaned at his own stupidity, but then realized he had heard something heavy and metallic hit the floor. It could not have been the ring, which had been made for a child, nor the gold coins. There was something else. Perhaps it had been hidden in one of the books, or perhaps he had not seen it as it lay in their shadow.

Rikkar eased himself onto the floor and, on hands and knees in the blackness of the chamber, he used his hands as a blind man would to discover what had made the sound on the smooth earthen floor.

Rikkar reached out and patted the floor in an arc around his knees. He found the pouch and the lock of hair, and put them to the side. He moved forward and again extended his arm out and around. This time he found one of the coins, which he put in his steadying hand and continued. As he neared the plank that served as a bed, he carefully put forth his hand on the floor until it found an edge. He traced its line along the floor. Suddenly, he felt the unevenness of an object that was neither coin nor ring. He drew himself close and picked it up, shifting it in his hand. A key.

He scrambled to the door on his hands and knees. Breathless from the exertion, he listened with an ear to the door. No sounds greeted his anxious ears. He stayed upon his knees and used his hand to find the lock. With the other hand he guided the key to the lock and inserted it, then slowly turned it. A small spark of excitement shot through him. The initial resistance came with a grinding squeak. When the lock clicked open it sounded like a clap of thunder in the quiet room.

Rikkar opened the door a fraction. No one stood where he could see. The dim light from the hall shone as brightly as the sun after his time in blackness. He opened the door wider to let more light in and squinted as he looked around. He picked up the two gold coins from the floor. They'd still be of some use to him.

Rikkar pulled himself up and carefully peered out of the chamber. His luck held. The corridor remained empty. He took his first few unsteady steps toward the rectory and freedom, moving as silently as his battered body would allow. When he came to the storeroom he searched for anything of use. He draped a dark woolen blanket over his head and shoulders, wrapping himself tightly. Fine robes were meaningless to him now. He moved on to the armory. Without much thought, he grabbed a sword and slid it through his belt, and then rewrapped himself. Though he dearly wanted food, he could not take the chance of entering the kitchen and risking discovery. Rikkar listened at the door to the outside. Nothing. No sound. He pushed it open and exited the temple.

He limped in the direction of the stable, but heard men's voices within and quickly changed course, stumbling into the woods. Rikkar fell headlong into the snow, but struggled to his feet again, striking out on the very same course he had taken less than a full moon cycle before.

Snow clung to each of his heavy footfalls. The laden branches lashed at him as if offering their own punishment for his pride. Rikkar trudged on, praying his escape had not yet been discovered.

∾

Biera was annoyed to see someone approaching on foot from the woods. The figure was shrouded, but not in furs. *Either crazy or a beggar or both*, he thought. Either way, Biera didn't have time or interest to spare him. He continued working until a croaking voice called his name.

Biera stopped, shocked to see the priest standing before him. "Apotti?"

The figure nodded. "Biera, I must get to. . ." he began, and then he seemed at a loss.

Biera shook him from his stupor. "Apotti?"

Roused, he continued, "Biera, I must get to safety."

"Well, Apotti, you are safe enough here. Vannes has gone."

"Vannes?" The priest choked on the name.

"He gave me nothing but bother, but he's gone, and I was glad to see the back of him."

The shrouded man shook. "What do you know of Vannes?"

"I know he's a nasty fellow and quick to use his sword," the farmer grumbled.

The priest lunged toward Biera, taking hold of his coat with trembling hands. "But Biera, how do you know him?"

Biera stumbled back. His face grew hot with indignation. "Well, you sent me there, didn't you? And he returned with me at the other's bidding."

His retort brought the priest up short. Biera watched the man as he seemed to come to some kind of conclusion.

"I must reach the Brethren of Hunters."

"But I've just returned from there," Biera complained.

"Biera, this is a matter of life and death. Your company is not required. I merely need a mount. I will journey on my own."

The farmer shook his head. "But if I give you a mount, I'll have none for myself."

"Then guide me and return with your mount. . .and a reward." Desperation overtook the priest's voice.

"What kind of reward?"

The priest drew himself straighter. "I cannot speak for the Brethren, but I will give you such compensation as my position affords me."

Biera appeared to consider the proposition and then agreed. "I'll take you."

"I am ready to leave," the priest answered.

The farmer snorted. "Ready to fall over's more likely."

"Regardless of my present state, I am ready to depart immediately," the priest assured him.

"You might be ready, but I must prepare the sledge and supplies."

The priest acknowledged this with an impatient shake of his head. He waved his hands as if to encourage his guide to get moving.

~

As Biera headed off toward the barn, Rikkar took in the burned home and the mound of earth carelessly piled up. A wave of regret washed over him. He couldn't undo what he had done, nor could he acknowledge it. Instead, Rikkar said a prayer, then made his way toward the barn.

In its shadowed interior, Biera gathered food and furs and gave his work horse some grain. Rikkar sat upon a chopping stump just within the doorway. What little energy he possessed drained away.

"What is the mound out there?" he asked, knowing the answer.

"It's Sohja's grave," the farmer replied, as he continued to work.

"There is hardly any snow upon it."

"That Piijkij made me dig it up so he could look at the bodies." Biera wheezed, heaving the sledge harness upon the horse's swayed back.

Rikkar swallowed, his tongue thick. "And what did he find?"

"He found one body, is what he found."

"One body?"

"The child's body wasn't in the grave."

The priest leaned forward. "What did the Piijkij say about that?"

"Nothing. He tossed the digger to me and told me to fill in the grave again, and he left."

The two men fell silent. Biera concerned himself with the tasks at hand as the former priest thought of how best to use this information.

Rikkar closed his eyes and nurtured a new hope.

CHAPTER THIRTY-SIX

"HE IS MOVING," THE Noaidi stated. "We have heard him. We have also heard the infant's voice. It is strong."

Mord, the leader of the Taistelijan, nodded.

"I am glad you see the importance of my request," the head of the Council of Elders said. "His continued presence threatens us all, and he may not be acting on his own."

"I understand, Noaidi," Mord answered. "We will leave immediately." His jaw clenched reflexively. "We would not have waited this long had we known."

The Elder frowned. "Do not concern yourself with Okta. His deception is a matter for the Council to consider."

Mord inclined his head once more.

The Noaidi held out his arm. "We will await your return and pray for your success."

Mord grasped the arm and then left the Chamber of the Elders, pleased the Taistelijan once again would wear a mantle befitting their heritage.

~

The binna's slow ambling motion, combined with Kalek's fatigue, worked to lull him to sleep as he rode into the night. When he woke, it was with a start. Dreamy visions of Aillun still swam before his eyes. But it wasn't the visions that had startled him awake, rather it was the Taistelijan chorus, suddenly strong and resonant in the Song of All.

Kalek stopped his reindeer and sat and concentrated. Their voices poured into him as if he were part of them.
We are the Taistelijan.

> *We are the warriors of the Jápmemeahttun.*
> *Our swords serve our kind in death,*
> *Our knowledge our continued life.*
> *We ride with purpose renewed.*

When chorus faded into the background, Kalek realized he was shaking. Mord and his men were riding—no doubt to find the Olmmoš and the baby. But what would happen if they found them? He had himself told Okta he would kill the Olmmoš, and Mord would likely do the same. Kalek felt no concern on that point. But what of the baby? What of Aillun's baby? What would Mord do with her?

A sick feeling of dread crept up Kalek's spine, telling him that, though he didn't know for sure what Mord would do, he had his suspicions and they frightened him. He shook himself free of the dread and spurred his mount to pick up speed. There was still a chance he could honor Aillun's memory. If he could find Mord and his men before they found the child, then perhaps Kalek could get to her first.

CHAPTER THIRTY-SEVEN

"IRJAN." AN INSISTENT AND familiar voice hovered above his head. "Irjan!"

Slowly he came to awareness and found Gunná hunched over him with a worried expression on her face.

The widow sat up and gave him another nudge for good measure.

"I thought you were dead. I could not feel the beat of your heart. Hardly a breath escaped your lips."

"How long?" Irjan asked.

"How long have I been here or how long have you been like this?"

"Both," Irjan shook his head to fight off grogginess.

The widow frowned at him. "I found you this way when I arrived, and I have been back long enough to be worried! It is hard to say how long you were on the floor before that."

"The babies!" Irjan cried. He tried to sit up quickly, but succumbed to dizziness and fell back down.

"They are fine," the old woman reassured him. "But the fire has gone out and they are no doubt hungry. You take your time, and I will start a fire and get some milk for the little ones."

Gunná stood up slowly to let her limbs catch up with her intent. "What happened?" she asked.

Irjan shook his head. "I don't know. I must have passed out. It has never happened before."

"I will make you a strong cup of broth, and that will hopefully put your feet back under you." Gunná laid tinder in the hearth.

Irjan sat quietly and retraced what had brought him to the darkness. It all came flooding back: the voices, the song, and then the one voice—a new one, different in quality from the ones he had heard before. He tried to remember what the voice had said, but the only part that came back to him spoke of a balance of life and death.

But Irjan could not be sure if it was a threat or if it was even intended for him.

When he looked up from his thoughts, Gunná was heading in his direction.

"Come, come," she said. "I will give you a hand to stand and you will sit with us by the fire and get your strength back."

At another time, Irjan would have rejected this offer, but in his current shaken state he welcomed it. She held out her hand and gave him a steady tug, more symbolic than effective. Nevertheless, Irjan rose to his feet and followed her to the fire.

"There now," Gunná said, as she sat down by the flames and ladled out the thick broth. "You drink and I will feed the babes."

Irjan took the offered cup and expressed his thanks.

The old woman brought Marnej into her lap, and offered Dárja some words of comfort. "Do not worry, pretty little one, I will not give him more than you, and next time you shall go first."

Irjan remembered Gunná's journey. "How was your daughter?" he asked, feeling the warmth of the broth in his hands.

The old woman laughed heartily. "Strong like her mother and twice as stubborn. I could no more take care of her than I could you when you first arrived."

"And her baby?"

"Loud and pink-faced like his father," she said with satisfaction. Gunná fed Marnej and he took the milk in greedy slurps. "Since there was nothing for me to do, I kept myself busy with the happenings of the village."

"And what of that?" Irjan asked, more to keep the conversation going than from any real interest in village gossip.

"Most congratulated me on my daughter's son." Gunná put Marnej down and picked up Dárja, busying herself with the girl's milk. She snuck a peek at Irjan. "But I managed to pick up a couple of interesting bits of information." When she noticed he made no reaction, she repeated herself.

"There were a couple of items of note. One in particular you might take interest in."

Irjan looked at Gunná through the steam of his broth. His eyes bored into her. "And what makes you say that?"

Gunná fed the hungry girl, and kept Irjan waiting.

"Gunná, what makes you say that?"

The old woman scrutinized Irjan as she had at their first meeting.

He met her gaze straight on.

"There was talk in the village of a man, a stranger, who was searching for another man, an escaped prisoner." Gunná paused to feed Dárja. "The man he described could have been you."

Her accusation rested between them.

"And what exactly is known of this stranger?" Irjan asked.

"He traveled on a horse, he carried no markings of the Order of Believers, and he wielded a sword," the old woman replied.

"What kind of sword?"

"Does it matter?"

"Yes."

"I do not know enough about swords to answer with certainty," the widow admitted with a furrowed brow. "But some said the markings were like a bird."

Irjan's jaw clenched "An eagle?"

Gunná shrugged. "I do not know."

"And the man himself?" Irjan asked. "What of him?"

Again she shrugged. "I do not know, other than he was described as thick and dark."

Irjan nodded, but said nothing.

"Is it you whom he seeks?" The old woman kept her eyes on Irjan. "Are you an escaped prisoner?"

"A prisoner would hardly be traveling with two babies, particularly if he had just escaped." Irjan shook his head. "And no, I am not a prisoner. I am a man, like any other, with a past and a present and, the gods willing, a future."

The old woman waited for him to continue, but he did not.

"But he seeks you?" she asked finally.

"Yes."

Irjan looked at the widow, fearing there would be no future for him or those in his care.

"Well, it is good, then, no one knows you are here with me." The old woman smiled.

Irjan stared at her for a while, deciding how to proceed. "Do you not want to know why the man is trying to find me?"

"If you care to tell, I will listen," she said. "If you do not, it will not change my feelings toward you and your little ones."

Irjan nodded and looked to the fire for guidance. "I fear I may have brought trouble to your peaceful life."

The widow cocked her head. "I do not hear it knocking. Besides, I did not choose a peaceful life. It chose me when my husband died."

"The man who searches for me is one of the Brethren of Hunters. He looks for me because I broke my oath to them in search of a life free from death."

As Irjan explained how he had left behind the life of a Piijkij for the binna and later for his life on the farm with Sohja, he watched the old woman's face to see if it would change.

"I thought I could have a life that a man should have. A wife and family and job to do that could support life. But I was wrong, and the gods took my beautiful Sohja. I could not return to the other life again. I cannot," he said with finality.

"What will happen if they find you?" Fear showed in her eyes for the first time.

263

"I can only imagine. They can crush my spirit and body, but I will not kill for them again."

"And the babies?"

"I have thought about nothing else since I took this path through the woods. I am at a constant struggle to stay with them for their protection. But am I not also the source of their danger?" Irjan's hands cupped his head, trying to keep his rising desperation at bay.

"I think of escaping to the binna and the Pohjola, but you know as well as I it is no place for babes. It barely allows a grown man to enter and survive."

"And what of your family?" Gunná looked hopeful.

"They are dead, all of them—long ago in my childhood. And my wife's father was all she had, and he too is gone."

"Then you shall stay here and I will be your family," Gunná affirmed.

Irjan shook his head. "I cannot."

"You yourself said the Pohjola is no place to take your children, and for the moment you are safe here." The widow crossed her arms, signaling her mind was made up.

"But what happens when it is no longer safe to be here?" Irjan shook his head, refusing to take what she offered.

The widow leaned forward and rested her gnarled hand upon Irjan's knee. She smiled, kindness radiating in her eyes. "Then you will go and I will care for the children."

"But I cannot ask that of you." Irjan shook his head again.

The widow slapped his knee and pushed herself back. "You would ask it of family!"

Irjan agreed with a shrug of his shoulders.

"I choose to be your family!" Gunná looked at him, daring him to disagree with her.

"But how will you explain two babies in your care?"

Gunná laughed. "I am an old woman with enough grandbabies that to have two in my care would be a very normal thing."

"And if your daughter visits?"

"I have not lived this long life without learning a few tricks. My daughter has not seen the children of her brothers in the north. These babes could as easily be theirs as yours, and for the same reason. The Pohjola is made for stout men with strong hearts and a will to live. It is not for babies newly entered into this world."

"I have no way to repay your kindness and your trust," Irjan confessed.

Gunná smiled at him. "It is what family does."

CHAPTER THIRTY-EIGHT

VANNES TRAVELED NORTH, SNAKING through villages and crossroads, searching for signs of his long-lost, faithless Brother in arms. He had no sightings or hints to where Irjan might be. In truth, Irjan could cross into the Pohjola at any point along the forested edge before the gate, but, if he traveled with an infant, he would need to stock up before entering the wild Northland. However, with no clear trail to follow, Vannes would not enter the Pohjola on his own.

Instead, he doubled back and retraced his steps, checking on new developments during his absence. In Ullmea, he stopped at a travelers' hut along the northern trade route to wait for reinforcements. He had been there before and knew the hutkeeper to be a sharp woman, and a decent cook.

The keeper greeted Vannes with cautious respect. "We welcome your return."

Vannes nodded.

"Do you require lodging for yourself, and perhaps another?" she asked without a hint of greed and only an interest in what would be required.

"For myself alone," Vannes answered, and sat before the fire. "But I expect to be joined by my men, and would like to be informed of their arrival." She nodded and waved to a youth who poured Vannes a warmed juhka, which he took, savoring its heat. The keeper stood across from Vannes and waited to see if anything was needed.

When the Piijkij said nothing, she busied herself with work. Other travelers arrived, as well as a few local men, looking for an excuse to avoid their farms. A pair of them had already had enough juhka to make them loud and boisterous. One bumped Vannes, causing him to spill his drink. The Piijkij stiffened, but the keeper quickly proffered a new drink and a cloth to dry himself.

"Please excuse the interruption," she said, shooing the offender away. The local, however, would not be curbed.

"Who is he that you need to fawn over him, making me move along like some moose blocking the cart path?" the local said, loud enough to be heard.

His friend agreed with a drunkard's nod and mumbled, "S'right."

The hutkeeper shushed the man, but the villager would not be put off. The keeper hissed, "He is the man looking for the escaped prisoner."

"What escaped prisoner?" the drunken friend asked.

Again the hutkeeper tried to quiet the men down.

"Let them speak freely," Vannes called. "Perhaps they know something."

The two men became quiet as all the attention narrowed on them.

"In good faith let me buy them each a juhka," Vannes continued. "Come, sit by the fire with me."

The two, suddenly bashful, tottered over and did as Vannes asked. When they each sat with a fresh drink in their hands, Vannes leaned forward with his elbows on his knees.

"You both look like men who have your wits about you. I am sure little goes unnoticed in your world. I am searching for a man. Perhaps you have seen him?"

Vannes let the flattery sink in, along with their first few deep draws upon their drinks.

The pair, warmed by juhka, let smiles enliven their faces.

The first raised his cup. "You are right about that. We see a lot."

"Well, the man I am looking for is an escaped prisoner who is very dangerous." Vannes regarded the two before him.

"There's nothing dangerous in Ullmea." One drunkard laughed and his friend joined in. Vannes allowed them their joke.

"So you have seen no one? No stranger you did not recognize?" the Piijkij pressed.

"Only you!" the first man ventured, nudging his compatriot for congratulations on his wit. His friend let out a loud guffaw, but stopped when he saw Vannes looking at him.

The man choked on his laugh, causing his friend to roll with hysterical delight. The laughing friend received a quick clap to the head from his compatriot. Vannes's displeasure must have shown because the atmosphere changed and the men seemed to momentarily sober. Vannes leaned back and considered the two men.

"I saw someone at Gunná's," one of them offered.

Vannes leaned forward again, prompting him to continue.

"I think it might've been her son, because he cared for two babies," he went on.

"What did he look like?"

"Well." The man drew out the word for longer than Vannes had patience. The Piijkij coughed.

Roused, the man continued. "I couldn't see him too well. I was checking my traps, and sometimes I stop at the old woman's because she gives me something warm to drink. The door was ajar, which was strange, so I looked in to see if she was there and I saw the man. But only the back of him."

"And?" Vannes prodded.

"Well, he's dark like you and maybe taller. But it's hard to say since I haven't seen you standing."

Vannes stood to accommodate him.

"Yes, definitely taller. Maybe by a head."

"Well, Gunná's husband was a tall man," his friend piped up. "Didn't they call him Ulvá Treetopper? It could've been their son back from the Pohjola."

"No, you are talking about Áivvit," the drunkard answered. "Besides, why would Gunná's son be back? It's the middle of the dark time. He'd still be up there with the binna."

"Still," the other protested, "he could be."

Vannes's mind sparked with interest and possibility. Irjan was both dark and tall—taller than himself by a little less than a head.

"And where does this Gunná live?" he broke into the men's bickering.

"She's a half a league or so to the east of here," one of them offered before draining his drink. "You'll have to search for her place, though. It's deep in the woods. Don't see why she wants to stay out there when she could live with her daughter here."

"Perhaps," Vannes said, "you could check your traps tomorrow and guide me to Gunná's. Your assistance would not go unrewarded."

The drunken man considered. "Well, I wasn't planning to go, but I suppose if there was fair compensation I could be persuaded."

The other interrupted before his friend could agree. "You couldn't find the moss on your backside!" To Vannes, he said, "I will guide you. This drunkard's sure to get you both lost."

The two men fell into a heated argument, fueled by drink and age-old grudges.

Vannes fairly bellowed, "You shall both guide me, and receive compensation for your labors."

The two men smiled at one another, suddenly friends again, and called for more drinks.

The hutkeeper stood with her arms crossed and gave the two a dark look before going off to fetch them their drinks.

~

A shaking in the darkest hour of the morning woke Vannes from a restless sleep. He rose swiftly, grabbing his scabbard.

The hutkeeper jumped back, barely managing not to drop her candle. "Your men've arrived."

Vannes relaxed and she added, "They're in the stables."

Without another word, the Piijkij dressed quickly, eager to meet with the others. Reinforcements meant they could expand the search.

Vannes left his furs in the corner and strode out into the dark main room, past a small, struggling fire. He pulled open the outer door and pushed into the cold dark morning, eager to take advantage of men and a promising lead.

"What news?" he hailed Bihto.

The other Piijkij clasped Vannes's arm in welcome. "The Avr sends men and greetings. He is impatient to have this matter resolved and hopes you have succeeded."

"As am I." Vannes chafed under the implied censure, but he swiftly took command by adding, "There is a lead to follow this morning, but not all are required. I want you, Bihto, and you five to accompany me. The rest, I want to fan out north to the Pohjola boundary. There were no sightings of Irjan along the trade route, but he travels with his child, so he will need supplies."

If the men were surprised to hear of Irjan's child, they did not show it. They kept their thoughts to themselves and prepared their mounts for more travel.

~

The night of drinking had made his local guides all but useless and the delay had soured Vannes's mood.

"There it is," one of them finally said. He started forward, but the Hunter's hand stopped him.

"I can travel from here by myself. No doubt you both must be anxious to get back. I have taken too much of your time already. I thank you, as the gods thank you."

The men, at first surprised, ultimately agreed with a shrug.

Vannes held out his hand and the men took the offered coins. They didn't look at their bounty while he watched, but the Hunter knew that when he turned his back, they would eagerly size up the merit of their day's labor and realize it was enough to keep them in warm cups for some time.

Vannes watched the two locals disappear into the woods, then gave a signal to his own men. The one drunkard had been right; without their assistance he would have never found the old woman's place. A strong billow of smoke rose from the chimney. If the local's report held any truth there could be as many as four within; but only one would pose a problem, if indeed he was Irjan and not the woman's son.

Bihto drew alongside. Vannes continued to scrutinize the hut. "I want the men to maintain a close perimeter." He stopped, watchful of the door. "I will approach alone, but I want you close in case Irjan is within. If he is not, and there is no son either, we must be alert for Irjan's return."

Bihto nodded and withdrew to convey the orders.

Vannes watched the small shelter from the cover of a tree. He could feel his pulse rising. *It could all be over soon.* He heard foot falls behind him. Bihto was once again beside him. Vannes waited a beat before slowly approaching the hut.

At the door, he knocked loudly, then repositioned his hand on the hilt of his sword. If Irjan answered, Vannes would be prepared. The door opened a fraction and he saw an old woman's face, but nothing beyond.

"I have come from Ullmea. I have word from your daughter," Vannes lied.

The old woman cautiously opened the door, revealing the interior. There appeared to be no one but her and two infants, sleeping near the fire.

"What word do you bring?" she asked.

"You are Gunná?" Vannes inquired.

The old woman nodded.

"I was told you might offer me something to warm myself after my journey," the Hunter pressed.

Gunná eyed him with suspicion, but allowed him to enter. She walked behind him toward the fire and only when he was seated did she turn her attention to his request for something to warm himself. "I have nothing stronger than *muorji* tea," she said, placing the water upon the fire. "What news of my daughter?"

"She is well. She had heard tell her brother and his children stayed with you. She wished to know his news and perhaps see him."

The woman's face betrayed her surprise. "How did she receive word of this?" Her voice wavered.

This time, Vannes spoke the truth. "A hunter checking his traps told her he had seen her brother in the house as he passed."

Her eyes narrowed. "Why has my daughter sent you to discover the news? I don't know you to be of her village."

"I was traveling in this direction, and the others were still drunk from the night before. I said I could be of service." Vannes spread his hands in a gesture of benevolence, but he knew her suspicion was growing.

"I do not see him here," he continued quickly, "has he gone back to the Pohjola?"

The old woman gave a non-committal shrug as she handed him the currant tea.

"It must be a burden for you to care for the little ones by yourself," he added.

The old woman's body tightened visibly at the mention of the infants. Vannes took a sip of his tea and expressed his appreciation. He looked at the two sleeping babies, noting that, though close in age, they did not resemble one another.

Vannes pointed at the sleeping infants. "They are not paired?"

Gunná shook her head, but offered nothing more.

Vannes placed his drink upon the floor and leaned forward to examine the two—the dark-haired girl and the pale boy.

"My daughter wishes to know if her brother remains?" The old woman spoke up, drawing his attention.

He looked up. "Yes."

"Well, it is true he was here," she said quickly, "but he has returned to the Pohjola. You can tell her."

Vannes's gaze dropped again to the boy, noting the blanket wrapped around him. It bore the same markings and colors as the shroud of the woman in the grave—Irjan's wife.

Vannes leapt forward from his seat and scooped the child up in his arms. As he did, he saw the woman staring at his sword.

"Let my son's child go," she commanded, though her voice shook with fear.

"Hardly your son's child, old woman. This is the child of a murderer and a traitor."

The woman jumped to her feet. "Marnej is the child of my child! You have no right to touch him or to fill this house with your lies."

She reached to take the baby from Vannes, but the Piijkij pushed her back, and she fell to the floor. The woman cried out, trying to rise to her feet again. She hurled abuse upon Vannes, but the tip of the Piijkij's sword, pricking her throat, silenced her.

"Where is he?" he demanded.

She continued to glare at him "My son is in the Pohjola."

"You know the man I mean, old woman." He dug the point in farther. "Where is this baby's father?"

She gasped when Vannes drew a trickle of her blood, which slowly moved down her neck.

"He is in the Pohjola," she whispered hoarsely.

"You mistake me for someone who has time for the lies of a pathetic old woman." Vannes spoke through gritted teeth.

"He is in the Pohjola," she repeated. "He is in the Pohjola."

Vannes brought his hilt down upon her head in a fit of frustration. The crone slumped to the floor and the small dark child began to wail. He grabbed a thick fur and wrapped the boy in it, then left the hut.

Bihto came out from behind the cover of the trees and strode forward.

"Take him," Vannes commanded, handing off the bundle. "Return with the child to the Fortress. Tell the Avr you bring him Marnej, son of Irjan.

Bihto took the squalling child, "And Irjan?"

"He's not within, but I am certain he is close. Warn the others."

Vannes scanned the surrounding woods. If his supposition proved true, Irjan would, in due course, come to him. If he were mistaken, then the Brethren of Hunters had just acquired its newest recruit.

~

The Avr of the Brethren of Hunters sat in his chambers, reflecting on the state of affairs. A fortnight had passed since the Apotti of Hemmela had crossed his doorstep, hoping to trade information for clemency.

Rikkar had pleaded his case, claiming to be the victim of his acolyte's machinations; that the young man had stolen the letter intended for the Avr and delivered it to the Vijns of the Order of Believers.

Dávgon had listened to the man's excuses and wondered what further use he could be. And then, Rikkar said something worthy of a reprieve.

Irjan's son lives.

Dávgon's mind had jumped to the possibilities. If Irjan's son lived, then Irjan would likely be with him. The child would slow down the traitor's escape. Moreover, a man and babe traveling would be noted, particularly in the dark time. If Irjan sought refuge on his journey, it would not be missed. Dávgon could almost feel the man in his grasp, and yet, Vannes and the others remained abroad.

CHAPTER THIRTY-NINE

KALEK HAD NO TROUBLE following the song of the Tais-telijan. It was strong and proud and all but beat down upon his own chorus. They remained north of him still, but he doubted they could be far. He could almost hear the satisfaction in their song as the word *purpose* lingered in his mind.

But Mord and his men were not Kalek's only concern. For some time he had been aware that he drew close to some Olmmoš village. The woods around him were littered with their hunting traps and he was careful to avoid their menacing iron jaws.

Finally, as night approached, he took shelter in a tight circle of trees, hobbling his binna close, but not next to him, in case the veil of the Song of All faltered. Kalek burrowed deep into the snow, creating a cave, which he lined with evergreen branches. When he was situated for the night, he took out a little bit of food and chewed it absentmindedly, thinking about his next step and Mord.

Loud voices from beyond his encampment caught Kalek's attention. At first, he thought they were the Olmmoš hunters who had laid the traps, but it was far too late in the day for them to be checking on their bounty.

"Vannes really believes he will turn up?" asked one.

"His son is here," the other answered.

"And what if he doesn't?" the first one pressed.

"Then we have about as much chance of finding the Jápmea as finding a patch of summer berries in this snow," snorted the other.

The two moved off, and their voices grew fainter. Kalek quickly gathered his possessions, cursing the Olmmoš and their insatiable desire for bloodshed. He doused his fire and chased after them. The Olmmoš had lives little longer than a mayfly's, and yet the ancient Jápmemeahttun had opted to hide. The Olmmoš should have been crushed like the insects they were.

The two Olmmoš stopped near a small hut. Kalek hid behind a copse of leafless trees, even though he remained within the Song of All. Two more Olmmoš joined the first pair. He strained to hear what they said, but could not. The conversation, whatever its subject, was short and to the point.

The men dispersed.

Kalek stayed rooted, fearing discovery if he moved, and waited. He watched the stars shift in the sky as the cold night stretched out endlessly. Numbness invaded his body, beginning with his feet. He looked around and could not see any of the Olmmoš. Presumably, they lurked about, but where, he could not tell.

In the distance, smoke rose from the small chimney of the silent hut and he assumed there were more Olmmoš inside. Kalek shifted and felt the relief of movement. He did not know how much longer he could or should stay. His training told him the best thing to do would be to tell Mord and the others of his discovery; he could reach out to them in the Song, and if they were paying attention they might hear him, or he could try to find them. Of the two options the first seemed the least risky, but it would put an end to his journey.

As Kalek weighed his options, they became more like burdens than true choices.

Finally, he called out to the Taistelijan through the Song.

You are the warriors.
You are the survivors of the battles of the Olmmoš.
Your sword serves our kind in death,
Your knowledge our continued life.
I see those who would undo us,
I see those who must be stopped.

Kalek waited and listened. He heard.

We hear the call.
We answer with our swords ready.

He'd made his choice. Mord would find him and it would all be over soon. Kalek resigned himself to the future awaiting him.

He sighed and his own breath was overshadowed by the cry of an Olmmoš. Mord and the Taistelijan must be closer than he had realized. Another loud gasp came from a different direction, followed by the eerie quiet of death.

Behind Kalek, an Olmmoš man rushed past, calling out, "He is among us! He is among us!"

The door to the hut flung open and a man emerged with his sword drawn.

"He is among us!" the runner cried, breathlessly.

"From which direction does he approach?" the other asked.

"From every direction!" Fear made the runner's voice shake.

"Have you seen him?"

He shook his head. "I saw Viellja and Hánnas dead. I have not seen the others."

"Go find them and warn them to be on alert," the man from the hut instructed.

The foot soldier did not seem eager to carry out the task, but in the end he did as ordered.

The man from the hut scanned the surroundings and seemed to be listening to the sounds around him. Kalek did this as well, believing the Taistelijan would soon be among them, but he did not hear the familiar sounds of his kind. Rather, he heard a shriek from the far edge of the woods.

"Irjan," the man called out. "Do not hide in the trees like some Jápmea."

Silence reigned. The man circled the hut, keeping his back to it and his sword facing out.

"Irjan," he called again and before he could make another sound, another man came bounding out of the woods. It was as if he had been invisible and had suddenly appeared.

Kalek gasped.

The apparition had his sword drawn and stopped directly in front of Kalek's line of sight. He was tall and dark and dressed like one who ran with the binna.

"Vannes," the man called out. "You have grown, but only a little."

"And you, Irjan, smell like the binna," the man named Vannes sneered. "You betrayed your Brothers for *this*?"

"I would not expect you to understand, Vannes. But I would find better company in a pack of wolves than with my so-called Brothers. Wolves do not use their young for bait." He raised his sword to eye level.

"Yes. Your son, such a fragile little thing, but don't worry, Irjan, he is safe. The Avr will raise him to be a true Piijkij, not a traitor like his father."

Irjan lunged at the taunt and Vannes countered easily. Their swords clattered as the edges met. Each man put all his effort into the traded blows. The two raged across the snowy clearing.

Vannes pushed forward, upsetting the other's footing, and brought a crushing blow down upon the prone man.

With only a second to spare, Irjan managed to bring his blade up enough to parry, but he would not be able to move or protect himself from the next blow.

Kalek, acting on the whispered voice of instinct, jumped up from his hiding place and released himself from the Song of

All. He plunged into the disquiet it brought—the heaviness, the lifelessness—but he pushed on. He ran forward with his sword drawn, bellowing "No!"

Kalek reached the pair before either could react. He pushed his sword deep into Vannes's half-turned back. Kalek felt the man's flesh and bone resist and he pushed harder, determined to stop only when the man was dead.

Vannes gasped and tried to reach out with his sword, but his life force drained and he crumpled to the ground beside the other Olmmoš.

Kalek trembled. His sword was lodged deep in the man's back. Irjan got up quickly, ready to continue the fight. Kalek reached for his sword and tugged at it. It refused to move. Quickly Kalek placed his foot upon the Olmmoš's back, leveraging himself to pull his weapon free. A tremor of revulsion ran through him, but he did not have time to give it much thought.

Irjan faced him, sword drawn. "Do not stand between me and my child," he growled. "I have killed more of your kind than you have seasons of snow in this life."

"Do not think that because I saved your life I will not gladly take it," Kalek spat back.

Irjan gestured toward Vannes's body. "I know what he wanted from me, but I do not know what you want." The man stared at Kalek, his sword raised to heart level.

Kalek felt skewered by the Olmmoš's scrutiny, but he did not look away. Instead, he tried to calm his pounding heart. Unfortunately, Kalek had control of neither his mind nor his body.

"If you have nothing to say to me, then I will end this now, because more than one life is balanced here," Irjan said without emotion.

"Aillun." Kalek shouted her name. "Did you kill her?"

"Aillun?" Irjan's sword dropped slightly, as if the name struck a blow upon him.

Kalek took advantage and moved quickly to bring his own sword to Irjan's neck. The man did not try to stop him, but he also did not back away.

"Did you kill her?" Kalek repeated.

"What is she to you?"

"Answer me!" the young almai shouted.

"I did not kill her."

"But you were there when she died!"

"Yes, I was there when she died."

"The child?" Kalek pressed on. "What did you do with her child?"

"When last I saw her, she lay within the hut alongside my son in the care of a woman who loves them as her own." Irjan glanced over his shoulder toward the hut.

Kalek's attention wavered as he glanced toward the yawning door. His soul wanted to believe the man, as if the Olmmoš's words could remove the black stain upon his heart, but his mind cried out with suspicion.

He tossed his head and nudged the man. "Move ahead."

The two moved cautiously forward. At the entrance to the hut, Irjan looked through the opening and saw an old woman slumped in her chair, her arms bound behind her. Heedless of the possible danger, he rushed inside, leaving Kalek behind. He went around and cut loose the old woman's bonds. She tumbled forward, and Kalek reached out in time to catch her. The almai leaned her back and Irjan gently patted her face.

"Gunná," he whispered. "Gunná."

The old woman's breathing was shallow.

The man patted her face and called her name once again.

The woman's eyes fluttered, and when she could focus, she called out. "Irjan, it is not safe! You must leave. There is a trap. They took your son. I could not stop them." Her warnings came out like water rushing in a spring stream.

"Do not, Gunná," Irjan soothed her.

Tears flowed down the lines of the old woman's face. "I could not stop him. He took Marnej. Please forgive me."

Irjan hugged the old woman as she continued to cry.

Irjan held Gunná away from him. "How long ago did it happen?"

"I cannot be sure because I awoke on the floor. The fire was cold and Dárja was crying." The woman looked over her shoulder. "She was so cold and weak with hunger. I thought I had lost her too, but she is stronger than she looks." A hint of pride filled her voice.

At the mention of Dárja's name, Kalek followed the woman's gaze until he spied a small wad of blankets in the corner. He scrambled forward to pull back on the swaddling. Kalek blinked, staring, as he took in the babe's dark hair and eyes—so much in Aillun's image. He gently laid a hand upon her and offered a prayer of thanks to the gods, before letting his song rise, he hoped, to Aillun's soul.

I am the seeker.
I come to find the truth.
I have lost my heart, but know I will find her legacy.
I have chosen the path of warrior and healer.
I will balance life and death.

From somewhere beyond the little hut another voice called out in the Song of All.

We answer with our swords ready.

～

Irjan saw the Jápmemeahttun's head snap up.

"We must leave immediately," the Immortal said, grabbing Dárja into his arms.

Gunná protested and Irjan leapt to gather up his sword.

"I do not have time to explain," the Immortal cried. "If we stay, you will die!" He looked directly at Irjan, and Irjan saw truth in his face.

Irjan gathered the frail woman into his arms and headed toward the stable. "Follow me," he called.

"Irjan, put me down. I cannot go with you," the old woman spoke up.

"Gunná, no!"

She cut him short. "I am old, and now not as sure of myself as I once was." She faced the Immortal. "I know what you are. My Ulvá spoke of your kind and told our children fanciful stories of those who lived forever within the Pohjola. I suspect Dárja is more of your flesh than Irjan's, and can only guess how this has come to pass." She shifted in Irjan's arms. "It is time I rejoined my family."

Irjan reluctantly placed the woman on her feet and stood up, kissing her forehead as he did.

She put a hand on his cheek. "I am sorry for Marnej. Now go!"

Irjan started for the door and motioned to the Immortal who held Dárja. They followed him to the barn, where he harnessed the nag to the sled, grabbed the reins, and pulled them out into the open.

"You guide us away," he ordered. "If we are followed, I will fight. Take Dárja back to your kind."

Irjan hopped onto the back of the runners and the Jápmemeahttun cracked the reins. The lone nag may have been spry enough to carry an old woman on her errands, but it struggled to pull the added weight.

Irjan looked over his shoulder and saw nothing, but knew he could not trust his eyes alone. If they were followed, he could only assume the Immortal who had saved him did not travel alone and it was his kind who lurked in the shadows. Irjan could not fathom why this Jápmemeahttun had decided to intercede, but did not doubt he had his reasons.

~

Kalek kept their pace consistent through the small rises and falls of the cart path. He listened to the sounds around them, but did not enter into the Song of All. He hoped the little one would not either. He looked carefully for landmarks. Although he had not passed along the road, he had been near it. He needed to retrieve his mount. He could not let the beast perish, and they needed its strength and speed if they hoped to escape from Mord and the others. The idea of escaping struck him as a cruel jest. There would be no escape in the end, because he needed to bring both the baby and the man back with him to the Jápmemeahttun, and, sooner or later, Mord would confront him. But he would rather it end that way than in the woods.

Kalek brought the sled to a stop. "I have another mount tethered beyond these trees. Move on and I will catch up. We can join or switch the animals."

Irjan nodded, and took the space vacated by Kalek. He snapped the reins and headed north once again. Kalek traveled through the forest, taking a shortcut, ducking under branches heavy with snow, and was rewarded with a cascade of cold powder upon his head and shoulders.

Kalek shook off the snow as he continued. For an instant he entertained the thought that perhaps Irjan had doubled back to escape from him, but he dismissed it. To turn back would guarantee an encounter with Mord and his men and, although Kalek hadn't had time to explain exactly who and how many followed, he had conveyed the danger.

Kalek ran up a small crest. At the bottom he saw his mount, nestled in the copse where he had rested briefly the previous night. He ran down the berm and loosened the reins of his hobbled binna. The beast snorted its warm breath in protest.

Kalek patted its neck, saying softly, "Ride. I promise you will feed later. But for now, ride!"

As they approached the cart path, Kalek hoped he had traveled far enough north to intersect the path Dárja traveled with the Olmmoš. The binna stomped its hooves, seeming anxious to move. Kalek patted its neck, reassuring it. In the distance, to the southwest, Kalek could see the sled approaching. He nudged his reindeer and the beast galloped toward the oncomers.

Kalek waved the sled over and quickly set about adding his binna to the harnessed nag.

"We must hurry," Kalek said. "We must keep a steady pace through the night. One can sleep while the other steers us ahead. We can put more distance between us and Mord and the other Taistelijan."

Irjan remained seated. "You have not told me what you want with me. Why did you protect me from Vannes, and why do you want to protect me from your own warriors?"

"Does it matter?" Kalek demanded. "If you want to live. . .if you want to save your son, then your best chance is to trust me."

Irjan scoffed. "I could kill you now."

"Yes," Kalek agreed. "You could. But then you would be facing a troop of Taistelijan alone, with Dárja to care for. I do not know you, but I know of your kind and your capabilities. Yet, I saw you fighting your brother for what you held dear. We are not so different. I too honor what is close to my heart. As you have said, you could easily kill me, and yet I am willing to close my eyes and trust I will wake. If I can do that for you, can you not do that for me?"

Irjan seemed to consider Kalek's challenge. "You will need to give me direction so I know where I am to go."

"For the moment, it is best we head north, as quickly as we can," Kalek answered.

Irjan snapped the reins and they started with a jerk. Kalek held on to Dárja. Neither looked back, wanting to put the past behind them, and yet, neither looked forward to the future awaiting them.

At the small hut, Mord and his men found the snowy woods littered with the bodies of Olmmoš. The leader of the Taistelijan knelt beside one after another and examined their wounds. There had been no fight, no exchange of blows. The footprints suggested one deadly strike felled each of the Olmmoš. They probably never saw their attacker. The killer had been swift and efficient. Had they arrived sooner, they would have faced these Piijkij themselves, and part of the old warrior regretted the lost opportunity.

Mord shook himself free of what might have been. What mattered to him was that the Olmmoš they sought still traveled freely and, it would appear, with impunity.

Mord stood and walked to the body closest to the hut. Unlike the others, this one had fought back. The snow was trampled all around, and a sheen of sweat had crystallized upon the dead man's face. He picked up the Olmmoš's sword and held it for closer inspection. A sword of the Piijkij. Mord spat upon it.

"The hut is empty," one of his men called out. Mord let his attention drop from the sword. He was about to let it fall back to the earth when he thought better of it. If proof were needed by those who lacked the courage to confront the Olmmoš, he wanted to be prepared.

"Gather the swords," Mord called out, watching his men respond to his command. It felt good to be out in the world. *Good to have men and a purpose once again.*

Mord entered the hut and appraised its shabby contents. By the cold hearth he saw a basket of woolen knitting and swaddling clothes. He picked it up. The knitting was a baby's bunting. *The child and her captor must have taken refuge here recently.* He looked back through the door to the feet of the dead Olmmoš. Clearly, he and his men were not the only ones tracking the man and the child.

He walked out of the hut, stepping over the dead Piijkij. He stood still and listened. The earlier voice remained silent. Mord had not yet questioned his men to see who among them had given the warning, and the matter would have to wait. They needed to track the Olmmoš who'd prevailed among these Piijkij. He could not be allowed to live. As the Noaidi had predicted, this man had the potential to bring death and destruction to their kind.

"Gather the mounts," Mord called out. "We follow the trail leading northwards." The binna of the Taistelijan warriors stomped and grunted, as if begging to be unleashed upon the forest. When Mord gave the command, they thundered off. *The time for hiding is over*.

～

Weak from blood loss and fearing discovery, a man held his breath. When finally alone, he crawled out from the undergrowth. He slowly stood, shaken by everything he had witnessed. Not only had their ranks been decimated by one of their own, but the Jápmea once again took up arms. The man could only hope he would survive long enough to relay this information to the Avr. Though they had failed to apprehend Irjan, they would find their place and fight the Jápmea as they once did. The time of the Brethren had come.

CHAPTER FORTY

KALEK AWOKE TO QUIET murmuring. The sled was stopped and the Hunter hunched over the baby. At first, he couldn't make out his words, but then, as he became more aware, he realized their importance. The Olmmoš spoke the birth song of the infant—the song which defined the the soul of each individual Jápmemeahttun—the song which had come from Aillun's heart at the time of birth and her transformation.

As he listened to each tender word, it dawned on Kalek that this Hunter was the child's biebmoeadni —the one entrusted to raise the child. But it was impossible.

"Where did you learn that?" he demanded.

Irjan, who had been focused on Dárja, turned around in surprise. "Aillun taught me."

The sound of her name pierced Kalek's heart, and his guilt flared as doubt and distrust.

"How did you come to be with her at her Origin?"

The Olmmoš stopped repacking his provisions. Finally he said, "I was tracking her."

Kalek lunged forward and tore the supplies from his hands. "We go no further until you explain yourself."

~

Anger flooded to the surface, but then Irjan let it go. Although it was not the best time to walk through the past, he knew they couldn't move ahead until he gave the Jápmemeahttun an explanation.

"For twenty-five seasons of snow I was one of the Brethren of Hunters. I pledged an oath to kill those of your kind who survived after the wars. I was good at what I did." Irjan broke off, expecting an outburst from the almai.

When none surfaced, he continued, "There came a time when I could no longer do what I had been asked to do. I walked away into the Pohjola and spent six seasons of snow with the binna. After that, I sought the company of men, believing my past to be behind me. I became handmate to Sohja, I had a child, a son, and I lived as a farmer. But my past was not forgotten by others, and they sought me out and tried to convince me to return to it. I refused." Irjan paused again.

"I came home one day to find my wife and son dead." His voice broke. "I was desperate when I heard Aillun's song. I recalled the tales and legends of my childhood, and I put my faith in them. I prayed they might be true; prayed they might save Marnej. I tracked Aillun. I found her and the warrior. They believed I had come to harm them and they fought bravely, but I had come not to hunt—I came to find life. I did not know what would happen."

After a long silence, Kalek said, "Your son lived and Aillun died. She could not transform."

Irjan nodded. "The old warrior burst into light and I ran forward with Marnej in my arms. We entered the light as Aillun began to give birth." Irjan's voice dropped to a whisper. He felt sadness draining his will to continue. His actions appeared rash, and now, all for naught.

If he could have accepted his place in this world, none of this would have happened. If he had remained a Piijkij, Sohja and Aillun would both be alive, Dárja would be with her mother, and Marnej, though he would not be the son of Irjan, his soul would be in this world, perhaps with a family who could have loved him more and kept him safe.

Had he continued to be an agent of death, he would have saved the lives of those he loved most. However, he could not go back and undo what had been put into motion so many seasons of snow before; he could only go forward to whatever future awaited, and try to save his son from his past.

"But how did you hear her?" Kalek asked finally, his expression caught between anger and confusion.

"I heard her," Irjan replied, searching within himself for the answer. "I don't know how, but I heard her. I heard the warrior as well. I cannot explain. I also knew you or someone else from your kind searched for me. It is as if the wind carried the voices to me."

Kalek snorted—with disgust or impatience, or perhaps a combination of both.

Suddenly, it became important to Irjan that this almai understand him.

"I cannot tell you how or why it happens, but it has been this way since I was a child. When I trained to become a Piijkij, I was the smallest and weakest, and yet the most effective, because I could see and feel and hear things which the others could not. I did not question the meaning, because it did not matter to me. The only thing that mattered to me was to kill as many of your kind as I could, as payment for the death you brought to my family. When I walked into the Pohjola, I heard voices—songs in the distance. I believed they were a fabrication of my own lonely soul. But when I sought Aillun, I realized it was something else— something I could not explain. I could not only hear her, but I lost time. I traveled through time that was not my own, and yet I found myself within my body as if I had never left it." Irjan waited to see if the young Immortal understood, but the skepticism on his face drove Irjan to keep speaking.

"And not only could I hear Aillun, I could see things which had happened in the past."

Irjan thought about the warrior's vision and the baby. He had believed the warrior had left a helpless babe to die, but Aillun had corrected him.

Irjan met Kalek's gaze. "She asked if I could hear the Song of All."

The almai's eyes widened.

Irjan picked up Dárja and rested her against his shoulder.

"I think I can," he finished, shushing Dárja softly.

～

Kalek's chest rose slowly as he struggled to find breath. He stared at the Olmmoš and realized the danger the man represented. Wisdom told him this man should not be allowed to live, that he must be killed for the sake of all Jápmemeahttun. None would be safe until he was gone, and yet, he could not use the knife at his side to bring an end to it all. He knew, in his heart, he couldn't kill this man. It would have been a final betrayal to Aillun. She had made this man the keeper of Dárja's song, and he couldn't take that away from either of them.

Kalek handed the reins back to Irjan. "We follow the eastern track of the stars now."

CHAPTER FORTY-ONE

THE AVR WAITED IMPATIENTLY for the return of his men. In particular, he awaited the homecoming of Irjan, the prodigal. In his quiet moments, Dávgon relished the idea of breaking the man's will. He knew he could easily do it. He had the man's son, and this would be his failing. Vannes, however, did not return. Instead, Heidid made it back, wounded, to report that Irjan had mercilessly killed their men, and Vannes had died at the hands of a Jápmea.

Resting in the arms of one of the Brethren, Heidid looked up into Dávgon's face as he spoke.

"Vannes had all but defeated Irjan," the exhausted Piijkij whispered, "when suddenly, as if from the air itself, the Jápmea sprang forward and thrust his sword through Vannes's back. The coward plunged it deep, and Vannes never had a chance to face his attacker."

Heidid attempted to spit with contempt, but only brought a bit of spittle to the corners of his mouth.

"Irjan faced the Jápmea and surrendered without cause. Then the two disappeared into the hut. I don't know what became of them, but as I struggled to regain my feet, the woods filled with reeking Immortals. I did not fear death at their hands for my own sake. But I did keep cautiously to myself, knowing I must get word to you."

The dying man panted, trying to get enough air to continue. The Avr knelt beside his Brother. In this public place, his men had given their leader a wide cordon of privacy, despite their curiosity.

Though weak and overwrought, Heidid was clear that the Jápmea once again rode as warriors.

"None are safe," he coughed, then smiled. "The time of the Brethren has come."

Dávgon, the Avr of the Brethren of Hunters, looked down at the face of his man and watched the light leave his eyes. The man's soul went on to the gods, but a smile remained upon his lips.

As the Brothers stepped forward to remove Heidid's body and prepare it for honors, Dávgon reflected upon recent events and what they presaged. Blood began to course through his veins as his breath came quicker and his heart began to beat faster. Their time had come. The Brethren would rise to meet the Jápmea.

Aloud he said to the retreating backs of his men, "The gods are on our side."

~

Bávvál was preoccupied. The High Priest of the Order of Believers scanned the reports before him, which contained news of the movements and sightings of the Piijkij. The Hunters had been seen traveling the Pohjola, which puzzled the High Priest. No one but reindeer herders willingly went to the Pohjola.

What are the Hunters up to? he wondered.

Were they actually searching for Jápmea? And if so, why? The peace remained unbroken. And though the Immortals likely roamed about unseen, they seemed to have little interest in the affairs of the Olmmoš.

Bávvál looked at the letter from Rikkar, the traitorous former priest of Hemmela. It annoyed him the man had escaped his due, but it did not change the fact he had engaged the services of a Piijkij to locate the Jápmea. Bávvál could not see why the priest chose this particular man, but clearly the intrigue centered on him, perhaps at the behest of the Brethren of Hunters.

Admittedly, Bávvál had been too lax in his supervision of the Brethren, but he had believed they would die a natural death. No marauding Jápmea had bothered the Olmmoš in a generation or more, but he should have expected the Hunters would not fade away like their prey. Now, he needed to confront the problem before it became more of a threat.

To his advantage, Bávvál had the village Hemmela to act as an outpost from which to monitor the Brethren. He had no doubt Siggur, the newly appointed Apotti, would remain loyal only as long as it played to his advantage. But there were ways to ensure that the young man's ambition was curtailed to the proper avenues.

The focus, however, needed to remain on the Brethren. Their numbers, though greatly reduced, still represented a force to be reckoned with; particularly when one considered their training. For too long, Bávvál had not concerned himself with the methods of the Brethren, but now, in light of their looming presence, he saw his shortsightedness. The fierceness of their training and their isolation combined to make the Brethren a loyal and a lethal force; moreover, the deeds of their glorious past served to bolster their pride. The Avr, no doubt, used the tales of Piijkij heroism to sow a seed of renewed ambition among his men.

But the Brethren would need a reason. They could not step forward to claim power out of hand. The Olmmoš, though seemingly placid, had more of a friend in the church than they had in the Piijkij. The Hunters' isolation had hurt them there. The Brethren were not called upon to aid the sick, bury the dead, or pray for the living. This was the role of the church. If called upon, the Olmmoš would side with the Order of Believers against the largely unknown usurpers. But Dávgon, the leader of the Hunters, was no fool. He must have surmised this. The Jápmea must then be the Hunters' gambit for power.

Well, the Order of Believers would be ready for them, Bávvál thought.

The power over the souls in Davvieana belonged to the gods and therefore to the Order. They would have their own army of loyal Olmmoš trained and ready to meet the challenge of the Brethren. Bávvál drew his ink and vellum close. He would immediately call on the village priests to prepare their charges for the future. When he finished writing, he held the document to the fire and looked at the dark curling marks.

"I will see the end of the Brethren," he said out loud. But before the nascent vow could soothe him, another thought shattered his thin veneer of confidence.

Unless they have already found the Jápmea.

Part Four

THE SIDE OF THE GODS

CHAPTER FORTY-TWO

"Einár, cast your anger at me! Kalek did my bidding based upon my falsehood," the ancient healer entreated, stepping between his assistant and the Noaidi. "He believed he acted on the behalf of the Council of Elders. He should not be punished for my actions."

"Of all, Okta. . ." the Elder started, but seemed unable to make his way through his conflicted feelings.

"I sent Kalek because I did not trust Mord. I did not trust he could see through his own ambition—his own lost glory—to make the right decision."

"What of you?" the Elder demanded. "What about your ambition? Were you not serving it by believing you were right, by interfering in the plans of the Council of Elders? What about your own glory, Okta?"

Okta took a step forward. His eyes were slits, his jaw tight with tension. He wore the mask of a warrior, not a healer. "Before you accuse me, Einár, look to yourself. You may speak with the gods, but you are not one of them. Perhaps you have forgotten all the bloodshed. If you remembered, you would not be resurrecting the Taistelijan with such blind faith."

"No, Okta! I was blind to you, but I will not make that mistake again. I told you I do not seek war."

"But you started on that path! Each step you take brings you closer to it."

"I act to save our people!" the Elder boomed.

The healer took a step closer, "I act to save lives. Are we that different then, Einár?"

The Noaidi did not answer, but rather stormed out of the room, leaving Kalek shaking.

~

"He cannot be allowed to stay," a voice spoke up.

"He cannot be allowed to go," another rose.

Murmurs grew among the Council of Elders.

"What really needs to be said is that he cannot be allowed to live," someone growled. The voice belonged to Mord.

"It is not for you to decide, Mord," Okta, the healer, replied softly.

Mord turned his grizzled face toward the old medicine wielder, ready with his reply, when the Noaidi interrupted.

"For more time than many can remember, the Song of All has been our solution and our haven from the Olmmoš, but I fear we cannot rely upon it in the future." Whispers rose all around him. He raised his voice to be heard over the din. "I do not seek war. I merely seek to keep our kind alive. I cannot, however, assure that blood will not be shed."

The whispers grew in volume, yet no one dared to raise his voice among the group, not even Mord.

The Noaidi continued, "The Song of All has given me a glimpse of the future, but not its details. The past, however, is something we all know well. We once believed ourselves to be on the side of the gods. We cannot make that mistake again. This Piijkij will remain with us until either his worth or his threat can be proved. Only then will his fate be decided."

The healer bowed his head and kept his feelings hidden, while Mord let all those around know of his disapproval.

The Council of Elders stood and slowly withdrew.

The Noaidi remained standing, stilled by the burden of responsibility. "Mord. Okta. Remain," he commanded.

The two aging warriors halted, then approached from opposite sides.

In these two, the head of the Council of Elders saw the difficulty their kind faced. If war were needed, they would be unprepared, and if peace required more sacrifice, the risen warriors would be hard to quell.

"We have before us a dilemma which must be resolved before we can move forward," he said.

"Einár," the healer began, but the Elder's raised hand stopped him.

"Okta, let me be clear, this is not a discussion. That time has passed. You have managed to insert your will, and we have among us an Olmmoš and the child."

Disgust pinched Mord's face.

"Your disapproval is noted, Mord, and perhaps it will soothe your pride to have the Olmmoš as a prisoner."

The Elder turned his attention to the medicine wielder, expecting an objection.

Okta did not protest; instead he asked, "And what of the child?"

The Elder considered the matter. "She is one of us and she will live as we do. She will live with her biebmoeadni and she will be observed."

The healer cleared his throat.

"You have an objection, Okta?" the Elder snapped.

"It would appear the child's guide mother is the Olmmoš." The healer lowered his eyes humbly, his look of satisfaction going unnoticed.

～

Irjan sat alone in his cell. When he'd first arrived among the Jápmemeahttun his mind had been bombarded with voices and songs overlain into a cacophony. Irjan could not find a quiet moment within himself and it almost drove him mad. As time passed, however, the voices moved to the background and he could finally hear his own thoughts. But his thoughts did not bring him comfort or relief; instead, they pulled him into the darkness of guilt and remorse. He was as much the prisoner of his own anguish as he was the ward of the Jápmemeahttun.

Irjan's every waking thought centered on his lost son. So much had been sacrificed for Marnej to breathe life, and that joy—that indescribable joy Irjan had felt—had been crushed. He sat upon the wooden plank that served as his bed and hung his head into his hands. He pressed the heels of his palms deep into the sockets of his eyes, trying to wipe away the images emerging from his darkest imagination.

He tried to reason with himself that if the Brethren had taken Marnej, they'd kept him alive, if only to further their own plans. But Irjan feared those plans. Surely their interest in the child went only so far as to exact revenge. Irjan had walked away from them, from his duty, and worse: by his choice of actions, he'd killed one of his own. Kalek might have been the one to drive a sword through Vannes, but Irjan would have done the same, given the chance. The Brethren would spare Marnej only until they managed to avenge themselves.

Irjan raised his head and looked about his cell. The dizziness and blurring he had initially experienced was gradually fading. Now when he looked about, he could clearly see that his cell shared all the same qualities of an Olmmoš prison: stone, bars, and stout wooden door. The solid door before him hung by sturdy hardware, and neither light nor shadow filtered through its edges. He could hear the muffled sounds of movement and voices, and it served to push him further into the realm of the forgotten. He expected no friendly face to present itself any time soon.

Irjan lamented not seeing Kalek or Dárja since they'd joined the Jápmemeahttun; but then again, their homecoming had not raised the heralds. Kalek had tried and failed to bring them directly to his master. As soon as their trio entered the stronghold, guards set upon them. While not welcome, they certainly were anticipated. When the guards' firm grip had closed upon him, Irjan found he lacked the will to fight, and he let himself be led away without a struggle.

It was only when the door to his cell opened that the reality of his imprisonment sparked him to life. Irjan twisted and pulled and tried to free himself from the guards' steely hands, but the harder he fought, the more his own body seemed to revolt.

The guards threw him into the cell and he landed on the floor in a scattered heap of arms and legs. He scrambled uneasily to his feet and was met with the force of the slamming door. Irjan beat his fists against its hard and ancient surface. His protests went unanswered, fueling his rage. He continued to pound upon the door until he wore his skin raw. Finally, he slumped to the floor and became lost to the sensations flooding his body and soul.

Now, Irjan understood the length of his days as the time between his meals. Two meals marked the passage of a day, and instead of the sun and stars to chart time he had the quick knock and the opening of the door to tell him another bit of his life had slipped away. His meals were placed on the floor in front of him, and then the armed guards withdrew to leave him to his solitary repast.

Irjan could not complain of the food's quality or content. It was more than enough to sustain him. But the question nagged him: sustain him for what purpose? He marked what he believed to be the days of his confinement, and they had grown and grown to fill the moon cycles leading up to Skábmamánnu and its darkest days.

Early on, he believed each knock signaled his last breath. Irjan had prepared himself to meet his death with evenness and acceptance, but the summoning had not occurred. Over time, he began to wonder about his fate. If death had been the order, it would have been swift; the Jápmemeahttun would not have wasted precious resources on his continued existence. They must have some purpose for him, and yet he could not be sure what it might be.

Perhaps they planned to use him against the Brethren?

But if they wished to have the secrets of the Hunters, they had yet to extract them from him. They had not even spoken to him beyond the simple questions of his basic needs. Food arrived and his pail of waste was taken. Otherwise they left him alone to pace the small confines of his cell and count the stones that imprisoned him. A bed, a bucket, a blanket, and some furs for warmth, these counted as the elements comprising his world.

A loud knock stopped Irjan's musings. He sat and stared at the door, awaiting the expected delivery of his food. The door opened and, as usual, the points of swords entered his chamber first, but this time, no food appeared; rather the face of an aged Jápmemeahttun came through the hulking backs of the guards.

Irjan looked at the unfamiliar face and noted its craggy lines, topped with a shiny pate and blanketed by a closely trimmed beard.

Irjan rose quickly to his feet, causing the guards to lurch forward with swords leveled. The ancient one raised his hand in a gesture of forbearance. He lowered his hand and the swords haltingly dropped away.

"We have much to talk about," the Jápmemeahttun said. The sound of his voice startled Irjan. It seemed to come from both within and outside him. "But this is not the most appropriate environment for our discussion." He regarded Irjan's narrowed and suspicious eyes.

"I see your mistrust," the Immortal continued. "I guarantee your safe return, if you give me assurance you will perpetrate no violence in a foolish attempt to free yourself."

Irjan inclined his head.

The Immortal nodded to the guards. Their ranks parted and from them emerged buckets of steaming water and folded garments and furs.

"You will be escorted to my chambers when you have readied yourself," the ancient one said, then left the cell. The guards withdrew as well, and the door closed with a firm thud and a scratch of the bolt.

Whatever their motives, they trusted him only within limits. As he stripped off his soiled and ragged clothing, he acknowledged the wisdom in this. He dripped hot water from the soaking rag down his shoulders. He sighed at the feeling of something he once considered so normal. Sohja always had a bucket of boiled water waiting for him after his day's toils. She would take time and care to remove the grime and sweat caked upon him, even in the coldest of days. His lost, lovely Sohja. He had brought her no good, and she had given him a son, a home, and a family. This painful thought pierced him. He was like the stag brought low by a single arrow.

Irjan plunged the rag into the bucket and quickly and fiercely scrubbed himself as if each of the red marks he made served to absolve him of his crimes. When he finished, he dressed and then pounded upon the door with his fist. The sound of the bolt pulling back seemed to echo in the small stone cell. The door opened and, as it widened, he stepped forward to face the questions that dogged him.

Irjan walked down the corridors flanked by guards. As he emerged into a wide hall he looked around for clues to where he found himself. The sound of voices filling the hall gradually faded to a low murmur as those around noticed him. Irjan felt their stares. He knew their whispers concerned him, and could only imagine what they thought. He had killed their kind—killing had been his life. Surely they must hate him. They could not know he had forsaken his past and the path of death. Nor did they know the turmoil his past actions caused him. It would have been meager compensation to offer his suffering to them.

Irjan looked about at those he passed. He could sense fear in the ones who lowered their eyes, and contempt in those who met his gaze. He finally stopped looking into their faces and walked forward. Irjan and his escort crossed the hall and entered another long series of corridors that ended in an alcove. It appeared as if they stood at a dead end, when before them the panels of the wall parted and hands pushed him forward into a large, torch-lit room.

Irjan looked up. It seemed the roof had given way to the sky and its stars, and yet the room was warm. He looked about again, to gain his bearings, and he realized the guards surrounding him had been replaced with a retinue of old Jápmemeahttun. They guided him forward as if he lacked a will of his own. Finally, they stood before the Immortal who had visited his cell.

"Irjan of the Piijkij, you stand within the Council of Elders," the Immortal intoned. "This may be the first meeting of our two kinds outside the bounds of violence since the Olmmoš brought hatred into our world." The Council of Elders drew back in an ever-widening circle from Irjan, until he and the Immortal were surrounded.

"We know of your deeds and there are many of us who believe your death would be small compensation for what you have done," the Elder intoned.

Irjan nodded, accepting the scales of judgment that balanced his future.

The Elder continued, "There are others who believe your death would ensure our safety. But I wonder, Irjan of the Piijkij, what you believe? What do you know of your destiny?"

Irjan waited to see if he was expected to answer or if the questions served another purpose. When nothing more was forthcoming, he cleared his throat and answered. "It would appear my fate is in your hands."

The Immortal remained motionless as he considered the response. "Were you ever master of your own future?" he asked. An odd look of interest graced his expression.

Caught off guard by the question, Irjan gave himself a long moment's reflection. "I have made the choices which have shaped my present," he said finally.

A slow, enigmatic smile spread across the Immortal's aged face, but he did not immediately reply. Instead, he beckoned Irjan to join him on the low bench in the center of the room.

"No doubt you must be curious about your future with us," the Jápmemeahttun said. "But we, the Council of Elders, are as interested in the past as we are in the future, and we believe much can be learned about one from the other. We have heard much about you from Kalek. He has told us Aillun spoke to you of the Song of All. He said you can enter it as well."

Irjan nodded, but said nothing, wary of what might happen next.

"I wonder if you can see the significance of this?" the Immortal asked. From the quiet circle of the Council of Elders a hushed concurrence rose.

This question obviously troubled the other members of the Council.

Irjan quickly scanned their faces. "I am more a threat to your kind now than I ever was as a faithful Piijkij," he answered, trying to bring the subtle probing to an end.

The Immortal nodded. "Yes, it is true."

"Then why have I been left to live?" Irjan pressed.

"That is something best seen with your own eyes," the old one responded.

Irjan looked around the room for something or someone to shed light on the inscrutable response he had received, but noted nothing different about the room or those there with him.

Irjan sat still, waiting for something to be revealed. The Immortal quietly studied him. The silence of the room overwhelmed him with its portent, but it was not really silence. Irjan could hear something, but its nature eluded him. He quieted his thoughts and slowed his heart to hear the refrain lingering in the air.

Finally, as if emerging from the deep water of a lake into the world above, he heard what seemed to be all around him.

We are the Elders.
We are chosen to guide.
We listen to the voices of the gods.
We seek to avoid the mistakes of the past.

From deep within him, Irjan felt his own voice rise up unbidden, to add another refrain.

I am the son of the gods.
I am brother among my kind.
I started my life at a crossroads.
I traveled the winding path of those who are lost.
I will return to fulfill the forgotten destiny of one who should not exist.

Suddenly, Irjan saw a young man running through the woods, calling out playfully to someone hidden from him. From the air behind a tree, a beautiful young Jápmemeahttun appeared and reached out to grasp the young man in a long embrace. She rested her head against his chest and he kissed the top of her head. Somewhere beyond his ability to comprehend, Irjan felt a pain radiating from deep within him. When the two broke their embrace, Irjan saw she was pregnant. The man knelt before her, lowering his grief-stricken face; this time she placed a kiss upon his crown before disappearing into nothingness.

The image then seemed to melt and blend with another, more familiar to him—one he had seen not so long ago. He saw a Taistelijan with his sword drawn and a young Olmmoš—a Piijkij. The two fought without mercy, but in the end, the Taistelijan bested the Olmmoš.

Irjan's heart beat faster, just as it had the first time he'd witnessed this vision. He watched the wounded man struggle to crawl away, helpless as the Immortal thrust the dagger into his chest.

With a start, Irjan recognized the dead Olmmoš as the same heartbroken man of his previous vision. Though still youthful, in death the man wore a mask of infinite loss. Irjan's attention wandered back to the Taistelijan as he found the child and uncovered its face. Irjan realized the child must belong to the couple of his vision.

He watched the Taistelijan walk away, only to stop and retrace his steps. The Jápmemeahttun picked up the child, great sobs racking his large frame, and headed back through the woods. Irjan felt his inner mind jump, and the warrior reached a crossroads. The familiarity of the place tugged at Irjan, but he was more in tune with what his eyes showed him than what nagged his intuition.

The Taistelijan walked purposefully until he came upon a hut set off in a clearing, then carefully moved toward the door and gently laid the babe before it. The warrior gave the infant a long look before withdrawing into the ether.

Irjan's vision stayed with the child. A plaintive cry rose from the small body and he felt drawn to it; he wished he could soothe it. He peered into his vision, frantic for a sign of anyone, but distrusting the shadow ahead that seemed to be moving toward the hut. Then the shadow distilled into the shape of a man and his cart.

As the man drew closer, he slowed to a stop, then sprang from the wagon and ran toward the crying baby. When he stood up with the child in his arms, Irjan gasped at the familiar shape of his jaw and the wide set of his eyes. It was a face he never thought he would see again. A tremor ran through him.

Irjan waved to get the man's attention, but the man's focus stayed with the infant. Irjan tried to move forward to touch the man's shoulder, but he found he was rooted in place.

He cried out, "Father! Father!"

As these words entered the Song, Irjan was pulled headlong from the scene. His stomach rebeled, and suddenly he found himself seated in the circle of Elders with the Immortal's hand firmly grasping his.

Irjan stood, shaking. It took all his strength not to fall to his knees. He expected the ancient one to say it had all been a dream, but the Immortal did not speak, nor did he release his hold on Irjan's hand.

"Have you always known?" Irjan asked, his shattered voice a hoarse whisper.

"No." The old one shook his head.

"How can that be?" Irjan struggled to understand.

"We do not know all the measures within the Song. Only the gods do, and they are revealed in their own time. Sometimes the refrains are known and the meaning is unclear. In your case, Irjan, you were revealed to us only when you joined Aillun."

"That is why I could hear her. Why I can hear Dárja." Irjan felt a growing understanding rise up in him. "That is why I could find your kind when others could not."

Irjan felt the Immortal tense, but his face remained unchanged.

"Yes. You are both Olmmoš and Jápmemeahttun. You were able to find us because you are a part of us." The revelation hung about the room like the smoke of a wet fire.

"Djorn killed. . ." Irjan whispered, but could go no further.

The fractured parts of the Hunter warred with each other as he tried to grasp the story of his birth.

"The words I sang earlier. . .?"

"Were given to you by your oktoeadni?" the ancient one provided.

Irjan nodded, unable to continue.

"We believe she gave you your song. And before you ask, I must tell you Máre did not return from her Origin."

"Like Aillun," Irjan said, barely above a whisper.

"Yes, like Aillun."

"What about. . ." Irjan was going to ask of his son Marnej, but stopped himself. Something made him hold back the name, as if it would protect his child from some unseen force. It could be that Kalek had already mentioned him, but for now Irjan would remain silent.

The Elder looked at him, waiting for him to continue.

"What about now?" Irjan said. "What is to become of me now?"

"I have been persuaded to keep you alive."

The matter-of-fact tone brought Irjan abruptly to his present condition. Whatever kindness he had seen in the being before him was an illusion of his own making. Irjan remained a threat to the Jápmemeahttun. The Council of Elders drew close to Irjan, and it became clear his time in their midst had come to an end. What they hoped to achieve by revealing his Origin, he could not tell, and he was not ready to look within himself to see how this knowledge might have changed him.

Instead, as the guards led him from the room, Irjan thought of his son and what must be done to save him.

~

The Council members watched as the Olmmoš retreated. When the door to their chamber closed, they spoke in turn.

"What do you make of the prisoner?" one asked.

"It is hard to say what the truth will do to him," the ancient one answered. "If we are to bind him to our cause we must give him reason to feel he is one of us and not one of them."

"And if that cannot be done?" another member asked.

"Then he will be killed," the Noaidi answered without hesitation.

CHAPTER FORTY-THREE

SINCE HIS RETURN, KALEK had been quiet and withdrawn. When Okta tried to draw out the events of the journey, Kalek answered in short clips. He presented facts, but not feelings. The old healer worried he had asked too much of the young almai and hoped, in time, the youth would seek him out to discuss what continued to trouble him. But for now, he would keep to the work of healing.

"Kalek, could you check to see what stores are low?"

"Yes," the almai answered, walking off without a backward glance.

Okta worked quietly, cutting dried herbs and combining them for different ailments. He had all but forgotten about Kalek when he finally reappeared.

"I have a list of what is needed, but much will have to wait until spring. There are a few plants I can forage for now, unless you have a more pressing task."

Kalek's blank expression troubled Okta, but he said nothing about it.

"I have nothing that needs immediate attention," the old healer answered, and his young assistant nodded and left the room.

~

Kalek knew Okta worried about him, but he couldn't share his feelings. He was angry at his master for making him responsible for the turmoil welling among their kind. Those who knew of his actions blamed him for bringing danger to their door. Kalek, in turn, dodged everyone. Old friends may have wondered about this change, but what could he say? He had failed Aillun and betrayed his own kind. What could they offer him in comfort? And Irjan? What of Irjan? He'd brought the Olmmoš to his imprisonment. What of his fate? Kalek could've asked Okta, but it would have meant talking to him, and he wasn't ready for that. He wasn't sure he could contain his resentment.

Kalek moved quickly through the corridors, keeping to those he knew were sparsely traveled. He desperately wanted to breathe in the cold air of the forest. He needed something fresh and new, and not tainted with regret.

Kalek drew his furs closer to him and pulled his hood up over his cap. When he got to the door, the guards let him pass unhindered, but he felt their rancor. Kalek had defied Mord. He would be forever marked by it.

Outside, his feet crunched upon the hardened snow and Kalek stopped to watch the white fissures grow. It was like surveying his life—one misstep and it all had fallen apart. He shook his head to free himself from the gloom that traveled with him. Enough darkness already filled the world. Kalek put his mind to his task and searched for the plants he needed: *ránesjeagil*, the grey reindeer lichen which Okta boiled to soothe breathing, and the *uulo* shrub, for a tea to calm stomachs and nerves. Kalek gently brushed the snow from the ground-hugging plants, looking for the pointed, clustered leaves. Moving forward, he set a rhythm of bending and standing that finally allowed his mind and soul to find some peace.

The wind picked up, swirling loose snow into the air. Though his satchel hung largely empty, Kalek knew by the cold in his bones the hour had come for him to return to the great hall and Okta. Reluctantly, he retraced his steps.

A creaking slit of light greeted his knock, then the door opened wide and Kalek walked in. As the door closed behind him, one of the guards murmured, "We should have left him out there."

Kalek faced him, as if he faced all the accusations leveled upon him. "If I had the courage, I would have stayed out there," he answered, then slowly walked away.

Kalek was so immersed in his own remorse he did not notice the head of the Council of Elders approaching. Kalek had not seen the Noaidi since his return. The unannounced meeting seemed to bode ill.

"Noaidi," Kalek said, bowing before the ancient one.

"Okta told me I might find you here."

It did not even occur to Kalek to ask how he knew the right time to find him there. He assumed any number of spies kept the leader informed. These were his new thoughts, ones he would have never before considered possible. But now, the darkest notions did not surprise him as they ought.

"I will walk with you as you bring the herbs in your care to your master," the old one said.

Kalek nodded, and the two moved forward through the torch-lit corridors. The Noaidi's silence disturbed the young almai, and Kalek snuck a couple of quick glances at the Elder. As they neared the healers' chambers the Noaidi stopped and confronted Kalek.

"I think it is time you honored your duty to Aillun's child. She should know and learn from her biebmoeadni. You shall take the infant to the Piijkij. Aillun chose him and we must respect her wish." The Elder paused before adding, "I hope you know, Kalek, I am entrusting you with a great responsibility in this endeavor. The Piijkij must feel a connection to us, for all our sakes."

The Noaidi stood still, but seemed to vibrate with energy.

"You will take the child and explain to Irjan his duty as a bieb-moeadni, and then you will ensure he provides the proper care and instruction."

Shaken by the encounter and unable to fashion artifice, Kalek blurted, "But why me?"

The long, thin hand of the Elder reached out and rested on Kalek's shoulder. "Because he just might trust you."

~

Troubling dreams plagued Irjan upon his return to his cell. His nightly visions were filled with those he had known and loved, and those he had not known but somehow recognized. He wished for peaceful darkness in his mind. In truth, he wanted oblivion. Were it not for Marnej, he would have figured out a way to achieve it. Irjan, however, could not bring an end to his life when there was a chance of freedom for his son.

Lost in his despair, he failed to hear the knock upon his cell and the creaking of the door as it opened. When he looked up, Kalek stood before him, holding Dárja in his arms. The guards closed the door behind them, and Kalek walked forward, holding out his arms, waiting for Irjan to take the infant from him.

Irjan hesitated, watchful of the Jápmemeahttun standing before him. Finally, he stood and took Dárja into his arms, looking into her dark eyes. He staggered back slightly, feeling like he'd been stabbed. Kalek moved to steady him, but Irjan regained himself and let the longing he felt for his own son melt into his feelings for the girl in his arms.

The child's gaze locked on his face. It seemed to him that she was considering him for some important but unknown task. She smiled, teeth peeking through the gums, and he realized just how much time had passed since he'd last seen her. He bounced her in his arms and she smiled even wider.

"She has grown," Irjan stated, watching the baby.

"Yes," Kalek answered.

Irjan looked up at the almai. "I don't understand."

At a loss, Kalek answered truthfully, "You are her bieb-moeadni."

Irjan's brow furrowed.

"Aillun chose you to be Dárja's guide mother," Kalek explained.

Irjan shook his head. "No. She did not choose me, Kalek. You know that."

"Perhaps it was not her choice, Irjan, but she gave you Dárja's song. It does not change the fact you are the child's biebmoeadni."

"And what does that mean?" Irjan asked pointedly, all the while caressing the infant's back.

"You are her guide in this life, her teacher, her comfort."

Irjan shook his head. "I am in prison, Kalek. I am a Piijkij—a killer. How can I. . .What can I teach this innocent?"

"How is this different from when you traveled with her and your son?" the almai asked, wearily. "What would you have taught her in that life that you cannot teach her in this? Were you any less a killer then? Were you any freer then than you are now?" Kalek reached out and smoothed the dark hair upon the child's head.

"Irjan, I cannot tell you what you should offer the child. It is for you to decide. I can only tell you what I would do with this gift. I would treasure it."

Irjan tried to hand back the child. "I do not ask for this, Kalek. It should be you, if anyone. You are the one who can share her mother with her."

Kalek pressed Dárja back into Irjan's arms. "Her birth mother is gone and would have been gone regardless if she had survived. You are her biebmoeadni, Irjan; there is nothing more to say on the matter."

"Did you know?" Irjan asked suddenly.

Kalek slowly faced him.

"Did you know?" He repeated forcefully.

Kalek shook his head. "No. I did not know."

"Do you know what will become of me now?" Irjan thought about the future awaiting him.

"Yes, Irjan." Kalek reached for the door. He opened it and walked through. Over his shoulder he answered, "You are to be the biebmoeadni for Dárja." He closed the door behind him and Irjan was left alone with the child.

~

Kalek strode down the corridor, his mind still with Irjan and Dárja.

"I see you are the deliverer of the innocent to the slaughter," a voice hissed from the darkened hall ahead.

From the gloom, a large figure emerged—Mord, the Taistelijan tasked with finding and killing Irjan.

"I do as I am asked," Kalek answered, hoping to avoid a further confrontation.

The warrior blocked his path. "Yes, that's right, you are the slavish underling of that coward, Okta." Mord's voice rose as he spoke. "You both betrayed us all!" He spat at Kalek.

Kalek tried to pass the warrior, but Mord blocked his way.

"What conniving plan has he set in motion now?" Mord demanded.

To silence the Taistelijan, Kalek said the only thing he could. "I am here at the request of the Noaidi. If you have an objection then you should bring the matter before him."

A look of fleeting doubt played across the ancient warrior's face and he shrank enough for Kalek to continue—but before he could pass, he felt his shoulder pulled backward, and the hot breath of a fierce whisper on his ear.

"Do not count upon the protection of others more powerful than you. Who knows what the gods have fated for them."

With his shoulder released, Kalek fell forward and stumbled away. He gave every appearance of being anxious to be rid of

Mord, but at the first tee in the corridor he pressed himself to the wall to listen. When he felt certain no one followed, he quietly retraced his steps toward Irjan's cell.

Kalek got within range to hear Mord demanding the guards open up the prisoner's cell. Dread shot through Kalek, and he propelled himself headlong down the corridor in search of someone who might be able to stop the warrior.

～

When the door opened, Irjan cautiously stepped back as Mord's hulking frame entered. Mord seemed to take up all the space in the cell, and Irjan felt very much like a trapped animal.

"I see the very best a Piijkij can do these days is to hide behind a babe," the warrior taunted.

"I do not hide. It is clear you can see me, and I cannot help but see you," Irjan answered calmly, giving a moment's glance to the child in his arms.

Mord sneered. "You like to parry with words."

"You find me armed with nothing else." Irjan shifted to the left to have a smooth wall at his back. The infant yawned and rubbed her eyes with tiny, balled fists.

Mord laughed to himself. "Apparently she is no more impressed by you than I am."

"I make no claims that require notice. And yet, you are here." Irjan gave Mord a wry smile. "That is, of course, unless you pay a visit to each of those who find themselves behind bars. It is one way to assure yourself an audience for your. . .I might say bulk, but then your bulk could not be missed, or wit, but your wit is too small for any space but a tinderbox, and so I would say for your sleight of hand, that makes others believe you have skills worthy of being called a warrior."

Mord lunged across the tiny room, arms outstretched to throttle Irjan. Just as he did, the door to the cell flew open and the guards rushed forward to restrain the warrior. He shrugged off their hold and once again went for the prisoner, who had stepped quickly out of the way.

"Mord!" a voice in the doorway bellowed.

The warrior whirled around. Okta stepped forward with his sword drawn.

"I see your shadow ran to you for help!" Mord hissed. Then he let out a single mirthless chuckle. "Ha! You hold your sword like the feeble old one you are. See how it trembles. Be careful, Okta. You might cut one of the guards." Mord laughed again. "At least you will be able to stitch him back up again, Healer." The last word he spit out like foulness in his mouth.

The guards surrounded the Taistelijan and, though they seemed conflicted, escorted Mord toward the door. Okta kept his sword raised and cross-stepped in a circle to make way for all to exit.

Mord looked over his shoulder and said, "Don't think this action of yours will go unpunished."

"I will keep it in mind, Mord," the healer answered, "as long as you remember I have dispatched more souls to the gods than any other, so including yours will not add sleepless nights to my numbered days."

When the guards left, Okta lowered his sword and faced Irjan. The healer regarded him and the child wordlessly. His expression gave no indication of his thoughts.

"Thank you," Irjan said. "I don't understand why you stopped him. But I thank you."

"I did it for all our sakes," the other said, then left the cell, closing the door firmly behind him.

Irjan sat down upon the cot and rested Dárja on his furs. He stared at the door, wondering what would happen next. When time passed with no more interruptions, he turned his attention to Dárja's long, deep breaths. While her small chest rose with surety and evenness, Irjan felt his own breath catch and grow ragged. Heat grew behind his eyes, and before he could stop them, tears rolled down his cheeks, dropping away from the edge of his chin like the first drops of rain upon the trees.

Without thinking he began to sing:

Daughter of the gods.
Sister among the Jápmemeahttun.
You started your life at your Origin, with sadness and joy as your com-
panions.
You braved dangers and met enemies and can see the truth of friend-
ship.
Go into the world to meet your destiny, knowing that the stars watch
over you.

His heart took over when his voice faltered, and for the first time since discovering who he truly was, he opened himself fully to the Song of All. It flowed into him and he followed strands until their melodies ended. On the edge of it all, he knew there was another song that needed to be sung. It rose from his heart effortlessly.

Son of my heart.
Vessel of a father's soul.
You journeyed into the realm of the dreams of the dark sky,
And traveled back in a blaze of light.
Go into the world to meet your destiny,
And know that you have been touched by the gods.

CHAPTER FORTY-FOUR

WHERE WAS HE? THE Avr of the Brethren wondered.

It had been several moon cycles since Bihto had brought Irjan's child to them, and Dávgon had been anticipating Irjan's appearance ever since. And yet, the traitor had not shown himself. *Had he truly abandoned his son after all his previous effort? Or, was he biding his time among the Jápmea?*

As a precaution, Dávgon had reinforced the guards at the gates. He knew his men would be vigilant. The bitter taste of treachery was not quickly forgotten, and if any still harbored compassion for the man, the massacre in Ullmea served as a reminder that tender thoughts received no rewards. Irjan had not forfeited his bloodlust; he'd merely exchanged the blood of his Brethren for that of the Jápmea.

Bastard, Dávgon swore to himself.

Dávgon could accept villainy as a cold reality, but not when coupled with insult. A rogue Piijkij was something for the Brethren to deal with swiftly and quietly, but Irjan's reappearance in a brackish little village, embracing the calling of a farmer, had made it impossible. It was as if he enjoyed taunting the Brethren.

And now, there was much more than pride at stake. The Order of Believers knew of him and their weasel-chinned High Priest had used the intelligence to press for more presence in

Hemmela. Dávgon was certain the Vijns's men watched their comings and goings.

Well, he can watch all he wants.

He walked through the halls and accepted the solemn greetings of his men, searching the faces until he found the one he sought.

"Ah, Rikkar, just the man I was looking for."

"My Avr." Rikkar bowed.

"Join me in a walk about the inner circle."

The leader of the Brethren strode ahead, knowing the scurrying man could hardly say no. Dávgon could have asked the man to strip naked and bleat like a sheep and he would have done it. Rikkar was neither able as a fighter, nor useful as a servant. The best the disgraced priest could offer was to trade on what little information remained from his former position within the Order of Believers.

At the gate to the inner circle, the Avr walked out from under the low roof. He turned his face heavenward and felt the sickly sun upon his face. The snows had given way, but just barely, and their fickle nature couldn't be trusted. Still, after the darkness, the weak light almost blinded him.

"You have been with us many moon cycles now, Rikkar."

"Yes." The man foundered upon the single word.

The Avr began to stroll, forcing the other to follow. "How do you see your place among us in the future?"

Rikkar hopped to catch up. "My place, my place is of your choosing."

The Avr nodded. "You are right. It is of my choosing." He continued to walk but let the silence grow between them. Finally, he said, "I have been thinking about your usefulness. When you first came to us with news of our missing Hunter, I was surprised and suspicious, but then ambition can make brothers of even the rat and the raven, and while our plans have not borne the fruit we had hoped, indeed quite the opposite, I believe there is still something that might redeem you."

"I am ready to be of whatever service you deem necessary," Rikkar quickly answered, although his voice wavered.

"I am glad. Come closer and let me explain what I believe to be your redemption." With a tight smile, the leader of the Brethren held out his hand to the one-time Apotti of Hemmela.

CHAPTER FORTY-FIVE

"KALEK, EVERY DAY I am here I feel the pull of my son!" Irjan protested. "I am powerless to stop whatever harm may have befallen him, and it is killing my soul."

The two sat in a small courtyard outside the prison, surrounded by four watchful guards. Dárja tottered between the two of them. Her steps grew surer each day.

Dárja looked to Irjan for approval. When he did not immediately acknowledge her, she furrowed her brow until he realized his oversight. He swooped down, picked her up, and held her high in the air until she laughed. With her good humor restored, he placed her upon the ground and she wandered off toward the guards.

"I know it is difficult for you, Irjan," Kalek said, "but I can offer no platitudes to make it better. I cannot say he will be fine, and I cannot say your circumstances will change, but you should take comfort in the service you do Aillun's child and be grateful for that."

Kalek's reprimand stung.

"I am sorry. I did not mean to offend you or Aillun. I am truly grateful for my time with Dárja. If not for her, I would have gone out of my mind, but she is more than a distraction to me, Kalek. She is the daughter I might have had, and I cherish her."

Kalek nodded. "Good."

They both sat quietly watching Dárja make a game of running head first into the legs of the guards and then looking up at them in surprise. The stoic guards were no match for the sweet little mánná and smiled helplessly at her antics.

"Look," Kalek said, pointing in the direction of the guards. "She can win over the stoutest of souls."

Dárja had a force about her that could not be denied, and Irjan knew it went way beyond her sweet smile and endearing manner. She drew souls to her as if she had cast a spell upon them.

"Is she like her mother in that way?" the Piijkij asked softly, keeping his eyes on the child.

Kalek shook his head. "No. Aillun was not one to draw attention to herself. She was quiet and shy, well suited to work with herbs. She found comfort in using her hands. She had an open heart and I was lucky enough to know it."

Silence grew between the two as they listened to Dárja's voice cooing and laughing beyond them.

"Is she yours?" Irjan asked, broaching a subject he considered delicate and fraught.

Kalek's brows furrowed. "She is all of ours," he said slowly as if the question was new to him. "She is Aillun's, Djorn's, mine, yours. We all have our part in her life."

"But you are her father?"

Kalek shook his head again. "I had my role. I could not give Dárja life as Djorn did. I am not the one to guide her to her future as you do." He stopped and observed Irjan. "It is not as you have experienced. That is perhaps why I cannot give you the answers you need with regards to your son."

Irjan nodded, trying to put himself in Kalek's place. "If Aillun had returned. . ." He started then stopped. He tried again. "If Aillun had returned, what would she have been to you?"

"We would have both been almai." Kalek sighed, as if he had revisited this thought many times in the past.

"Sometimes the birth so transforms the nieddaš that as an almai her thoughts and feelings are altered, and the almai starts a new existence in body and in spirit. Other times, old feelings are preserved and lovers are reconnected."

"What about you, Kalek?" Irjan asked, realizing for the first time that Kalek had been both mother and father in his life already.

"I did not have a heart-pledge with anyone before my journey to my Origin. It was easier for me."

Irjan watched Dárja, who still played with the guards. "Was it easy for you to give up your child?"

"Yes, I was an almai and could not be her biebmoeadni."

"But you still have feelings for your child?"

"Yes, I have feelings for her, as I do for Dárja, as I did for the child for whom I was a guide mother. I have feelings for all, but my roles were done and I had new ones to honor." Kalek waited a second before adding, "Perhaps it is time for you to consider this as well."

Dárja came running at them before Irjan could reflect on his answer. Kalek grasped the little one, spinning her as she loved, and then placed her within Irjan's arms.

"I must get back to Okta. We have much gathering to do to restock what the winter depleted. I will return later to take Dárja to her quarters."

Kalek stood and walked between the guards who opened the gate for him.

Irjan's mind swam with thoughts and questions. The explanations Kalek had offered left him wondering about himself. He was supposedly half Jápmemeahttun and yet he could not imagine becoming a man from a woman or forgetting he was a father.

Irjan would always be Marnej's father and the boy his son, no matter the distance between them.

Kalek longed for the quiet of the woods to calm him, and the herbs to give him purpose, especially after his conversation with Irjan. He'd never put into words the events of his life and he was unnerved by the feelings that had surfaced.

Kalek entered Okta's work room without knocking to find Einár, the Noaidi, in deep conversation with the healer.

"Excuse me," Kalek said, attempting to withdraw.

"No, no, Kalek," the Elder called to him. "Please enter. Okta and I have finished our discourse and I would like to speak to you."

The almai flushed as he reentered the room. "I will knock in the future," he apologized to his master.

The ancient healer waved his hand to dismiss the idea. "There is no need to knock to enter your own quarters." He gave the Noaidi a long, meaningful look. "Shall I give you some privacy, Einár?"

"My interests do not exclude you, Okta, unless you feel Kalek would benefit from a private conversation."

"It is for Kalek to decide, Einár. I have no say in his actions."

"If only it had always been that way," the Noaidi said, letting his voice drop.

Okta appeared to ignore the comment, moving to his work table and making preparations for their afternoon's foraging.

Kalek grew more uncomfortable as the silence in the room deepened. He felt as if he were reliving his ill-fated return. Now, just as before, Okta and the Noaidi stood in these chambers, with himself caught between them.

The spell that had taken over the room broke when Kalek heard the Elder's voice.

"What news can you give me of Irjan?" the Elder asked.

Kalek hesitated, peering between Okta and the Noaidi. "He feels the burden of his confinement," he answered finally, "but he is heartened by his time with Dárja. The little one grows quickly."

"And what do you speak of when you are together?"

"We talk of the past."

When Kalek did not expand upon his statement, the Elder pressed, "What of the past concerns him?"

Kalek was about to answer that it was Irjan's son, but something stopped him from mentioning Marnej.

"Each of us has many regrets," Kalek said instead. "Irjan struggles with a past he cannot change and a present that gives him no peace."

The Elder picked up a flask and shook its contents. "Does he harbor resentment toward us?" The old one's eyes slid down from the flask to meet Kalek's watchful ones.

"Not that he has expressed to me. He is trying to understand what it means to be half of one and half of another. He is very much an Olmmoš in his thinking and in his heart."

The Noaidi's face clouded with concern.

"I do not wish to suggest that he feels he is one more than the other," Kalek spoke quickly. "It is more the case he does not know what it means to be Jápmemeahttun. Today, I tried to explain our life changes and I knew Irjan could not fully understand my intent. Perhaps he cannot, because he is also Olmmoš." This last comment seemed to be what the Elder wanted to hear, because he nodded as if to say, 'it is as expected.'

Kalek's stomach knotted and he quickly added, "Who can know what it means to be one of a kind?"

If the Elder heard him, he did not show it. Instead, the Noaidi looked toward Okta, before thanking Kalek for his service.

When the Elder left the room, Kalek stood alone with his master, waiting to hear Okta's opinion of the conversation. But Okta continued checking the jars and bowls.

"So you have nothing to say," Kalek finally prompted.

Okta shook a small jar in his hand. "I think I have made a complete list of what we need. If we leave now, we may be able to finish within the day and not have to stay abroad at night."

"You know that's not what I meant."

The healer gathered his bags and knife and made to leave the room, but then stopped and faced his assistant. "What would you have me say, Kalek? I have risked you for my own device. I will not continue in that vein."

Kalek gathered his own satchel and knives and joined his teacher at the door. "So you will not comment on the Noaidi's questions?"

"What do you wish to know, Kalek?"

"I want to know to what end I am being used. I want to know if I am bringing harm by what I do."

"I suppose it remains to be seen," Okta said with a sad smile, as he walked out toward the wilderness.

CHAPTER FORTY-SIX

"I NEED INFORMATION," THE AVR said. "Nothing a man of your skill couldn't find out."

Rikkar assured the Avr he would gladly do whatever he could for the Brethren, who so generously protected him.

"I want the writings of the Old Ones." The Avr cut him short.

Believing the Avr toyed with him, Rikkar hedged. "But they were burned. You know, as well as I, the Order of Believers destroyed all the Jápmea texts."

"Surely not all of them, Rikkar. And what of the writings of your own learned men? Those must still exist." The Avr's lips curled with dubious superiority.

Rikkar was at a loss. "But I cannot access the libraries of the Believers."

"I am not asking that of you," Dávgon replied.

"Then from where?"

"From Hemmela."

"But there is nothing at Hemmela." Rikkar stopped short, wondering how the man had known about his own library, and then, with a shudder, remembered Vannes. Vannes had been in his chambers. *What had he told his leader?*

Worried now he had fallen into a trap, Rikkar proceeded with deference and caution.

"Perhaps it is a matter of a question I might answer."

"I want to know the ancient gathering sites," the Avr said flatly, making it clear there would be no easy escape.

"But I don't know where to begin," Rikkar confessed.

The Avr's taut jaw became even more squared. "A priest, as well-versed as you are in the ways of the Jápmea, would know their ancient sites; those places the Believers cleansed with fire to build their temples upon."

"But not all temples were built on gathering sites," Rikkar said unwittingly, realizing his error only too late.

"Begin with maps. I want detailed maps. When you have provided them, then you will concentrate on the ancient writings and whatever else you have hoarded."

There was nothing else to say but, "Yes, Avr," which Rikkar did, bowing.

~

Rikkar now sat in his chambers thinking about what the Avr of the Brethren had asked of him. On the surface it seemed simple, but if he peeled the layers back, it was evident he would be placing himself at great risk.

He cursed his ambition. He had sought out the Brethren for their raw strength and power and their knowledge of the Jápmea. He had believed that with their help he could free himself of the capricious and slow-witted among his own order; in the end, however, Rikkar had to admit it was he who had proved to be dull and dense. Were it not for his misguided notion of his own importance, he would still be within the safe confines of Hemmela—warm, respected, and blissfully unaware his next breath might be his very last.

He paced the six steps of his room and back again. The task before him was impossible. The old documents and maps from bygone days existed, but they were locked within the chambers he once called his own. Those chambers now belonged to Siggur.

The treacherous little fool was likely too arrogant to read them. He had already gotten what he wanted. *Damn his soul!*

Everything Rikkar needed was lost to him, including maps. He could tell the Brethren where the church had built temples, but he could not remember which had originally belonged to the Jápmea. Hemmela had been one, which is how he first became interested. But little remained there in the way of ancient writings. Those had been burned. He had found some reference to them in other church documents but he had only his notes, not the actual texts. And now, shut within the fortified walls of the Piijkij stronghold, he had no access to his old network of informants. He couldn't summon anyone without raising suspicions.

Rikkar agonized over his miserable fate. Then he remembered Biera. Biera had helped him before and with the proper leverage he might again.

But that didn't change Rikkar's underlying problem. He could not bring Biera to the Brethren.

But I could go to him.

As soon as he thought it, Rikkar wanted to dismiss the idea. The Vijns's men swarmed like pestilence about Hemmela, and he had no desire to become the High Priest's unwilling captive. He much preferred being the willing prisoner of the Brethren, as fraught as this situation was.

A missive, he thought.

And then found himself stupefied at this own foolishness. A missive had been his very undoing. *No. I must speak with Biera in person.*

Rikkar wasn't sure how long the Avr would give him to provide the information requested, but he couldn't afford to wait to find out. As much as he feared the wrath of the Avr, he feared equally his own loss of courage.

Once, he had considered himself both a man of the world and a servant of the gods; but his time with Vannes had relieved him of both illusions. Neither the gods nor the Piijkij had listened as he had screamed to make the pain stop.

Rikkar shivered as he readied the sullen horse and looked around to see if anyone had taken note of him. The southern stable was occupied with only carts and nags more interested in their feed than in the man skulking in their midst. The priest pulled the Brethren's cloak up around his head and led the animal afoot toward the east gate.

When he reached the first trees, he mounted the mare and looked back to see if he were followed. When he saw no one behind him, he gave the horse's rough sides a sharp kick, urging her forward.

It took a hard day's ride to reach Biera's farm, and Rikkar was relieved to see smoke rising from the man's chimney. He slid awkwardly off the nag and rubbed his weary body. The horse grazed contentedly on lichen, and he tethered it among the trees.

Slowly, careful to make no sound, Rikkar approached the hut. When he reached the structure, he pressed himself flat and inched his way to the small window opening. He quickly peeked into the hut, then ducked out of sight, sliding below the sill. As he crouched, he thought of his visit to Irjan's wife. It seemed long ago. He had been so sure of himself then, filled with confidence—arrogance really, he forced himself to admit. But he could not undo what had been done.

Rikkar gathered himself up in front of the door, trying to recapture some of his lost pride and assurance, before pushing the door open without knocking.

"Apotti," Biera exclaimed, stunned to see who interrupted his peace and quiet.

Rikkar strode to the fire and removed his gloves, letting his chin rise with confidence. "Biera, I have need of your services."

The farmer recovered from his surprise and his eyes narrowed in suspicion. "What do you want from me?"

"A simple matter really," Rikkar assured him with a careless gesture of his hand.

Biera snorted. "Well, tell me what it is you want, and I'll decide whether it's a simple matter or not."

The fallen priest grabbed the farmer by his collar and squeezed. "Do not forget how you got this farm. It could easily disappear. A letter to the Vijns, stating your role in the deception, might have you answering more questions than you would like."

Biera squirmed. He grunted out, "Fine. What do you want?"

Rikkar released the man, brushing off his shoulders and straightening the collar calmly. "I need you to get me maps I have stored in my chambers."

"You mean the Apotti's chambers," the farmer corrected, seeming to take a measure of enjoyment.

Rikkar drew back, insulted. "I can see getting this farm has made you bold, Biera, but you should not believe yourself to be anything more than what you are—a boanda who, through intrigue, gained a valuable piece of land. What would your neighbors do if they knew your part?"

The farmer said nothing in response, but the man's jaw tightened.

"Now," Rikkar went on, "it should be a simple matter for one as motivated as you are to keep what you have worked so hard to obtain. Get me the maps within the fortnight, and you get to keep it all. Fail and you lose everything you see around you."

Biera protested, "I can't do what you ask in so little time."

"Nevertheless, I will return and I expect you to have the maps."

Biera took a menacing step toward him and Rikkar pulled out his dagger.

"Do not think of harming me, Biera. Is the surest way for your secrets to be revealed. If I do not return this evening, letters detailing your assistance in my escape will be sent to the Vijns and to that upstart in Hemmela."

Biera stopped short, scowling.

Rikkar swelled with the thrill of having power again. "I wonder what you will do then?"

CHAPTER FORTY-SEVEN

FTER KALEK LEFT, IRJAN returned to his cell with Dárja.
She'd fallen asleep and he'd watched her tiny chest rise
and fall. He marveled at the sense of peace she radiated
and prayed his own son, Marnej, lived blissfully unaware of his
own danger.

But Irjan couldn't shake the unfairness of the situation. One
child slept, safe and loved; the other lived alone and in peril. He
couldn't turn his back as Kalek had done—merely accepting that
his role had changed, and others would guide his son toward the
future. He couldn't accept it, because he knew what Marnej's
future would entail. He had, himself, experienced the cruelty,
the isolation, and the constant fear of death that came with being
raised among the Brethren. Irjan had chosen it for himself as a
small boy filled with rage, but he would not choose the same for
his son. Marnej deserved the happiness and pleasure of an ordinary Olmmoš—the simple joy of being spun in the air by one who
loved him. He deserved to have the same as Dárja.

Released suddenly from his thoughts, Irjan realized the little
girl had awoken and stared up at him with deep concentration.
Her eyes blinked but they did not waver from his. They were so
dark, as if they had captured a starless night. Deep within Irjan

something unexpected gained strength: a sense—a feeling—telling him something.

And then he clearly heard the words in his mind, *We shall be together.*

Before he could stop to think what he was doing, Irjan sprang from the bed and knocked upon the door to summon the guard.

The door opened and he stepped back, picking up Dárja and saying, "Kalek has not returned to take the child."

The guard reached out his hands toward the little girl and said, "I will take her to him," but Dárja pulled closer to Irjan, and as the guard touched her, she began to wail. The startled guard flinched as if scalded.

Irjan patted Dárja's back to comfort her, but when the guard suggested getting one of the nieddaš to take the child, she screamed even louder.

"Let me take her to Kalek," Irjan suggested. "She is content in my arms." To prove his point, the little girl drew her arms around his neck and buried her red face in his shoulder.

The shaken guard agreed and called to the others. Irjan moved forward into their midst and they headed for the healers' quarters. As they walked, Irjan kept his mind clear and tried to find the spark within himself. His heart beat faster and it was all he could do to keep in step with his guards.

When they reached the healers' chambers, the guards knocked upon the wooden doors, but any response was drowned out as Dárja started to wail once again. Irritated and uneasy, the guards readily agreed when Irjan suggested he would go in and give her to Kalek.

Irjan opened the door and slipped in, calling out, "Kalek, I have brought Dárja to you since you cannot remember to keep your appointments." He shut the door behind him and the child gave a deafening scream.

As they moved further into the healers' sanctum, Irjan knew Dárja's screams were the only things loud enough to reach the guards.

He scanned the rooms quickly for a way to escape. Doors. Windows. Finally, through a narrow corridor, he saw a way to the outside. Irjan placed Dárja on the soft bundles of cloth stacked upon a chair. She sat there crying as he grabbed one of the cloaks by the door.

He bent and kissed her face and whispered, "Thank you, my sweet one." Then he slipped out through the garden and into the twilight. When he reached the cover of the forest he ran and didn't look back. Irjan didn't know what would happen, but he knew he had to try to get his son back, so he could watch the child sleep and know he did so in peace.

He ran until he could no longer hear Dárja's cries; then he stopped, breathless, to find his direction. The long and deep shadows of the fading spring day made him feel as if he were already surrounded. But if luck stayed with him, the night sky would be cloudless and the moon would allow him to travel under its light.

~

Kalek finished building the fire. He wanted it ready, because Okta was an old soul and the cold still chilled the spring night.

"I could always come back tomorrow," Kalek suggested, as Okta sat himself close to the fire and withdrew something to eat from his bag.

"No," the healer declined. "I have not instructed you on the proper harvesting techniques, and if it is done incorrectly, the plant's medicinal qualities are lost."

"But you could just explain it to me. That way you wouldn't have to spend the night out in the cold air, and on hard ground."

Okta laughed. "Do you think I have not experienced this before in my long life? I have spent more nights like this than I have in the comfort of my bed."

Kalek hastily agreed. "Yes, yes, I know, but not recently."

"I am old, but I know what capabilities remain to me; and spending the night sleeping out under the stars will not tax them.

Now go fetch us some water so I may make tea for us. I may be fine with sleeping in the open air, but I am not above wanting to have something warm inside of me."

Kalek took the waterskin, shaking his head at the vagaries of his teacher's desires. At the stream he knelt, careful not to fall into the dark water flowing over smooth stones. He dipped the waterskin into the stream and let it fill, feeling, for the moment, at peace. The sensation was like a lost friend come home—familiar and yet filled with anticipation.

The shadows lengthened and bent through the birch trees, and a light wind rustled their budding leaves. Out of the corner of his eye, Kalek saw something moving through the forest—too big to be a wolf or a fox and too small to be *ealga*. Besides, a moose would not move in such a smooth, fluid manner.

Kalek stood for a better look. He peered into the twilight. *What is an Olmmoš doing here?* A sense of dread washed over him. He knew that shape and stride. More importantly, he knew what the Olmmoš must be doing.

"Irjan!" he called out, but either the man didn't hear or chose to ignore him.

Kalek ran after him, but stopped. His sword was at the camp. He wasn't going to approach Irjan without some sort of protection. They may have come to an understanding, but he wasn't certain they were friends.

Kalek hurled himself in the direction of camp, jumping over stones and felled trees. He reached a startled Okta, out of breath, then fumbled for his sword and hurriedly twisted himself into his satchel.

"Irjan has escaped," he exploded in his haste. "He has escaped and I must stop him."

Okta protested, suggesting that others should have the task of capturing the prisoner, but Kalek shook his head.

"It is my fault," he said. "I did not tell the Noaidi about Marnej."

Kalek did not stop to explain his answer, but sprinted off in the direction in which he had last seen Irjan. As he ran, he slowed to look for signs of his predecessor's passage. He followed freshly snapped twigs and overturned rocks, but as he ran forward, he also looked back to see if others pursued.

One thought repeated in his mind. *It's my fault.* He knew Irjan was heartsick about his son, yet he'd ignored it, preferring to believe it a temporary condition—that Irjan would accept his role as all Jápmemeahttun did. But Irjan was not simply Jápmemeahttun. He was also Olmmoš and, more importantly, a Piijkij. Irjan went to free his son from the men who had trained him to be a killer.

Kalek deeply regretted his lapse in judgment. If he'd told the Elder about Marnej, then this would not be happening. But Kalek couldn't shake the feeling that if he had told all he knew or suspected, then Irjan's future among their kind would have been brought to a quick end. Irjan's existence posed a threat, but a controlled one. Marnej, however, represented the real danger, because he underscored the fact Irjan could not be controlled. Kalek knew the Noaidi would not have allowed such a risk to continue unanswered, and so he'd remained silent.

Though his lungs burst with effort, Kalek's pain went far deeper—directly to his core. It was the agony of not knowing the right thing to do. Irjan had caused Aillun's death, and yet she'd entrusted Dárja to him. But what choice did she have? Yet, Irjan had upheld his promise and kept Dárja safe. He was a killer, and yet Kalek had killed to save him. Kalek had believed he was doing the right thing, and yet he couldn't discount the Noaidi's fears and concerns. Irjan could lead their enemies to them, simply because of who he was—perhaps not for his own sake. But if it would save Marnej. . .he couldn't be sure.

The one thing he was sure of was where Irjan was headed, and by the looks of the trampled ground, he wasn't slowing down.

Kalek drew upon all the anger, all the injustice, stored within him to push his speed, but he feared it wouldn't be enough to keep pace with the love of a father intent on saving his son. Still, Kalek ran on, through the pain and the self-doubt. He had to find Irjan before the others did.

As the night sky became full with a heavy moon, Kalek slowed to discern the direction Irjan traveled. A faint odor of smoke drifted toward him, giving him a moment of pause. It could be the Piijkij or it could be an Olmmoš—or worse, a group of them.

Remaining within the Song of All, he slowly moved forward, threading through the trees to where a fire burned within a small clearing. At this distance, however, he couldn't discern who occupied the camp. Kalek moved closer, pressing himself against a tree, feeling its comforting thrum, then cautiously he peered around it. He saw no one at the fire, but someone had been there: a bedroll, furs, and a satchel lay in the camp. *Another Olmmoš.* Irjan hadn't any of these things when Kalek had spotted him earlier.

Kalek took a step toward the fire and felt a sharp point at his back. He slowly pivoted and found himself facing Irjan.

He shouldn't have been surprised. Irjan had told him he could enter the Song, but Kalek couldn't help feeling a great break in the order of things had occurred. In that moment, he truly understood the Noaidi's fears. Before him stood someone who should not exist.

"You should not have come, Kalek," Irjan said, winded from his exertion.

"I cannot let you escape." The almai took a step back from Irjan and his sword. "Did you take that from the guards?" Kalek nodded toward the weapon.

"No. It belongs to the builder of this fire."

"Did you kill him?"

Irjan's eyes narrowed. "I see you still don't know me well, Kalek."

"I know you are desperate to save your son, Irjan, but I don't know how far you are willing to go."

"Are you worried for yourself, then?" The man's voice hardened.

"I am unsure of what you will do. I cannot let you go and you cannot leave me behind." His hand crept toward his own weapon.

Irjan saw the movement and parried it with the tip of his sword.

"So, you would fight me, is that it, Kalek?" Irjan's hardness gave way to disappointment.

"What option do you give me, Irjan?" Kalek demanded. "By escaping, you have proved yourself the danger the Noaidi believes you to be. I cannot help but believe he is right."

"Kalek, the only one in danger is my son. Come with me! Help me save Marnej and I will gladly, willingly, return to your prison. I am asking you to understand the bond between a father and his child. I cannot turn my back on him. You must know you will have to kill me to stop me.

"If you cannot understand the hold my son has on me, then consider this—if we do not save him, he will be turned into a killer—one who will be trained to hunt and kill your kind. The Brethren will try and make him everything I was and more, if they can. By helping me, you will end that threat and the threat you believe I pose."

Kalek's resolve wavered as he considered Irjan's fevered argument. There were as many advantages as flaws, but he didn't want to betray the trust of the Noaidi. Kalek knew he should kill Irjan, and if he died in the process then his debt would be paid in full. But he also knew if he did not succeed and Irjan lived, then the danger to his kind would be doubled.

Kalek could see no other way than to once again help this man—this Piijkij. He couldn't understand why his life had become so entwined with this killer and halved being, but it appeared their journey together was not yet at an end.

"I do this for my kind," Kalek said finally.

⁓

Irjan lowered his sword slowly. He knew what he was asking, but he preferred that price to the one that would have cost Kalek his life. Despite their differences, Irjan had forged a connection with Kalek. He knew the almai had tried to make life better for him in prison. He brought him small tasks and projects to keep him occupied in the long idle time between Dárja's visits. And he encouraged the guards to let them be outside when the weather permitted. But most of all, Kalek talked to him. He shared his thoughts and listened.

Irjan had betrayed the nascent friendship and suspected he might never have the chance to regain it, but he was willing to make this sacrifice to give his son the chance to know what friendship meant.

The earth beneath Irjan's feet suddenly shifted, as if solid ground had turned into a fast-moving river. He put his arms out to steady himself. When his body recovered its balance, a leaden silence suffused him. He tried to turn to look for Kalek but before he could move something shimmered in the corner of his eye. He doubled over and Kalek steadied him. For the first time since he had discovered his true nature, Irjan began to understand the potential and the perils of moving within the Song of All.

"Where is the Olmmoš who belongs to this encampment?" Kalek asked, making no mention of their shift out of the Song.

"He ran off," Irjan said, trying to replace his sword in the loop of his belt.

Kalek regarded him with suspicion.

Irjan ran his hand across his face, reminding himself of his own solidity. "He thought I was the spirit of the dead when I appeared, and ran off into the night."

The almai peered into the dark perimeter of the camp.

Irjan anticipated the almai's next thought. "I very much doubt he will return."

"And why is that?"

Irjan grinned, feeling his confidence returning. "Because I said something to suggest his soul was in danger if I saw him again."

"Actually, it is not a lone Olmmoš I am most concerned with," Kalek muttered, still peering off into the darkness.

"Mord?"

"If he knows of your escape, he will surely want to be the one to catch you."

Irjan nodded. "Then we had better leave. The man was kind enough to provide us with a horse—a nag really, but faster than being on foot."

"Grab what you see here." Kalek pointed to the scattered items. "I will douse the fire and clear our tracks."

Irjan packed the food and supplies neatly into the satchel. He brushed away his own marks, then mounted the horse with the satchel about his front. He offered his hand to Kalek. Before Irjan gave the reins a snap, Kalek stopped him.

"If they catch us, you know they will kill us," he said.

"If they catch us, we will fight." Irjan flicked the reins.

~

Okta was gathering his supplies when the first guards came upon him. Even in the gloom, the healer saw eagerness in their eyes that made him uneasy.

"We search for the escaped Piijkij," their leader announced, his chest and chin pushed forward with importance. Okta saw the guard's braid.

One of Mord's men, he thought with distaste, and then, for the first time in ages, the healer acted the part of the old and frightened.

"Yes! Yes! Indeed. I saw the man running through the woods." Okta made his voice breathy and excited. "I was just gathering my supplies to return and inform you. You have not missed him by much!"

The puffed leader stepped forward and Okta shrank a little, exaggerating the Taistelijan's towering stature.

"Which direction did they go?" he demanded.

The healer stretched out a wavering arm toward the north.

"He must be heading for the Pohjola," the leader surmised. "He cannot be far ahead. We should spread out to widen our search so as to not miss his tracks."

The guard turned to Okta. "One of my men will escort you back."

"Oh no!" the healer protested. "You will need all your men. I will manage on my own and will report your course to the other guards." He let himself shrink further. "You are not alone in tracking this dangerous Olmmoš?"

"No," the leader affirmed, "others follow. We are the vanguard."

As Okta watched the guards' backs disappear, he regained his true stature and allowed the age to drop away from him. "What have you done, Kalek?" he whispered.

There would be consequences for deceiving the guards, but Okta owed Kalek more than he cared to admit. He only hoped he was in fact aiding the young almai and not condemning him to a horrible end.

CHAPTER FORTY-EIGHT

RIKKAR WAITED THE FORTNIGHT with a mixture of wariness and impatience. Every day he expected the Avr to approach him and demand the maps he had requested. Rikkar had sketched what he could and hoped he might stall the man by describing the drawings as the rough first draft. But the Avr hadn't visited him. Indeed, he hadn't seen the man at all.

When the time came for Rikkar to repeat his earlier clandestine foray, he fell in with a small group of Piijkij leaving to forage in the forest. Gradually, he fell behind before finally angling off to make the long trek to Biera's.

In almost perfect repetition, Rikkar brought his mount to a stop beyond the farmhouse. Again, as before, he saw the smoke rising from the hearth and it seemed to him a signal that all was going according to plan. If he could produce the maps before the Avr requested them, then perhaps he could gain some favor with the man.

Rikkar tethered his horse and surveyed the open fields. Nothing stirred. He skirted the trees, then darted across the unprotected land between the hut and forest. He stole a glance through the window. Biera sat with his back to him, facing the fire. On the table sat scrolled papers.

The maps, he thought with relief.

Rikkar relaxed against the wall of the dwelling. For the first time since his disgrace, he felt his luck was about to change.

Rikkar stood straight and pushed open the door with anticipation. "Biera!" he greeted the farmer heartily. "I see you have succeeded!"

The man rose, and for a moment Rikkar couldn't believe his eyes. "It cannot be."

Even when the voice greeted him, Rikkar could only repeat, "It cannot be."

"My apologies, Rikkar, but Biera could not be here to meet you." The Vijns of the Order of Believers remarked. "He did ask me to give you his regards."

Rikkar's horror was so complete he could say nothing in return.

"I am so glad we could have this little meeting," the High Priest continued lightly. "It was rude of you to run out on me earlier." He circled Rikkar and appraised him head to toe. "You are too brazen by half," the Vijns scolded and then added, "or is this the foolish attempt of a man with frayed nerves?" The High Priest stopped. "Has Dávgon grown weary of you?"

A sudden flash of anger surged through Rikkar.

"Yes, I thought so." The Vijns eyes flashed. "Were I less of a forgiving soul you would be dead for your faithlessness. But I understand your eagerness to serve the gods made you rush into an unfortunate decision." The High Priest ambled over to a chair by the fire, making himself comfortable, before pointing to a chair across from him. "I am offering you the opportunity to make the right decision, Rikkar. I am offering you the chance to undo what you have done."

Rikkar walked, corpselike, toward the proffered chair. He hovered momentarily before slowly easing himself down.

"I would like to undo what I have done," he said in a hoarse whisper.

"I am pleased to hear that." The Vijns rested his crossed hands upon his chest. "It will save me the trouble of killing you, something which I was prepared, but quite loath, to do."

Rikkar swallowed, as if trying to move a mouthful of sand downward. "What would you have me do?"

"Excellent!" the High Priest exclaimed brightly, leaning forward in the chair to slap Rikkar's knee. "I do appreciate your initiative."

Without waiting for his former priest to respond, the Vijns continued, "I want you to spy on the Brethren. I want to know everything that goes on within their walls."

Merriment sparkled in the man's eyes. It was a game to him, but a game whose stakes were very dear to Rikkar.

"You see, I have reason to doubt the Brethren's loyalty," the Vijns commented, gesturing with a causal wave to the rolled maps. "Something you may know a bit about." His eyes narrowed, then he smiled. "I don't have the time to torture you for all that. In any case, it would be difficult for you to explain the bruising to Dávgon. But fail me again and I will make certain you suffer for what feels like an eternity."

Rikkar drew back from the menace in the man's playful tone.

The High Priest let out a laugh. "But I'm not a man strictly driven to command by violence. Give me what I want, Rikkar, and I will give you what you want. It is really quite simple."

"You will bring me into the Court of Counselors?" Rikkar balked.

Vijns inclined his head. "Indeed I will."

"But why?"

"Because the habits of a traitor are hard to break, and keeping you close will ensure you will not be tempted again. Now, if I have answered all your questions, I believe you have some maps to take back to Dávgon."

The Vijns stood up and walked to the plank table.

"You are giving me the maps to the temples and the ancient Jápmea sites?" Rikkar asked incredulously.

"You'll need to strengthen your understanding of guile if you are to succeed, Rikkar," the High Priest said. "I am giving you what Dávgon seeks. I am not giving him what he needs." The

Vijns held out the scrolls. "You will come here and deliver your information."

"Biera is to be trusted to bring it to you?" Doubt bubbled up through Rikkar's voice.

"Biera has already been rewarded for bringing to light your less-than-cunning attempts at intrigue."

Rikkar nodded then looked toward the door.

"Go," the High Priest commanded. "And remember to practice a little more discretion."

CHAPTER FORTY-NINE

KALEK AND IRJAN RODE south, staying off the well-traveled tracks and outside the Song of All. Though neither had wanted to, they'd stolen a small, sturdy horse from a farmstead. They needed two mounts to successfully outrun their pursuers and have a chance of getting to Marnej.

Although it nagged at him, Kalek hadn't questioned Irjan about his plan. Instead, he focused on their immediate predicament. Mord and the Taistelijan could catch up with them any day, bringing an end to more than this foray, but each day they moved farther south, the threat Mord posed grew less important, while the plan to save Marnej became more central.

Finally, Kalek was moved to speak. "I joined you from necessity, but we are at the point where necessity requires a plan."

"It is a matter of slipping in and stealing away with my son," Irjan answered, preoccupied with boiling water in the small fire.

Kalek shook his head. "That is no small matter, nor any kind of plan."

Irjan mumbled a careless response.

"We cannot barge in upon the Brethren armed only with your righteous indignation and my need to protect my kind!" Kalek's voice cut through the night air, compelling Irjan to look up from his tea.

"I know every inch of the stronghold. I know where they will have my son," Irjan spoke with impatience.

"Fine. But how will you get in? Presumably they have guards at the gate, or are all Piijkij as arrogant as you, and believe foresight is not necessary?"

Irjan scowled. "Of course there are guards. But I will get past them."

"How?"

Irjan groaned. "Kalek, you are worse than a spring mosquito intent on blood!"

～

It annoyed Irjan that the almai insisted everything be planned. Plans went awry. Still, he had to admit, some preparation was needed.

"I can slip in using the Song of All," Irjan spoke, as if suddenly inspired by the thought.

Kalek frowned. "Irjan, you haven't had much practice with the Song."

"I have had more practice than you might wish to acknowledge!"

Kalek's expression darkened. "It takes more than you imagine to control it." He shrugged. "Fine. Let us assume you enter the Song of All and sneak into the fortress."

"I will not have to sneak—"

Kalek's stony voice cut him short. "How will you bring your son out undetected? You cannot bring him into the Song."

"What do you mean I cannot bring him into the Song?"

"Irjan, it is not that simple. It is not some game you are playing. Olmmoš and Jápmemeahttun are not the same. The Olmmoš have no part in the Song."

"Why?"

"Irjan, I do not know these things. I'm not an Elder. Perhaps, because they cannot believe."

"Believe what?"

"Believe the gods gave life to everything and not just to them."

"But I am both!"

"That is all well and good, but you've no idea whether Marnej shares your abilities. You may be one of a kind."

"So I can't bring Marnej into the Song? What then?"

"I do not know, Irjan. This is for you to decide."

"I will bring him out in my arms then!" Irjan snapped. Then, when his irritation receded, he added, "We will need a diversion at the gates."

"All right," Kalek agreed, "what kind?"

"One that draws the guards out and occupies them."

"A fire, perhaps?" the almai suggested.

"Yes! A fire! If we can light a fire in the eastern stables where carts and winter hay are stored, it will take the effort of many to put it out. Those not immediately engaged will be distracted and won't recognize an infiltrator of their own bearing and costume."

Kalek's brows knitted. "And where will you get this disguise?"

"The first to notice will likely respond alone," Irjan quickly answered. "I will subdue him and strip him of the essentials."

"And if he is not alone?"

"Then I will subdue both, and you shall have a costume of your own." Irjan smiled.

Kalek ignored Irjan's attempt at humor. "What of armament?"

"What of the legendary prowess of the Jápmemeahttun warrior?"

"I am not a Taistelijan, nor do I claim prowess with a sword."

Irjan tried to interject, but Kalek's icy expression stopped him.

"I will not hang the matter of our lives and the lives my kind on a thread of pride. I'm a healer's apprentice who has trained with a Taistelijan. I have fought, but not in battle. I have killed an Olmmoš, but I am not a killer like yourself."

Irjan took Kalek's hesitation to heart and nodded. They were two against many.

"The temple at Hemmela has a well-stocked armory. We can take what we need, and set up multiple caches. The fire should provide enough of a distraction for me to enter undetected."

As if to anticipate Kalek's next question he continued, "If I don't emerge within a reasonable time, then use the caches to loose arrows and make the Piijkij believe they're under attack from a greater force. If I haven't emerged before the supplies are exhausted, then give me up for dead, because I will make sure I do not survive." Irjan paused. "Ride then like the northern winds for home and prepare yourselves for war—pray it does not come. I promise you my dead body will not lead them to you, nor give them any hint where to find our kind."

~

The softened spring snow had turned the dirt pathway into a bog, and Siggur, the new Apotti of Hemmela, lifted his robes to carefully step where he believed the path to be driest. But the ruts and ridges of the cart track mashed under his foot, and the mud sucked downward as if it meant to swallow him whole, starting with his feet. Siggur wrenched up his leg, cursing the mud, the town, and its people. He should be in his chambers, in front of the fire, commanding his acolyte to attend to the needs of the villagers. But he had no acolyte to charge with daily duties. The Vijns of the Order of Believers had decreed the village of Hemmela needed only a priest.

Siggur had tried to maintain an even expression as he listened to the High Priest, but when the Vijns smiled, he knew he had not succeeded.

"Besides, Siggur," the man added, "I would hate for you to fall prey to the wiles of an ambitious assistant. It seems Hemmela is a wellspring of intrigue that requires me to leave a unit of men behind. For your safety, of course."

Now, as Siggur trudged toward the temple, he silently raged. *Useless mouths to feed.* He knew the guards spied on him and reported back to their master. Aloud he muttered, "Tale tellers," before coming to a stop in front of the temple, where the guards showed no inclination to descend and assist him. Siggur wished the pox upon them, but did not openly berate them. To do so would offend the Vijns. Instead, he squeezed his face into an approximation of a smile. "If you would kindly open the gates, I wish to enter the temple."

Siggur lifted the hem of his robes, prepared to ascend the steps. For what seemed an eternity, neither guard moved. Then the guard on the left rolled his eyes, sighing loudly as he pushed open the heavy wooden door. A cold fury suffused Siggur. With jaw clenched and chin held high, he turned abrupty on his heel. A sniff of indignation escaped him as he strode passed the front steps to seek out the temple's side entrance, where there would be no sniggering guards. Blood coursed through his ears, as his anger pulsed. But not even Siggur's anger could mask the squelching of his sodden boots.

Away from prying eyes, Siggur hoisted his ungainly robes up above his knees. He slogged forward once more hurling invectives at the mud and the guards and the injustice of his burdens. He edged past the stables, muttering and cursing, all the while focused on the warmed elderberry cider awaiting him, never once aware the shadows watched him with eager interest.

⌁

"I recognize him," Irjan said in a low voice, although no sounds could reach beyond the Song of All. "He was the Apotti's acolyte, but it looks as if he no longer is. He wears the robes of a priest now. It was this man's master who wished me to once again hunt the Jápmea for the glory of the Olmmoš."

Kalek's face clouded. "You speak of us as if we are some other, having nothing to do with you."

Irjan came up short. "It is the habit of a lifetime."

"Well, let us hope you live long enough to learn a little more respect," Kalek shot back. Before Irjan could respond, Kalek continued, "What interest would an Olmmoš priest have in us? We have lived apart from each other for more than a generation."

Irjan thought back to the occasion. "I didn't ask his reasons, because I had no desire to reclaim my title and its burden. When I was willing, I had my own reasons and cared not about the whys and wherefores of a priest. I was thinking only of Marnej."

Irjan walked out of the shadows and motioned to Kalek to follow. The two strode forward cloaked from the eyes of the priest by the power of the Song.

The priest withdrew a long iron key and inserted it into a lock. Metal ground upon metal and the swollen wooden door creaked with resistance. The priest pulled recklessly on the handles while Kalek and Irjan waited, like the gods, unseen and yet observing all.

When the stubborn door gave way, the young priest tumbled back into the mud. His watchers were in no position to give aid— first, because it did not serve their cause, and second, because they could not transcend the Song without leaving it. When the priest's feet finally found a steady point and his arms stopped flailing, his face glowed red with effort and anger.

The priest tumbled through the open door, his unseen companions at his heel. The man then slammed it shut with the force of frustration and stormed off down a corridor to his right, trailing mud for any who cared to follow in his footsteps.

"The armory is ahead, and beyond it, the kitchens," Irjan said over his shoulder, leading the way. "With any luck, we will find the area unguarded."

When they finally reached the armory, Irjan swore when he saw the posted soldier. He motioned to Kalek to keep moving toward the kitchens.

"How do we approach the guard?" Kalek asked, slipping through the open kitchen door.

Irjan looked around the room. The evening meal had yet to be prepared. His stomach lurched in hunger as he eyed the food laid out upon the table. "I don't relish the idea of attacking. It raises too much suspicion."

The almai agreed.

"What herbs do you carry with you?" Irjan abruptly asked.

"Those for wounds and comfort."

"Any to cause a man to fall asleep?"

The young healer nodded.

"Quickly, we don't have much time."

Irjan let the Song of All slip from his mind and felt the uneasy shift in his body. His limbs were heavy and awkward, as if he had just awoken from a long, deep sleep. He took a step and reeled forward. Kalek, standing close to the fire, rushed back and steadied him.

"It will get easier to make the transition," the almai reassured him. "There are points in the Song better suited for shifting."

Irjan nodded and straightened himself, silently appreciating the trust Kalek's encouragement indicated. He grabbed the grey cook's smock off the peg where it hung and awkwardly slid his arms into the too-short sleeves.

He glided quietly across the kitchen. "I'll keep watch at the door," he whispered.

Kalek grunted in answer, working with his back to Irjan.

From his position by the door, Irjan cautiously peered out into the empty corridor. A poke at his back jolted him nearly out of his skin, and he whirled around.

Kalek held out a tray with three cups. "Take the tray to the guard at the armory and tell him the priest asks him to deliver the warm drink to those who stand guard in the front, as a sign of his gratitude for their service. And tell the guard to return the tray to the kitchen when all are done."

Irjan gave his ally a knowing look of approval. "You work like a healer, but think like a Hunter."

Kalek ignored the praise. "I will follow in the Song."

Irjan took the tray and walked briskly down the hall, dividing his attention between the tray he held and the man he approached. When he was within a few feet of the armory guard, he slowed to take in the man and his weapons.

"The priest sends these drinks, to warm yourself and your fellows at the front gate," Irjan said with what he hoped was the tone of a harried cook. The guard reached to take one and Irjan pulled the tray back.

"You may have yours with the others," he said, "I need to get back to the kitchen."

The guard protested, but Irjan cut him off. "The longer I stand here talking to you, the longer it will take me to prepare the food for tonight. So, if you have a thought for your stomach, then take the tray and let me get back to my kitchen."

The man groused, but finally took the tray and walked toward the front of the temple.

"Bring the tray back when you are all done," Irjan called after him. "I don't want to leave the kitchen to look for it." The guard waved him off without a backward glance.

Irjan rested his hand upon the door's iron latch, but did not move until the guard disappeared from sight and even then he listened for any returning footsteps.

Kalek materialized within the gloomy corridor. "Is it locked?"

Irjan pushed against the door. "We'll know soon enough."

The door swung slowly open under his weight. Kalek entered, waving a torch toward the black corners. The room looked as Irjan remembered it, and once again he was struck by how much had happened in the short time since he had last stood here. The last time he'd had no need for its contents, save for a sword; this time he had use for it all.

Irjan shrugged off his smock and laid it upon the ground. He gathered bows of varying length and their paired arrows. He ran his hands across the smooth wooden handles of the cudgels, wondering if they could be of use, but decided against them. If it came to battle close at hand, then it would mean all had been lost. Throwing spears and arrows offered the best option for Kalek.

"Take off your cloak and do as I have done. Load what you can," Irjan said, not looking back to see if his example was followed.

"Hurry, we don't want to be caught by the returning guard," Kalek answered, peering out down the hall. "We still need to make it out through the kitchen and into the stables."

"That is what the sleeping draught and the Song are for," Irjan replied, adding more arrows to his growing pile.

"I cannot guarantee when it will take effect, and the Song will not hold you if you plan to take all that with you." Kalek snorted.

Irjan whirled around. "What do you mean?"

"You are barely skilled at bringing yourself through. You don't think you are going to be able to shift all of that?" Kalek chided.

Irjan hovered over his pile of weapons, pointing down at them. "But I have seen you bring beasts with you into the Song, why not this?"

"The animals have their own song and I can join them to mine. It is much easier to bring the living into the Song," Kalek explained. "These are metal and wood."

"But so are armor and shields!"

"Stop," Kalek hissed, "we do not have time for this. Trust me when I say we must plan to leave here on our own effort."

Irjan quickly bent down and tied the corners of the cook's smock. He picked up the bundle. "I am ready," he said, barely containing his frustration.

Kalek lifted his own bundle and peered into the hall. No one approached in either direction. "Quickly."

Kalek led the way back to the kitchen. At the door, they listened for sounds of food being prepared. When they heard nothing, they entered, relieved to see the room unoccupied. They swiftly crossed the space, winding their way through the cold storage and out into the garden.

They reached the stables out of breath, but stood quietly, listening for sounds of alarm. They heard only their own hammering heartbeats mixed with the foraging of the animals around them.

"How are we to get through town unobserved?" Irjan finally demanded in a hoarse whisper. "We can't exactly ride through with satchels overflowing with weapons. Why didn't you tell me the Song wouldn't hold all this?"

"I did tell you," Kalek replied, examining the stable.

"At the last minute!"

"You did not share your plans with me fully, so you do not need to blame me. Keep it to yourself." The almai turned his attention elsewhere. "Here. Come and help me harness the hay cart."

Irjan let go his irritation long enough to consider Kalek's request and realized the almai had already found a solution to their problem. Without hesitating, he helped Kalek harness the cart to their pair of mismatched horses and loaded their cache into the wooden trundle. Then they piled hay upon it.

"Here, take my cloak." Kalek climbed into the back of the cart.

"Where are you going?" Irjan asked, surprised.

"I will ride in the back, within the Song. A lone man is less of a presence to note."

Irjan nodded and surrounded himself in the woolen wrap. He led the horses and cart out of the stables and onto the rutted path. The mud slid under his feet, but the horses were sure of themselves. He hoisted himself up onto the running board and sat down, taking care to obscure his features with the hood.

～

Siggur sloughed off his mud-stained outer robes and stood before the fire in his thin inner ones. The new Apotti of Hemmela held out his hands toward the flames, his attention drifting down, first to the fire itself, and then to his feet. He still wore his boots. Siggur snapped his head around, taking in the muddy footprints he'd tracked through his chambers.

"Gods be cursed," he shouted, kicking off his offending, mud-encrusted boots

Beleaguered by the day's frustrations, Siggur reached for the jug of elder cider and poured himself a healthy dose of the strong drink. He downed the heady liquid in a single gulp, then repeated the pour again and again, until he felt pleasantly wooly-headed. He sank into his chair and closed his eyes, allowing pleasant visions to sparkle just beyond his conscious mind.

A sharp rap upon the door broke through Siggur's tired musings. He sorely wished to ignore the knock, believing it to be another problem, but perhaps he'd taken the wrong attitude. Perhaps the cook stood outside with his meal.

"Come," he called out, readying himself to receive his meal.

When a guard and not the cook entered his chambers, Siggur fell back into his chair. "What do you want?"

"The armory has been ransacked," the guard answered, crossing the room to stand before the priest.

"The armory has been what?" Siggur demanded.

"Ransacked!"

The priest stood abruptly, knocking his chair back. "When did this happen?"

"Just now."

"How is that possible?" Siggur boomed.

The guard shook his head. "I don't know. The cook came, bringing us tea on your word and it. . ."

Before the guard finished his explanation, Siggur broke in, "On *my* word? I gave no such order!"

"The cook said you sent drinks to warm us," the guard insisted. "I took the tea to the men at the temple entrance and we drank together. I awoke inside the front passage not more than a moment ago."

"You fool!" Siggur fairly shouted at the guard. "The cook is not a man. The cook is a woman!"

The guard gaped, ready to protest, but Siggur cut him off. "What did he look like?"

"He was tall and dark. He wore the cook's smock," the guard answered.

"Tall and dark. That is all you observed? That could be anyone." Siggur scowled. "What was taken?" he quickly added.

The guard shrugged. "I'm not sure. I came directly to you when I discovered the armory had been ransacked."

Siggur threw his arms up in frustration. "So, you don't know what, if anything, has been taken? And the Vijns places his faith in you!"

"But—" the guard began.

Siggur held up his hand, "Lead me to the armory so I can see with my own eyes."

The guard spun on his heel and Siggur followed him out into the drafty corridors. The priest shivered and wished he had thought to take a wrap or his robe.

Too late now, he thought and added aloud, "Nothing but problems."

When they came to the armory, Siggur saw the door stood wide open. He took a torch and held it in the doorway. Pikes lay scattered across the floor. He stepped inside and waved to the guard to enter. "Look around and tell me what is missing."

The guard's quick movements caused the torch to flicker, casting fleeting shadows across the wall. The shadows pricked at Siggur's doubts and fears.

Who took the weapons? he wondered. *And for what purpose?*

"Bows are missing. Both long and short, as well as their arrows." The guard called out. "There are slings missing, and throwing rocks." The man picked up prone shields and replaced them against the wall. "Several of the long arrows are missing."

Siggur grew irritated. "And what are they?"

"They are like spears, but have fletching on the ends. They are meant to be thrown long distances with. . ." here the guard picked up something that looked like a stick with a hooked end. "With this," he finished.

"Bow, arrows, slings and spears," Siggur listed the items. "But what does it mean?"

"They are good weapons for hunting game," the guard suggested.

"So you think this was the work of villagers?" Siggur scoffed.

The guard shrugged. "Possibly."

The priest's thoughts raced ahead. What if the weapons were not for hunting? Was he, perhaps, a target? Perhaps Rikkar had returned to seek revenge? But the old priest would not risk getting caught by the Vijns.

No, he thought, *it was someone else.*

But Siggur couldn't shake his apprehension. The ease with which the weapons had been taken made it clear that, guards or no, the temple was not safe.

"The weapons could be for a siege." The guard spoke up.

"What?" the priest cried out.

"There were no close combat weapons taken."

"A siege? Are we in danger?"

"No." The guard shook his head. "The numbers of weapons taken would not be enough for a siege."

"Then why did you suggest it?" Siggur admonished the man.

The guard, however, stood his ground. "Because they are the kind of weapons that would be used for a siege and not for close combat. No pikes were taken, nor shields, nor axes."

"Fine then," Siggur snapped. "No close weaponry was taken. What does it mean?"

"It means we should inform the Vijns." The guard straightened to stare down his nose at Siggur.

The last thing new Apotti of Hemmela wanted was the further scrutiny of the High Priest. He pushed down his frustration long enough to ask, "Who would benefit from the use of these weapons?"

"Any brigand," the guard quickly replied. "They would be ideal to attack cart paths and traveling merchants or soldiers."

But could just any brigand walk into the temple unopposed and leave unseen, carrying what had to be armloads of weaponry? the priest wondered

He was inclined to believe not—not just anyone could do what had been done. *It took skill and planning and a purpose. . .* Siggur's breath caught. . . *the Brethren.*

Rikkar had aligned himself with a Piijkij. He could very well have kept up the alliance after his ousting. In fact, where else could Rikkar have turned? The former priest could have given the Brethren a detailed account of the temple.

The guard shifted his weight, Siggur noticed.

"Review the standing inventory and make a complete list of everything taken," he said to the man. "Then report to me the figures. I will inform the Vijns of today's events."

Siggur handed his torch to the guard and stepped out of the armory.

"But I do not have the standing inventory," the guard called out after Siggur's receding back.

"Then follow me to my chambers and I will supply you with one," the priest bellowed.

CHAPTER FIFTY

CROUCHED MOTIONLESS IN THE trees, neither Kalek nor Irjan would have wagered on their future. They watched the guards at the gate, each trying to perceive relative strengths and weaknesses.

"We gain nothing by waiting," Irjan said finally. "I'll follow the forest boundary until it reaches its closest point to the fortified walls, then I'll draw out a fire from my tinderbox. When you see the guards move in that direction, give me a raven's warning. Do not stay beyond the means of your weapons," he instructed.

Kalek nodded.

Irjan scampered off through the trees toward the eastern edge of the wooden fortress. He stayed low and hidden in the shadows.

Kalek divided his attention between the guards and the first sign of smoke, which indicated their plan moved forward. These quiet moments gave Kalek time to examine his choices. Admittedly, it had been reckless to run off after Irjan; but he also had good reason to want to bring Irjan back himself. Unfortunately, Kalek had allowed himself to be persuaded by the Olmmoš's arguments, and now he was party to this doomed rescue attempt. He couldn't imagine they would actually succeed. But if they did, Irjan had promised to return without protest. And whatever his reservations, he knew Irjan would keep his word; if not for his own sake, then for Marnej.

Gods, he thought, *what would the Elders do with not one, but two half-beings?*

Kalek didn't have time to contemplate the question, because the first dark tendrils of smoke climbed skywards. The black streaks curled up, thin and wavering, as if they might not survive. But as he watched they grew darker, more ominous, until they caught the guards' attention. First one and then another guard left the gate to investigate the source of the smoke. Kalek cupped his hands and imitated a raven's caw. He lowered his hands and listened. At this distance he heard no resistance, no struggle, but he doubted there would have been much. Irjan was skilled.

Suddenly, Kalek saw a Piijkij running toward the gate, calling out, "Fire! Fire!" There was no mistaking Irjan's stride and bearing. For an instant, Kalek wondered if the costumed artifice would rekindle Irjan's link with the Brethren. Then Irjan disappeared into the stream of Hunters rushing forward to douse the blaze.

∽

As Irjan moved through the gates, his pulse hammered. This place had once been his home, whatever may have come after. To be back within its walls stirred him.

He ran through the gathering numbers of curious Piijkij, calling, "There is a fire in the stable. We need water and buckets." He dashed on ahead as the others raced to lend their hands. Irjan needed to find a quiet corner where he could slip into the Song unnoticed. His heart skipped a beat at the thought. If he somehow failed to enter the Song of All, he would have to continue as he was, disguised, but certainly recognizable to any who had once known him.

Finally, he found the niche he searched for. How many times had he hidden here as a boy? And now, its sanctuary served a greater cause. He leaned against the cold stone and its chill trickled down his spine. He slowed his breathing and focused on the sounds of his world. In no time, his mind and body hummed with the living energy of everything around him, and he opened his eyes. Even in the darkened recess, the unnerving glow of the Song blurred his vision.

He stepped away from the wall and immediately missed its steadfastness, but he didn't have time to become comfortable within the Song. His stomach lurched as he ran through the empty passageways.

When he entered the corridors of the eastern hall, he slowed his pace from a run to a brisk walk, taking in the changes around him. But little had changed. The dormitory for boys was in the most northern part of the fortress. He'd once lived there himself and could walk there with his eyes closed. But he experienced no nostalgia of happy times or halcyon days, only the chill of cold determination, made harder by brutality. He would not allow his son to come into his boyhood in this chamber of horrors.

As Irjan moved deeper into the stronghold, he felt more at ease within the Song of All. Its double vision loosened its grip and he felt surer upon his feet. But he knew he wouldn't be able to remain veiled forever. He would have to come out to get Marnej.

He'd always known his greatest challenge would be to explain his presence in the dormitory. A handful of elderly Piijkij quartered with the boys; in theory, tending to their needs, but his own recollections were more of merciless beatings than tender mercies.

At the door to the dormitory he released the Song from his mind. All at once his body felt heavy and leaden. The vibrancy of his perceived world gave way to a thick silence. Irjan felt rooted in place, but forced himself to move. He burst open the dormitory door, hoping surprise would aid his efforts.

Two aged Piijkij oversaw the afternoon duties assigned to the boys. The oldest among the boys were outside training, leaving only the youngest inside. Young and old alike looked up from their tasks to take in the figure at the door.

"Brothers," Irjan said in a frantic voice, "there is a fire. We must get the children to safety." Then he quickly scanned the room for Marnej. In a shadowed corner he saw a cradle. The startled men regained their composure, and before Irjan could advance, they drew themselves up before him, blocking his way.

"A fire?" one of the wizened monitors croaked. "We have neither heard nor smelled fire."

Irjan took a step forward. "Truly, Brother! There is a fire that, as we speak, grows and threatens us. We must gather the children and move them to a safe place."

Irjan observed panic spread through the young ones, as they added their own anxious cries to the mix. The weak utterances of the two elder Brothers could barely be discerned in the din. Irjan strode forward, beckoning to all the boys to head toward the door, saying, "Go to the Great Hall!"

Finally, he wove his way to the bassinet. His heart skipped a beat to see his son staring up at him. The boy had grown. But he was still small, smaller than Dárja.

Irjan scooped him up and moved into the throng of boys, pushing out of the dormitory. The insistent calls of the old ones for calm went ignored by their unruly little mob, and the boys appeared to relish the opportunity to bring fear and uncertainty to their ancient guardians.

As they entered the Hall of Hunters, Marnej grew restless, and Irjan tried in vain to comfort him and still his movements. But the tighter he clutched the child, the harder Marnej rebelled. Irjan had mere steps to go before he could move into the Great Hall and from there to the eastern gate where Kalek waited.

"You there! Stop!" a voice commanded from behind Irjan.

The deafening shout brought the fretful chattering of the boys to silence and heightened the pitch of Marnej's screams. Irjan was suddenly gripped by indecision. He knew he could easily make the Great Hall and from there run until he reached the forest. *But what of Marnej?* Irjan was overcome with visions of an arrow piercing his beloved child.

He froze and, with racing heart, slowly turned around, as if some unseen hand gripped him and made him move against his will.

"Where do you go?" the voice demanded.

"We go to safety," Irjan replied with a breathless desperation

"You are quite safe here," the man answered, moving closer as he spoke. "I do not recognize you," he added, pulling forth his sword.

"I am newly joined and not known to many," Irjan offered quickly, hoping it would suffice, and dreading what would happen if it did not.

The Piijkij narrowed his eyes and scrutinized him. The boys in the hall whispered, vibrating with primal anticipation. "I have seen you before."

Irjan smiled as if greeting a friend. "In the rectory," he suggested.

The nascent smile of recognition drained from the Piijkij's face when he realized who stood before him. "Irjan," the man whispered with surprise.

Irjan hesitated. In that instant, he confirmed his identity to everyone in the hall.

The Hunter advanced in a lighting strike of force. Irjan spun and took the full point of its impact in his arm, sparing his son's life. He grabbed his own sword, wrenching it from its scabbard, as he ducked to avoid a sweeping blade.

Another lunge by his opponent left Irjan scrambling to keep his balance and protect Marnej. He crouched, raising his blade in time to take the crushing weight of a downward strike, and looked in horror as hilt ran into hilt. In a panic, he pushed back and swung wildly, his eyes straying to his son, who remained red-faced and relentless in his squalling.

The bitterness and frustration that had dogged Irjan since his wife's death finally broke free. He roared with rage, bellowing like a wounded beast as he savagely slashed at the Piijkij who stood between him and his escape. The man cried out in pain, grabbing his side. Blood oozed between his fingers, but no one crossed the red-slicked floor to intervene. The boys, once emboldened by the safety of their numbers, cowered in a corner, while their ancient guardians shrank back, gawking.

Irjan knew he was winning, but he also knew his chance for escape was slipping away. He still needed to break free and make it through the eastern corridor and gate where, if he had not exhausted his time, Kalek would give him cover under a rain of arrows.

After a great flourish of blows, he made his move. As he ran, the cries of alarm grew behind him. It had been eight seasons of snow since his name had echoed in these halls. In those days, it was because he was a hero. Today, it was because he lived on as a traitor. And today the odds were decidedly against him.

"Irjan!" a voice cried out. "It is over."

Arrows sailed into the gathering crowd of men who stood to challenge him and Irjan focused his eyes long enough to see Dávgon. Surrounded on all sides, Irjan batted away timid strikes, then spun in a circle, fending off men he had once called Brothers. He kept Marnej close to his body, but the child screamed and arched away.

"Kill the child if you must," Dávgon commanded from behind his wall of men.

"No!" Irjan roared with the voice of one defeated.

Then from behind him another voice cried out, "Come, Irjan, you cannot save him!"

Irjan heard the sickening screams of men dying, and then Kalek was beside him.

"Go!" Irjan yelled. "This is not your fight." He slashed at the face of the man before him, cutting him to the bone.

Kalek whirled and sliced through the midsection of another Piijkij, bringing him to his knees. "You made it my fight when you escaped," Kalek shouted back, swinging his sword up to block the downward slash of two more Brethren.

Kalek staggered back into Irjan, but sprang forward again.

"Leave me, Kalek!" Irjan barked. "It will end here." He blocked a slicing cut, but lacked the speed to parry the second. He spun, sacrificing his arm again to protect Marnej.

Kalek lunged forward. "It will not end here."

From the corner of his eye, Irjan saw a flash of steel and turned in time to see it cut through Kalek as if he were made of air and not flesh. Kalek gasped and lost his footing. Blood gushed from the wound. Kalek grimaced and fell to his knees.

Irjan met the almai's horror-stricken gaze. "No!" he screamed and hacked at the man who stood between him and his friend.

The ranks of Piijkij closed in on them. Without a moment to think, Irjan raked the man, then pushed past him, running to Kalek.

In one careful motion, Irjan laid Marnej upon the ground and looped Kalek's arm around his neck. "Find the Song," he cried out, unsure he was heard. Irjan pulled the almai roughly to his feet, ready to embrace his end.

Then time seemed to stop. Swords hung high in the air and faces were distorted. Irjan saw his son lying on the ground and Dávgon mere paces away, confident and sure in his stature.

"I will always love you, Marnej," Irjan cried out, taking a step toward his son.

Then everything dissolved into movement and chaos. Those who had surrounded him spun in circles, looking confused. Marnej sat upon the ground, crying, his fists curled in tight balls. Dávgon rushed forward, cursing the gods and all around him.

Irjan took this all in from beyond the shimmering veil of the Song. The voices resonated within, filling him, but his heart ached as it called out to the living world around him. Irjan looked over his shoulder at Marnej. *He would live*.

Kalek stumbled beside him. Irjan looked at his friend and felt fear creep into his pulse. He shifted the almai and took one step and then another away from his son and the Piijkij.

Irjan cursed under his breath. Aloud he panted, "You were supposed to leave me to my fate."

Kalek lifted his pale, sweat-cloaked face. "I could not leave you."

"Why?" Irjan whispered his thought.

Kalek lost his footing and groaned. "I could not tell Dárja I had let her bieba die."

Irjan swore again, blinking away his own tears and frustration. He pulled the Jápmemeahttun up under his arms and dragged him deeper into the forest. He wanted to run for the horses, but he did not want to leave his only ally, his friend, alone.

Irjan told himself that if he could keep his eyes upon Kalek, then Kalek's spirit would not leave his body. They reached the horses, drenched from the exertion, and he struggled to hoist Kalek over the smaller horse's back. Irjan's own blood loss was taking its toll. When he finally succeeded in heaving Kalek into position, he pulled himself up on his mount, caring only to put distance between themselves and the Brethren.

～

Irjan did not know how far they had traveled, nor if they had been followed, but he knew they could go no farther without tending to Kalek's wound. Irjan stopped near a streamside copse of trees. He eased the almai down and rested him against a slope, then tore open Kalek's blood-soaked shirt.

Kalek stirred and complained. "Just like a clumsy Olmmoš," he said with a cough.

There was a long upward cut along Kalek's ribs. The skin's edges were pulled jaggedly apart and he thought he saw the white glint of bone. He needed to stanch the bleeding.

"Kalek," he nudged his friend, "I need you to tell me what to do."

The almai opened his eyes and from a far-off place pulled himself into the present.

"You are cut to the bone and bleeding," Irjan told him, "but I cannot tell more."

Kalek nodded. "You must clean and close the wound," he croaked. "Boil water and douse the area. Take my shirt and cut it into strips. My satchel contains honey and a roll of pitch. Heat them. Then pull the wound tight. Cover the gash with the honey, then the pitch, and then bind me tightly." The effort of explaining was too much for Kalek, whose eyes fluttered closed.

"Kalek," Irjan shook him. "Tell me again what I must do."

Though he was already well into the preparations, Irjan feared that if Kalek slipped to the other side he might not return. He blew on the nascent embers of a fire, but kept focused on the almai, whose chest rose with labored breath as he continued to softly explain his care.

Irjan pulled out the metal pot they had gotten from the unfortunate Olmmoš hunter and filled it with water from the stream. He looked at Kalek's blood-soaked shirt. It wouldn't serve to bind the wound. He tore his own over his head, and with quick flicks of his knife, he reduced his shirt to long linen strips.

While the water began its slow rise to a boil, he impatiently reached inside Kalek's bag and rooted for the honey and roll of pitch. His hands couldn't identify any of the objects, so in a fit of frustration, he dumped the contents of the bag on the ground and found what he needed.

The water finally bubbled to a boil and Irjan drew a cup of it out to cool. Kalek's voice continued to mumble in a breathless whisper, his lips barely moving. Irjan looked at his friend's pale and drawn face; blond locks lay plastered to his forehead. He brushed aside the hair and felt the clammy mixture of death and cooling sweat. Irjan tested the water on his own arm, and flinched at the heat, but fear made him believe it was tolerable.

"Kalek," Irjan roused the almai to warn him. "I am going to clean the cut now."

The almai tried to nod his head, but only manage to let it loll to one side. He groaned.

Irjan slid his hand under Kalek's back and slowly poured the water down the length of the gash. The Immortal contorted in shock and pain, but even as he twisted away, Irjan continued to pour the hot liquid along the cut. The water, stained pink with blood, flowed into the ground below them, absorbed into its mossy softness.

Irjan placed the pitch roll near the fire. He quickly dripped the amber-colored honey onto Kalek's wound, and as he pulled the pitch from the fire, he allowed its sticky drops to fall upon the edges of the ragged gash. He repeated the administration of the pitch until he could add no more.

Gently, he shifted Kalek toward him, careful to keep the edges of the wound together. With the clumsiness of one unskilled, but desperate to do right, Irjan wound a strip of cloth around the almai and tied it taut. With one binding in place, he moved quickly to wrap one after another of the cloth strips around Kalek to seal the gash entirely.

When he finished, Irjan laid a fur behind his friend, leaned him back against the slope, and wrapped the ends of the fur around him to keep him warm.

Kalek opened his eyes and blinked slowly.

Irjan felt regret's weight upon him. "I'm sorry, Kalek."

Unable to meet his friend's penetrating stare, Irjan turned away to dig within his own supply bag. He pulled out a strip of dried reindeer meat and slid it into the pot of boiling water before him.

"Irjan." Kalek's voice was weak but insistent. "I don't blame you."

Irjan protested, but was cut off by the wounded Jápmemeahttun. "We all have our parts. And mine is over."

Irjan crawled next to the Immortal, putting his hand upon Kalek's chest to feel the almai's heartbeat. He watched Kalek try to take in air and his own breath caught. He could not be the cause of this Jápmemeahttun's death. He could not allow his friend to die without doing everything in his power to save him. He owed Kalek not only his life, but many lifetimes of debt. He thought of Marnej, lost to him, but alive.

Irjan shook his head, denying the power of destiny, the power of the gods. "No! It is not over. You will not die here."

Irjan kept his hand upon Kalek's chest and quieted himself, letting the voices he once sought find him. When they surrounded his mind he called out into the Song of All.

I am the son of the gods.
I am brother among my kind.
I started my life at a crossroads.
I traveled the winding path of those who are lost.
I will return to fulfill the forgotten destiny of one who should not exist.

I travel back with a heavy heart.
I travel back with a wounded soul.
I bring my brother to our kind.
I bring myself to my fate.
Search for us south as we ride north.
Life depends upon our meeting.

The answering chorus flooded through Irjan like a river freed from a dam.

We ride to save the lives of our own.
We ride to bring those lives home.

Irjan leaned forward and rested his head upon Kalek's slowly rising chest, feeling the sweetness of relief. He sat up and looked toward the twilight sky. There were no stars to guide. He took a deep breath and slowly released it.

Whatever my future, I have made it.

CHAPTER FIFTY-ONE

THE VIJNS OF THE Order of Believers stood across the garlanded hall and studied the Avr and his flanking retinue. He considered his words carefully.

"The Order of Believers thanks the Brethren of Hunters for joining us to confront the grave danger we all face," Bávvál began, inclining his head ever so slightly to honor those around him. He paused to hear the response, rote as it may be.

A murmured, "We thank you, as the gods thank you," echoed and faded into silence.

"Dávgon, much time has passed since we last met. We have in the past not always agreed, but I hope our disagreements are behind us."

"The past is where it stands," the Avr replied.

The High Priest allowed the corners of his mouth to curl up into a half smile. "I see time has not dulled your tongue," he remarked. "It still cut both ways."

The Avr nodded. "As you no doubt know from experience, Bávvál, time can be like a whetstone. It can hone what is put to it."

Bávvál's smile hardened as he spoke. "Yes, it is true the grain of sand can either wear down the blade or sharpen it to a point, but I hope we find ourselves without need for a blade at this juncture.

It serves neither of us to waste our energy fighting one another when a greater cause lies before us." He gestured to a feast-laden table. "Please join us first in food and then in conversation."

The Avr chose the middle chair in the length of the table and his Brethren fell into place on either side of him.

The High Priest sat across and signaled for the juhka to be poured. He lifted his cup, "To the health of the Brethren."

Dávgon, the Avr, repeated the gesture, replying, "To the faithful."

A rustling filled the hall, and then the rafters echoed with the sounds of men enjoying the meal before them.

The High Priest noted the Avr ate sparingly and drank even less. Dávgon watched his men and those belonging to the Order. He was wary. Bávvál expected no less of the leader of the Piijkij. Their watchfulness had served them in the past, but their particular skill had not been required for some time. In name, they still acted as the protector of the Olmmoš, guardians against the Immortals. But to most, the Jápmea existed only in ghost tales told to frighten the young and wayward. They had not been seen in generations, and memories of them had faded and twisted with time and invention.

But Bávvál knew the truth. He had read the old texts—the ones that spoke of the battles and the defiance of the unnatural creatures. The Immortals had been defeated, but they had not been purged. He knew the Jápmea hid themselves away. And now he believed they were no longer content to remain apart.

There had been too many odd occurrences and unexplained sightings recently. At first, he had suspected the Brethren of Hunters of fomenting fear to give credence to their existence. But the carnage outside of Ullmea had disabused him of the notion. Not even the Piijkij would kill their own as a ruse.

"Perhaps," Bávvál said in a loud and clear voice, "it is time we talked."

A general grousing rose from those who hated to see a good meal shortened by words, but even among the disgruntled, curiosity overcame hunger and the hall became quiet.

"Brethren," the High Priest began, "for too long we have been at cross purposes. As trained and vigilant protectors it cannot have escaped your attention the Jápmea walk among us once again. I speak for the Olmmoš, whom you are sworn to safeguard, when I say it is an evil we must address. The time has come to share this burden—to share our knowledge." Bávvál looked in Dávgon's direction, but saw no reaction one way or the other.

"At the present, most Olmmoš are largely unaware of shadowy movements, but it is only a matter of time before they too realize they are in danger once again." Bávvál squared his shoulders. "As the High Priest of the Order of Believers, I am sworn to protect their souls, and so I call upon you, the Brethren of Hunters, to pick up your mantles, so bravely carried in the past, to help secure Davvieana in this crucial time."

The High Priest's voice reverberated, and then silence overtook the hall.

"Is that what you really want from us, Bávvál?" the Avr of the Hunters asked, leaning forward to scrutinize the man across from him.

"Yes, Dávgon," the Vijns answered. "We need you to lead us—lead us in battle."

The Avr sat back and appeared to reflect on the Vijns's proposition. "You give us such power and ask nothing in return?" the leader of the Piijkij asked.

This time, the High Priest leaned forward. "We ask you to lead. We ask you to share your insight. Alone, you have neither the men nor the resources to defeat them."

Dávgon snorted. "What do you know of it?"

"You have neither sufficient men nor resources," Bávvál repeated. "We do."

The Avr looked ready to protest again.

"Let me finish!" the High Priest demanded. "We know that resources and manpower are also not enough. We know the Piijkij have the skill we, the simple Olmmoš, lack. Neither of us can confront the Jápmea alone and hope to win, but together we will succeed."

"So how do you envision this fated alliance?" the Avr inquired, sitting back in his seat, resting his hands upon the arms of the chair.

Bávvál inwardly scoffed at the man's pretense of ambivalence. He knew they had reached the crux of the matter. Bávvál moved to the edge of his seat and allowed his voice to be rounded by solemnity. "In the past, the Brethren alone were responsible for victory. In the past, the Avr alone made the decisions that saved us. But in the past, you were an army and the Order had little to offer. Now it is we who can provide you the army you need, and together we can make the decisions that will remove this threat once and for all."

An uneasy tension permeated the hall. Men on both sides were prepared to engage those whom they had, not moments before, shared a meal with. Chairs slowly eased back and hands rested upon hilts in readiness.

"You will give us men and weaponry, and we are to make decisions like brothers," the leader of the Piijkij summarized. "I wonder, Bávvál, in battle, will you be at my side when decisions are made to lead men to their death? Or, will you leave that to me and await the success you are so sure is our destiny?"

The High Priest felt his anger surge, but he did not rise to the taunt. "I bow to your expertise in battle, Dávgon. I know nothing of it. But I understand the needs of the Olmmoš. You know how to keep order among the trained. I know what it takes to keep order among the ordinary. Our continued existence is maintained by both. I ask you to keep me informed of all developments so I can protect the souls in my care. I will offer my opinion as I see fit and will defend it when I feel it imperative. I would expect the same from you." Bávvál sat back, signaling this was his final gambit.

～

Dávgon considered the High Priest's overture and knew the decision rested with him. He believed the priest's true aim was power over souls and not their protection, but he could not find fault in that. Most Olmmoš were little better than the binna when threatened by wolves. They would bolt in any direction available to them, even if that direction were ultimately a trap. Still, it could not be denied that if the Brethren were to succeed, they would need weapons and manpower. They needed what the Vijns offered. But with any luck, it would be the Vijns who would be beholden and not the Avr.

"Perhaps we should discuss the latest developments with the Jápmea," Dávgon said, leveling his gaze upon his newest ally.

～

It had been foolish of Rikkar to risk coming to the Order while Dávgon and the Brethren were in their midst, but Bávvál had to admit the information he brought was valuable and timely.

The High Priest regarded his newest spy. "The gods thank you, Rikkar."

"As I thank the gods," the man answered, bowing.

"And Rikkar," the High Priest spoke to his receding back, "Dávgon and his men have a half day's lead. Do try not to get caught returning to our friends. We both have much to lose."

Rikkar faced Bávvál, and the High Priest could see his point was taken.

When the door shut behind the man, Bávvál considered what he had learned from both Dávgon and his spy. The Avr of the Brethren had been circumspect.

Training foray. Bávvál snorted at the ruse.

The Brethren tracked one of their own—one who had betrayed them—this Irjan. And the full force of the Piijkij had failed to make a prisoner of one man.

But the man had not been alone, Bávvál amended his thoughts, *he traveled with the Jápmea.*

Despite the warmth of the spring night and the fire before him, Bávvál felt a chill overtake him. If the Jápmea were preparing to regain their place, then he would have to be ready not only to push them back into obscurity, but also to make sure the Brethren of Hunters joined them.

Part Five

THE CALL OF DESTINY

CHAPTER FIFTY-TWO

"**S**top!" Irjan called out. "That is not how you thrust your sword! If you do that you open your broad side to a quick spin and slicing cut!"

He drew back his own weapon and stepped away from his opponent.

"You are too eager to deliver the last blow," he criticized. "You have to take each moment as it is presented and fight that moment while looking to see if another will follow." He spat upon the ground and raised his sword. "Again," he yelled.

He parried the quick jabs and thrusts of his opponent and then began his own attack.

His opponent slipped back and then ducked under the next arc to thrust, turn, and slice, finding the soft portion of Irjan's flank exposed.

Irjan felt the flicker of heat and the pain it brought. He stopped short and drew himself up smiling, despite the discomfort. "Good. Well done." He gathered Dárja into his arms, squeezing her. "I will make a swordswoman out of you yet," he teased.

She pulled out of his embrace and scowled. "You mean, I already am one. I just humor you until I can no longer allow pity to occupy my mind."

Irjan laughed heartily. "It will take more than your sixteen seasons of snow to best me."

Dárja's stern look crumbled and she laughed as well, falling into him and allowing him to embrace her once again.

They walked comfortably together toward the guards.

"I would like to return to my cell," he said to one of them. The guard nodded and led the way. Dárja followed. At the entrance to his cell, he stopped. "My heart, would you allow an old man to lick his wounds in peace?"

Dárja hesitated but then quickly nodded, saying, "Of course, bieba!"

"Go and torture Kalek and Okta," Irjan chided, kissing her on the forehead. The guard started to close the door behind him, but Dárja raced forward and stopped the door with her hand.

"I'll be here tomorrow," she said.

Irjan smiled, "I am already looking forward to it."

~

Dárja released her arm and stepped back. She stared at the door's smooth surface and continued to work on a problem she'd been unable to solve. In the recent moon cycle, Irjan had become more withdrawn. She worried about him. Despite her best efforts, she couldn't lift his spirits. She knew it went beyond his imprisonment, because, though he was confined, Irjan had made a life for himself within the walls of the Jápme-meahttun world—a life he built upon her—and she recognized her responsibility.

He was her bieba. He'd raised her, cared for her, given her her song, and most importantly, he loved her. She'd always known that sadness lurked within him. As a child, she believed it was because he was in prison, and he couldn't move as he pleased; but now, she knew that even if he'd been free to go where he wished, he would still be in prison. Irjan was chained by old memories and regrets, and though she'd tried, Dárja could not erase them.

This failing pushed her to try harder, to become what he most needed—his son.

Dárja wasn't supposed to know about Marnej, but she'd overheard Kalek speaking to Okta and it had triggered in her some deep, wordless memory that clung maddeningly to the edges of her consciousness. And though neither Okta nor Kalek wished to speak of it, Dárja was determined to make them do so, today—now.

She strode down the corridor and was surprised by the frenzied activity all around her. Dárja looked and felt out of place as she stood still in the center of the flurry. She called out to one of the passing nieddaš she knew.

"Úlla, what's happening?"

"Have you not heard?" Úlla answered in disbelief. "The Elders say the Olmmoš are leading their army in our direction. We must prepare for war."

"What?" Dárja replied, stunned.

Exasperated, Úlla called over her shoulder, "Perhaps if you did not spend your time in the jail with that half-being, you might know what is happening to your own kind."

It wasn't the first time Dárja had heard such words, words meant to hurt her by questioning her relationship with her bieba. In the past, she would have quickly countered it, but in her present frame of mind, she wondered if she'd not just heard a piece of truth from some silly nieddaš. Dárja rushed in the direction of Kalek's quarters, her urgency lost among a crowd of others.

"Kalek," she called out, bursting through his door without stopping to knock. "Kalek!" Her own echo greeted her. Dárja swore under her breath and raced off to the only other place he might be.

At Okta's door she stopped and knocked and was summoned to enter. The old healer looked up from his work. "Well, you are a sight," he laughed.

Dárja touched her face and hair. Her carefully plaited braid must have loosened during her training, and what had been loosened had become wild in her mad dash to find the truth.

"Where's Kalek, Okta? I must find him," she exclaimed.

Unfazed by her frenzy, Okta answered, "He is about his business."

Dárja fidgeted under his scrutiny. "Where did he go?" she demanded. "I must find him."

"You look as if you are about to run off in a hundred different directions," the healer commented, then came around his work table and stood before her, putting his hand on her shoulder. "You know you carry your mother's spirit," he said quietly.

She shook off his hand. "I care not for my mother's spirit," she said brusquely. "I'm only concerned with finding Kalek."

The old healer took a couple of steps back and asked, "And what do you hope to achieve when you find him?"

This question, posed so gently, so filled with feeling, disarmed her. Dárja was forced to ask herself the same thing.

"I need to know. I need to know the truth," she said finally.

"But what is the truth?" Okta mumbled and then seemed to regret his severe tone. He nodded reluctantly then agreed, "Yes. About what matter do you wish to have the truth?"

She looked at him and without hesitating said, "Marnej."

Dárja watched the healer's face as she said the name. Although nothing moved, it was as if darkness had overtaken the old one.

"If we are to speak of this," he started, "then humor my old bones while we talk of the past." He moved to the chairs by the cold summer hearth and beckoned to Dárja.

She followed, unexpectedly hesitant. If the truth required her to sit, then perhaps it was something so enormous that she might never stand again. Dárja wanted to spring to her feet and run from the room.

"Marnej," Okta spoke the name with soft reverence, "is at the heart of so many lives. I had hoped this was something relegated to the past, but devotion, I have learned, endures."

As she listened to the story unfold, Dárja heard a tale of loss and hope and heartbreak. Kalek had nearly lost his life to save

Marnej. Irjan had killed for him and would end his life imprisoned by guilt. And Dárja had unknowingly been a part of it all.

Anger flared within her. Who was this Olmmoš boy who had shaped her destiny, who deserved such sacrifice from all of them? She hated him for existing and hated him even more for being beyond her grasp; he was among the Piijkij who sought war and the destruction of her kind.

Dárja's heart pounded with the futile hatred of one besieged by injustice on all sides. But her anger, so quick to boil, cooled into icy resolve. She knew she couldn't remake the past, but the future still lay ahead. *He will not have a hand in it*, she promised herself. *He will not have a hand in it.*

Kalek then burst into the room, breaking the spell of silent intention. A torrent of questions tumbled from him before he realized Okta had company.

Dárja stood, slowly. Though her heart beat with determination, she wasn't sure her legs were ready to stand and carry the burden she'd taken on. When she reached her full height, she leaned over to kiss Okta upon the forehead, then faced Kalek with a knowing smile. "We're at war," she said, leaving the healers to their arts.

~

Kalek seemed caught off guard by Dárja's manner, and he did not stop her. Instead, he looked to Okta for an explanation.

The old healer had known for some time their lives would be changing in a way he could not control. He had believed the Piijkij and other Olmmoš to be the biggest threat to the future of their kind. Now he wondered if it wasn't something less obvious, but no less powerful, like the bond of love.

"She knows the truth," he finally said by way of an explanation. "She knows about Marnej."

"And you let her go, just like that?" Kalek exclaimed.

Okta felt overwhelmed by sadness, "I have interfered too much in her life."

"But Irjan!" Kalek sputtered. "What will she do?"

"I do not know," Okta said. "I do not know."

~

The soldiers grumbled and Marnej couldn't blame them. They'd been scouting for days with no success, and while he and the other Piijkij rode on horseback, staying just ahead of the biting flies, the foot soldiers walked through the thick of them.

Marnej squinted up at the sky to sight the sun, and groaned. It had barely passed the midpoint. They had hours to go before they would make camp. He focused his attention on the dust swirling around the horses' hooves and tried to forget about the passage of time, but a sense of unease tightened about him, making him wary and suspicious. Straining to look in all directions, he could see nothing, but he could definitely *feel* something—a presence he couldn't explain.

Marnej spurred his horse toward his commander.

"Sir." He stopped abruptly beside the older Piijkij. "There's something in the woods to the northeast."

The commander scrutinized the tree line. "I see nothing."

"Sir, I'm sure of it," Marnej insisted.

The commander, though skeptical, called out to one of the foot soldiers, "Take your men there." He pointed to where Marnej had indicated. "Scour the undergrowth."

The soldier jumped to action, taking a dozen men with him. Marnej followed behind. The soldiers beat the bushes with their swords, moving further into the forest.

Perhaps I imagined it, Marnej thought as he rode toward the trees, seeing nothing around him.

A cry, like that of no animal or bird, pierced the air. Marnej dropped off his now alert horse and ran in the direction of the sound with his sword at the ready. He quickly came upon the body of an Olmmoš soldier. He knelt, placing his hand upon the man's neck—then something moved beyond his sight. Marnej stood up, and a branch cracked under his weight. In an instant, arrows rained down and the Jápmea materialized from the shadows, their swords cutting a great swath through the group of soldiers before vanishing back into nothingness.

The surviving soldiers scrambled to their feet and scanned the area around them.

"Accursed demons!" one of the men yelled after the ghosts. "You are cowards."

Marnej and the foot soldiers retreated warily, their swords at the ready.

The Piijkij commander rode up, calling out, "Marnej! At my side, now!"

Marnej quickly stepped over to the commander, but his eyes wandered back in the direction the Jápmea had disappeared.

"Explain how you knew they were there!"

The boy, though as tall and broad as any among the Brethren, bowed his head in the face of scrutiny. "I saw them," he answered, though he knew it wasn't the truth.

The commander looked at him with suspicion. "I did not see them."

Marnej's throat tightened. "I'm sorry sir, I just. . .saw them."

The commander eyed Marnej again and then dismissed him, saying, "Since you have vision well beyond the rest of us, you will have sentry duty during the darkest hours."

"Yes, sir."

Marnej retreated to get his horse. Discouraged and shaken, he pulled himself up, conscious of the shadows, but aware that the threat had passed for now.

~

"Get me Marnej," the Avr called to one of his men, and threw himself into his chair.

It had taken them too long to get to this point, and Dávgon refused to allow the rat-faced Vijns to step into the forefront. Fifteen seasons of snow, hunting and tracking and building small skirmishes into battles, and now, as they stood poised on the brink of a successful campaign, the Order of Believers was attempting to stall. The Avr of the Brethren of Hunters would not bow to someone who had never held a sword in his hand, much less had the strength to use it.

The tent flap parted and a guard leaned in. "The boy, my Avr."

Marnej stooped through the parted canvas, but still caught his head on the fabric. Dávgon could see the boy was nervous.

Good, he thought, *keep him unsure of himself for the moment.*

He allowed the silence to grow thin and taut before finally speaking. "Your commander informed me of yesterday's occurrence. He is at a loss to understand how you, and only you, were able to see the Jápmea before you were set upon."

"I can't explain, sir. But I saw them." Marnej spoke quickly, but with firmness to his answer.

The Avr smiled behind his steepled hands. "Yes, I am certain you saw them. You seem to have the same gift your father had."

At the mention of his father, the boy's jaw tightened. "I'm not my father."

The Avr bounded out of his chair and stood directly in front on the boy. "No, indeed." Dávgon clasped Marnej's shoulders. "You are not your father."

The boy twitched but did not look away.

The Avr released him and paced the short distance between him and the tent wall. "Let's put your skills to their test. To win a battle we must first have a committed enemy. The Jápmea have been content to strike at us in fits, because we have not truly cornered them. But to corner them, we must find where they hide, and they cannot hide from you, Marnej."

Dávgon watched his flattery work upon the boy. The fruits of a life sculpted by loneliness and isolation were coming to bear. Marnej was anxious to prove himself.

So much like his father at this age, Dávgon thought. *Right down to the Jápmea blood they shared.*

"You will leave immediately, taking my most trusted men, and follow whatever track is available to you," the Avr said. "Find them and bring me the knowledge I need to win a battle—to win back what is rightfully ours."

~

Marnej left the Avr, feeling at once emboldened and at a loss. His talents had finally received the recognition they deserved, and yet he felt uneasy. Marnej had never quite fit in with those around him—a cloud of whisper and gossip always seemed to follow him. But it went beyond the undercurrent of his heritage. He knew he was somehow different; he sensed and saw things the others didn't, and he suspected the voices he heard were unique to him as well.

While Marnej shared what he could see, he had never shared what he'd heard. The revelation risked too much, calling into question the state of his mind. And while he might speculate on his own sanity, he wouldn't allow others to do so. It was bad enough to be ostracized because his father had betrayed the Brethren; to be seen as mad would've been more than he could bear.

But Marnej had to admit the voices were there. As a child, they comforted him when no others did and kept him company when no one ventured to speak to him. And even now, they echoed somewhere far in the background. If he stilled himself long enough, he could, at times, make out its parts, but since the campaign had started, he'd not had a moment's privacy to give himself over to silent contemplation. Surrounded as he was by Piijkij and other Olmmoš soldiers, he could not risk a resurgence of rumors. Men depended on him. He couldn't lead them if they doubted him, if they feared treachery.

Gods, he groaned inwardly, *will I never be free of my father?*

Irjan, traitor and murderer. How many lives had he ruined? *His own. Mine! My mother's.* Marnej thought of his mother, dead at his father's hand. Villainy upon villainy. And now, Irjan had joined forces with the Jápmea to attack the Piijkij and his own people. His father was a damnable plague upon his every day.

Marnej gathered his bedroll and his mount and joined the men who awaited him. They would travel west and north, looking for signs of movement. Villages in the region had reported odd occurrences, and the Vijns of the Order of Believers had passed on the news to the Brethren. Many in Marnej's group grumbled that the High Priest led them astray, to keep the Piijkij spread out so they would be no threat to the power of the Believers. But the news couldn't be overlooked by the Avr or by Marnej.

⁓

From the moment they crossed into the western boundaries, Marnej felt ill at ease. The voices he often heard in his mind became louder and more pronounced. In the day, he could silence them with action, but at night, in the quiet crackle of firelight, he couldn't ignore them. At first, they came as a jumble, as if voice upon voice were overlaid; however, the more he sorted through the layers, the more they seemed to accommodate his efforts.

Huddled in his furs, awaiting sleep, Marnej finally heard the words clearly.

We are the Jápmemeahttun.
We are the guardians of the world.
Our memory stretches back to the start of days.
Our vision reaches beyond all tomorrows.
We sing together as one, so that our one may always survive.

We have waited.
We have watched.
We have rejoiced.

We have mourned.
Our journey begins.

The voices repeated and echoed and Marnej fell into them. He saw men and women in the shimmering distance. They walked forward with intention, as if nothing could distract them.

He tried to see their faces, but they remained shadowed, all save one—a girl, who rode upon a binna, wearing a man's armor and carrying the weapons of a soldier. She sat ramrod straight. Slowly, she turned her head and he felt her eyes upon him. He was powerless but to stare, as she held his gaze. Then from within him he heard a voice.

I am the voice of one brought to life by truth.
And by my sword that truth shall be set free.
I am watched over by the stars, but my destiny is my own to make.

She turned away from him, and in that instant, whatever spell held him broke. Marnej sat up abruptly, shaking. He looked around him. Everything had a fine dusting of snow. Sweat dripped down his face despite the cold, and he could neither draw breath in nor let it out.

Had it been a dream or had he truly gone mad?

Marnej shrank back into his furs as if the delusion resided outside of him and he could somehow hide from it. His eyes flew from one shadow to the next, looking for evidence of what he'd witnessed, but the shadows were just the flicker of the firelight against the dark night. The men around him slept soundly, as though they were alone in the forest.

But they weren't. The Jápmea were out there. He'd seen them; so had others. His latest vision. . . Marnej stopped himself. He couldn't explain what had happened to the others. Visions. They would scoff. He could barely believe it himself. No. He would stay silent, and let luck, and not his strange gifts, guide his future.

~

"They're not here," one of the Piijkij groused.

A murmur of agreement rose in the group. Some of the men looked at Marnej, but he avoided their sidelong glances and said nothing. He'd had no further visions, but felt sure the Jápmea were nearer than any believed.

He spurred his horse forward and scanned the forest floor for tracks upon the snow. He was desperate for some tangible sign to prove what he'd known in his heart for days: the Jápmea moved among them.

Why did they not attack? The young woman in his vision had been armed, perhaps a real soldier, although the idea of a woman fighting seemed cruel. But then again, who knew the extent of Jápmea barbarity? Perhaps their small group of men posed too little of a challenge for them, though it was unlikely they'd overlook an opportunity to strike at an enemy. *Unless.* The word hung in his mind. *What had the voice said?*

"Our journey begins." He almost shouted as the refrain popped into his mind, and then spun to see if any were within earshot. Relieved to find he was alone, Marnej settled his horse.

Where do they journey? They already lived in the mist, where else could they go? And then it occurred to him. *Beyond our reach—beyond my reach.* His heart beat faster as he considered his next actions. He'd never tried to conjure the voices when they were silent, but he had to know. He had to try.

Marnej dismounted, moving into the gloom of a snow-laden thicket. He wanted no prying eyes to witness his efforts. He tethered his mount to a low-slung branch and the horse tossed its shaggy head, shaking free a cascade of snow. Finally, standing in the center of the clearing, he listened.

He heard the horse's deep snuffling breath and the far-off cry of a bird, but no voices. He stilled himself even further, willing his heart to quiet, his breath to slow. He let go of whatever tension he held in his body and felt his muscles soften.

Around him, sounds became sharp and precise and the far-off could be heard. Then the sounds were no longer outside of him, rather the bird's call echoed within him and the wind whistled through him. He was the sound and it filled his heart, urging him to call out to the world. He was at a loss, and yet he was content, at peace, accepted.

And then, a lone voice broke through his reverie.

Son of my heart.
Vessel of a father's soul.
You journeyed into the realm of the dreams of the dark sky,
And traveled back in a blaze of light.
Go into the world to meet your destiny,
And know that you have been touched by the gods.

Marnej's eyes snapped open. "Irjan."

CHAPTER FIFTY-THREE

As Irjan rode westward with the Jápmemeahttun, his thoughts matched the swaying gait of his binna. He knew he occupied a unique position in the Jápmemeahttun world. He was, at once, hated by many, begrudgingly accepted by some, and befriended by only a few. But he drew satisfaction knowing at least one, among all the Jápmemeahttun, loved him wholly—Dárja.

She was his beacon, lighting the way forward. She was willful and tenacious and demanding, and he loved all these parts of her because they made her alive. He looked over his shoulder and watched her riding, straight-backed and determined. Unlike the rest of the nieddaš, she rode with a sword at her side. Many among the Jápmemeahttun disapproved of their relationship. He'd heard the comments and often agreed with them. A prison was no place for a nieddaš. Nor were his skills as a parent to be lauded.

But Kalek had tried to assuage his doubts.

"A cell is just a room, no different than another when it is filled with love. You, of all of us, have shown the depths to which you are capable of love. That is perhaps your best quality as an Olmmoš, and being an Olmmoš is not something that should be held against you. Besides, she may need to know more of what it means to be among your kind than to be among ours."

At the time, Irjan had missed the almai's meaning, but the passing seasons of snow made it clear there was a growing disquiet among the voices in the Song of All.

Irjan had not ventured to ask the meaning of it, because he knew the Immortals did not believe he merited an answer. Even Kalek would have been reticent to speak openly and so Irjan had not pressed him. Instead, it was Dárja who made Irjan think about the emerging future.

~

"Bieba," Dárja called out, rushing past the guards, "you must teach me to fight."

Irjan laughed at her request, "Mánná, why do you wish to fight?"

She looked at him with the intensity of one who knew she was not being taken seriously.

"I must know how to use a sword if I am going to fight in a battle."

It was Irjan's turn to regard the child gravely. "What battle do you speak of?"

"The one between us and the Olmmoš."

Dárja's matter-of-factness chilled him to his core.

There was no battle that day or for many days following, but then gradually the skirmishes began and more Jápmemeahttun were taught to wield the sword. Though she was barely into her eighth season of snow, Irjan finally acquiesced to her demand. He had not been able to protect Marnej, but he could teach his mánná the skills she would need to protect herself, should it ever come to it.

Dárja's education gave him new purpose, and Irjan threw himself into it wholeheartedly. He went so far as to offer his services to the Noaidi and the Council of Elders.

His offer, however, was soundly, though gently, refused.

~

"You have honored your promise to us, Irjan. And you have made a great effort to abide by our rules, but we cannot accept your proffered services," the Noaidi answered for the Council of Elders.

"But I know how they think and plan," Irjan persisted.

The ancient one agreed. "Yes, that is true. But your son is among them, and as long as he is, the true loyalty of your heart is unknowable."

"You believe I will not fight by your side." Irjan shook his head in disbelief.

"I believe you would, until the moment your son's life were before you."

Undaunted, Irjan promised, "If it comes down to a sword, then you will have mine. And though I may not be able to take my son's life, I can let him take mine."

The Noaidi shook his head and stood up. "We will not need such sacrifice from you, Irjan. You have given enough—yes, though you have taken much, you have given enough. It is the Council's decision to move away from here."

"But the Taistelijan?"

"They wish to fight, and it may come to that. But for now, we move forward in peace. The Song still holds us and perhaps moving away from the Olmmoš will let us rebuild."

"There are few places where the Olmmoš do not thrive," Irjan pointed out.

The Noaidi gave him a rueful smile. "It is true. Your kind spreads everywhere."

"My kind are but two, that I know of," Irjan remarked, and the Noaidi acknowledged this by bowing his head.

On the way back to his cell, Dárja came bounding down the corridor toward him and rushed headlong into an embrace. She looked up at him beaming.

"I heard from the guards that Mord leads more than one thousand warriors now, and they are ready to fight," she said with a child's simple pride. "One day, I will be one of them."

Irjan froze and then quickly recovered. "Let's hope it's still many seasons of snow in your future."

Dárja looked crestfallen. "Bieba, don't you believe I will make a good warrior?"

Irjan knelt and pulled her close to him once again. "No, mánná! On the contrary, you will make a fine warrior. It is only a bieba's wish to have as much time with the one he loves."

Her good humor restored, Dárja jumped back and grabbed her sword. "Then let us practice!"

Over the next seven seasons of snow they practiced and sparred and studied the strategies of war, but each day Irjan wished it wasn't necessary. He longed for the vision of peace the Council presented, but in the end, as the number of skirmishes increased, he came to believe an all-out battle was inevitable.

～

Irjan looked at Dárja upon her binna, her dark hair plaited down her back. He sighed for the child he was destined to release into the world. She had grown into a beautiful and strong nieddaš and he could only begin to imagine what her future might look like.

If Irjan was one of a pair in the world, then Dárja was truly unique. She'd survived birth, but without receiving the full force of life because he'd intervened. In a fit of guilt, he'd once asked Kalek what would become of Dárja as she grew.

The almai had shrugged, not wishing to answer, but when pushed, Kalek had confirmed Irjan's suspicions. "She will not be like the others. She has shared the spark of life with another and I cannot believe she will ever be anything besides a nieddaš."

"She will not transform then?" he'd asked, hoping he'd misunderstood.

"Irjan, she will not become an almai. Her destiny is singular within our Song." Kalek must have sensed the burden he'd placed upon Irjan, because he added, "I believe that is why you were chosen to carry her Song. You can give her what none of us can—a new way to the future."

But he had made her a warrior, though she would never be a Taistelijan. Irjan withdrew into the deep strains of the Song of All, hoping to forget the past, forget his regrets. But it gave him no relief. There was a discordant and unfamiliar note within its regular melody.

He scanned the faces around him, but none seemed to have noticed it. He listened closer, trying to pick out its parts and then a voice came bursting into his mind like a clear picture.

I am alone in this world.
The child of death and treachery.
I carry the burden of history changed
And a promise unfulfilled.
I will right the wrongs of the dark nights.

Irjan's heart skipped a beat. The unfamiliar refrain repeated, and the image it brought to his mind was precious—Marnej. Fifteen seasons of snow had passed since his failed attempt to rescue his son and yet he knew it was Marnej. Irjan had chosen to save Kalek's life over his son and he would not change that. But what about now? Was there a chance now for Marnej?

Irjan quickly glanced back at Dárja. Her focus remained ahead. Then he looked around to the others riding beside him. Before he could stop himself, Irjan sent his voice into the Song.

Son of my heart.
Vessel of a father's soul.
You journeyed into the realm of the dreams of the dark sky,
And traveled back in a blaze of light.
Go into the world to meet your destiny,
And know that you have been touched by the gods.

The words flooded out of him and an instant later Irjan regretted his carelessness. He'd put them all in danger. The Noaidi was right. When it came to Marnej, he was powerless before the love he felt for his son.

~

Marnej stood alone in the clearing, panting with fear and anger. He'd heard his father—Irjan, the traitor to the Brethren. He wanted to turn and run, but he had to continue; he had to recapture the feelings flowing through his mind.

If Irjan still favored his notorious ways, then perhaps Marnej could both lure him forward and gain knowledge of the Jápmea whereabouts. He stilled himself, envisioning the morning's reconnaissance, placing its details in the center of his mind. If what he believed was true, or even possible, then he'd opened up his brothers to ambush. But the risk was worth it if he could, once and for all, rid himself of his father.

Later, when Marnej recovered his comrades' trail, he kept a keen eye about him. But as they traveled through the dimming light of day, he began to doubt his plan. Perhaps it was madness, after all, that had overtaken his mind. He shook his head as if to clear it of its misgivings and out of the corner of his eye he saw something sailing through the air.

One of his men cried out and fell from his horse. With swords drawn, the Piijkij circled, looking to face their attackers, but saw no one. Then the world seemed to split wide open as a wave of armed riders came at them. Marnej froze, looking from one face to another.

At the forefront, a wild-eyed man charged ahead of the others.

Vindication grabbed hold of Marnej. He drew his weapon and moved to engage. Then he stopped. The man he believed to be his father wasn't advancing to attack. Rather, he was advancing as someone pursued, and the Jápmea behind Irjan seemed just as surprised to see the Piijkij as his own men were to see them.

Before Marnej could make sense of it all, a sword swung down at him. His mount screamed in pain and reared, clawing the air. Marnej barely managed to hold on.

As he regained firm ground, he parried his attacker, dispatching him with a graceless hack to his neck, then turned in time to see Irjan drop off his binna and slide under the girth of a mounted Piijkij. With a deft flick of his wrist, Irjan sliced through the saddle's leather straps. The rider slid off with a sickening thud, and was finished off by Irjan's blade.

Marnej lost track of his father as a wave of attackers came at him. He pulled hard upon the horse's reins, and the pair of them narrowly missed being cleaved in two. Marnej spurred his horse to charge, and slashed with deadly accuracy. The Jápmea warriors fell to the ground and Marnej growled with satisfaction. He whipped about, looking for his father once again.

At first, Marnej didn't see him in the thicket of fighting men, but then he came into view. Marnej urged his horse forward, but stopped abruptly when he saw a girl ride into the melee with her sword poised to bring death.

She rode balanced upon her binna as if they were one, and then she spun and dropped and ran just as Irjan had before.

Marnej stared, amazed. This young girl was as reckless as his father and clearly had been trained well. Irjan came back into Marnej's field of vision and he quickly spurred his horse forward, charging right over the Jápmea girl.

Startled by her sudden appearance, Marnej drew himself up short and she quickly raced under his horse. But Marnej was prepared. He jumped as the saddle slid and fell and rolled into a fighting position. The girl bared her teeth and charged him. He fought off her blows, surprised by their strength, and he returned in kind.

She deflected his onslaught with effort, but not with panic. Whatever her intentions, they were no less stalwart than his.

He moved to rush her and she slid low under the sweep of his sword, coming up with unexpected swiftness to attack.

"No!" a distant voice rang out.

~

Irjan looked up from his own fight to see Dárja in the midst of heated struggle with a young boy. The sight filled him with horror.

"No!" he cried out again, realizing the blond young boy had to be Marnej.

Irjan ran headlong, heedless of who followed, cutting at everything in his path.

"No," he screamed, coming between the two. "It cannot be this way. Marnej, I cannot undo the past, but I beg you to believe that I have only loved you and tried to protect you."

The boy lowered his sword for a split second, his face alive with pain, his fury wavering.

"Marnej," Dárja gasped and the spell was broken.

The boy lunged forward with his sword and Irjan blocked it.

"Leave here, Dárja," Irjan commanded.

"I am not leaving you, bieba," she cried back.

"If you do not leave now, Dárja, I cannot guarantee any of us will live!"

~

Marnej brought all he had to the blows he rained down upon his father and still the man did not fight back.

"Fight or you will die!" he screamed in frustration.

But Irjan continued to block blow upon blow, letting himself be pushed back further and further, all the while staring at Marnej.

"It may come to that," he answered, "but not today." The man deflected another thrust, closed his eyes, and vanished into the mist.

Marnej stood apart, his heart pounding and his head spinning. He fell to his knees in the thin, wet snow. Panting, he pulled himself up from all fours to look at what remained of the battlefield. Wounded Piijkij called out for assistance, and this brought Marnej back to himself. He jumped to his feet and bounded to the closest of the Brethren in need of assistance.

CHAPTER FIFTY-FOUR

RIKKAR STOOD BEFORE THE Vijns of the Order of Believers and recounted his news.

"As you know, the Avr has sent patrols to the north, and they have just returned with news of skirmishes."

Bávvál looked at his spy and saw that the man enjoyed the suspense he was creating. "Hurry up with it, Rikkar! I would hate for the Brethren to question your absence."

Chastened, the man spoke quickly. "The word is the boy was among the patrols and met his father."

"And?" Bávvál pressed, wondering if Rikkar might have finally lost his usefulness.

"They met in battle. The boy's loyalty is now sealed, and the Avr has put him at the forefront of the campaign."

"Dávgon places his campaign in the hands of a mere boy?" Bávvál shook his head with disgust. "It appears I have given him too much credit by allotting him so much of my attention."

Rikkar hurriedly broke in, "You do not misplace your energies, my Vijns."

The High Priest was about to reprimand his spy for impertinence, when Rikkar blurted out, "The boy has Jápmea blood, like his father!"

Bávvál sat stunned. "What? How can that be?"

"Of Irjan I do not know, he is said to be the only survivor of a Jápmea raid. But I overheard the Avr, before he left on campaign, to say that while they had failed to turn Irjan's Jápmea blood to the cause, they had succeeded with his son."

As the High Priest silently gathered his thoughts, Rikkar continued, "Many have noted the boy is as oddly skilled as his father before him. They say he claims to see things others cannot. And when the Jápmea attacked, he alone was ready."

Bávvál put his hand up, stopping the man from going on. "So Dávgon harbors the Jápmea within the Brethren. What do you know of his plans for the boy?"

"I suspect the Avr believes the boy can somehow lead the Brethren to the Jápmea, just as I believed his father could." Rikkar hesitated. "It appears my assumption would have borne out."

Bávvál ignored the man's need for praise. "Yes, and it appears Dávgon may be right as well. If the boy can lead the Brethren and our soldiers to the Immortals, then the Jápmea may finally be at an end." To himself, the High Priest savored the possibilities. *And if it were revealed the Brethren harbored not one, but two, of these foul creatures, the honor of the Piijkij would be ruined.*

Aloud he concluded, "We will let our fine Brethren deal with the Jápmea, and then we will expose their rotten core—their unholy union with the Immortals. The girkogilli will clamor for justice. We will be duty bound to do what they ask."

The High Priest leaned back. "Rikkar, after all this time, you may have finally proven yourself worthy of the power you covet."

～

Marnej's resolve wavered as he traveled north again with the remaining Piijkij. The encounter with the Jápmea had unnerved him. But in truth, it was Irjan and not the Immortals that caused his disquiet.

Who was Irjan really? His father had begged to be believed, professing his love, yet he acted in concert with the Jápmea. Still, he'd refused to fight Marnej. It was impossible to see the truth of the man, but in the end, Marnej couldn't ignore the fact his father remained a traitor to the very men Marnej had sworn to serve, and couldn't let doubts cloud his vision. The next time he encountered his father, he vowed he wouldn't falter. His future depended on his doggedness.

Marnej turned his attention to scouting for signs of the Jápmea. They were on the edge of the Pohjola now and, despite the long days of sun, he and the others felt an unnatural chill. Few ventured beyond this frontier. And then the thought occurred to him: *my father did.* His father had roamed these desolate lands with the binna; perhaps even then he was in league with the Jápmea.

"Do we make camp here?" one of the men asked, shaking Marnej free from his speculations.

Marnej was about to say no, they had plenty of light left to continue; but then he remembered it was Evenday, and the men had need of some connection to the lives they'd left behind to come north, if only to maintain their morale.

"Yes," Marnej answered. "Let's build the bonfire and drink the juhka and give thanks to the gods." He slid off his mount and saw the men were pleased by his decision. Even after many moon cycles of travel, Marnej felt uneasy in the role of leader. He knew the men thought him too young, and then there were his particular skills, which, though they pretended otherwise, bothered them.

Marnej let his horse forage on the low mounded shrubs and was surprised to see the men had already raised the fire. Good cheer flowed through them as the flames grew, and no doubt the juhka being poured added to it. Marnej stepped up and held out his cup, filled to almost overflowing. He took a sip and closed his eyes, savoring its heady sweetness. Around him he heard the laughter of his men and their ribald jokes.

He was sinking into the sound of their voices when he felt an unseen hand pulling him. He opened his eyes and saw his men smiling and joking. They raised their polished horn cups to him and drank deeply. Then, as if he were already drunk, his vision turned hazy.

Marnej tried unsuccessfully to focus his eyes, and when he attempted to take a step, he found himself rooted. Finally, he willed himself forward and swayed. He tried to brace himself upon the closest man, but his hands found neither flesh nor firmness and he tumbled ahead, landing upon the ground next to the fire.

The earth under Marnej's hands pulsed like the veins of a man. In horror, he pushed off its warm, throbbing surface, landing on his back unable to scramble away from the fire, which inexplicably radiated life itself.

Voices echoed in his mind, surrounding him, swirling like the wind, and he tried to focus on them. He stood up and took a step forward into unfamiliar lightness, listening to the beckoning voices. Soon he was running, trying to catch up with fragments of images. But as Marnej rushed ahead, the voices seemed to withdraw further.

Onwards he ran through blurred visions, until he found himself before beautiful carved wooden spires. He raised his hand and touched their dark wood surfaces, marked by the yellow of a lichen bloom, and felt the hum of life within.

We are the Jápmemeahttun.
We are the guardians of the world.
Our memory stretches back to the start of days.
Our vision reaches beyond all tomorrows.
We sing together as one, so that our one may always survive.

Inside these walls resides a creature older than time, Marnej marveled, and he'd found them. By the gifts of the gods, he had found them.

Marnej's joy, however, crumbled into frustration as some force pulled him backward against his will. He reached out to grab anything as the world blurred around him. Then his stomach lurched, and his body fell hard upon the ground. When he finally managed to stand, Marnej found himself before the mounted Brethren, their swords poised to strike in his direction.

"I've found them," Marnej said, in a voice barely above a whisper. "I've found them."

~

A collective knowing spread quickly through the Council of Elders. One among their group said, "He has come."

Einár, the Noaidi, nodded. He had hoped the skills of the father would not be shared by the son. But he had heard for himself the voice of the young Piijkij within the Song. He feared they were facing their last days of peace.

The fact that their fate rested upon the actions of one soul was maddeningly unjust. The history and wisdom gained through countless Jápmemeahttun lifetimes would be pitted against the arrogance of one young Olmmoš.

Einár considered his choices, looking to find a path that might have brought them to a different place. Each time the end was the same.

"We must offer counsel," he said finally.

~

"We have run and it has cost us." Mord's voice boomed. "Our only course now is to fight."

"We listened to the messages from the gods and tried to preserve our promise of peace," Einár spoke for the Council of Elders.

"Then the gods have deserted us!" Mord declared, and a collective gasp shuddered among the gathered Jápmemeahttun.

The old warrior turned to face the others, many of whom shared his view. "We fought the Olmmoš once and then retreated, only to find ourselves once again threatened by their hatred and aggression. If we turn away, then we doom ourselves. We should not blindly walk into obscurity."

A voice rose from the back. "If we fight, will we not end in the same obscurity?"

A chorus of agreeing murmurs traveled through the room.

"Then we shall have to make the battles of the Jápmemeaht-tun the matter of legend!" Mord exhorted. "We shall fight with valor like the ancients and wreak havoc among those who dare to stand against us. Our arrows shall fall like sleet and our swords will pierce their souls, sending them to eternal darkness. We shall not run except to battle and we shall not withdraw unless it is in victory. If we are to meet our end, then let us leave the world in the manner of Jápmemeahttun—proud guardians."

This time, a swelling of support arose for the warrior's vision and Mord drew strength from the rumbling.

"Allow the Taistelijan their place in this world!"

～

Within the crowd, Kalek sat beside Okta. He felt sadness emanating from the old healer. He put his hand on his mentor's shoulder and Okta looked at him with eyes lost to the past.

"Our end has come," he said quietly.

"We are strong and resourceful," Kalek answered. "We may have lifetimes ahead of us yet."

Okta nodded. "I have seen this before. We will have much to do. We must prepare ourselves while we can." He stood up and waited for Kalek to do the same.

～

"Mord. Remain," the Noaidi called out to the backs filing out from the great hall.

The old warrior stood to attention, his expression triumphant.

Before he could say anything Einár came to the point. "The boy has discovered us. He leads the forces of our destruction."

"You are certain?"

The Elder nodded. "I am. He has entered the Song."

The old warrior looked taken aback, but reserved his response as he appeared to give the matter more thought. "They will be travel-weary by the time they reach us. It will be to our advantage. We can strike at them along their route like a dog nipping at the heels of the herd."

"It will take more than distance and skirmishes to diminish their power," Einár pointed out.

The Taistelijan scowled. "You speak with too much authority for one who has given little thought to the strategies of a war."

"I am speaking as one who sees these as the last days of our kind."

Chastened, Mord bowed his head to the Elder. "We will fight to our last."

Einár sighed. "Yes, I am afraid we will have to. If they attack us here, then everyone will need to be armed. The Song is no longer strong enough to protect us. It is fracturing and beginning to tear apart."

"It is not my intention to let them reach us here," Mord explained. "We will be the ones to choose our battles, and, with the gods' favor, we will walk away victorious."

The Noaidi envied the confidence of his eminent warrior, but he feared there would be no victory. If the Jápmemeahttun somehow managed to prevail, it would be an interlude, a momentary triumph, followed by the plaguing shadow of the Olmmoš.

Einár had resigned himself to this future when the warrior broke into his thoughts.

"You said the boy has just entered the Song?"

"Yes."

"There is, then, every reason to believe he is close." Before Einár could object, Mord continued. "The boy is at best the half-fling of a half-being. He could not have the power to enter the

Song at great distances and sustain it. We ourselves struggle to do this."

"If the boy can be found. . ." Einár began.

"Then he can be dispatched before disclosing his knowledge," Mord finished.

"Their strategy would suffer a setback."

"It would be at an end," Mord corrected.

The Noaidi met his gaze. "Gather your men."

CHAPTER FIFTY-FIVE

Dárja waited anxiously for Kalek and Okta to return from the gathering. When they entered their temporary quarters, she bounded off the cot to stand directly in front of them.

Though she desperately wanted to blurt out her question, she knew she needed to find some tactful way to ask it. As she searched for the right approach, Kalek looked at her and said, "We are to fight."

Dárja stopped in her tracks, unsure of how to respond. She could see from their faces the healers weren't pleased with the outcome of the gathered council, but she supported the decision.

"Can it not be for the best?" she asked, not wanting to disregard their feelings.

"War is rarely what is best," Okta answered, moving toward his table of medicines.

Dárja approached him. "But Okta, you fought, and most would agree you were one of the best Taistelijan."

"Do not think I am flattered by such regard," the healer snapped, without looking up from his herbs and potions.

Dárja stiffened at the rebuke. "So you're not proud you were a Taistelijan?"

"I see no reason to build my pride upon meting out death," he barked.

"Dárja, we have much to do," Kalek interrupted, trying to diffuse the growing tension, but she would not be dissuaded.

"Well, I will be proud to be a Taistelijan," she challenged Okta.

Okta waved her off. "I do not know who fills your head with such notions."

Kalek tried to stay his mentor's words, but the old healer spoke over his objections.

"There is no honor on a battlefield. There is only death and silence. Even if our days continued to the last sunset of this world, you would not stand among their ranks."

The finality of this pronouncement stunned Dárja. She looked at Kalek, whose eyes pleaded with her to leave off.

"You don't believe I have the spirit of a Taistelijan," she spoke through gritted teeth.

Okta banged his palms down upon the table, causing bottles to rattle and fall. "If you wish to hear you have the soul of one who can take the life of another, then I say: yes! But you shall not know the life of a Taistelijan." His anger spent, he turned away. "And I am both sorry and thankful for that fact."

The healer left the room, closing the door behind him with a resounding thud.

Dárja felt the weight of Kalek's hand on her shoulder. "What did he mean, Kalek?" she asked, dread folding around her chest.

His hand dropped away. "You are unique among us, Dárja. You survived birth without receiving the full essence of life." Kalek frowned, then added softly. "We do not believe you will be able to make the transition."

Dárja heard what Kalek said, but the enormity of his meaning took time to sink in. "I'll remain a nieddaš for the length of my existence?"

"Yes, so we believe." Kalek hung his head.

Dárja was caught up in her collapsing world, but came back to herself in time to hear, "But we have no way of knowing with certainty. For, as I say, you are unique."

Pride and hurt made her stand straighter. "When were you planning to tell me this?"

"We hoped you would become a biebmoeadni and experience the joy of it, before. . ." Kalek stopped. "The truth is, I hoped I would never have to tell you. I hoped you would have a normal life as your mother did—become a biebmoeadni, fall in love, find your Origin, and bring life back to us. I wanted all this to be true for you. It still may be, I don't know."

"But. . .Okta." Dárja sputtered, regaining some of her anger.

"Okta has witnessed more tragedy than you or I can ever imagine. He lived through it, believing it was over, and today he had to face the fact it is not. To have you, to whom he has given so much of his heart, take on the cause of war. . .it is just too much for him." Kalek exhaled into the room's quiet tension, "I do not say he spoke kindly or with much thought, but I do ask you to believe he acted from a place of lost hope."

Dárja nodded, but said nothing. She stood silent, gazing down at the floor. Finally she asked, "Why did I not receive the full life essence?"

"You must ask your bieba," Kalek answered softly.

❧

Walking down the long passage to Irjan's prison cell, Okta's judgment replayed in Dárja's mind. She clenched her teeth and fought back against it.

I will be a Taistelijan. Maybe not in body, but at least in spirit.

"I would have won if he hadn't stopped me," she muttered aloud, reliving the recent skirmish with the Olmmoš. Then she realized what she really meant. *I would have killed Marnej.* But Irjan had stepped between them and she'd been forced to turn and run.

Dárja reached the door to Irjan's cell. His foray had cost him what little freedom he'd acquired, and now she wasn't allowed to enter his chamber; but they couldn't stop her from learning the truth. She banged loudly.

"Bieba," she called out. When there was no immediate response, she banged again and this time called, "Irjan."

With her ear pressed to the aged wood, she could hear scuffing footsteps approach the door.

"Dárja." His voice could barely be heard through the door.

"Yes, bieba. I've come for the truth."

"I will not speak of truth to you like this. Words have less meaning separated from the face of the one who speaks them."

She heard his footsteps move away from the door. She pulled back, whirling around to face the guard. "Let me enter."

"Dárja, you know he is allowed no visitors," the guard answered.

"I'll leave my sword and my knife," she offered with a frantic gesture to her weapons. "You may search me. I don't care, but I must see my bieba. Please, I've known you my whole life, allow me this one favor."

The guard grimaced.

She pulled the knife and her sword from her belt and held them out to him with her head bowed. She felt their weight taken from her hands and looked up to see the other guard opening the door to Irjan's cell.

As she crossed the threshold, the anger that fueled her quest drained. Sadness hung upon Irjan like a heavy woolen cloak, drawing his shoulders down with its weight. It was all she could do not to rush to him and embrace him as she'd always done. But she was no longer a child; she was a nieddaš, and her future rested upon the questions she needed answered.

"I need to know the truth, bieba."

Irjan grimaced when he heard the endearment. He kept his head lowered and then released the breath he had been holding. He looked up at her. "Ask what you must."

Dárja hesitated. "Kalek and Okta told me I will likely never become an almai, because I lack the life force necessary to transform. Kalek told me you must be the one to explain why."

Irjan nodded. "I wish I could say I would have chosen a different course had I known the outcome of my actions. But I cannot, because, at the time, my love for my son drove my every step."

"Marnej," she spat out bitterly.

"Yes, Marnej. Your quarrel, however, should be with me, and not with him. I sacrificed many lives to save him from the darkness of death."

Irjan explained how he had heard the voice of Aillun when he was consumed by despair and loss. He spoke of the spark of his idea, coming from the lost legends of the Jápmemeahttun. He explained, with the slow heaviness of lament, how he had tracked Aillun and found her at her Origin.

"Your oktoeadni fought bravely to protect you. She believed I had come to kill her and Djorn, the life bringer. But I was not there to take life. I was there to find life. I was trying to put the breath back into the body of my precious son."

Irjan's voice cracked, but he drew himself straighter. "When Djorn transformed, I placed Marnej within the explosion of his light. You were born, and Marnej reborn in that moment. I didn't know my actions would cost Aillun her life, nor you your future. I have lived with this guilt for all these seasons of snow. I thought I had taken your mother from you, but now I know what I took was something far more. . ." He stopped as his breath caught.

"I took from you the life of a true Jápmemeahttun and doomed you to an existence only you will know. For this I am truly sorry." Irjan hung his head.

Dárja looked at the bowed crown of the man who had raised her and cared for her, and tried to find a feeling alive inside of her. She wanted to find anger, to unleash a torrent of outrage, but she felt no anger, nor fear nor sadness nor any recognizable sensation. She felt numb.

She turned from Irjan without uttering a word, and left the cell, then regained her weapons and walked down the hall toward some unknown future.

CHAPTER FIFTY-SIX

MARNEJ HAD NOT HESITATED once he was certain of his visions. He'd gathered the Piijkij and ridden as if chased. They rode for days, stopping only for the sake of their horses. When they finally encountered the gathered armies of the Avr, Marnej and the men in his party were exhausted. They fell from their mounts and struggled to find their feet. The leader of the Brethren strode out to welcome them.

From his prone position upon the ground, Marnej beamed with satisfaction. "I've found them," he said with the certainty of accomplishment.

The Avr helped him to his feet. He clapped the boy solidly on his back. "I have waited a lifetime to hear this."

He called out orders as he stood supporting Marnej. The Brethren moved quickly to roust the rank and file. Meanwhile, the Avr spoke to Marnej.

"You have brought honor to your name, and now we will bring honor back to the Brethren."

～

Dávgon left the boy to rest and rode to the top of a hillock to look into the distance. His men rode ahead of the *varis* soldiers, supplied by the Vijns, which, in the Avr's opinion was symbolic of the righting of the order. The Brethren were natural leaders. The foot soldiers were a ragged allotment, mostly farmers more interested in their now untended crops than fighting the Jápmea, but they would fight, either by threat of evil or by threat of a Piijkij sword.

His own men, by contrast, stood prepared, fearless and determined. The skirmishes had transformed any apprehension about fighting the Immortals into resolution. The loss of their brothers made the cause personal.

One of his men rode forward at a gallop. "We are being attacked at the advanced front flank," he said, bringing his horse to an abrupt stop.

Dávgon masked his surprise. "What numbers are engaged?"

"We are thirty trained and half again as many varis."

Before the Avr could respond, another of his men rode forward.

"The Jápmea have attacked our contingent to the east," the new arrival shouted over the sounds of his approach.

"It appears they have chosen to fight," the Avr commented, with a trace of satisfaction. "Losses?" he demanded.

"Few of our own, but many of the untrained," the first answered.

"Likewise," the second confirmed.

"We have the luxury of lives to spare among the varis," the Avr replied. "Return to your *chuoði* and inform other regiments along the way to be prepared. Send word back and keep me informed."

The two Piijkij nodded and rode off. Dávgon was taken aback by the early contact. They were still a fortnight's ride from where Marnej had discovered the Jápmea, and he trusted the accuracy of the boy's vision. To be hit upon two flanks was more than happenstance—it was an intentional foray. The attacks could be a diversion from a larger planned assault, or, more likely, an attempt to weaken and divide his troops before they reached their destination.

Dávgon thought about the various tactics the Jápmea might employ and realized he had the means to gain a clearer picture of their intentions. He spurred his horse toward the rear guard unit and rode along the outer ranks looking for Marnej. He found him near the front and gestured for the boy to join him.

The young Piijkij stopped his horse and waited for the soldiers on either side to pass by. Then he made his way to Dávgon.

"I have a need for your skills, Marnej." The Avr's tone was clipped.

The boy, though curious, followed without asking questions and entered the Avr's tent on his leader's heels.

Dávgon whipped around. "They have a plan and I want to know what it is."

Seeing the boy's confusion, Dávgon slowed to explain himself. "Jápmea have attacked at two flanks, and I want to know if this is a diversion or an attempt to weaken us."

"I don't know their minds, my Avr." The young Piijkij sputtered.

Dávgon waved off the boy's modesty. "If you can see them and hear them, then what is to say you cannot understand them?"

Here the boy faltered. "You wish me then to. . ."

"I want you to do what must be done."

"Now? Here?" Marnej looked around him.

"The present moment is upon us," Dávgon prompted and then, sensing the boy's unease, he added, "There is no shame in what you can do, Marnej."

~

Marnej bobbed his head, then took a deep breath, which he released slowly. He closed his eyes, unsure of what would happen, and tried to still his thoughts, but they raced ahead of him. What if he failed? What if he couldn't find the answers or even hear the voices?

Marnej shouted down the doubts with his own internal voice, willing himself into a precarious silence. Gradually, his breath grew sustained and deep, and his heart slowed until he wasn't sure it still beat within him. Then sounds rushed into his mind crowding out his own will. Something inside of him yearned to be set free, to fly out, and without making a conscious decision, Marnej let go and felt himself pulled apart at his core.

He opened his eyes and the world around him swirled, awash with a glow. He tried to focus and realized the glow was actually his blurred vision. He could see the Avr standing before him, turning in frantic circles.

Marnej wondered at the man's fright. Looking around the tent, he could see nothing to cause concern. He took a step toward his leader and dizziness overwhelmed him. He swayed and lost his balance, tumbling backward through the open tent flaps to land upon his backside with his palms upon the ground.

The earth pulsed. This time the sensation caused Marnej no fear. Rather, he took it to be a sign—a sign the Jápmea were near.

He stood and was pulled through a muddled world. When he stopped, he stood above a ridge looking down upon a vast army, gathered in ranks, preparing to march.

Marnej tried to move forward, but he found he couldn't. Each step he took toward the Jápmea brought him back to the same spot.

We are the Taistelijan.
We are the warriors of the Jápmemeahttun.
Our swords serve our kind in death,
Our knowledge our continued life.
We walk into battle to end what was long ago begun.

One voice built upon another, until Marnej's every fiber vibrated with the power of the chorus filtering through him. He felt the heartbeats of those below, their pride and their power. He saw the flashing swords and green fields. He felt the pull to join their ranks and then, just as he seemed to break free from whatever constrained him, he fell forward and found himself in front of the Avr of the Brethren of Hunters.

Marnej tried to speak, but his voice wouldn't come. He coughed.

The Avr handed him a waterskin, from which he took a long drink and coughed again as the water tumbled over his parched tongue and throat.

"They've gathered an army," the young Piijkij finally said.

"And what of their strength?"

"Their numbers are far less than ours, but their strength is vast." Marnej answered like one recalling a dream.

"They're within our reach?"

"They are within the Great Valley, gathered in ranks and preparing to move." He coughed again.

"That's less than a day's ride from here. How can they have moved so close in such great numbers?"

Marnej shrank under his leader's critical eye. "I don't know, my Avr. We've been scouting ahead, looking for signs. But the distances are vast and their means of approach many."

The Avr's eyes narrowed. "But you did not see signs when you were in the North."

Marnej shook his head. "No, I saw no indications, but the approach from the Northland is broad and it could have happened along many routes."

"If the Jápmea are in the Great Valley, there are but few inlets and even fewer outlets. If we can travel with speed, we can block their advance at the narrow western point while sending part of our forces to circle in from the north and cut off their retreat. They would be surrounded," the Avr said aloud with some liking.

Marnej frowned. The Avr laughed.

He clapped the young Piijkij on his back. "Don't worry about my jumbled thoughts. I have what I need to bring about the end of the Jápmea. And you have been my greatest asset."

The young Piijkij tried to smile, but the corners of his mouth quivered.

"I want you to stay within my retinue," the leader of the Brethren said as Marnej moved to leave the tent. "I may have further need of your skills. Check with Gáral for where to bunk and tell Feles you will no longer be within his ranks."

"Yes, my Avr," the boy answered and left the tent.

❧

Dávgon watched the back of the young Piijkij disappear through the canvas slit. Once again, the boy had proven himself useful, and yet, this time, Dávgon weighed the knowledge gained with the manner in which it was gained.

Until now, Marnej's skills had been the subject of rumor and speculation. The few who'd traveled with him in the Northland had reported his disappearance. But Dávgon had discounted the report as the product of imagination and drink. Now that he'd witnessed the strange phenomenon for himself, he couldn't ignore the unease it caused him.

❧

Outside the tent, Marnej breathed in the cool evening air and let it fill him, profoundly conscious of what had transpired in the Avr's presence. Though he couldn't know what the man had actually seen, he was genuinely relieved the Avr didn't know what Marnej had felt.

Marnej had wanted to join the ranks of the Jápmea. He longed to be one of them. This desire went beyond everything he knew or understood, and it frightened him. It gave life to unspeakable doubts and unanswerable questions. Why had he been drawn to them? And more importantly, could he be trusted to remain loyal to the Avr when some unseen part of him wished to rebel?

～

In the still forest, beyond the watchful eyes of the scouting Brethren, Mord stood beside a score of Taistelijan upon the ridge overlooking the Great Valley below. The soft glow of the dipping sun cast shadows across the wide green field.

"You are sure they will come?" one of the warriors asked.

"Yes. He has seen a vision of our great army," Mord answered, still watching the changing light upon the valley.

"How can that be?" asked another of the younger almai.

"We shared with him a long-ago memory—a memory of those who marched from here into battle and glory." Mord opened his soul to the remembrance of that time.

"We will again," he whispered to himself. "We will again."

CHAPTER FIFTY-SEVEN

DAWN BROKE, THOUGH THE sun had never truly set. The men who formed the ranks of the Piijkij-led army were restless. Although their leaders had extolled the glory that was to be theirs this day, these soldiers did not dream of glory; instead, in the privacy of their hearts, they prayed to live to return to their families or to whatever life they had come from.

When the order to move forward arrived, both horses and men were glad to do so, if only to rid themselves of the unwanted feelings of foreboding. As wave upon wave of man and beast marched ahead, they became a great stream of bodies, coursing through the countryside, caught up in the events of a history too far-reaching to comprehend.

At the junction before the Great Valley, the mounted portion of the eastern army split off. They would ride to the far northern entrance of the valley and block the escape of the Jápmea, should it be needed. The remaining foot soldiers and their mounted Piijkij continued forward toward the southern entrance to meet their enemy.

~

High upon the ridge the Jápmemeahttun waited. They remained within the Song of All, listening, perhaps for the last time, to all the voices that held their world together. The polished armor of ancient warriors shone in the rising day's sunlight. Had the Olmmoš been able to see them, they would have been blinded by the magnificence surrounding them, but the Olmmoš were as blind to this as they were to most things.

Mord and the others watched as the Olmmoš emerged into the valley with banners and pikes, moving like ants toward a carcass.

Impatience flared among the Jápmemeahttun. The slow advance of their enemy was almost too much to bear.

Dárja surveyed the ranks around her and embraced the relief that she hadn't been discovered.

When Mord prepared to lead the army from their northern stronghold, Dárja knew she had to follow at all costs or lose any hope of ever counting herself among the Taistelijan. As she polished the armor of those bound for the battle, she slipped aside pieces that would fit her. But her slim build had made it impossible to find a complete set to fit. She'd had to settle for using her leather jerkin layered with others of larger size, hoping it would be sufficient protection in battle. When the food wagons prepared to leave, Dárja hid among them, concealing her armor in one of the last carts.

Now, as she waited for the battle cry, she prayed to prove herself worthy.

～

Unbeknownst to Dárja, Irjan had also managed to stow away with the army of the Jápmemeahttun. He had joined the ranks of healers with the full knowledge and consent of both Kalek and Okta. It had taken many agonizing discussions to convince the two his sword served the Jápmemeahttun more upon the battlefield than it did in the prison cell he occupied.

"Grant me the chance to live and die as a free man," he had begged Kalek. "I am no friend to the cause of the Brethren, and you know I am their sworn enemy, not only by my choosing, but by theirs. Whatever harm I have done is fully realized. I can do no more damage and can only repay some small debt I owe to others."

Kalek had listened with his head bowed. When he had looked up, Irjan saw he had indeed caused even more pain to those he professed to love.

"I will not ask you to stay behind for my sake," Kalek had said with the weariness of acceptance. "I know you will go. It is who you are. But I ask you to think of Dárja."

And Irjan told himself he was thinking of Dárja and the last time they'd spoken.

Kalek had ultimately agreed and proposed Irjan develop a sickness to remove him from his cell and bring him into the care of the healers. On the appointed day, Irjan drank the tincture Okta had prepared for him. Within minutes, he doubled over in pain, frothing at the mouth. At first, his calls to the guards went unheeded and Irjan feared the plan would go awry, with dire consequences, but the door finally creaked open, and just before Irjan succumbed to darkness, he felt himself being carried off.

When he awoke, he was within Okta's chambers. The old healer stood over him with a concerned expression that broke into a smile as Irjan's eyes fluttered open.

"I thought perhaps you had moved beyond my reach," the ancient one said.

"Many would have thanked you," Irjan croaked.

"Yes, but I have stood between you and death too many times to lose you now."

Irjan sat up and felt the aftereffects of whatever illness the healers had brought upon him.

"You will be fine in a few moments," the old one assured him. Kalek smiled ruefully.

"You are enjoying my discomfort?" Irjan inquired.

"Never," the almai answered, "upon my oath to heal."

"The guards?" Irjan wondered.

"Too busy with war preparations to remember you," Kalek replied. "We too must gather our things and move to the sick wagons. You will be in the back with me, Irjan. When the moment is right, you may emerge, but for now it is best for you to stay out of sight."

Irjan noted Kalek's resigned tone. He reached out and took the almai's hand. He squeezed it, feeling its reassuring warmth, recalling how this gentle hand had saved his life and comforted him. Kalek gave a little tug and Irjan let himself be led to the wagon where he hid behind layers of supplies.

The long bumpy journey gave him plenty of time to reflect upon his past and contemplate the future. The Jápmemeahttun faced possibly the last battle of their existence. If they did not defeat the armies of the Piijkij, then he did not believe they would have the strength to fight off the onslaught that would follow. They needed a decisive victory to crush the spirit of the Olmmoš so they would not dare repeat the error again.

Irjan didn't know whether victory was possible, but he was certain he would lend his sword to the effort. On the morning of the battle, he took the hands of both Okta and Kalek, looked deep into their eyes, and saw his likeness. None of them held countenance with death, because they had been forced to keep its company too often.

Irjan could not express the truth of his feelings, and so he let an embrace speak for him. He mounted one of their binna, lowered his face shield then joined the closest rank of Taistelijan without looking back.

～

The first several rows of the Olmmoš army swept into the valley, expecting to meet the gathered Jápmea. Confusion quickly spread through their ranks when they saw the open valley before them.

The Piijkij vanguard sent riders back, and as they did, a ripple ran through the ridgetops and a rain of arrows flew through the air, momentarily darkening the clear, blue sky.

The men in the valley stared up at the heavens and then at the hills in terror. The arrows plunged toward the earth and men fell all around. Some writhed in agony, and others lapsed into a silence. The strongest felt their knees weaken, and the weakest men broke ranks, running in all directions. Those who looked up saw an unbroken line of blazing light burst forth from nothingness. They saw and felt the sickening sound of the battle cries of their enemy and the powerful gait of their beasts.

Their commanders' shouts did nothing to keep the varis soldiers in line, but within a matter of moments there was no place for them to run, because swords and cries and death seemed to be everywhere.

～

News of the battle in the Great Valley reached the rearmost ranks of the Piijkij army. The Avr charged forward on his horse, looking for Marnej, catching sight of the boy as he spoke to one of the front riders.

When Marnej's eyes met the Avr's, the boy's surprise was clear.

Dávgon didn't have time to consider the possibility the boy had, like his father before him, turned traitor; instead, he rode forward, urging his men to engage the Jápmea. But as he wound his way to where he could see the fighting, it was obvious his soldiers were hampered by the narrow valley entrance they had once assumed would be their advantage.

Dávgon looked to the ridgeline and saw no easy route to climb and gain a vantage. He sighted the position of the sun and, though it was past its zenith, it was hard to gauge how much longer it would take for the eastern branch of his army to engage from the north. For now, his troops would have to keep moving forward and hope they would succeed in their current strategy.

❀

Marnej couldn't believe what he was hearing. The Jápmea lined the ridges and not the valley. He'd led the Brethren into a trap, and the realization cut him to the quick. Marnej sat upon his horse, paralyzed by dread, as the press of the ranks moved him and his mount forward without his consent. He looked up and saw the Avr staring at him, but couldn't explain what had happened. His visions had never failed him before.

News that the Jápmea had gained the upper hand finally freed Marnej from his torpor. He spurred his horse into action, moving to the side and along the edge of the varis soldiers. The only thing that mattered to him now was vindication. He had worked too long to gain the trust of the Avr only to let it slip through his hands.

He pushed his way past comrades and trembling soldiers, not stopping until he made it to the border of the melee. On one side, a crush of bodies tried to push into the fight; on the other side there was the most horrific sound of carnage. Marnej could barely distinguish the cries of man and animal, both were so frenzied.

When he squeezed his way through the barrier, he reeled back, stunned. The ground was pitted and churned by hooves and feet. In the crevices and valleys, all manner of bits and pieces of bodies lay—some protruding in grotesque ways, others trampled under the press of men fighting.

Marnej didn't have time take in all the horror, because he was set upon by the hacking cuts of a Jápmea warrior. Though he managed to fend him off, Marnej felt off guard and unsteady, and when he finally exacted a fatal blow, it surprised him—but there was no room to dwell upon it because behind him came another Jápmea, and then another. He had no time to think, only time to react—to slash and move and slash again.

~

Irjan fought through the ranks of the Olmmoš soldiers. They were farmers, as he had once been; and though he pitied them, he cut through them with his blade as surely as if they were the Piijkij. The bravest among them had a frenzied look in their eyes, telling Irjan they were beyond understanding, beyond caring about anything except killing, and he obliged them with death. He would have preferred to exact his revenge upon those truly deserving of it, but these soldiers stood in his way and so he cleared them, one by one.

It didn't surprise him that killing came back to him so easily. The vengeance he felt as a boy was reborn, but this time, the object of the hatred had shifted. He raised his sword to block the blow of a Piijkij; he did not recognize the man, but it would not have mattered if he had.

Irjan snarled and unleashed his own barrage, which ended with the Piijkij clutching his throat as blood filled his cries. Irjan sliced his sword upward, catching the soft opening under the man's raised arm, and then the body toppled sideways.

Irjan looked out at the sea of faces, bloodied and smeared with dirt, intent upon the struggle for life and death, and dove into them with the abandon of one who no longer cared about the outcome.

~

At the northernmost edge of the battle, Dárja entered the fray, carried by all of her anger. She spurred her mount ahead and found herself surrounded by foot soldiers. Those with weapons attacked her, and those without clawed at her with their hands. She kicked at the unarmed mercilessly as she blocked on both her left and right flank, then grabbed the reins of her binna tightly and spun her mount in a circle with her weapon outstretched like a lethal whirlwind.

Those who reached up found themselves missing their hands, and those who wielded weapons were pushed back. Dárja fought her way forward toward the heart of the battle, knowing that in its midst lay her destiny.

~

How many times had Mord looked up to see more Olmmoš clamoring to be spitted on his blade? He was more than willing to oblige, but he'd begun to wonder how long he could continue at the pace he kept.

He wiped his sweat-clouded eyes and lashed out again and again. And still they came, like a swarm of insects nipping and biting at him as he swatted them away.

Suddenly, the throng of Olmmoš gave way to mounted riders, and Mord knew a battle worthy of his skill was at hand. His weathered face broke into a wide smile.

~

Alongside Mord, Irjan fought on foot. Long ago, his mount had fallen wounded, to thrash among those who lay dead and dying. Undaunted, Irjan moved ahead, dispatching a pair of witless foot soldiers who had found themselves alive and surprised by the fact. He killed them before either had time to realize their end had indeed come.

Irjan saw Mord still upon his mount ahead. The ancient Taistelijan cast a ragged shadow across the melee. He fought through wide swaths of soldiers, crushing some, slicing others, and running through the most unfortunate. Mord was an impressive sight to behold, but Irjan could see his strength was flagging. It would only be a matter of time before the great warrior would be overcome by the sheer numbers he could not hope to repulse.

Irjan entered the skirmish beside Mord, vowing to himself he would fight and give the warrior the last of his strength.

The two fought side by side, one high and one low, to cut down the ever-growing horde of Olmmoš. They worked as a team, although only one of them knew of their partnership. The other was consumed by the glory of battle and the chance to relive a life from long ago.

The mounted Piijkij pressed through, trampling soldiers to reach the two warriors. Both Irjan and Mord were stunned by the blows they received, but fought back to take their attackers down.

Irjan had seen a thrust out of the corner of his eye and turned quickly to block it. In that moment, as his arm reached up to deflect a downward blow, another unseen sword lunged forward, finding the unprotected flesh under his arm.

Irjan felt the burning heat of the steel cutting his sinew and the gush of his blood. He tasted the iron in his mouth and felt a sickening twist in his gut. Blood rushed past his ears, drowning the sounds around him. He was falling forward. He saw the faces of men, the dark hooves of horses—and then there was nothing.

～

Mord turned in time to see his fellow Jápmemeahttun fall forward, dead. It released in him the last reserve of his hatred. He spurred his binna forward into the overwhelming number of Piijkij and cut at them as if they were wheat and he the reaper. They fell all around him, but still more came. He thrust and cut and rounded to parry, then turned into the sharpened pike of an Olmmoš.

The pike ran him through.

He looked down at the long pole extending from his body and then out into the Great Valley. He saw the battle still raged, but realized his own battle was over.

～

Marnej carved his way to the very center of the fighting. All around him varis and Piijkij lashed out at Jápmea. His dream of

432

victory had become a nightmare. He had no sense of who was winning. Winning, in fact, was no longer important to him. There was nothing but death, and if he stopped, then he would join the ranks of the dead.

Marnej continued to fight and continued to live. Though his muscles screamed in pain, he lifted his sword and brought it down with all the strength he could muster; he repeated this over and over again, until a hand stayed his and he dropped to his knees.

~

Dárja looked up, and in the distance saw Marnej upon his horse without a helmet, fighting with wild abandon. Marnej swung wide, losing his balance, and tumbled off his horse, becoming lost among those who fought on foot.

Dárja ran toward him, heedless of the danger around her, cutting at anything standing in her way. But she was blocked by numbers too overwhelming to push through, so she battled and sliced and swore at the gods who kept her from her true enemy. From behind, she heard a thunderous sound she couldn't place. She turned to see what it was, and in that instant, her heart sank.

Countless mounted riders advanced under the banner of the Piijkij. Instinctively, Dárja's thoughts reached out for the Song, even as she swung her sword. She wanted to hear the voices of her kind one more time. But all she heard were the grunts and screams of those around her. *I am lost to the Song*, she thought, and in her despair unleashed a torrent of blows against the Olmmoš she faced. She cut viciously at the man as he crumpled. She kicked his body over and sought the next.

CHAPTER FIFTY-EIGHT

When the Piijkij returned from the Northland in triumph, they did not tell the tale of the true end of the battle. They spoke of their honor and the hard-fought victory over the Jápmea. They described the ones they killed and the ones they left to die. They even brought one back as a captive to display before the cheering girkogilli.

But triumph could not hide from discerning eyes the fact the returning Olmmoš were a weary and ragtag lot whose numbers had suffered greatly at the hands of the Immortals. Many families accepted their returning men with tears of joy, but many more were the families whose men would not be returning.

The Piijkij were welcomed home by Brothers too old to fight and boys too young to wield weapons. The halls echoed with their homecoming and all were glad to have a warm bed and a solid meal. The returned Hunters found comfort in the small things, after the horrors they had seen, although none among them would have admitted a need for comfort.

Marnej had traveled back with the Avr's retinue. The journey had given him plenty of time to review the battle and the events leading up to it. His false vision had plagued him, but he took

comfort in knowing he'd acquitted himself well on the battlefield.

He couldn't begin to tally those he'd killed, but he'd fought
until there were none left to fight. And even then he would've
continued fighting ghosts if the Avr hadn't stopped him. To
see pride in his leader's face that day had been a vindication for
Marnej, because it meant he had finally proven his loyalty.

Still, Marnej couldn't help but revisit his doubts along with
his victories. He had to admit the voices had been tempting. Part
of him had yearned to join the Immortal warriors, and the more
he tried to reconcile what he knew with what he'd felt, the more
he fought against those feelings. He'd sworn his loyalty and he
clung to it, dismissing his urges as fleeting and imagined.

But then there was the girl—the Jápmea captive—whom
he'd recognized from his vision and his brief, but fierce, encounter with her before his father had interceded. She'd been caught
upon the battlefield and brought to the Avr kicking and fighting,
though she bled from a wound. Marnej had watched her from a
distance. She rode with her chin held high. Her long dark plait
hung in a ragged mess of dried mud and gore. Her sleeve and bind-
ings were stained rust with the blood that seeped from the gash
upon her arm. The fact she hadn't disappeared like she had the
first time he had come across her puzzled him. He wondered if it
was because of her wound. Perhaps she was not strong enough or
had lost too much blood. He'd looked back to her often on their
journey home, knowing she represented the last link to the truth
about his father and possibly himself, but had neither spoken to
her, nor of her.

He hadn't dared.

～

Returned to his chamber, the Avr enjoyed the quiet, his dreams
still echoing with sounds of the battle, most particularly the

screams of the wounded. Their victory had come at a great price, but he had been willing to pay it.

A knock sounded at the door and he called, "Enter."

"I bid you welcome and hail your great triumph," said Rikkar, the former priest.

"Thank you, Rikkar," the Avr said graciously, and then waited. "Was there something else you wished to speak to me about?"

"It is just a matter of curiosity, really, which I had hoped you would indulge," the man replied with an obsequiousness that both gratified and grated at Dávgon.

"The girl," he said finally, "is she really Jápmea?"

Dávgon's jaw tightened in annoyance. *All this time and the man still does not know his place*, he thought. But before he could address this overstep, the meddlesome former priest spoke again.

"Rumors abound, and I would not like to perpetuate what is not true," the man stammered.

The Avr stared at Rikkar, but he said nothing, hoping he would take his leave.

"I have disturbed you," Rikkar mumbled, seeming to realize his blunder. "I will not speak of it again, and I honor the gift you have bestowed upon us all." He bowed and quickly withdrew.

The man's departure returned the room to enjoyable silence. Dávgon relished it, closing his eyes and soaking it in, but Rikkar had planted a seed in his thoughts—the girl. Dávgon had planned to use her to give the villagers a face to go along with tales of their enemy, and her haughty demeanor would only serve his cause. He thought of her riding—unbowed—her hands trussed behind her. He had to give her kind credit. They were fiercely proud.

Much could be learned from her about the Immortals, Dávgon mused. On the other hand, the Jápmea were gone, defeated, so there was no longer need. *Still*. It was interesting to consider what might come of a pairing of the two Jápmea—Marnej and the girl.

～

Dárja sat in her cell, weighed down by the leaden silence of the Olmmoš world. She shivered, feeling the lifelessness of everything around her, and tried to find the Song of All. She let her voice go out in search of her kind, but heard no answer, no other voice but her own. Desperation drove her to try again and again to find that precious connection she craved. *Not all had perished.* She knew that in their stronghold there were nieddaš and mánáid and the Council of Elders, and those too old among the almai and Taistelijan to fight. But perhaps they weren't enough to keep the Song strong. Or perhaps she wasn't strong enough to find it any more. Either way, even if the door to her cell weren't locked, Dárja knew she couldn't just slip away into the Song. But what truly compelled Dárja to keep on trying to find the Song was Irjan. She desperately wanted to hear his voice.

She thought of the last time she'd seem him, standing in his cell, his head bowed. Her heart ached to think of their conversation. The truth had been too much for her and his part in it unavoidable, but she'd discounted the guilt he must have felt. That Irjan was safe in the Pohjola was the one small comfort Dárja could draw strength from. If she ever managed to make it back to him, she would tell him she forgave him and, more importantly, loved him as her bieba. *I am so sorry. Please forgive me*, she silently called out to him, hoping he could hear her.

But even if she never made it back North, Dárja had fought and proved herself. Although no one would know of it, her actions gave her the satisfaction she needed to dispel all her self-doubt, and embrace the truth—Irjan had always loved her for who she was. Even her anger toward Marnej had receded to the background. She'd watched him on their journey south. His mop of straw-colored hair fell across his eyes, but couldn't hide that something troubled him. He often looked back at her, but hadn't approached. At the time, she'd been grateful. Now she was merely curious.

Dárja lay down once again. She willed sleep to take her away from her imprisonment. She closed her eyes and pictured those she'd left behind. Kalek, with his broad shoulders and proud brow. Okta, bent over his herbs, muttering to himself. Irjan.

Noises in the shadows broke through Dárja's visions. She tensed and pricked her ears. Alert now, her skin tingled with apprehension.

"If you wish to watch me, then come out of the darkness," she said. But the figure stayed hidden.

She sank back into her cot and closed her eyes. Whoever it was would soon grow tired of watching her sleep.

"Who are you to Irjan?" a hoarse voice whispered.

It took Dárja a moment to understand. The hushed tone made the thick Olmmoš accent even more pronounced.

Dárja turned her head, but did not rise. "I don't speak to those I can't see."

She heard a quick step, and a figure came into the dim candle light, then receded into another shadow.

"I said, I don't speak to those I can't see."

The figure suddenly strode forward into the light. "Do you know who I am?"

"You are Marnej," Dárja said with more than a trace of bitterness. "Irjan's son," He grimaced, but whether his distaste was due to Irjan or herself, Dárja couldn't tell.

"Who are you to Irjan?" he repeated, this time with force behind his question, even if his sharp features wavered.

"Irjan is my bieba," she added but didn't elaborate.

"What's that?"

Dárja sat up to peer into the darkness. "He's the one who cares for me in this world."

Marnej's eyes narrowed, as if he were trying to understand her words. "Your guardian?"

"If that's what a guardian does."

Marnej said nothing but his breath escaped him in noisy bursts, like he had run the entire way to be in front of her. Then he abruptly turned on his heels and stalked away. His footsteps faded on the dirt floor before stopping all together.

Dárja laid back down on her cot with an annoyed sniff. Whatever comfort sleep might have given her was lost to her now. She took a deep breath and tried to still her thoughts and calm her heart. She reached out with the first line of her Song, hoping this time it would work. She listened deep within herself, feeling something beyond her. She struggled to hold on to it.

"What do you know of my father's past?" Marnej's roughly spoken demand shattered the silence.

Dárja's eyes flew open. He stood before her again, tension radiating from him like the sun's heat on a long hot day.

"Release me and I'll tell you."

"No."

"Then we have nothing to talk about."

"Why were you on the battlefield?"

Dárja rolled to her feet and walked in his direction. She glared at him through the crude iron bars which separated them. "I was on the battlefield because I am a Taistelijan."

"But you're a female," Marnej scoffed.

"I'm a warrior and I wouldn't let you take that from me. Even now I can see you're afraid of me; that's why you won't let me out. Me, a nieddaš. And you, afraid. I can see now what kind of fighters the Piijkij truly are."

"We were good enough to best your kind," Marnej said as he crossed his arms in front of him, smirking.

Dárja snorted. "*My* kind? Is that what you tell yourself? Or is it because you don't know the truth?"

～

Marnej hesitated a moment before answering, "What do you mean?"

"Ah." The Jápmea girl drew out the word. "You don't know, then."

"Know what?"

She smiled, her short, even teeth catching a glint of torch-light. "That you are Jápmemeahttun."

Marnej leapt forward to stand a hairsbreadth away from the girl. "Lies," he shouted. But even as the word escaped his lips doubt began to creep in around him, cruel and susurrus. The visions. The voices.

"The voices," Marnej repeated his doubt aloud.

The girl's hand shot through the bars to grab his sleeve. "You can hear the voices?" Her question sounded oddly formal and patronizing to his ears.

He stiffened and pulled his sleeve away. "Yes."

She shrank back as if burned but she continued to badger him with her irritating interrogation. "Can you hear them now?" Her dark, angled eyes bore into him.

Wary, Marnej shook his head. "No."

The girl seemed to sink into herself, like she had used the last of her energy.

"Can't *you* hear them?" Marnej taunted more than asked.

The girl slumped onto her cot. "No."

"What does that mean?" He stepped closer, genuinely interested.

She bowed her head. "I don't know. Perhaps our kind is at its end."

"Stop saying that," Marnej exploded, pushing off the bars as if he were pushing her physically away. "Stop saying *our* kind. I'm not your kind. I'm not a traitor."

The girl jumped to her feet, her fists balled at her sides. "No, you're right. You're like all the other Olmmoš, too stupid to see the gifts you were given."

"You call these gifts? They're a curse. I'm shunned because of them."

"Then why do you choose to be with these men?" Her voice rose, making Marnej feel as if he'd just been scolded.

"Because I am loyal," he said with enough force to almost quiet the truth within him. He would never tell *her* he stayed because he wished to belong somewhere.

"I am a prisoner," she said with an unexpected softening of her tone. "But you are free." Her puzzled expression was maddening.

Marnej slowly shook his head even as he considered the possibility. "I'm not free. I've never been free. My father made sure of it."

The Jápmea girl suddenly rushed the bars as though she meant to pass right through them. She stopped at the door's limit but her penetrating stare cut right through him. "Your father is in a cell like this." She pointed around her. "He has been for the whole of my life. Because of you. While you," she spit contemptuously, "you've gone about your days, however you Olmmoš spend your days, placing blame at the wrong threshold."

"My father is a traitor," Marnej spat back.

"My bieba is no traitor," she hissed. "He is a man who made the mistake of loving *two* children instead of one."

Marnej started as if he had been slapped.

He wanted to pull open the door separating them and shake her, make her understand what his father had done to him. But she'd landed a blow more painful than any weapon could inflict. It was as if she'd been able to see inside of him. To find that hidden corner where he held his most cherished wishes and his darkest fears. She spoke of his father as if Irjan belong to her. Her claim had all the certainty that could only come from feeling loved.

Marnej shook inside. He looked at the girl, her mud-streaked face, her challenging gaze. His throat closed, choking back the howl rising from his heart. But he couldn't stop his mind from screaming, *Why her? Why not me?* Marnej hated himself for this weakness. He grabbed the bars of her cell, his knuckles white and taut. He was so tempted to open that door to her cell and make her take him to his father. To prove to her, to himself, he deserved more.

For one brief moment he imagined himself among her kind. Their kind. He repeated cautiously to himself, *Their kind.* The memory of how he'd felt in his visions swept over him. The thrum. The connection. He recalled hearing his father's song, before Irjan had burst into view with a trail of Immortals in his wake.

Son of my heart. Vessel of a father's soul.

Those had been the first words he'd heard from his father and at the time they sounded like a cruel joke.

But now, a part of him that he'd kept small and isolated, began to wonder if it might not be true.

"What will happen to me?" the girl asked, breaking into his thoughts.

His focus came back to her and Marnej realized he'd been staring. The girl's proud expression was marred by the concern she couldn't keep from her voice. They had been this close when Irjan had stepped between their raised swords. She'd been fearless. And the way she'd said his name, as if she'd known all about him. He'd known nothing of her. Marnej released his grip on the bars to step away. He rubbed the back of his neck with his hand, reassuring himself of his own body, and his presence here. He needed to be sure he was not lost in one of his visions.

"I don't know, Dárja." Marnej said, then paused, realizing that, for the first time, he'd called her by her name.

ACKNOWLEDGMENTS

I would like to thank the following individuals for helping make this book possible:

Grant Kalinowski for putting *The Hobbit* in my hands so many years ago and introducing me to fantastical worlds. He is my champion on this quest as both a friend and a reader.

Sage Lee for his mentorship and encouragement that this was the right path for me even after reading my first draft.

Thomas Tomcat, Sita Saxe, and Nicole Martensen for their kind devotion while reading the various iterations.

Stevie Mikayne, Sunah Cherwin, and Melody Moss for making me a better writer through their editing.

Mark Gottlieb of Trident Media Group for his unparalleled support and guidance.

Jeremy Lassen of Night Shade Books for his staggering wealth of knowledge and judicious use of praise and critique.

Cory Allyn of Skyhorse Publishing for keeping me on target.

Deborah A. Wolf for her early and enthusiastic praise of this book.

Irvin Lin and S.B. Hadley Wilson for their unfailing support at our monthly writers' meetings

Scott James, Shana Mahaffey, Katy Lefroy, and Melina Selverston-Scher of the Castro Writers' Cooperative for giving me a quiet place to write and the support to keep going.

Kay Myers for always suggesting I should be a writer even when I was convinced I was a surfer.

Benjamin Thompson for using a red pen on each of these pages and walking the fine line of loving husband and merciless editor.

And finally, The Muse for whispering in my ear and then shouting when I did not listen.

My gratitude knows no bounds.

TINA LeCOUNT MYERS is a writer, artist, independent historian, and surfer. Born in Mexico to expat-bohemian parents, she grew up on Southern California tennis courts with a prophecy hanging over her head; her parents hoped she'd one day be an author. Tina has a Master of Arts degree in History from the University of California, Santa Cruz. She lives in San Francisco with her adventurer husband and two loud Siamese cats. *The Song of All* is her first novel.